ABOUT THE AUTHOR

Grant J Everett is a writer from Western Sydney. He writes science fiction comedy novels for a couple of reasons: one, because we all need an escape almost as much as we need a laugh, and two, because it's easy to be witty when you have a fortnight to think of a comeback.

ALSO BY THE AUTHOR:

SCUM OF THE UNIVERSE
WHERE HAVE ALL THE HUMANS GONE?

PRAISE FOR SCUM OF THE UNIVERSE

"There is nothing to dislike about "Scum of the Universe", every page delivers hilarious and quotable prose. It is jam-packed with science fiction Easter eggs and tropes.

"Under the warped humour and scummery, Everett directs his precision-edged satire at modernity, extrapolating our present wastefulness and indifference to suffering into the far future where education is a one hundred percent passive transaction between student and teacher, and politicians are as self-serving as ever." Sci-fi and Scary.com

TOTALLY, UTTERLY SCREWED

Grant J Everett

Black Cockie Press

Totally, Utterly Screwed.

Published by Black Cockie Press

Copyright Grant J Everett 2022

The moral right of the author has been asserted

Cover design Black CockiePress 2022

Distributed by Ingramspark

ISBN: 978-0-6454896-2-0

CHAPTER ONE PETTY THEFT & FANCY LATIN WORDS

A squeal of static broke the church-like stillness of the enormous supplies area like a pipe bomb in a China cabinet. A voice made from soggy cardboard hopped between tens of thousands of squawkers as it gradually droned its message from one end of the warehouse to the other. As the aisles of this emperor of a storage facility stretched for a total of thirteen kilometres between office goods and luxury cheeses, it took quite some time for the broadcast to finish echoing all the way.

Its words were a very, very bad omen.

"Sanitation engineer Robert Tuesday is to see the Captain immediately."

There was a throaty snort and the smacking of gums deep among the fluorescent yellow shelves. At an altitude of three hundred metres, situated so far above the armies of automated forklifts that their flashing hazard lights were barely embers, a scruffy head popped out from behind a towering pallet of vacuum-packed spinach puree. A chlorine-flavoured cigarette sputtered offensive green smoke from Bob Tuesday's mouth, a horrid pit made up of blackened teeth and frequent obscenity, and his eyes darted about in rat like paranoia.

He relaxed at the realisation he was all alone.

Tuesday stretched, yawned, and stepped out from his hiding spot. Like all civilian janitors serving aboard starships that belonged to the all-powerful human regime known as The Unison, Tuesday was dressed in orange coveralls and steel-capped cricket-leather boots. Unlike other janitors, Tuesday's uniform was striped with patches across the shoulder blades, breast and both sleeves that declared PAROLEE in blinking red block letters, and a tracking device was locked to his left ankle. The tracker's batteries had conveniently run flat for the sixth time this week, even though they'd been graded to survive a solid century of use.

The thirty-metre-tall pile of liquefied spinach that Tuesday had been hiding behind for his eighth smoke break and power nap of the morning was but one monolith in a storage area so immense that it generated its own weather among the upper tiers. Looking up, a few wispy clouds curled about at the very extent of Tuesday's eyesight, but at least it didn't look like rain today. Glancing down, Tuesday wondered if that stowaway who went missing in the haberdashery section six days ago had died of dehydration yet.

Taking a second to rub at his gummy eyes, Tuesday ditched his chlorine cigarette in a wheeled bucket of neon-green cleaning fluid, jammed a suspiciously clean mop into its maw and pushed towards the closest gantry. As you'd expect from an era where Work Health & Safety and litigation had both gone utterly mad, the bright-yellow freight elevator was specifically designed to prevent compensation claims. Stepping into a roll-cage, a pair of over-the-shoulder shock absorbers slammed into place on both sides of Tuesday's turkey neck and the metallic bottom of his bucket was stuck fast with a magnet. One hundred and thirty-seven stories blurred past without a sound, and the g-forces were so intense at one point that the soles of Tuesday's boots were four inches above the weathered grid work. Stepping off with a wobble, Tuesday pushed his bucket onto a conveyor belt that instantly recognised his near-theoretical security clearance. In a matter of seconds he'd crossed a full tenth of the warehouse and been deposited within eyesight of the primary exit.

Tuesday knew that the request he'd heard over the PA was a portent of doom. He may be lazy, dodgy, light-fingered, disrespectful, smell like an expired tin of smoked oysters and have no talents beyond amateur flower arranging, but Tuesday had the survival instincts of a cockroach and could smell trouble. And while some crew members might hope that they were being called in so the Captain could congratulate them in person for some amazing achievement, Tuesday was certain that this summons was for the exact opposite reason. After all, Tuesday hadn't achieved one thing worth remembering in his entire life, and his chances of promotion were around the same as winning the Lotto without buying a ticket.

Reaching the unattended sign-in book, Tuesday paused just long enough to snort, hawk, and spit a disgusting brown glob of phlegm into its open pages. A moment later the laser tip pen bolted to its cricket leather cover vanished up his sleeve chain-and-all, sliding neatly into one of the many secret elastic pockets he'd sewn into his coveralls. This theft was committed as casually as breathing, and his skill bordered on magical. An eye witness wouldn't have noticed a thing until Tuesday was well and truly gone.

Passing beyond the flappy rubber curtain of the supplies area, whistling the offensive theme song from the controversial immersive vid-show Wildest Xenosexual Celebrities Revealed, Tuesday rattled his mop and bucket down a broad, slightly curved corridor. The boffins who designed this starship had apparently acquainted "high-tech" with "no straight lines", so as soon as Tuesday had escaped the perfect right-angles of the supplies area every surface suddenly ranged from slightly rounded to completely circular. As this was officially a Navy ship, needless decoration wasn't a high priority, so despite the emphasis of curves, its design would be best described as utilitarian and efficient....within the less important areas, anyway.

Continuing to whistle, Tuesday casually headed towards a turbolift that was currently spewing out twenty or so Navy scientists. Like all the tech staff on board they were dressed in midnight-blue uniforms weighted down with far too much gold piping, and they all seemed to be in a massive hurry to get to wherever it was they were headed. Most of them were tapping away at holographic displays projected from tiny Omni implants buried in the meat of their left hands, flicking their eyes at retinal screen readouts that only they could see, or snapping tongue-twisting jargon at distant workmates over the omnipresent Unison-wide network known as the Link. Whatever had kept everybody so busy for the last few days was lightyears above Tuesday's paygrade, but he had no interest in such things anyway. If he couldn't smoke it, sell it or get hammered on it, Tuesday's general care factor was nil.

Wearing a totally neutral expression, Tuesday gently made his way through the dark blue mob from the opposite direction, innocent as a dove as he brushed against them too softly to detect. The crowd abated for a moment as Tuesday made it to the empty lift, and as the triple doors slammed closed he bared his rotten teeth in a horrible smile. Reaching into the orange sleeves of his coveralls, Tuesday extracted three gold watches, four diamond-studded wedding rings, a pair of designer sunglasses, five of those retro-style matchbox-sized mobile phones that had been all the rage yesterday, and a single pair of pearl earrings. He sleeved the phones again and dumped any water-resistant treasures into his wheeled bucket. The stolen items sank beneath a layer of thick froth and disappeared.

As you'd expect from something called a "turbolift", the pod shot across six-hundred-and-seventeen stories in a matter of four point three seconds. Tuesday experienced half a second of weightlessness around the middle of the trip as the capsule hit full speed, but his voyage was over so quickly that nothing tipped over or spilled. In those brief moments Tuesday got a fantastic view of the outside of the ship through the transparent outer walls of the turbolift: it was two immense glowing white lines that seemed to go forever, a middle finger brandished at physics and a raspberry blown at the immensity of space, the greatest starship ever conceived: it was the Carpe Astrum.

And then the view was gone.

Although this starship served as a monument to the genius of Tuesday's species, for the last three weeks it had also served as the formal location of Tuesday's work-release parole placement. And no matter how gilded the cage, a prison is still a prison. So, in his own way, Tuesday had made the most of things. Admittedly, those things technically belonged to other people, but a lifetime of scummery was hard to break.

Tuesday slouched out of the capsule and dawdled along a much nicer part of the ship than where he usually worked. Bucking the Navy's normal ascetics of function over form, this level was designed to impress visiting VIPs and had been decorated like Xanadu itself: there were orchids sourced from a hundred worlds with colours so vivid that looking at them for too long could cause permanent eye damage, huge post-modern gabba-gabba abstract paintings that had a lot in common with the scribblings of a colour-blind five-year-old, and even a range of living thought-reactive sculptures that would twist and change in hypnotic ways depending on how the passing humans were feeling at that moment. In addition to that, every square inch of floor was carpeted by stain-resistant shag so thick you could sink all the way up to your shins if you didn't walk fast enough.

The mood of this most opulent of levels was further reinforced by soft, calming violins and pianos that had been digitally slathered over the top of some intense subliminal messages. While the human ear was unable to consciously pick up any of the underlying white noise, the brain would lap up these sounds like a thirsty dog at a bowl of tap water. Designed by the finest aural engineers, the underlying messages were able to actively boost all of your cognitive processes while reducing your stress levels. There were plenty of urban legends about Vegan Extremist terrorists hiding harmful "depth charges" within these brain-altering compositions, but it was pretty common knowledge that Vegan Extremists preferred nerve gas and chainsaws, and so nobody actually believed the rumours.

Pushing the tools of his trade up to the elegantly bare secretary's desk situated outside of the Captain's loft, Tuesday went as slowly as humanly possible without actually coming to a complete stop. There was a reason he was going at such a lazy pace: if he put a bit of pressure on just the right spot with his mop, the wheeled bucket would make a noise like a dagger's tip being drawn down a chalkboard. And although he was sure to keep his gaze averted from the secretary's face, Tuesday could clearly see her expression of agony in his peripheral vision. The shrieking bucket continued to claw at the inside of her teeth until Tuesday finally halted in front of the grandmotherly lady's desk. He looked up with a sleazy smile.

"Sanitation engineer class nine Tuesday reporting, Love."

The secretary's eyelid twitched as her line of sight darted between Tuesday's horrid teeth, his sloshing bucket, and finally towards a cluster of holographic displays being projected from her Omni implant. She swiped at one of the intangible screens a couple of times with the index finger of her right hand before looking back up at Tuesday. It was clear that whatever she'd just read had soured her view of the janitor even more than his deliberately horrible entrance.

8

"Take a seat."

No please? Interesting...

Turning on the spot, Tuesday squeaked his bucket all the way to the furthest point in the waiting room. Casually as though he had no idea how annoying he was, Tuesday sat on a padded chair bolted to the carpet and calmly watched a Ugandan cockroach dart between hiding spots.

Although he'd been ordered to turn up immediately, fifteen minutes silently passed without anything happening. After the life he'd lead, Tuesday knew all about waiting games: they were a basic psychological technique designed to make the guilty party sweat and worry, keeping them off balance before the interrogator went in for the kill. Unbothered by doing nothing (after all, it was his fourth favourite thing), Tuesday continued to wait with the patience of a man well accustomed to being on detention.

Five more minutes passed before the Captain - a snooty nerd in a midnight blue uniform decorated with five kilograms of gold edging - appeared in the ivory doorway. Glaring down at the janitor, he gestured sharply over his shoulder. Tuesday smiled at the secretary one last time and walked inside.

The size and comfort of the Captain's loft would put most seven-star Presidential suites to shame, and the office was dominated with what may be the greatest treasure trove of video game memorabilia from the late-21st and early-22nd Centuries. All the items were displayed on polished oak shelves and arranged both according to genre and alphabetically. They were all in their original shrink-wrap and protected by thick, unbreakable glass. The pride of the Captain's collection was a sealed-in-the-box Beyond console from Miyamoto-Kojima, an almost non-existent piece that the majority of collectors would sell their entire families just to be able to see it with their own eyes. The Beyond was the very last console that the Japanese gaming giant had produced, as a slight design flaw in its cortical shunt had the unfortunate tendency of converting one third of its users into serial killers. Miyamoto-Kojima was quick to release a corrective software patch that was 100% guaranteed to completely nullify the problem. Unfortunately, as the patch carried a price tag of $9.95 and took half an hour to download and install, the update was seen as nothing but a cash-grab and was wildly unpopular. Most users decided that two-out-of-three were pretty good odds, and their German yen would be better spent on games. All of the Beyond consoles were thought to have been hunted down and destroyed after the infamous Mushroom Kingdom Massacres, so how this one slipped through the net was a mystery.

An intelligent alien shrub extended a blue frond towards Tuesday as he walked past, and made a depressing little whimper as he ignored it. The double doors shut behind Tuesday with a thud, and four Enforcers positioned themselves between him and the only way out of this room. The war-criming roid-monkeys were dressed in your standard sapphire-coloured riot gear and armed with stunners, sting cuffs, burn spray and pain batons. One of them snatched his mop without a word, as though disarming a deadly weapon.

Crap...

While Tuesday had guessed that this morning wasn't going to end well, those already low hopes suddenly nosedived. The Captain spent a full thirty seconds silently glaring at Tuesday from the other side on an immense mahogany desk, the rage in his eyes indicating that he was barely restraining himself from throwing an ergonomic chair. When the Captain finally took a seat, Tuesday went to do the same without an invitation. However, the look on the Captain's face made it clear that the janitor would keep his butt cheeks elevated unless he wanted them to be surgically removed. Despite all the obvious hostility Tuesday waited patiently, trying not to smile despite the bleak situation. After an Ice Age, the pompous Captain finally spoke.

"Robert Tuesday," the Captain began, narrowing his eyes. "A defective, no-hope two-bit parolee of no fixed address that some backwater legal system had the audacity to jam into my ass in the name of, hah, rehabilitation."

Tuesday saluted smartly.

"Reporting, sir!"

The Captain was taken aback by this unexpected enthusiasm, but only for a second. Tuesday had that effect on people. It was hard to tell if he was a total moron or the smartest guy in the room. The Captain rolled on towards his point.

"The Carpe Astrum is the most expensive object ever created by man, bar none. She is important beyond measure. What happens aboard this vessel will impact our descendants for all time." The Captain got to his feet again and began pacing behind his desk, a sure sign of being on edge. "Do you know why we have janitors on this starship, Tuesday?"

"Class nine sanitation engineers, sir," Tuesday corrected, somehow keeping a straight face.

"Do you know why we have class nine sanitation engineers on this starship, Tuesday?" the Captain repeated with twice as much aggression. Tuesday shrugged. "No? No idea? We have class nine sanitation engineers because the experimental technology we're testing requires that we keep everything spotlessly clean if we want to remain at peak efficiency, that's why. Because if things aren't clean, that means they're dirty. And if they're dirty, that means they're unsafe. And if a single component is unsafe with the godlike levels of science we're messing around with out here…" The Captain trailed off before making a ripping gesture with both hands. "Boom, that's what."

"Boom?" Tuesday repeated.

"Boom."

"Ah." Tuesday sucked at his sad little teeth. He glanced at the Enforcers, who were still standing there impassively, then back at the Captain. "Boom. Noted. So…is that all, Cap'n? We got a hot tip that Jimmy Slummer is heading to Muchacho Taco for the All You Can Eat Burrito Deal again, so all us sanitation engineers need to be prepared for any serious projectile poop-related emergencies what may arise. Also, I'm due to go fumigate the…"

The Captain cut Tuesday off mid-sentence with a hand motion, squinting his piggy eyes in hatred.

"Oh, I haven't even started."

Veins visibly throbbed on the Captain's shiny forehead and neck, and drops of sweat weaved through his bushy eyebrows. A flick of his left hand instructed his Omni implant to create a holographic paperback book in mid-air, which he then snatched as though it was a physical item rather than sculpted light.

"Your continued placement as a parolee on board the Carpe Astrum relies on regular reviews once every six months. As you've only been here for three weeks, your first review isn't due for quite some time. However, due to, mmm, factors that I'll come to in a second, I've decided to bring your review forward to…right this moment." The holographic book was so well formed that the Captain was even able to rustle its pages with believable sound effects. "We've been recording every single microsecond you've spent aboard the Carpe Astrum from a dozen different angles, and what I'm holding right now is a summary of your more…notable activities."

Tuesday's eyes widened, and the Captain instantly assumed a look of triumph and spite.

"What's that, sanitation engineer class nine Tuesday? Is something the matter?"

"I…"

"Oh, so you weren't aware that we are constantly recording everything that every crew member does while they're aboard the Carpe Astrum? Or that these recordings are closely monitored by an army of AI watchmen around the clock?"

Tuesday glared.

"Our surveillance system is the best ever created, Tuesday, boasting fourth-dimensional high-def. video, flawless surround sound, infrared, night-vision, x-ray and far, far more. Just to spell out the sheer depths of how utterly boned you are, we've also been using no less than fifteen different kinds of classified scanners

11

that are so far above your paygrade and comprehension that I'd be forced to kill you if you even knew what they were called, let alone what they do." The Captain placed his hands on the desk, hard. His arms were shaking. "So as you may have surmised by this point, Tuesday, we know what you get up to, what laws you've broken, how many days it's been since you last brushed your teeth, and the exact wingspan of the Ugandan cockroach currently living in your Cornflakes box." The Captain smirked. "Twelve centimetres. Seems she's been eating well."

"I..."

The not-book's pages rustled as an interruption.

"I'll begin with what appears to be your definition of a standard shift. You start by getting to work two hours late, though you're always sure to use an illegal code-smashing device to cook the books when you think nobody's watching. Once you do get to work, the six hours that remain of each shift are broken up into various sequences of drinking, sleeping and smoking. You've engaged in so many variations of dereliction of duty that even after all my years with The Unison's Royal Navy I don't even know what to name half the things you get up to. To make matters worse, you are also partial towards illicit narcotics such as Shatter, Spaceman, Nirvana, Blink and Purgatory, but quite a few of the chemicals in your system don't even have an official classification yet." The Captain tapped at his holographic book. A page flipped over. "But the thieving is on another level altogether! Starting less than four damned minutes after you first stepped on board, we've had thousands of items go missing from just about every vending machine, deep freeze, medical fridge and personal locker from arse-to-armpits, and crew members have posted so many Lost Property reports for precious items that I've had to ban public bulletin boards. Until we looked closely at these recordings, however, we never could have guessed just how extensive your..."

"It wasn't me," Tuesday grunted, interrupting the tirade with what may be the most flimsy denial in the history of petty crime.

Both of the Captain's manicured hands thundered down onto the aged mahogany. Blue veins pulsed along his maroon neck and face, as though about to burst like water mains. An Enforcer brought Tuesday's mop bucket over without needing a prompt, reached into its green depths with a Kevlar glove and fished out Tuesday's haul for today in one big handful: there were rings of all sizes encrusted with gems from a dozen worlds, chains made of gold, silver, platinum and more exotic metals, earrings, designer sunglasses, a string of pearls...

A second Enforcer grabbed Tuesday by the sleeves and violently shook his arms until a whole appliance shop of electronic devices tumbled onto the Captain's desk. Besides the personal organisers, media players, those kitschy retro-style mobile phones and a few other devices, Tuesday couldn't even name half of what he'd stolen, only that they looked as though they were worth something.

The same two Enforcers pushed Tuesday down into a chair at a motion from the Captain. They wordlessly resumed their place at the double doors with the remaining pair of armoured thugs. On the bright side, it looked as though he was allowed to sit down now.

The Captain pinched the bridge of his nose. His triumph over the sanitation engineer was obviously warring with his extreme anger, so it took a few calming seconds to cool down enough to talk.

"To put it simply, Tuesday, we have endless reams of incriminating surveillance footage, we know where all your stashes are, and every stolen item we've recovered thus far has been slathered with your genetic markers. We've gathered so much evidence that I've had to place three Admin people on full-time shifts in 'The Wednesday Department'."

"The Wednesday Department?" Tuesday clarified.

The Captain raised his nose imperiously.

"Yes, so named because their job is to come after Tuesday." The Captain's eye twitched, possibly because he'd silently thought the 'The Wednesday Department' was a really clever name, but was now having second thoughts about its true level of wit. He shook this away. "Now, have you got anything mature and appropriate to add about being a one-man crime wave before I stick you in a coffin cell until you die of a combination of old age and terminal boredom?"

"Yeah."

"What?"

Tuesday casually mouthed a chlorine cigarette from his crumpled packet, drew at it until the suck-burner auto-ignition tip glowed neon green, and put his filthy steel-capped boots on the expensive antique desk. He bared his little brown teeth in a hideous smirk.

"Two things. Firstly, dickhead, tell your mum to stop telling everyone what a good lay I am. Secondly..."

Tuesday was interrupted by a grinding noise: the sound of fingernails digging into lacquer. When the Captain straightened up there were ten permanent scratch marks gouged into the desk's thick varnish.

Then he snapped.

The Captain leapt over his desk, scooped Tuesday up by both shoulders, kicked the chair from beneath him so hard that one of its wooden legs went spinning away, and pounded the class nine sanitation engineer into a wall of unbreakable glass. He growled, teeth bared and spittle flying, into Tuesday's ear.

13

"Go on. I'm very, very interested to hear what you have to say next, Tuesday."

Pinned in place, Tuesday calmly raised a sexy, lacy pair of neon-pink panties to face level. He smiled at the Captain's widening eyes.

"Secondly: are these delicates regulation issue?"

Snapping his head down so fast he almost got whiplash, the Captain made a gurgling, choking noise at the sight of his unbuckled trousers lounging around his ankles. Somehow, impossibly, the frilly knickers he'd secretly been wearing were now spinning around on Tuesday's index finger. Stunned, twitching, his brain seizing up as he tried to comprehend how Tuesday could have accomplished this impressive magic trick, the Captain let go of Tuesday's throat as though the janitor was radioactive and staggered backwards.

"How did you...how..."

Hearing the beginnings of a snort, the Captain swivelled towards his four Enforcer bodyguards and almost tripped over the crumple of his ankle-height trousers. Sadly for his security detail, it took a second for the Captain to regain the presence of mind to cover up his shame. If it was any consolation, there wasn't much to write home about. Despite this being the funniest thing any of the Enforcers had ever witnessed, somehow they were professional enough to keep staring straight ahead, poker-faced.

Unable to speak for a moment, deflated from a humiliation that would doubtlessly follow him for the rest of his career and beyond, the Captain half-whispered, half-growled three words as he tried to wrestle the lower half of his uniform back into position.

"By the ears."

As instructed, Tuesday was picked up by both ears – one Enforcer on each - and physically dragged out the door and down the hallway. It was difficult to tell if he was laughing or screaming.

CHAPTER TWO WORK EXPERIENCE

Lana Slade had been creeping along at two percent of light speed for almost three days now, and after seventy hours of being alone in the empty black she was on the very edge of blasting herself out the bulkhead scissor doors just to break up the monotony.

As a Cadet of the local naval branch of The Unison, Lana's crude shuttle actually belonged to her school. The Junker was painted a dull bruised-banana yellow, had an interior layered in eight decades of student graffiti and chewing gum, and was powered by a sub-light drive that was mostly composed of duct tape and putty. In short, the shuttle wasn't worth a second glance. What Lana had been approaching for the last three days, however, was without a doubt the greatest wonder ever built by mankind.

From fifteen thousand kilometres away the Carpe Astrum looked like two equilateral triangles hooked together at an invisible central anchor point. One of them was whiter than the driven snow, while the other was so dark that space itself looked grey in comparison. And sure, while the colossal triangles were exactly thirteen kilometres long on each side, mankind had built plenty of big things throughout the galaxy. "Big" happened a dozen times a day. "Big" was nothing new. "Big" wasn't what made it special.

At a range of five thousand kilometres, Lana could see that the six vertices of the Carpe Astrum were each interlinked with a much smaller equilateral triangle. The half-dozen minor triangles might have only been two kilometres a side, but besides their scale they were identical to the major pair. All eight of the triangles constantly revolved in hypnotic, seemingly random patterns, never touching as they remained the perfect distance away from one another. At Lana's best guess they were being kept in place by incredible magnetic and graviton forces, but her clearance wasn't high enough to confirm her suspicions.

On the upside, she was almost at her destination. However, her proximity to the giant starship had automatically caused the school shuttle to slow down to a more polite speed, so if Lana thought she was crawling before, this was an even more fiery level of Tartarus. Her fingernails cut into the cricket-leather armrests, but she otherwise controlled herself.

Once Lana got close enough to see the twisting details of the Carpe Astrum's superstructure, things started to get uncomfortable for her eyes and her brain. Each of the eight separate segments that made up the starship were actually Penrose triangles, which meant they were geometrically impossible shapes that were only meant to be able to exist as two-dimensional images. Since being created by psychiatrist Lionel Penrose back in the 1930s, Penrose triangles had been used by mathematicians and artists to mess with people's minds, to make statements about the way our brains perceive the expected and to represent impossibility "in its purest form," as Penrose himself had once stated. It was the kind of thing that had made MC Escher rich in his day. Somehow the builders of the Carpe Astrum had made this impossibility into something solid, as though their collective goal was to bully physics and steal its lunch money.

15

When Lana reached point-blank range she could see that all eight of the triangles were covered by a constantly-shifting labyrinth of countless palm-sized tiles. Unsurprisingly, every last tile was an equilateral triangle. Layers upon layers upon layers of them rearranged non-stop, performing some sort of mathematical dance that even the greatest of human minds could barely understand, a higher form of pure logic that made calculus look like adding up a lunch bill at a MacDeath burger joint. Being able to understand something that lay right on the knife edge between gibbering madness and God's own cheat guide was not compatible with most human brains, and even the best of the best paid the price for this terrible and beautiful treasure. After all, the true reason the Carpe Astrum had taken so many decades to build wasn't just its borderline ridiculous scale and impossible architecture, but because the mathematical geniuses who worked on the project had the unfortunate habit of throwing themselves out of airlocks. Beyond money being no object, the sheer prestige of working on this greatest of structures, this peak of human accomplishment, meant that there was never any problem finding more sacrificial goats to march into the abattoir.

Lana knew that the Slicer Drive that allowed this vessel to hop about instantaneously was actually a direct descendant of the Wattson-Rice Drive, mankind's original FTL breakthrough, the scientific miracle that had made the early days of interstellar travel possible, if not very safe or reliable. While both the Slicer and the Wattson-Rice operated on the same principal - folding the fabric of space and tying it together like a high-tech needle and thread – this was like comparing the ceiling of the Sistine Chapel to a hand-smear of Neanderthal excrement across a cave wall. The difference in sophistication made relating the two laughable. Saying that the Wattson-Rice wasn't all that safe was a massive understatement, as early space farers quickly nicknamed it the Deathwish Drive after hundreds of ships disappeared mid-transit for no apparent reason. They soon found that the further you pushed a Wattson-Rice Drive the higher the chances the ship and everything on it would cease to exist, so anything beyond a million kilometres per hop was rolling the dice. Worse still, this inherent level of risk made it impossible to get insurance from a reputable provider, which meant using a Wattson-Rice for business purposes hadn't been commercially viable for centuries. As Lana had already learned, the Slicer Drive aboard the Carpe Astrum was proven to be utterly reliable, and was projected to remain that way for as long as it existed.

Lana had to force herself to look away from the glowing ripples and patterns once her headache became unbearable. Even after closing her eyes and relaxing into the cricket-leather seat, Lana could still feel the wrongness of the looming monoliths.

She wasn't some alarmist anti-tech Luddite or anything, but anyone with a brain bigger than rabbit droppings would be worried about what this starship represented. To date, the Carpe Astrum had already shattered hundreds of previously-immutable laws of physics in test after test, and the horrible potential of what mankind could unleash upon all of creation if something went wrong was well beyond her imagination. If their reality-bending somehow backfired, somehow went wrong...

Best not to think about it.

Lana's head still really, really hurt from foolishly trying to comprehend the Penrose triangles, so she closed the transparent window with a slight twitch and sat back in the darkness with her eyes shut. Deciding to take a few quiet minutes to skim the Link to reacquaint herself with some facts that would hopefully help her to appear intelligent to the senior crew of the looming starship, Lana tapped at a bump on the meat of her left hand. The bump glowed a light cyan hue in recognition.

Like every other Cadet at the Academy, Lana had a personal computer the size of a grain of Basmati rice buried deep in the meat between her thumb knuckle and index knuckle. Known as an Omni, this was a relatively cheap upgrade you could get punched into your flesh in a matter of seconds at any accredited body piercer. While Lana's implant provided student-level access to the all-knowing Link no matter where she was in The Unison and was sufficient for her schoolwork, it was far from top of the line.

Firing up the retinal screens installed in each eye, with just one mental search command Lana was inundated by reams of information, and had to spend a few breathless seconds selectively scanning through cascades of three-dimensional schematics and news articles. Of course, while the Unison-wide Link was dominated by a million variations on the announcement that the Carpe Astrum was about to go on its very first manned voyage after eight years of exhaustive tests, this was technically untrue: Lana knew that the very first attempt had involved using boxes of cockroaches as passengers, followed by white rats for the second jaunt, then assorted types of monkeys for the third, fourth, fifth and sixth, until the Slicer Drive was safe enough to test on a bunch of feral zombies from the latest Australian outbreak. Today, though, the passengers would be the crème-de-la-crème of the human race, the bigwigs, and the movers-and-shakers. The list of VIPs was too long for Lana to read through in one sitting, but at a glance she saw the glitterati included high-ranking politicians, the most acclaimed aural engineers, a handful of traumatised survivors from last week's Olympic Deathsport Finals and a hundred captains of industry from the logistics, artificial intelligence, mining, cricket farming, and manufacturing sectors. Even the current CEO of the MacDeath Combine had waddled aboard.

Today was the fulcrum upon which mankind's future teetered, and the value of this final proving was beyond measure, beyond money. It would be the swelling of a new wave that would spread Lana's species across the galaxy, across the universe, infinitely faster than what had been possible yesterday. And while two thirds of its superstructure was composed of yawning, empty metal caverns, once the Carpe Astrum was judged to be viable for transporting sentient life it would be trucking time: crammed full of goods from distant corners of The Unison, this starship would spend its future jumping back and forth across the galaxy like a flea on a Chihuahua, only pausing in each system long enough to offload hundreds of millions of tonnes of resources and luxuries before collecting literal truckloads of German yen. The Carpe Astrum was going to be the ultimate commercial power in this galaxy, and was projected to pay for itself within a matter of years.

Nobody said it very loudly or very often, but there was little doubt the Carpe Astrum would soon be the ultimate military power in this galaxy, too. Combining the instantaneous communication capabilities of the Link with an omnipresent starship would provide The Unison with the ultimate weapon. Rather than taking weeks or longer to reach a hotspot, a few encoded messages on the military band and a handful of hours spent collecting a dozen far-flung fleets is all it would take to neutralise any issue. Mankind's reach across the stars would become infinite.

But Lana already knew the importance of today's jump, and the real motivations behind it. She needed obscure facts, something that most people didn't know, something exotic, something impressive. She wasn't going to earn any respect as some Cadet who'd won the student lottery. She needed to make an impact while she had the chance...

She noticed that one notable feature of the Carpe Astrum – or lack thereof, to be more accurate – was an almost total absence of conventional propulsion systems. Sure, there were a few patches of old-fashioned graviton jets here and there for the sake of keeping the whole thing from getting sucked into any old gravity well that came along, but their lack of power was laughable. This jarring design choice meant that there was no way the ship would ever be capable of moving faster than a waddle, a lame penguin-like shuffle that barely rated better than NASA's starships in the 22nd Century (before they'd been bought out by Tibetan organised crime, anyway). But this lack of functionality was deliberate. After all, the Carpe Astrum could seamlessly skip from point A to point Z without worrying about the rest of the alphabet, which meant rockets were as logical as strapping ice skates to a pigeon.

A three-dimensional interactive map of the Carpe Astrum jumped out of Lana's Omni. Her eyes danced and her fingernails twitched, making the scaled down triangles revolve, scouring away its invulnerable outer skin with her pupils. She plunged deeper and deeper through subsystems and corkscrewed up and down photorealistic corridors, her eyes twitching back and forth in the hunt for something she didn't know, something she hadn't seen before. Obviously, large chunks of the schematic were so far beyond being merely "classified" that the confidentially rating system being used was, itself, even more classified. These zones had been blacked out and riddled with vividly flashing red VOID lights so there could be no mistake that they were off limits. Lana kept well away from these spots on the schematic, as virtually crossing into a restricted zone without enough clearance would automatically cause the system to launch a tactile backfire right into her brainstem. Lana didn't fancy spending the next week fitting and vomiting from dump shock, but that would be the least of her worries: deliberately crossing into a VOID zone would make her guilty of treason against a dozen different wings of The Unison, which was ill-advised unless you had an interest in being skinned alive with a power sander.

Lana slumped in her chair. Besides the empty parts of the ship, ninety-five percent of the schematic was made up of classified blocks that had nothing to tell her beyond the word VOID, and the bits that she could access were mostly devoted to sleeping quarters, the Food Court, temperature regulation, anti-grav systems, oxygen generation and other boring-yet-essential areas, all of which Lana had already seen in one form or another in other simulations. Lana's security clearance was currently so low that she couldn't even see into the thirteen-kilometre-long supplies area, which she'd heard was the biggest ever built, so the chances of viewing anything mind-bustlingly awesome was highly unlikely.

Feeling a bit peckish, Lana zoomed in on the Muchacho Taco in the Carpe Astrum's Food Court on level four-hundred-and-fifteen, and had a look at today's choice of burritos. Unfortunately, her security clearance wasn't high enough for her to see whether the filling was lentils or chickpeas. She sighed in defeat.

Annoyed with herself, Lana decided to stop ruining this once-in-a-lifetime experience with pointless anxiety and pessimism and flicked off the display on her retinal screens with a small gesture. After all, today was a fantasy made real: Lana had finally completed her fourteen years of study at the Academy, and this meant she was now eligible for work experience placement on an actual starship. As every Cadet received the same educational uploads, the only reason she was heading for the majesty of the Carpe Astrum and not some sling barge or garbage scow was entirely due to a fluke win with the work placement lottery. From a class of more than six hundred, Lana was one of only fifteen Cadets who would be leaving this system for her first assignment, and the only one to be placed on the Carpe Astrum. Luck or not, the entire Board of the Academy had made the unprecedented move of personally seeing her off at the docks, and they had all watched her yellow shuttle arc into the sky until their eyes couldn't see it anymore.

In fact, now that Lana thought about it, it seemed as though the Dean had been more pleased at the prospect of Lana being situated on the other side of humanity's empire for the foreseeable future than about the career opportunities that her voyage might present...

...weird...

Lana had waited her entire life for a chance to prove herself. And while attaining a rank beyond the "Cadet" designation she'd worn since she was in self-cleaning nappies was a major part of her dreams, as was the romantic cliché of visiting distant alien worlds and annihilating their civilisations with mass driver weaponry, most of all Lana was looking forward to earning some respect. She wanted to be able to storm back to the Academy with golden stripes sewn to her shoulder so she could repay all those bitches who had endlessly tormented her. She'd return with the authority to rain down bloody vengeance on the thugs who'd made her teenage years a misery, and she'd do so without mercy. After all, Lana's ordeals at the Academy had been legendary: bullies had sprayed her granny undies and training bras with poison ivy extract, slipped a swarm of miniature piranhas into her foot spa, hidden Vegan Extremist literature in her bookshelf before dobbing her into the Antiterrorism Unit, and one time Lacy Chabbers had even replaced Lana's sugar-free breath mints with fast-acting gender reassignment drugs. To this day Lana had to fight the urge to stand up to pee.

She'd show them. She'd show them all.

Lana snapped out of her daydreaming when she felt a silent clunk through her chair. It meant that her shuttle had finally docked at an available pylon, and she could picture all sorts of umbilical lines automatically snaking up to embrace her shuttle like an amorous octopus with low standards. And while this was the 25th Century, the shuttle would still be stuck fast with relatively low-tech magnets. An enclosed walkway extended between the two vessels with a thud that could be felt rather than heard, and the bulkhead door scissored open. Lana hefted her backpack on one shoulder and did her best not to skip with joy.

Stepping out of the dented yellow pod, Lana brushed down her ebony uniform one more time, made sure her hair was still concrete-stiff in a bun that would require a crowbar to unroll, then took her first look at her new home. It took a moment for her to recognise that she was in a generic customs area, a tight series of corridors that led her through a total of fifteen security scanners. At the end of the line, after total silence from the scanners, an Enforcer wearing full sapphire riot gear and armed with enough non-lethal weaponry to take down a herd of elephants waved her through without looking. He didn't even bother to glance away from the softcore delights of his Sexy Sentients magazine.

Even though Enforcers were little more than rent-a-cops, Lana stiffened her spine, put her arms by her side and skewed her feet in a sign of respect.

"Cadet Lana Slade reporting. I begin my commission today, and I must report urgently to the Captain for duty. Could you please direct me?"

Yes. Yes, that sounded official enough. Mmm.

The Enforcer blinked lazily at Lana. He flicked a stunner towards the clearly marked EXIT sign and resumed reading his porno mag without a word. Lana was so taken aback by this disrespect that it took her a moment to follow up on her statement.

"I said, Cadet La-"

Sighing loudly, effectively cutting her off mid-syllable, the Enforcer angrily flicked his issue of Sexy Sentients at the ceiling. The holographic magazine disappeared to wherever it is deactivated programs went. He called out at some unseen person over his shoulder armour without breaking eye contact with the roof.

"Yo, Jenkins, some jail-bait work-experience kid's talking at me. From what I can tell she might be too young to bone. Suggestions?"

Jenkins' helmeted head popped up above the cubicle. He blinked at Lana in that same lazy way, carefully considering the matter before giving his official opinion.

"Ignore it."

Lana's mouth dropped open as Jenkins disappeared. She would never have expected such rampant disrespect from mere Enforcers, common mercenaries, of all things! They barely rated above discount-store security guards! The only reason The Unison employed them was so that the proper Navy officers could dedicate their time to duties that were far more important than unskilled grunt work like customs and basic law enforcement and kidney beatings. Lana prepared to launch a vicious salvo of verbal ammunition at these insolent spug-headed gummos that would shred them down to the bone, and took a deep breath to prepare for the tirade to end all tirades.

"You..."

The Enforcer interrupted Lana by flicking his wrist, which made the magazine reappear again. He began to casually cycle through a menagerie of inter-species pornography with zero shame. He didn't bother to make eye contact again. Lana opened her mouth to try again, and was cut off with an even clearer response.

"Piss off."

Glaring at the Enforcer with total death, she gathered up her bag and stormed out of the customs area.

*

Due to the fact this ship was hundreds of levels high and wrapped tightly with escalators and pneumatic turbo-lifts, a simple point in the right direction didn't really help Lana all that much, and she inevitably got lost. Not too worried about such a mundane obstacle with all the technology at her disposal, Lana flicked open the local auto-map function on her Omni to get directions from the Carpe Astrum itself. Her heart plunged down to the level of her toes when a written line of total doom appeared in front of her eyes instead of a friendly green arrow.

Insufficient clearance. Please do not attempt to access this system again.

It took Lana twenty attempts at asking directions to realise that nobody on board had a spare second to waste on her. Scientists, Enforcers, Navy and Military personnel, janitors, and even some guy wearing a full-body neon-purple Mister Drizzle furry costume fobbed her off before she could even finish asking her question. At best they ignored her, or snapped something along the lines of "I'm busy" or "ask somebody else." Her last attempt was with an Enforcer who was clearly on a break, and for her foolishness Lana copped a half-eaten MacDeath burger right in the face. With zero clearance at her disposal, the Information kiosks were just as useless as the humans, but in a more polite way.

Finally stopping at one of the many thousands of observation bays that displayed the more interesting aspects of space (as well as the boring empty blackness that composed 99.999999% of the Universe), Lana sat there for a time, watching busy people hurry by in the reflection. Staring out of a two-foot-thick transparent block of unbreakable glass in the direction of her home world - which wasn't even a dot from this distance - Lana shed two tears.

"May I be of assistance?"

Years of sustained bullying had trained Lana well, and she instantly sucked both salty drops back into her tear ducts. Turning, Lana came face to face with a man in a dirty straitjacket. A jolt of adrenalin suggested she start running immediately, but then she noticed a golden starburst icon dotted with dozens of rubies had been clipped to the leather straps holding the man's arms in place. This person was rated as a First Class Psy-Math, a qualification that only about twenty members of the human race possessed at any given time. His voice was highly educated, despite the fact it came from a mouth hedged by an unkempt beard saturated with yellow drool. It was at this point Lana finally noticed the stranger's face was covered in tiny mathematical equations carved into his skin, most likely by his own hand. Lana didn't have a chance to accept or reject his offer before the Psy-Math ploughed on.

"My name is Professor Jon Ames, and I am the Development Head of The Carpe Astrum Project." Ames's eyes blinked out of synchronisation. "The fifty-seventh Development Head, to be specific. As I'm sure you can appreciate, this Project has turned out to be a bit of a meat grinder. Now, before this conversation proceeds any further, I am legally bound to apologise for any inappropriate behaviour that I may exhibit, and The Unison is unable to be held accountable for any damage that I may inflict to your person or your possessions." Ames sighed at Lana's expression. 'You are familiar with Psy-Maths, my dear?"

Lana nodded stiffly.

"Of course. Psychotic mathematics is the highest form of mathematics," Lana managed, going into her default setting of regurgitating facts. "It's the only reason interstellar travel is possible. I was told that a key requirement of Psy-Math is that the mathematician needs to be in full-blown psychosis, the sort that involves visual hallucinations, paranoia and delusions, otherwise the equations cease to make sense and the resulting products don't work. Nobody knows exactly why."

"And did they teach you about the effects that prolonged exposure to Psy-Math has on the human brain?" Ames hinted.

Lana tried not to take a step back as Ames smiled at her with stubby, ground-down teeth. What she'd heard about the side-effects of Psy-Math was impossible to describe in a polite manner, so she just nodded and maintained a neutral expression.

"Good!" Ames said with relief. "That saves us considerable time. Now, what did you want to know? Ask me anything! I feel like sharing my knowledge with the sponge-like mind of a child right about now."

"Um, while I do appreciate your time, Professor Ames, I'm sure you're very busy, and I really don't want to keep you from your duties," Lana said diplomatically, trying not to be offended by being referred to as a child at eighteen years old.

Ames twitched a small smile. There was sadness behind it.

"Actually, once we complete today's final test, my work here is done," Ames sat down on a padded ledge beneath the massive unbreakable window. Lana wondered how he was going to stand up again without being able to use his arms.

"I hope you don't mind me talking to you. I've sort of, well, alienated myself from the rest of the crew, even the other Psy-Maths. You can only bite so many people before you stop getting invited out for coffee hypos."

"Mmm."

"So, Cadet, what would you like to know?"

Lana shrugged.

"Well, I was wondering if you knew where I could find the Captain?"

The sad smile immediately melted away into eye-bulging rage.

"You want...directions?" Ames face spasimed. "I offer you the opportunity to speak with one of the greatest minds of this era, to ask anything, to have an open slather to a modern Great Library of Alexandria, and you...you..." Ames turned scarlet. "You want directions?!"

Lana looked down at her too-shiny boots. She considered how quickly she'd be able to retrieve the small atomiser bottle of fire spray in the front pocket of her bag if this encounter continued to go south. Ames was important, though, so she did the smart thing.

"Sorry," Lana said meekly. "I apologise, Professor. I didn't think before I spoke. I could ask you a better question, if you're still happy to speak with me?"

The fury disappeared as quickly as it had arrived. The Professor nodded, once.

Lana took a moment to weigh up the potential wealth of information that Ames may offer against the possibility that he may freak out and cause a scene. Her day had already been far too embarrassing and demoralising without the prospect of getting into a fight with a severely impaired genius wrapped in a straitjacket, especially one who was more than one- hundred-and-eighty-seven levels above her non-existent security rating. Desperate to turn things around, Lana made the obvious choice: she would try to find out something that may be beneficial to her career, and hope that it didn't end with her getting her face bitten off.

"Professor, those triangular tiles that make up the outer layers of the ship...the ones that ripple like water...why do they form those complex patterns?" Lana knew that she was flying very, very close to the sun with such a question, but this was too good an opportunity to pass up. "It's just that I couldn't find an explanation on the Link, official or unofficial, as though the moderators didn't want people to broach the topic, let alone answer it. It's just hard for me to accept that something on the scale of the Carpe Astrum would indulge in something so...decorative."

Ames smiled darkly.

"Ah, straight to the classified stuff! Excellent! Well, here's something only a dozen people know for certain: the "liquid" effects caused by those trillions of tiles isn't just cosmetic. You see, the outer layers of the ship are actually a visual expression of seventh dimensionality that has been effectively 'dumbed-down' to our relatively mundane four dimensions. The complexity of the seventh dimension is almost beyond verbal expression and would require ridiculous hyperbole to even begin to explain. To put it in a way that won't result in your skull imploding, those ripples are the Carpe Astrum plotting its upcoming course through seventh dimensional space. Also, it must be noted that time – commonly known as the fourth dimension – cannot exist in seventh dimensional space, which is why the transition appears to be instantaneous, and why we do not perceive its passage."

Ames blinked. After fifteen seconds of silence Lana eventually realised that he'd finished babbling, and was eagerly awaiting another question.

"So…where are we going, exactly?" Lana began. "To tell you the truth, I've never actually left this system, so it's a bit of a big deal for me."

At that moment a bunch of armoured Enforcers went past. They were dragging a screaming man in orange overalls down the thickly-carpeted corridor by his ears, but Lana was listening so intently to the Professor that she barely glanced at the spectacle.

"Seven star systems across the Western line of the Galactic Plane, approximately ninety-one lightyears towards that bright point right there." As his hands were restrained, Ames had to point out of the window with his nose. "Existing methods of travel would take anywhere from weeks to years to cover such a distance, but for the Carpe Astrum it should be instantaneous...like I just said."

"Sounds fast."

Ames shook his head violently. This comment seemed to have struck a nerve, and the Professor's demeanour suddenly changed.

"No, no! That's not it at all, you imbecile! Velocity has nothing to do with it! The targeting systems of the Carpe Astrum identify the exact profile of the correct star, and the ship appears next to it. But we don't budge an inch. In a four dimensional sense, nothing changes. This ship, despite what so many defective people think, doesn't actually move at all. It simply ceases to exist in one place, and then begins to exist somewhere else." Ames blinked rapidly, almost like he was having a small seizure. "It has been postulated that the Carpe Astrum actually accomplishes this by destroying itself down to the atomic level before creating a new, perfect copy of itself somewhere else, but, well, that's neither here nor there and hasn't been substantiated by anybody of merit." Ames twitched again. "Happy now, you bitch? That's what you get for forgetting my birthday! Two parrots on a wire, and one of them is a koala! A koala! A bloody koala! Do you understand? A koala! A koala!"

Lana gaped as Professor Ames began to sing a loud, bawdy song. Passer-byes were looking at the scene, but none of them got involved. Lana knew she should have sprinted in the opposite direction the moment she saw the straitjacket.

"Um, I kinda need to go, Professor, but thanks for your time…"

Ames stopped singing and his face relaxed. The anger and offence melted away.

"You know, I'm actually a Professor." Ames whispered, winking. "I'm quite good with numbers, too. Do you know why?"

"Because you're a Professor?"

Ames smiled with far too much gum.

"I've got to go." Lana repeated, more firmly this time. Then she remembered she was lost. Against her better judgement, she decided to ask her initial question again and hope that Ames didn't wig out. "By the way, Professor, do you know where the Captain is?"

Ames paused for a moment and blinked out of sync again.

"The Captain usually works in his loft."

"Okay. And where is that, exactly?"

"The Captain's loft?" Ames scratched at his ear with a long toenail. It was an impressive stretch. "The Captain's loft is where the Captain usually works when he's working in the Captain's loft. But sometimes you can also find him in the Captain's loft."

'Yes, okay, I understand that but, but where is it?"

Professor Ames blinked, turned his head and indicated a doorway a little over fifteen metres away. Lana looked up to see a grandmotherly secretary sitting at an empty desk directly beneath a glowing neon sign that declared CAPTAIN. She'd been twenty rotten steps away this whole time!

Feeling silly, Lana shouldered her heavy bag and nodded in thanks to Ames, but her words were immediately interrupted by three Enforcers in special white coats who crash-tackled the Professor and began to drag him – screaming - down the corridor. Ames sank his teeth into one of their Kevlar gloves and began yelling incoherently about dingos, so Lana decided that not getting involved any further would be a good career move.

Lana reached the Captain's secretary's desk just in time to see the Captain emerge from his loft with fury chiselled into his face. He appeared to be adjusting his underpants through his flight suit. Heading straight past the Cadet without a nod, Lana decided to put an end to today's disrespect by defiantly blocking his path. This may not have been wise considering that he looked mad enough to rip her lips off with his bare hands, but Lana knew that she needed to start being more assertive or the rest of her placement would surely be a misery.

"Captain, I am Cadet Lana Slade from the local Academy and I am officially reporting for duty."

The Captain gave her a dark look before dodging around her.

"I am very busy at present, Cadet Slade."

Lana easily kept up, feeling a little confused.

"But sir, I was informed that upon my arrival I would be immediately issued with minimal security clearance and a probationary assignment so I can observe how things operate prior to a receiving a more permanent placement in line with my skills and talents. May I have my first assignment, sir?"

"I really don't have time for this," the Captain snapped, trying to dodge Lana both literally and verbally. "We're a matter of hours away from the most important moment of interstellar travel for this century. Go inject a coffee hypo, and I'll waste some time on you later."

Lana stood up straight, blocked the Captain a second time, and glared at him. Although small and young, there was a scary determination in Lana's eyes that she'd been working on for the last six months, a special facial expression she'd perfected for occasions just like this. The glare usually helped Lana to gain the upper hand, but little did she know that this was mainly because it made her look slightly insane. Years of solid training in the style of martial arts known as keri soko had helped Lana focus her fire into a white-hot point, but that obviously hadn't helped to keep all those equally-trained bullies at bay. With a flick of her wrist, Lana's Omni projected a holographic piece of paper into her hand.

"Captain, I have official permission in writing that says I am to receive my assignment the moment I report for duty."

The Captain glared right back at her, fished in his pocket for a laser-tip pen, scribbled a line of code on a chocolate-smeared Sludge bar wrapper, and thrust it into Lana's hands. It was unclear what the sequence of letters and numbers could mean.

"Where do I use this, sir?"

"Garage," was his clipped answer. "You now have full authority over lifeboat number thirty-five, as well as all its crew and systems. I trust you will not misuse your power, Cadet."

Lana blinked as the Captain stormed past with the tinkle of gold piping. A lifeboat? But that was just an automated escape pod, and a tiny one at that. It had no manual controls, no weapon systems, no star drives and was more boring than a boiled cardboard sandwich on stale brown bread. Lana tried to put on a brave face for the sake of her budding career.

"But..."

The Captain stopped like a dropped brick, and his words hit even harder.

"Slade, not only are you are thirty-four minutes late, but when I checked to make sure you hadn't died in some kind of catastrophic shuttle disaster, imagine my surprise to see that you've been wandering about the place like a spugging tourist. You had just one task today: get here on time. You have failed at that task." He bared his teeth before turning to storm away. "Block me one more time and I'll Brig you, understood?"

"Thank you, sir," she called to the Captain's back.

The Captain snorted and muttered, possibly to himself.

"Enjoy the lifeboat, Cadet."

Once he was gone there was no way Lana could stop herself from sighing and quietly grumbling about this farce that she had hoped to call a career.

"Great. Just...just great."

It was immediately clear to Lana what this situation called for: a jumbo decaf vanilla-essence Frappuccino with a double caramel shot, chocolate sprinkles and a curly straw served in an edible gingerbread mug.

CHAPTER THREE PSYCHOPATHY FOR BEGINNERS

Trace's job as an Enforcer was to prevent crime and general naughtiness on the Carpe Astrum by visibly patrolling the common areas of the ship. In the event that physical intervention was deemed necessary, she was authorised to act with minimal force. While Trace was renowned for finding trouble ten times as often as any other Enforcer on board, curiously, all the dramas that occurred during her shifts only seemed to start after she had arrived...

Looming at six feet seven inches, an expensive series of almost-legal genetic splicing treatments had altered Trace's physique into something similar to a queen-sized mattress stuffed with footballs. Almost all of her exposed skin was covered with tribal scarification patterns, and what little was left had been pierced with long, thin obsidian needles. She had walnuts for knuckles and ice for eyes.

Her solo beat was the sprawling Food Court that took up level four-hundred-and-fifteen, and her shift mostly involved walking a massive figure-eight over and over again until it was time to knock off. On average, her shift lasted forty-two laps, and involved three broken bones, eight concussions, and at least one person being repeatedly kicked in the kidneys. Like every other Enforcer, she was protected with thick layers of sapphire blue riot armour and a belt that rattled with an assortment of non-lethal, though highly unpleasant, weaponry.

Trace stormed through the packed, animated Java Jab cafe that served as the middle point of her beat, radiating hostility with every glare and stomp. This Java Jab was far from the only coffee den on the Carpe Astrum, but it was far classier than what most of the janitors, technicians, dock workers and mechanics were used to. For one, you actually had to wear shoes to get in. Strictly speaking, Java Jab would much prefer to be frequented by the rich, powerful, beautiful and brilliant people who were on board for today's final test, but it's a fact that off-duty labourers use the exact same colour of money (though admittedly a lot less of it), so the plebs were grudgingly served by the snobby baristas.

Calm mood lighting reflected off Trace's shaved head, facial piercings and layers of non-lethal weapons as she went about executing her duties. For some reason, Trace seemed to have decided that her "duties" should include bumping into people who were trying to inject coffee hypos or sip cocktails, then wordlessly glare at them in the hopes they'd be dumb enough to start something. Unfortunately for Trace's bloodlust, it was clear that everyone knew who she was, as it only took one glance for the customers to decide that hey, they might as well just accept the fact that their vodka thick shake had been spilled, and they should just buy another one.

Trace continued to make her way past the bar, nudging patrons just as they were about to inject caffeine-delivery devices into their necks. After a couple of uneventful minutes without a Barney, it seemed there was no fun to be had today…until Trace bumped a short girl wearing the ebony uniform of the local Navy Academy. Lana turned around with a surprised expression, as this jostling had spilled half a gingerbread mug of jumbo decaf vanilla-essence Frappuccino with a double caramel shot, chocolate sprinkles and a curly straw all over her best formal ware. She looked up at Trace with fury, a burning anger that had been building by increments her whole life.

"You're paying for my dry-cleaning," Lana snapped.

Trace blinked in a bored way.

"Interesting theory, kid. Well, it's only fair that I give you a theory in return: piss off before I belt you into a skank-flavoured puddle."

Lana looked at Trace like she was an imbecile.

"How is that a theory? That makes no sense whatsoever. Do those piercings go all the way through your brain or something?"

The whole Java Jab went quiet. All conversations ceased. Trace narrowed her eyes at the Cadet, who must have been quite a bit less than half her weight, and

29

everyone within reaching range casually moved a couple of metres away.

"I'm not kidding," Lana insisted. "You are exactly five seconds away from an official complaint."

Trace expressed her exact level of concern with this threat by yawning and turning to leave, but Lana's iron-tight hand snapped out to grip her forearm. The Enforcer smiled in ecstasy: this was exactly what she'd been hoping for!

Trace spun around, picked up Lana by her face with one hand, and slammed the back of her head into an Inject Responsibly poster until the laminate cracked. Holding the stunned Cadet up by the jaw like it was nothing, Trace threw Lana clear over the bar and into a bank of Frappuccino syrup bottles with a loud smash.

"Hey!"

Four chairs on the other side of the café squeaked loudly as a full pack of five male off-duty Enforcers got to their feet. Trace turned, her face glowing red and her eyes deranged with violence, and stared the entire group down until they slowly sank into their seats, cringing in defeat. Grinning with chipped teeth, Trace turned back towards the mess of syrup and blood she'd just caused to be greeted with a surprise: not only had Lana gotten up, but she was perched on the bar like a monkey. The young Cadet put pressure onto the ball of one foot and expanded her other three limbs in a praying mantis pose.

"Eight dans of keri soko coming your way, bitch."

Trace didn't wait for Lana to act on her threat, and threw the sort of haymaker king-hit that would usually finish any fight. Lana bowed forwards to take the blow on her concrete-tough hair, which had been reinforced with a brand of hairspray that was graded to survive cyclones. Trace growled as her wrist jolted painfully on impact, nearly breaking her hand.

And then the tables turned.

Lana's left foot flashed into the side of Trace's jaw in a stunning, invisibly-fast blow. Eyelids fluttering as she dipped towards being knocked unconscious, Trace's entire world suddenly became an endless barrage of open-hand blows and kicks. Although the individual strikes didn't have too much power behind them, it took Trace a couple of seconds to recover from the surprise of this prissy little Cadet suddenly turning into a keri soko master. Eventually, Trace managed to snatch Lana's extended leg by the ankle mid-kick, turned, and threw her at the wall. Lashing out mid-flip, Lana bounced off the same Inject Responsibly poster as before like the ghost of Jackie Chan, and tried to toe-kick Trace across the other side of her jaw. This time Trace ducked, clenched her knuckles white, and prepared to take a swing at Lana once she had sailed over.

And then something happened that changed both their futures.

30

Whipping through the air, the blade of her foot extended, Lana skimmed the top of Trace's shaved head by a centimetre. In a stroke of bad luck that bordered on Biblical, Lana only had a microsecond to register that her fight-ending jump kick was now heading straight for the Captain of the Carpe Astrum just before she connected with his mouth at top speed. The Captain had been reaching for Trace's shoulder, rage chiselled into his features as he went to wrap his fingers around her bulging muscles. His eyes had only begun to flick up towards Lana when the heel of her dress shoe pounded into his mouth, jolting his brain about so badly that he immediately went wall-eyed.

To make matters worse, Trace hadn't got the memo that it was the Captain touching her, so she twisted around and put all her strength into a punch. The dazed Captain had only just started to sag towards the tiles when Trace caught him flush on the nose and both cheeks with her whole fist, and there was the familiar sensation of cartilage breaking under her knuckles. The Captain's slump became a total redwood of a collapse.

Landing smoothly on the toes of both boots and the fingertips of her left hand, Lana whipped around in time to see the Captain's burst plum of a face hit the deck. He was snoring a chainsaw melody on the way down, which at the very least proved that he was still alive despite being sandwiched between two king hits. Beyond that, it was hard to tell how badly he was wrecked.

There was total silence. Everybody was gaping at the Captain with the same expression. Lana broke the aural void with a whispered curse.

"Oh, spug."

The Captain had barely been on the ground for three seconds when half-a-dozen apple-sized grenades bounced into the heart of the Java Jab. A soupy green cloud of concentrated sting gas instantly filled the coffee house, and all the customers were suddenly gagging and screaming a chorus of pain. Hordes of Enforcers in full riot gear and rebreather masks burst through the trendy saloon-style doors, jabbing stun batons at the coughing, blinded onlookers. Trace and Lana were tackled, doused with fire spray, handcuffed and dragged away, but even then the two women kept trying to kick and spit on each other. It was like trying to handle a writhing mass of poisonous snakes, and not fun for anybody involved.

CHAPTER FOUR BORN VICTIM

"Hey! Slummer! Wake up! Hustle!"

Jimmy Slummer blinked at the sound of his name, but kept on staring blankly at the shiny, twisting chrome maze of the Burger Highway. Installed in a billion MacDeath franchises across Known Space, the Burger Highway was an intricate silver labyrinth of chutes, slides, ramps and pneumatic tubes. It unified an army of automated machines such as self-tipping deep fryers, bun warmers, patty flippers, salad shredders, sauce rifles, salt shotguns, wrapping spools, and auto-baggers. The Burger Highway had been created by the MacDeath Combine to prevent the peons they employed as tax write-offs from screwing up any orders, as there was no chance that such dropkicks could possibly deliver what MacDeath's promised without serious artificial assistance. After all, as the flashing neon yellow badge on Jimmy's left breast proclaimed: "I'll Get It Right First Time, Or I Don't Work Here Anymore!"

As usual, Jimmy had zoned out. He'd been daydreaming about the All You Can Eat Lunchtime Burrito Deal at the Muchacho Taco down the other side of the Food Court again. This might remain a pipedream, though, as after that unfortunate business last week, he'd been expressly warned never to come back unless accompanied by at least one sanitation engineer with biohazard clean up equipment. Honestly, you projectile-spray neon-orange vomit just one time, and people never let you forget it...

"Mmm?" Jimmy managed, giving a twitch.

Now that Jimmy's brain had started to warm up from its dormancy, he began to process the reflection staring back at him from the chrome ramp. Two hundred kilograms of cellulite and bad posture gaped back at him with a slack jaw. His apple-like body was dressed in a regulation yellow MacDeath uniform: an apron plastered with the standard I'm Servin' It! tagline, matching pants and an old-fashioned chef's hat. His headgear was emblazoned with the famous Mac logo and the grinning, manic face of Duncan MacDeath, the Irish founder of the mega-chain. What Jimmy saw in the reflection was a loser, a hyper-obese chump with a five o'clock shadow you'd need a flamethrower to remove.

Jimmy turned his dull expression towards Pluris. Pluris was a jerk, but he was a jerk who wouldn't hesitate to dob in a co-worker if he might benefit from it. Jimmy was momentarily distracted again by some sort of commotion coming from the Java Jab across the Food Court, but he didn't have time to check for local safety alerts on his standard-issue retinal screens before Pluris launched into one of his usual failed attempts at cutting wit.

"Ah, awake, are we?" Pluris sneered. "Very considerate of you."

Jimmy could not comprehend why Pluris always acted so cocky. After all, it was common knowledge that Pluris had only started working for MacDeaths because he'd been fired from the terrarium store for sniffing the turtles one too many times. Like every other floater in the MacDeath employee pool, Pluris was addicted to Ultrasweet - the dangerously habit-forming synthetic sugar substitute that had been a key ingredient in every MacDeath product for two hundred years – and that meant he had a bodily morphism halfway between a walrus and a lump fish. As Pluris had a tendency to bring out violence in the most peaceful of people, his extremely punchable face had been banished to the back of the store where only Jimmy had to tolerate him. Sometimes, Jimmy's life just felt like one long encounter with Pluris.

Pluris rolled a fat finger at a blinking neon sign. It proclaimed HOPPER IS 94% OUT OF SLUG in blinking red lines.

"We've almost sold out of Fisherman Utopia Sliders," Pluris snapped, flicking his wrist towards a vault-like slab at the rear of the store. REPLER was stencilled above the armoured portal. "Go grow another batch." Pluris latched onto Jimmy's wobbly, hairy shoulder as he slouched past. "And remember, Slummer: mature it for exactly two-and-a-half minutes, be sure that the brain-stem doesn't have time to form, terminate it immediately, then hit PROCESS, followed by MOLD INTO SLIDER PATTIES. Got it?"

Jimmy's pudgy face creased in a frown.

"I know how to gestate a slug, Pluris. I've been here a lot longer than you."

Pluris sneered.

"You are aware that's not a good thing, right?"

Jimmy heard a loud, glassy crunch as he took a step, and glanced at the underside of his bare foot to assess the damage. Due to Jimmy's overhanging curtains of cellulite, this involved using a reflective floor vent. Jimmy grunted in annoyance at the yellow Catch-Up sauce splattered all over his heel, and managed to knock the broken glass shards out of his leathery skin by kicking a wood like toe against a deep fryer. Despite the fact he'd trod on a mass of little blades, there wasn't any apparent injury and he couldn't feel a thing. Years of constant pressure had squashed all sensation out of his abused feet and left their undersides tougher than oak.

Pluris laughed a super-villain laugh at this for no real reason. Jimmy sighed and waited for the sad insult.

"Congratulations, Slummer. You are now officially the fattest, ugliest, stupidest

Hobbit of all time. Rowling would roll in her grave." Pluris waved in dismissal. "At least put your flip-flops on. I'm not copping the blame if you deep fry your idiot toes into nuggets or something."

"It was Tolkien, dip-head," Jimmy muttered once Pluris had vanished again. "JK Tolkien."

Jimmy pushed the armoured vault open, grumbling dark curses at Pluris and his entire genetic line, and waited inside the darkness for a couple of seconds. Lines of fluorescent strips eventually lit up in an uncoordinated strobing pattern, revealing a round room that was mostly filled by a calm, green-tinged circle of liquid. As customers would never have any reason to come back here to the Repler Pool, the grimy industrial area was far removed from the cheery, idiotic, childish face that MacDeaths tried so hard to promote.

He approached a vending machine next to the heavy door and blinked at a series of crude push buttons. Scanning his eyes over a line of off-white squares stamped with exotic animal names like BEEF BIRD, OCTOCRAB, SQUIGGLER, MEAT-MICE, CHOC-O-RAT and SQUIRT-PIG, Jimmy's finger eventually found the TITAN SLUG option and jabbed it. A transparent capsule the size of a chicken egg rattled down the chute after a lot of noise and a burst of icy mist, and Jimmy carefully raised the oval to his left eye. The embryo of a Titan Slug, a multi-sectioned invertebrate no bigger than a witchetty grub, was suspended inside. It twisted a little bit in response to being out of the freezer.

Even if this was the first time he'd gestated meat for MacDeaths (and it wasn't), any imbecile could figure out how to use the Repler Pool simply by looking at the closest wall. Every vertical surface was decorated by detailed instructions in the universal language known as Unglish along with three-dimensional diagrams, timing charts, red blinking warning boxes and disclaimers. So, so many disclaimers. As MacDeath employees were so notoriously stupid that they were statistically guaranteed to die by misadventure in the first five years of their career with the burger juggernaut, this meant that everything had to be explained at a kindergarten level.

Jimmy casually flicked the see-through egg into the Repler Pool. Its casing melted on contact and the Titan Slug embryo began to grow like a time-lapse video. As Jimmy had already grown bored of watching this miracle by the time the invertebrate reached a metre long, the sight of something scurrying from a nearby vent easily captured his attention. Jimmy's breath caught in his throat as he realised what he was looking at, something that even MacDeaths wouldn't tolerate, something that could get this whole franchise closed down: a cockroach. Jimmy snapped his fingers.

"Ship, query," Jimmy requested to thin air.

There was an eleven-second pause as Jimmy's turn in the queue rolled around, followed by a polite, feminine voice.

"How can I assist you, James Slummer?"

"I thought this ship was meant to be cockroach-free at all times."

There was a pause.

"My records show that this ship is completely clear of all nineteen categories of infestive vermin," the ship confirmed without any offence or arrogance. "The class nine sanitation engineer allocated to this duty confirmed this in triplicate."

"But I just saw one! I think," Jimmy said, beginning to double-guess himself. Then something truly horrible dawned. "Wait, class nine? Who, exactly?"

Pause.

"Robert Tuesday was placed in charge of ship wide fumigation eight days ago."

Jimmy choked. Bloody Tuesday strikes again!

Jimmy nibbled his lip in anxiety, thinking dark thoughts. Even a low-ranker like him knew how dangerous it was to have vermin in the systems of a prototype ship like the Carpe Astrum. Anything could happen if roaches got into the wrong place, literally anything. But then Jimmy realised that this could turn out to be a twenty-four caret golden opportunity to make a name for himself. If he was somehow able to avert a cockroach-related catastrophe from taking place, if he could prevent something terrible from damaging the most expensive object ever built in the history of mankind…well, that smelled like a promotion! He could be running this whole franchise in a matter of minutes!

"Ship, I need to speak with the Captain!" Jimmy announced proudly, almost able to feel the medals getting pinned to his chest already.

Pause.

"That is impossible, James. Your security clearance is sixty-eight levels too low for such a request. And even if you did have clearance, the Captain is absolutely not to be interrupted during the final test of the Carpe Astrum, or until the following celebratory cocktail parties have run their course in a week."

Jimmy deflated.

"But it's an emergency!" Jimmy wailed. "People could die!"

"Please state the nature of your emergency, James."

"Cockroaches!" Jimmy yelled.

This time, the ship didn't even bother responding. It took Jimmy almost a minute to take the hint that the AI wasn't even going to bother dignifying his outburst with an answer.

"Fine, fine!" Jimmy snapped, getting angry. "I need to see Tuesday, then."

"Please be more specific or rephrase your question, James."

"I need to see Robert Tuesday in person. Where is he?"

The computer ticked over for a few moments.

"Robert Tuesday is currently in the Brig on level zero in a Cramper Cube. The Captain has disallowed all privileges, including visits, bedding, food, water, heat, adequate space and all other comforts."

Jimmy smiled. This should be easy enough with Tuesday trapped in a box.

Filled with determination (and about a litre of chocolate mousse he'd sucked out of a steel nozzle while Pluris wasn't watching), Jimmy marched out of the Repler Pool area and slammed the armoured door behind him. Remembering to slip on his worn flip-flops, Jimmy stomped past five thick columns of grumbling MacDeath customers and made a bee-line for the elevator banks on the other side of the Food Court. Pluris was so busy ineffectively trying to chat up one of the uglier check-out chicks that he didn't notice the human sphere known as Jimmy Slummer leaving the shop.

The turbolift was a bit tight for Jimmy's ample frame (after all, it was only wide enough to accommodate two average-sized people), but he managed to squeeze in anyway. A slapped button sent Jimmy's capsule plunging to the lowest point of the ship in a matter of seconds. Spiralling open to reveal a bare metallic hallway, the first thing Jimmy saw on the far side of the corridor was an Enforcer on guard duty reading a Judge Dredd comic. He looked up as Jimmy walked in and raised an eyebrow in a wordless question. Beyond the gaoler's desk, Jimmy could see the walls of this dingy metal cavern were lined with opaque boxes the size of luxury coffins. A twisted black Cramper Cube in the centre of the room was a lot more sharply angled than the other cells, but just as dark. The gaoler blinked, waiting to hear what Jimmy wanted.

"I, um, need to visit someone for five minutes," Jimmy managed.

Nervously sidling up to the wary gaoler, who was well known to be crooked as a series of compound fractures, Jimmy got out a handful of crumpled purple notes from his yellow apron – a total of twenty German yen - and scattered them on the guard's desk. Smiling at the bribe and tipping his hat, the gaoler whacked a button and left, whistling merrily.

It took a second, but all fifteen cells turned clear. Jimmy's eyes skidded over two boxes in the corner to see they were currently occupied by the sociopathic Enforcer known as Trace and some late-teens girl in an ebony uniform. The moment they could see each other the two women began to shout, and even though both of their boxes were soundproofed Jimmy could clearly tell their words were of the four-letter variety. The name LANA SLADE was digitally represented over the cell of the younger woman.

Jimmy gave a little smile when the Cramper Cube in the middle of the room finally turned transparent to display its sole occupant: Bob Tuesday. The Cramper was so low that Tuesday couldn't stand up more than halfway, but it was also so narrow that he couldn't sit down either, leaving him hunched over like a croquet hoop. The look on Tuesday's face proved that God hadn't designed humans to enjoy having their spines angled like boomerangs. While Crampers could be set to administer painful burning or zapping sensations every time the occupant came in contact with the walls, taking the punishment to another level, Jimmy wasn't sure if this option had been activated. Although not a sadist by nature, Jimmy enjoyed seeing the look of discomfort on Tuesday's face.

Wobbling over, Jimmy untwisted the Cramper's food slot and prepared to make his demands. Tuesday beat him to it, however.

"So I'm assuming you received all that cash I left with your neighbour and have come to thank me for paying back my debts on time and in full, Slummer?" Tuesday rattled off as soon as the slot opened, placing his black grin up against the hole. His breath made Jimmy take a step backwards. "Fella promised me you'd get it soon as you arrived home. Promised me on his mum's life! Mmm...hope he can be trusted, eh? Actually, nows I mention it, he looked a little bit dodgy, to be honest, so I wouldn't trust a word he says, right?" Tuesday gave Jimmy another smile. "Be sure to enjoy those German yen in good health, Slummer, in very, very good health! Go buy yourself something nice, yeah? Thanks for the visit, chum!"

Jimmy blinked away this verbal onslaught of sleaze and bald-faced lies. Glaring into Tuesday's rodent face, thoughts began to churn behind Jimmy's forehead cellulite until something relatively unimportant pushed the whole fumigation subject aside. It was the sort of lapse made every day across The Unison, but Jimmy's defective attention span was about to change the future history of all mankind.

"Hey! You still owe me two-hundred-and-fifty German yen, Tuesday!"

Tuesday's grin faded into a scowl. Jimmy didn't need to be a psychic to tell the janitor was mentally kicking himself for the slip.

"Like I just said, Slummer, I left it with your neigh-" Tuesday frowned. "Wait, I only owe you two-hundred-and-thirty. Don't MacDeaths teach you how to add?"

"I'm counting the bribe I had to slip the guard." Jimmy folded his arms. "Simple."

"Hey, the only thing simple here is you, Slummer. I'm not paying a single sen more than two-thirty yen."

"So pay up, then. I don't believe this 'I left it with your neighbour' crap for an instant."

Tuesday's mouth curved.

"Right. Soon as this cell is open, I promise I'll try and think of a way that I might manage to figure out how to get my hands on some money, if that's at all possible, okay? And then I'll seriously attempt to pay back certain parties who may possibly have it coming to them, yeah? Happy with that?"

"And when are you getting out, exactly?" Jimmy pushed.

"Probably got another ten years in here," Tuesday said morosely. "But, on the bright side, after that they'll fire me into deep space, so when I finish drifting through eternity I'll be sure to look you up. Can't ask for more than that, can you?"

Jimmy sighed.

"Well, that's a tough break," Jimmy conceded, pretending to look defeated. "Guess I'll just have to find another way to earn some cash, right, Tuesday?"

"Guess so, Slummer."

Jimmy clicked his fat fingers together with a wet noise.

"You know what? I might find out about being transferred down here to the lower floors so I can cook for the Brig. I heard they've had trouble filling that job."

Tuesday's face showed total dread. Jimmy's astonishing lack of culinary skill was common knowledge among the crew. Tuesday let out an unintentional moan before Jimmy started getting specific.

"Perhaps I'll start with some lightly boiled rat bladders stuffed with menthol cigarette butts?"

"Okay, that's enough, Jimmy..." Tuesday growled.

"And plenty of freshly-steamed broccoli on the side."

Tuesday retched at the "b" word.

"Broccoli! That crap's illegal for a reason!"

"I'll do it, Tuesday," Jimmy growled at the transparent aluminium, trying and failing to look menacing. "I'm sick of being your chump. I want that cash now, or I guarantee your tongue will commit suicide within a day."

At the rear of the Brig, Lana and Trace were still trying to yell at each other. Both women finally went silent and just glared when it became apparent that their cells were muted and they were wasting perfectly good insults on their own ears. As their only choice of entertainment was to watch Tuesday and Jimmy have an unheard argument, they observed in boredom.

*

Far above the Brig, on the opposite vertices of the Carpe Astrum, was the main observation deck. As this huge open area was designed and decorated to coddle the rich, famous and brilliant, it had been constructed of rare empathic marble and draped in velvet curtains dyed such rich purples that most worlds only allowed royalty to own such colours. It was entirely lit with the charming crudity of white, arm-sized candles made from refined cricket fat, and an upper gantry of huge, plush recliners awaited the caress of entitled bottoms.

Gaggles of celebrities, politicians and zero-use trust-fund yen-wasters were joined by stiff-necked Navy officers in gold-trimmed midnight-blue finery and nervous, sweaty boffins who were doing their best not to have nose bleeds from the anxiety of actual human contact. Despite their crucial importance to The Carpe Astrum Project, it went without saying that all of the Psy-Maths had been sedated and strapped into their padded penthouse suites for Quiet Time. If you paid attention, Professor Ames could still be heard laughing like a maniac and screaming about koalas from two corridors away.

The gentle tinkle of pianos served as a backdrop to the babble of conversation and occasional laughter, and near-psychic hospitality staff silently swooped back and forth with endless canapes. Of all the rich treats the white-gold platters had to offer, the velociraptor carpaccio and brie-infused zucchini flowers went particularly quickly. The glitterati washed down these morsels with sips from ludicrously fragile flutes of the very finest Passion Pop from the legendary vineyards of Griffith, Australia, careful not to stain their priceless polyweave sin-silks in the process.

Sinking industrial amounts of Chateau Goon with the VIPs, the Captain wasn't sure if he'd be able to tolerate these braying prats for the duration of the final test, let alone for six consecutive cocktail parties spread over a week. If it was up to him, these civilians would all be relocated so they could go and be useless elsewhere. Of course, it was little surprise the Captain was in the foulest of moods. Being humiliated in front of his entire security detail had been bad enough, but getting his jaw and nose broken in multiple places had really sent this day plunging into the deepest Stygian depths. It had only taken a couple of minutes for an AutoDoc to reset the bones of his face, inject fresh cartilage and sew everything up with molecule-thin organic thread, but his fury could not be sated as easily. Alcohol was doing its usual valiant duty, but the Captain's main solace came from the thought of what he was going to do with those three gonks down in the Brig when he had a spare day or two. Bolt cutters and blow torches may be involved.

A gentle harp thrummed to get everyone's attention. Thousands of cultured conversations dialled down several notches as the VIPs slowly took their seats in the upper gallery of the observation deck to stare up at the blank, three-hundred-metre-long ceramic wall that dominated one whole side of this plush area. Once everyone was seated (their stunning lack of efficiency eventually led to the Captain literally crushing an entire champagne flute in his hand) the unbreakable surface turned transparent for the viewing pleasure of mankind's elite, revealing the true grandeur of what was about to happening just outside of the Carpe Astrum's hull.

Taking his seat with everyone else, the Captain produced a code-locked hologram from his Omni implant and twisted it open. The ship's guidance system had already been loaded with the exact profile of the target star weeks ago, a glowing ball like any other that was situated seven systems along the Western curve of the galactic plane. An advanced shipping yard was ready and waiting on the other side to welcome the Carpe Astrum on her triumphant arrival, a trip that should occur instantaneously. As the ship's supercomputer had crunched all the numbers and checked its work so many times that it verged on ridiculous, moving the Carpe Astrum to its target would involve little more than the Captain giving the software equivalent of a nod. With a thirty-seven digit security code and six different identity confirmation tests, he gave the order to slide.

Electromagnetic discharges of a hundred colours skittered across the expanding event horizon being created in the deepest core of the Carpe Astrum's two major equilateral triangles, producing a few ahhhs and ohhhs from the glitterati. The starship's outer skin of tiles continued to whir and click in water-like ripples as they expressed a seventh dimensional set of coordinates, like God Himself was scribbling the meaning of life in pig Latin with a crayon.

But there was one unforeseen factor...

*

If Tuesday's reeking bunkroom had a motto, it would probably be Everything Is An Ashtray. And even though a pair of Enforcers had just ripped it apart not thirty minutes ago to recover Tuesday's stashes of ill-gotten gains, this glorified closet had already been in such an unliveable state of squalor that the violence had somehow managed to tidy it up a little. This had annoyed the Enforcers no end.

On Tuesday's breakfast nook, a thin shelf mostly dominated by ashtrays filled with blackened lung expectorations and charred filters, a box of Cornflakes rocked a little, as though something was rattling around inside of the cardboard sleeve. Tipping back and forth more and more violently, coming close to hitting an open

40

glass bottle of rancid cricket milk, the Cornflakes box finally hit a terminal angle and toppled onto a floor spotted with squashed-in cigarette butts. A fifteen-centimetre Ugandan cockroach, heavy with an egg sack of her offspring, skittered out of her cardboard prison and dashed for the far side of Tuesday's bomb of a room. Understandably distracted with the piles of jewellery they'd discovered (and subsequently skimmed) and laughing at the Captain's now-famous willy, both Enforcers had clearly forgotten to take care of the roach.

Dashing towards a tight vent, the roach used her mysterious bug abilities to search for somewhere nice and cosy to lay her burden. Skittering in and out of tiny drafty gaps, her antennae waving about as she tasted the air for temperature changes, after ten minutes she found herself on the roof of a massive chamber. This expanse was dominated by a huge swimming pool filled with some sort of liquid far colder than anything else she'd ever sensed. Feeling the cockroach equivalent of disappointed at how icy it was, her egg crying out desperately to be expelled somewhere warm, she had the surprise of her short life when a white sphere the size of a basketball rose out of the freezing liquid directly below her and began to slowly rotate. Stopping at the sudden movement and twiddling her antennae, the cockroach tasted the heat of this mysterious object and found it to be quickly reaching an optimal temperature.

Obviously there was no way for the cockroach to know it, but this creamy basketball was the most powerful supercomputer of all time. While personal computers like the ultra-popular Omni implant had reached staggering levels of power and sophistication in a profile the size of a grain of Basmati rice, they were less than pocket calculators compared to this beast. Filled with enough atomic-scale circuitry to easily stretch from the Sun to Pluto and back again fifty times, this unassuming sphere was responsible for running everything aboard the Carpe Astrum, including calculating its slides. This was a job that had to be done perfectly, immaculately, without a single fault, an accomplishment that would be beyond any other piece of hardware. In truth, the only downside to this beyond-genius construct was that an ill-advised naming competition on the Link had officially led to the spherical supercomputer being christened as Roundy McBallface.

Freshly soaked in a refreshing bath of liquid helium, Roundy McBallface checked its maths a few more times and decided it was ready to make history. Devoting its whole attention to the task at hand, Roundy double-checked the status of an enormous vacuum chamber of antimatter, and told the stockpile to allocate just enough fuel to form the soon-to-be-open doorway.

Unfortunately, a literal moment before the slide's exact co-ordinate geometry could be finalised, momma roach extended an egg case from her spiked rear and dropped it with pinpoint precision into a vent on top of Roundy McBallface. As the leathery ootheca slid home, jamming into place, a tiny stream of smoke snaked out to mark its entrance.

*

Back up on the observation deck, three seconds after the Captain gunned the ignition, hundreds of VIPs continued to admire the complex dance of electrical discharges as they waited patiently for the slide to happen. As you'd expect from the most spoiled of humans, they were already getting bored.

A hundred empathic marble columns began to vibrate softly, barely enough to sense unless you concentrated on it, but the tremors quickly grew in volume and violence. In ten seconds it reached the point where you could feel the juddering in your teeth, and a few of the more senior boffins glared at each other across the opulent viewing area with silent questions and accusations. None of them were brave enough to stop the test, however, as that would be the end of their careers, and perhaps even their lives. This project was far too high-profile to be delayed by nerves, by a little bit of shaking. The test would continue.

But then the time finally came for the Carpe Astrum to prove it could transfer sentient life, and on the other side of the transparent ceramic shielding an alien sky split into a million fragments like an exploding sheet of purple glass. The totality of the Carpe Astrum was sucked into this wound upon space/time in an instant. Breathless with awe as the indigo and lavender sky began to congeal back into a single piece, the Planetary Mayor of the world of Seven Suns managed to clap his hands together just once. Hundreds of others went to do the same.

And then everything went wrong.

A lot happened in two seconds. First off, a hundred tonnes of antimatter, a stockpile mighty enough to power this ship pretty much forever, was burned all the way down to zero capacity in an instant. Sensing the upcoming disaster but too slow to do anything useful about it, Roundy McBallface didn't even have time to start flashing any of its hundreds of thousands of red hazard lights before flames filled the ship's ventilation system with the breath of dragons. Blasting apart everything in its path and setting fire to anything that was "lucky" enough not to suffer a direct hit, chained explosions demolished entire floors and rent apart the eight triangles that made up the Carpe Astrum. The circulatory system of turbolift lines peeled away, uprooted like weeds, and went drifting into the void in pieces.

Reacting too late to save the majority of souls aboard the Carpe Astrum, the ship's mind reacted to this catastrophic internal temperature increase by automatically venting the curling flames out of a million white-hot exhausts before every last inch of its interior could be reduced to charcoal. Tragically, this flash-fried many of the dancing triangular tiles into useless lumps, meaning they would never move again, let alone plot another seventh dimensional slide. Millions of tiles were shucked away and orbited the ruins of the Carpe Astrum with growing violence.

The VIP observation level was taken out so quickly that the Captain and his glitterati guests didn't have time to realise there was a disaster taking place before they were dead. Their so-called "unbreakable" viewing window shattered like thin toffee, exposing them to the horrors of deep space, signing their death certificates in all sorts of cruel ways: decapitated by their own Martini glasses as they went tumbling into the void, smashing into their fellow trillionaires so violently that it was comparable to a head-on collision on a skyway, and the Captain was the first man to be fatally smooshed between two flying recliners since the 21st Century.

They were the lucky ones.

It must be noted that many things will happen to an unprotected human body unlucky enough to be exposed to the vacuum. This list is so long and so technical that it would take a good five minutes of jargon like "nitrogen bubbles forming in their blood" and "terminal hypoxia" to adequately cover. Suffice to say, none of these things are good, or painless. Long story short, the VIPs who survived getting sucked out of the ship were killed by the explosive decompression of their own lungs turning their innards into meat fountains. Thankfully, this spared them from experiencing the absolute zero of space freezing their eyeballs solid in their sockets or a lethal dose of radiation frying them into jerky.

*

Precisely thirty seconds before this total catastrophe, a frustrated customer in front of the neon-yellow MacDeath franchise on floor four-hundred-and-fifteen had tired of waiting patiently, and decided his best course of action was to verbally abuse the wimpiest, stupidest-looking employee he could see.

"Hey dickhead, where's my slider?" the dockworker demanded.

Pluris bristled, but couldn't do anything. He may be able to lord it over Jimmy Slummer, but that didn't mean much. Pluris had been panel-beaten about the face enough to know who to pick and who not to pick, so he stretched out a painful-looking smile in an attempt to hide the misery in his soul.

"I apologise for the inconvenience, sir." His left eye twitched towards the order board independently of his right eye, then returned. "Your Mega-Sized Fisherman's Utopia Slider Combo Meal will be here within the established window period from the time that you ordered, or the MacDeath Combine guarantees that we will all be immediately fired."

Pluris flinched as half of the crowd suddenly joined in on yelling.

"Hey, I've been here for fifteen seconds already!"

"He better not get his before me!"

"Mine first!"

"Koala!"

Pluris turned on his heel and stormed away from the counter. Weaving between the usual teenage drop-outs and lobotomised ex-cons that made up the workforce of most MacDeath franchises, Pluris mentally rolled over some of the horrible insults he was going to use to hit Jimmy Slummer right in the brainstem. Shoulder-charging the heavy vault door that led to the Repler Pool, Pluris prepared a verbal barrage that would make Oscar Wilde wilt.

"Hey Slummer, where's the Slug you fat f-"

Pluris didn't register the five interlocked rows of serrated jaws before they had scissored him into dead mulch and yellow scraps. This was actually a mercy, as the fully-matured female Titan Slug could have swallowed him whole and dissolved him alive over the space of an hour. Thirty metres of armour-plated invertebrate violence flared her glowing blue frill as she uncoiled from the Repler Pool and into the store itself, smashing the Burger Highway into junk and eating both of the checkout chicks in one lunge. By the time any of the stunned customers registered something was wrong, the territorial female was halfway through the crowd, insatiably swallowing one person after another.

If it was any consolation, they would have all been dead in twenty seconds anyway

CHAPTER FIVE SURVIVORS

Nobody noticed the Brig's safety bulkhead slam closed, as Jimmy, Tuesday, Lana and Trace were all a little distracted by a gravity malfunction causing the dungeon to do a double somersault. Thankfully, the cells, guard desk and prisoner property tubs were bolted down. Unfortunately, the four humans were not secured, so they tumbled about like odd socks in a washing machine.

The Brig was plunged into thick darkness as every light simultaneously lost power. When a dozen yellow safety globes flickered on a few seconds later, their colour wordlessly explained they were operating on backup juice. They illuminated a total of four prone bodies.

A sustained groan finally broke the silence. Finding himself wrapped around the gaoler's buckled steel desk, Jimmy managed to extricate himself from the furniture and staggered to his leathery feet. Tilting sideways, feeling like a well-tenderised steak, he crashed into the tubs used to house prisoner possessions and somehow remained upright.

Despite being mildly concussed, Jimmy immediately detected a foul, chemical odour in the air. Squinting at the only way in and out of the Brig, he could see the thick bulkhead was shimmering with heat. Worse yet, its black surface was clearly brightening towards red. His train of thought was derailed by the click of four deadlocks disengaging.

"All cells have been opened due to a nearby fire," the ship's supercomputer helpfully explained over the PA. "This is a Category Ten Emergency. Please abandon the Brig."

"Fire? What spugging fire?" Trace growled, crawling out of her cell. Standing up, she clasped her shoulder and winced. She tested the arm to find that nothing was broken, but her entire left side felt badly bruised. "And what in the name of Odin's Itchy Verruca is a Category Ten Emergency?"

For some reason, Roundy didn't respond to Trace's question. Trained from infancy to react like a flash to any question she was able to answer, Lana started talking as though racing against the clock.

"There's no such..."

Trace wordlessly shut up Lana with a glance of pure hatred. Feeling the unbearable pain of knowing the answer to someone's question but not being allowed to voice it, the Cadet's words petered off. She thought it wise to keep a low profile until Trace looked a little less homicidal.

Trace focused her growls towards Jimmy.

"You, blob. Is a Class Ten Emergency an asteroid strike?"

Being directly addressed by Trace, the Terror of the Food Court, was enough to stun Jimmy into insensibility. His lips wriggled and he managed to produce what may have been a syllable.

"Gub?"

Trace gave him a slow, unimpressed blink. Turning towards to the Cramper Cube, she regarded Tuesday with the usual expression people wore when they were forced to speak to him, but with even more hostility.

"You, dunny-scraper: what's a Category Ten Emergency?"

Tuesday was currently trying to slide out of the Cramper Cube, but his body's posture seemed to be stuck in its current setting. He somehow managed to add a shrug to his wriggles.

"Maybe the ship accidentally went through Hell?"

Trace snorted. "That's the stupidest thing I've ever heard."

"Warning," the PA system crackled, "Registering fires on all levels. Structural damage is critical. There are multiple hull breaches. Death toll is-"

"Death toll?" Jimmy repeated at top volume, turning the colour of whipped cream. His badly-timed interruption meant that nobody heard the exact number.

Finally extricating himself with an audible crunch and pop, Tuesday stretched out in total ecstasy as he got free of the Cramper. It took a series of revolting cracks to untwist his spine enough to be able to walk, but he'd clearly had experience with Cramper Cubes before.

"Well, time to flee for my life before the Captain comes to visit with a chainsaw. Any of you point him in my direction, and I'll say you helped me escape. Always nice talking to you, Jimmy. Be sure to punch it all up your arse. Toodles!"

Tuesday marched for the only exit out of the Brig, whistling merrily as he pushed the shimmering bulkhead. Jolting as though zapped with electricity, Tuesday let out an unearthly shriek and tried to recoil from the source of his pain. This didn't work, as metal door was so searingly hot that his fingertips and palm were stuck fast to it, but a violent full-body spasm managed to detach him from the reddening surface. Falling onto his posterior and blowing on the burnt-smooth finger pads of his left hand, Tuesday swore and spat at the bulkhead. His brown saliva instantly boiled away into steam.

"A bloody warning would have been nice!"

"Door's hot," Jimmy said helpfully.

Tuesday went to stick all five burnt digits into his horrible mouth, but Lana gripped his wrist and took a close look at them.

"Nothing an AutoDoc can't fix in a minute. But I don't think leaving this room is a good idea just now."

Trace loomed above the two of them. Looking up at Trace's expression, Lana was able to read that while the Enforcer wouldn't lower herself to actually asking her a direct question, she still wanted to know the answer to what a Category Ten was. Lana graciously shared her wisdom.

"Like I was saying, the Navy doesn't have a Category Ten Emergency. Category

Nine means the ship is crippled beyond saving, pretty much the entire crew is dead, get the spug away from Ground Zero before it all goes nuclear." Annoyed by something she hadn't quite figured out yet, Lana glanced up at the vents built into the roof and walls before cautiously making eye contact with Trace. "But the Carpe Astrum is experimental. The kind of tech they're messing with, who knows what could go wrong?"

Lana scowled at the vents again, and a look of realization crossed her face.

"We need to get out of the Brig," she said simply.

"Tried that," Tuesday hissed, holding his stinging hand. "Didn't go so well."

Lana nodded at the clusters of slots in the ceiling. "Well, we need to find a way. You hear that? That total silence? The air recyclers have packed it in. We'll be poisoned by our own exhalations in no time."

"Somebody find me a crowbar or something," Trace growled.

"Uh, fire?' Jimmy said. Ignoring a borderline-homicidal glare from Trace, he looked up at the ceiling to regard a series of twelve bone-dry nozzles. "On, uh, the subject of fire, how come the sprinklers didn't kick in already? Surely…"

Belatedly, a storm of gelatinous white fire-retardant foam roared from a dozen nozzles in the roof. Hundreds of litres of thick gunk expanded massively to drench the small group from scalp to soles until there was a kneecap-level pool of retardant filling the Brig. Waterfalls of the stuff sloshed down the walls, pooling and rippling, but once its job was done the gunk evaporated into nothing. The Brig was totally dry within a few breaths.

"Well," Lana managed, spitting out a substance that resembled liquefied marshmallows and tasted like wall putty. She nodded towards the bulkhead, which seemed to have cooled down to a less alarming black. "On the bright side, if the suppression system worked in here, maybe it fixed the corridor, too. But we should test that bulkhead with a stick or something first."

"Uh uh," Tuesday grunted in an inarticulate negative, heading for a dozen-high stack of prisoner property crates. "First, I'm getting what's mine. Not going so much as another metre without my stuff."

Lana and Trace made sounds of agreement as Tuesday began scanning his eyes over the thick metal slabs. He found his name displayed on a crude LCD screen within seconds. Thanks to a thick layer of antigrav wafers on the draw, Tuesday effortlessly slid his crate out from the stack. He wasted no time in pocketing a dozen half-empty soft packets of green self-lighting chlorine-flavoured cigarettes.

Trace's property crate was a lot fuller, as it contained her Enforcer-grade riot armour. Tucked beneath the protective plates was a clamshell case nurturing a small black ceramic device the size of an old-fashioned smartphone, which Trace instantly hid inside her chest plate before anybody got a good look at it. Curious, Jimmy was about to ask Trace what the object was when Lana surprised him by kicking one of the property crates hard.

"It's empty!" Lana whined, at her wit's end. "My whole bag, gone. My whole life was in that."

Noticing a familiar shape out of the corner of her eye, Trace glanced at the small space between the guard's welded-to-the floor desk and his bolted-down spinney chair to see a lethal air pistol. Obviously focused on the not-inconsiderable bribe Jimmy had slipped him, the putz had clearly forgotten his gun before strolling off to spend his illicit earnings. Using Lana's screeching explosion as a convenient distraction, Trace casually checked the air gun's pressure bulb - a golf ball-sized sphere wrapped in antigrav wafers – to see that it contained forty-three tonnes of highly-compressed air. Its slug magazine was loaded with enough Densite ball-bearings to reduce a lorry to flakes.

Jackpot.

Trace slid the gun under her riot armour without anyone noticing.

*

Leaving the Brig was more difficult than just deciding to head off, as it seemed as though the automated bulkhead wasn't receiving any power. Thankfully, its magnetic locks had switched off when the mains power died, or the small group would have been sealed away forever. It took a team effort to budge the slab far enough for a tight squeeze.

The corridor that led to the turbolift was still empty except for a considerable layer of blackened char. On the bright side there weren't any flames, and the sweet smell of fire retardant spelled out why.

"Hello?" Tuesday called out. "Do I owe money to anyone out there?"

"Yes!" Jimmy snapped.

"Besides you, Slummer."

"Why besides me?" Jimmy argued.

"Because you are the definition of a low priority, jiggles," Tuesday chuckled.

Jimmy wobbled and puffed up his cottage cheese chest.

"Don't push me, Tuesday."

"You trying to act tough?" Trace snarled at Jimmy with her usual hostility. "You look like a mark to me. Dumber than rat turds and weaker than milky tea."

Jimmy didn't glare at Trace, no matter how much he wanted to. Jimmy had heard far too many stories about this particular Enforcer, and most of these tales ended with somebody crawling away on their hands and knees looking for their own teeth. Even if Trace had been a stranger, though, the bald head, scarification and obsidian piercings would be enough to make anyone feel cautious. Honestly, just the way she was looking at him made Jimmy's bladder feel twitchy.

"That's not possible," Lana breathed, interrupting their disagreement.

The Cadet was mucking about with her Omni implant and wearing a very concerned expression. Five intangible screens were hovering an inch above the knuckles of her left hand, and all of them had the words LINK NOT FOUND superimposed over hissing static. No matter how much she flicked her index finger across the screens, they refused to change. Lana looked close to panic.

"Must be bad reception, or something," Jimmy suggested.

Lana looked at Jimmy like he was an imbecile. Five screens of static vanished with a twist of her wrist.

"The Link isn't a walkie-talkie. Whenever a human ship goes somewhere new, the Link permanently expands to that region of space. That's why the borders of The Unison have always been defined by how far the Link reaches. Long story short, if humans have been somewhere, then the Link will be there, too. Furthermore, the Link hasn't gone down even once in The Unison's entire history. Okay?"

"So...it's not bad reception, then?" Jimmy clarified.

"Then why isn't it working, genius?" Trace snapped, interrupting. "If it always expands wherever we go, then why isn't it here, where we are?"

Lana decided to do something more constructive than getting involved in puerile childishness. Ignoring Trace, she looked up, snapped her fingers at the ceiling and called out to the ship's mind.

"Ship, a question. How many people are left on board?"

"You are not authorised to query the ship, Unregistered Visitor," Roundy McBallface responded politely. "You are not a member of the crew."

"Answer the question." Trace snapped. A look of panic crossed her face for a moment. "Is Poxius Hilton-Disney still alive?"

"You are not authorised to query the ship, either, Trace. Your security clearance has been revoked due to dismissal and multiple criminal charges."

Trace kicked the wall with a jackboot. Lana gave her a weird look.

"Poxius Hilton-Disney?" Lana repeated. "The CEO of Happy Planet? Why do you care about him?"

Trace just gave her a look of barely restrained fury. She offered no other answer.

"How...many...people...are...left?" Tuesday yawled slowly, as though speaking to somebody who had a thick Croatian accent.

"You are not authorised to query the ship, Robert. Your security clearance has been revoked due to multiple parole violations and the fact that you are a total bastard." There was an embarrassed pause. "My apologies. That is the exact wording of your record, Robert."

Tuesday shrugged. "Got me pegged there."

Lana waved at the turbolift, the only way off this level. It didn't respond.

"So how are we meant to get somewhere safe if none of us have clearance?" Lana wondered.

Lana, Trace and Tuesday all slowly turned around to look at Jimmy. He looked back at them blankly, not understanding. All of this staring was making his bladder feel itchy again.

"Well?" Lana finally prompted, sick of the staring competition. "Ask the ship something. You work somewhere on board, right?"

"You mean…" Jimmy could feel tears forming in his eyes. "You mean you need me for something? As though I'm your…" Jimmy snuffled, trying to hold back the waterworks. "…as though I'm your only hope?"

Lana shrugged. "I guess you could loosely phrase it like that, yes."

For the first time in Jimmy's life he felt needed, he felt important, as though God had reached out after decades of uselessness and disappointment and made poor Jimmy Slummer into a somebody for once, instead of a nobody. Puffing up his chest in pride, Jimmy started to form a very, very rare smile as an unusual sensation flooded across his chest.

Trace chose to ruin this moment by backhanding him. Layers of cellulite wobbled across Jimmy's face in response, but it would take much more than a slap to push over such a well-fed frame.

"Just ask the question, you fat tub," Trace snapped.

Jimmy's little ego trip was now well and truly crushed. He sighed.

"How many people are left alive, ship? What's the death toll?"

"Four," the ship responded instantly.

Jimmy shook his head, looking sad. "Wow. Four people died. What a waste."

"Hope it weren't anyone I knew." Tuesday muttered. He paused for a moment. "Well, not really."

"I believe you have misunderstood my answer," Roundy McBallface replied. "There are only four people left alive, James. The accident has claimed every authorised crew member and all visitors except for the four of you."

Jimmy almost fell over onto his huge backside in surprise.

"We're all that's left?" Lana said somewhat more hysterically than she had intended.

"So this crate's got nobody piloting her?" Trace growled. "We could be heading

50

into a moon, or worse."

"What happened, ship?" Jimmy asked.

There was a pause.

"To qualify my answer, first you need to understand that my target was a specific star located seven systems across the Western spiral arm of the Milky Way Galaxy from my previous location," the computer began. "Unfortunately, there was a mistake in my calculations due to a hardware issue, and this resulted in a substantial navigation error. So while we have reached a star that is absolutely identical to the profile I was told to target, it has turned out to be, in actuality, a different star in a completely separate system. While I admit that this is, technically, the wrong star, it is an identical twin to the original profile in regards to mass, density, composition and all other factors. The only real difference is that this star is located somewhere else."

"Yeah, that's not a big issue or anything," Tuesday sniped.

"So where are we?" Jimmy pressed.

The ship seemed almost embarrassed.

"While my answer may be far from correct due to the extensive damage that has been inflicted on my systems, from what I can tell we appear to be seven galaxies away from where we are meant to be."

Jimmy nodded, made a mmm sound for ten straight seconds, and fainted.

*

Jimmy dreamed of his eight years at primary school on the agriculture world of Sprout, although "nightmare" would be a more accurate definition. In particular, Jimmy was reliving his failed attempts at understanding basic astronavigational terms. All of the theory work would seep into his head easily enough, but the moment Jimmy had to recall something he faced a solid wall of meaningless mental static. No matter how much repetition was involved, he just couldn't seem to learn. Teachers spent hours reciting basic precepts to him in the hopes that something would stick, but his pudding of a brain just didn't work like it was meant to. Thankfully, book-learning wasn't all that important on an agriculture world, so nobody really cared that Jimmy was a dullard.

Jimmy's ten-year-old face squinted in concentration as he watched a slideshow of illustrated pictures, doing his best to retain the information: a light-year is how far light could move in a standard year. The distance between humanity's first star (better known as the Sun) and our birth world, Earth, is eight light minutes. The distance between the star systems of The Unison, however, were on another scale altogether, and ranged anywhere from a handful of lightyears to in excess of five hundred on the wildest of frontiers. The Milky Way galaxy, humanity's birthplace, was roughly one hundred thousand light-years from edge to edge. Beyond that, though, there were plenty of other galaxies. Countless galaxies, actually, though the space between the Milky Way and those other galaxies ranged from a million lightyears to distances so insanely huge that humanity doesn't even have a standard name for numbers that high…

*

Jimmy awakened to a close-up of Trace's pierced and scarified face, which was a horrific fate you wouldn't wish on anybody. Rolling over like a dropped Skittle, Jimmy got to his feet with a lot of effort. Straining to lift two hundred kilograms of whipped cream and meat pies off the tiles, as soon as Jimmy got vertical he noticed that this corridor was getting really cold. Despite the handful of cheery fires that had sprung to life along the corridor after he had fainted, this chill was getting worse by the second. Covering up his high-beaming nipples so nobody could see them through his yellow MacDeath uniform, Jimmy looked up at Lana.
"Heating systems are gone, aren't they?" Jimmy asked, rubbing the goose bumps from his forearms.
Lana nodded. She was standing in front of the only turbolift that could get them off floor zero, waving her hand at a blacked-out screen embedded on its frame. It wasn't responding.
"Cactus," Lana snapped. "We're stuck."
A chime sounded from the PA system.
"I have disabled the turbolift system due to critical damage. It is inadvisable to use elevators in an emergency situation. Please utilise the stairs."
Lana looked back and forth. Behind her was the entrance to the Brig, the unresponsive turbolift was directly ahead, and there were solid walls on both sides.
"What bloody stairs?" Lana demanded.
"You are not authorised to query the ship, Unregistered Visitor," the ship's mind repeated. "You are not a member of the crew."
Tuesday didn't seem all that bothered as Lana flew into a rage and began to kick the elevator. He happily warmed his hands next to a fire curling out of a mess of charred wiring.
"Brings back memories of Earth, this. Get wrapped up in some nice thick blankets on a cold night, cook your cold hands over a blazing fire…"

"You had a fireplace?" Jimmy clarified.

"No. Used to be a hobo."

"What are we going to do?" Lana asked nobody in particular, finally ceasing her assault on the metal slab. She was breathing heavily. If it wasn't freezing, she might have been sweating.

"Space is really, really cold, isn't it?" Jimmy wondered.

Lana sighed.

"Look, if the temperature systems are busted everywhere on this ship, once all the latent heat dissipates from this floating coffin it will hit temperatures far below freezing. Absolute zero is fatal to an unprotected human body within a minute, maybe even faster." Lana said all of this as though reciting from a textbook. She sighed again. "We'll hit that point in a matter of hours, probably."

Jimmy looked down at his dirty yellow MacDeath apron.

"Wish I was wearing a shirt under this," he mumbled.

"So do we," Tuesday chuckled.

Lana sat down in a meditational martial arts pose in order to clear her mind. It came naturally.

"Okay. We need to review our options." Lana took a breath. "With the entire crew dead, there's no way for us to repair the ship, let alone fly it back to where we started. Even if we did have all those experts to help us, I doubt the ship has any fuel left after jumping seven bloody galaxies. This means evacuation is our only real option, and we need to do it now. You heard the PA: half the ship is in flames at best."

Lana's eyes popped open wide as the passage shook.

"So what do we do?" Trace snapped. "We're seven galaxies away from anything we know, the ship is about to explode at any given moment, the entire chain of command is gone...we're baked. Simple as that."

Lana snapped her fingers and got a crumpled Sludge bar wrapper out of her pocket. Jimmy immediately perked up at the sight of it.

"I love those!"

"This has an authorisation code for one of the lifeboats." Lana clarified. "It should hold all four of us."

"And go where?" Trace asked in a condescending way. "We're probably in the middle of deep space, hundreds of years away from anything of use."

"Wait," Jimmy interrupted, squinting in thought. "You know the original star the ship was meant to target? Did it have any habitable planets?"

Lana shrugged. "I guess so. Not much point dragging the Carpe Astrum to visit a system full of dead, rocky hell-balls, is it?"

"So..." Tuesday prompted.

Jimmy tried to stay latched on to his train of thought. He could feel his inspiration slipping away already. It was primary school all over again. But he pushed on.

"So the local star is identical to the one that we were meant to visit, right?" Jimmy confirmed, not waiting for an answer. "And if that sort of star has a world that supports human life...maybe even more than one planet..."

"Then there's a higher than average chance that this star might have developed a habitable world, too." Lana confirmed, trying not to get excited. "And if that's the case, the ship's supercomputer might be able to find it for us."

"Yes, but that's the same crazed supercomputer that just jumped us halfway across the uncharted universe," Trace growled.

Lana waved this negativity away.

"Like any ship built in the last hundred years, the Carpe Astrum will be installed with all the dedicated hardware and software it needs to detect anything of worth in this system," Lana rattled off. "It wasn't designed to get bogged down in deep space or in star systems without resources. She was meant to be a bridge to places of worth."

"Yes, but that still doesn't help us." Tuesday whinged, shivering. "Even if we get this stupid elevator working, for all we know every other level is in even worse shape than this one. It's a miracle we haven't wandered into the bloody vacuum already."

"Better than waiting here to get frozen and blown up, in that order," Trace growled.

Jimmy snapped his fat fingers with a sound like two sausages getting slapped together.

"Got it. Hey, computer, can you plot a safe course for us to follow if I say where we want to get to from here?"

"Define safe," the computer replied.

"Preferably not getting burnt to charcoal, frozen to ice, or suffocated blue?" Jimmy clarified.

There was a pause.

"Koala."

As you would expect, the survivors looked equally confused. Jimmy finally managed to clarify things.

"Come again?"

"I said yes, James," Roundy said innocently.

The survivors rubbed their frigid bodies and took a moment to figure out their current plan.

"Okay, first we need to check that the lifeboats are still there," Lana started.

"Surely we can do that remotely," Tuesday argued. "I say we gather our supplies first, starting with the essentials." Tuesday ticked off his fingers. "Cigarettes, alcohol and pornography, in that order."

"No, we're going to check the lifeboats first," Lana chided in her best kindergarten teacher voice. "I don't like to pull rank, but seeing as though we're on a Navy vessel without any living crew members and all of you are civilians, well, I'm obviously in charge." Lana pointed at her chin with both thumbs. "I'm the only one even vaguely qualified to take their place. None of you have undergone a single minute of Navy training, correct?"

The other three looked down at the eighteen-year-old. Trace snorted.

"You try to pull rank and I'll pull of your ears, understood?" she snarled.

"Nice try, jail-bait," Tuesday muttered.

"Ship, we need to reach the cargo area, please," Jimmy said politely to the ceiling. He shrugged at Lana in an apologetic way. "Sorry. Majority always rules."

"Not in the Navy it doesn't!" Lana exploded. 'The most basic fact they teach you, the first thing you learn on the first day, is that the majority does not rule!'

Looking a little alarmed at the outburst, Jimmy's only attempt at rebuttal was another shrug.

It took ten long seconds, but the ship eventually processed Jimmy's request by beaming a three-dimensional schematic to everyone's retinal screens. A wriggling bright green line appeared at the very bottom deck of the floating representation of the Carpe Astrum like a worm in an apple, efficiently munching back and forth between turbolift shafts, flights of stairs and even the occasional oversized vent. It went without saying that this indirect path was formulated to avoid dangers like firestorms or hull breaches. Nobody was watching the green line at the start, however, as they were all equally transfixed by the map itself: the two black-and-white equilateral triangles that composed most of the Carpe Astrum now resembled crumpled-up wads of cartridge paper that had been used to put out hundreds of cigars. Swarms of ceramic triangles were detaching from the outer hull by the hundreds of thousands, giving the effect that a massive dust storm was orbiting the wreck, and towering chunks of hull the size of apartment blocks occasionally snapped away from the superstructure, tumbling end over end like flicked matches as they bounced and crashed about. Flames belched out of hull rips at random.

"Oh," Jimmy managed, literally lost for words. He paused for a few seconds and tried again. "Oh."

"The most expensive object ever built," Lana added quietly. "The beginning of a whole new era."

The turbolift finally cycled open, but it took the survivors almost fifteen seconds to notice.

*

Following the catastrophe, every hatch, airlock, turbolift, bulkhead, manhole, drainpipe, ventilation shaft, bin lid and doggy door had automatically sealed as a standard disaster response by the ship, and it turned out Jimmy was the only one who could open anything. Trace found this out the hard way after colliding nose-first with a bulkhead and almost knocking herself out.

It was clear that without Jimmy the other three survivors would be stuck wherever they had the misfortune to lose the fat man, as none of them had enough security clearance to so much as use a bathroom without having to pry the door open with a crowbar. Lana did everything in her power not to think about how this fat, incompetent imbecile had effectively been promoted to Captain in record time, but Jimmy seemed too busy keeping his limited attention span on the floating schematic following him around like a lost, mewling puppy to feel joy at the fact he now effectively commanded the Carpe Astrum. Lana couldn't believe how little Jimmy seemed to care about his lightning-fast rise through the ranks, and jealousy seethed within her.

As the four survivors carefully made their way out of the interconnected bowels of the ship, it was apparent that the Brig had barely been touched by the atrocity that had killed everyone else. Most of the walls and ceilings had been shortened by a metre and burst under the amazing pressure, spraying cables, mysterious green liquid and blackened circuit boards in all directions like someone had whacked a giant papier-mâché piñata. They passed far too many broken bodies wrapped in shredded midnight blue uniforms along the way, and many of the bodies were dripping the sad golden remains of molten Navy medals and trimmings. As Tuesday was heroically bringing up the rear, he was able to give the bodies a good kick whenever nobody was watching.

The group finally reached their second active elevator within minutes. Jimmy was the first one on board, and once the other three had squeezed into the tight space he managed to press the Up button with a cold-hardened nipple.

"Neat trick," Lana admitted from deep within Tuesday's armpit.

Jimmy looked embarrassed.

"Uh, that wasn't actually intentional…"

The pod ascended smoothly for three metres, made a horrible grinding noise and stopped with a clunk. Tuesday rapidly hit the Up button with his nose four times, although admittedly Trace was shaking his head like a stress reliever, so he couldn't take all the credit.

"Great," Jimmy moaned, trying to pry his way out of the tube. "Twelve sets of stairs."

And then the lights went out.

"Great," Jimmy repeated, even more frustrated. "Twelve sets of stairs...in the dark."

It was like a wrestling match in a kitchen cabinet, but between them the survivors eventually managed to find the emergency release panel, pried it open, found the exit lever and yanked it. Their capsule spun open to reveal the orange back-up lighting was still operational outside of the turbolift, which was a great relief. Unfortunately, the turbolift had wedged itself between two floors so badly that it would never budge again, and this meant everybody was forced to crawl through a tight gap. While Tuesday and Trace were able to squeeze their way out, Jimmy got horribly stuck halfway, trapping Lana behind his derriere. It went without saying that she wasn't having any of that.

"Pull!" Lana commanded from the turbolift, jamming her neck and shoulders into Jimmy's butt crevice.

"Heave!" Trace barked, almost dislocating Jimmy's shoulder as she violently yanked his wrist.

"Ho!" Tuesday added, taking a smoke break in the corner so he could watch the fun.

"It's not working!" Jimmy tried to say, but all that came out was an asthmatic squeak.

He would have followed this up with the very best profanity he'd learned from working with Pluris, but his chest was wedged so badly that he could no longer breathe, and every ineffective tug was only making it worse. While Jimmy couldn't verbally tell his would-be rescuers that they were, in fact, killing him with their help, his bulging eyes and mulberry face conveyed the message quite clearly.

Flashing spots exploded all over Jimmy's vision, obscuring the sight of a grunting, flexing Trace and a grinning, smoking Tuesday as he began to lose consciousness. Jimmy's eyes rolled back in his head, his brain drifting into total nonsense as though he was falling asleep. Jimmy let out a sad gurgle and a trickle of saliva pit-patted onto Trace's jackboots.

Jimmy felt at peace. He was ready to die. And as his career had hit its absolute apex, he was okay with that. He would die a success, even though he'd been Captain for less time than it took to bake a pizza.

His vision faded to grey.

There was crunching noise as loud as a head-on collision and the entire level shook like the San Andreas Fault had decided to stop being gentle with California. Walls splintered, orange backup light globes exploded and the damaged, uneven floor dropped by another two feet. Trace was caught by surprise as the artificial gravity failed, losing her grip on Jimmy's arms and tumbling backwards. Tuesday's chlorine-flavoured cigarette was knocked out of his surprised face in a puff of green smoke as he was collected by the huge, somersaulting Enforcer and crushed into the opposite wall.

The gravity decided to flicker back on almost instantly, probably due to some sort of auto-repair function, and this meant Tuesday, Lana and Trace slammed onto the splintered deck with a sustained silence.

It took far, far too long, but the ship's supercomputer finally decided to do something about the fact it's only remaining crew member was about to suffocate, and the turbolift door slid open another eight inches with a crunch. Jimmy took the biggest breath of his life, a gasp that seemed to go for days. Sliding out of the clamping door and into the vent, his face rapidly transitioning from blue to purple to red and then back to its usual pink, Jimmy rolled about in misery. His eyes were badly bloodshot, and it felt as though he'd lost about twenty IQ points. As he inhaled and exhaled like an emphysemic cow, Jimmy realised he'd never noticed just how truly sweet air tasted, even when it was full of smoke. He considered writing a poem about the experience, but he guessed that was probably due to brain damage, so he put this idea on the backburner for now.

"I can no longer provide directions to the supplies area," the ship apologised.

Jimmy flipped onto his back.

"Why?" he moaned pathetically.

"The supplies area is no longer located on this ship," the computer clarified helpfully. "Would you like another destination?"

"No longer on this ship?" Jimmy said incredulously. "It's twelve kilometres long!"

"Thirteen kilometres," Tuesday's muffled voice corrected from beneath Trace's backside.

"Medical," Lana said, getting to her feet and staggering into a nearby wall. "I think I lost a couple of teeth." She reached down, picked up something tiny and gave a dazed smile. "Never mind. Here they are."

"Lifeboats," Trace snarled, dragging herself upright. She shoved Lana violently away when the Cadet staggered too close. "We're running out of time. We need to bail. This wreck is about to explode at any second."

"I don't want to play anymore, Mummy," Tuesday mumbled miserably, recovering a lit chlorine cigarette from the hole it was burning in his forehead. He dragged on it pitifully. "Wanna go home. Wanna go home now."

Jimmy sat up. It took a while, but he was already feeling much more lucid. Almost dying in such a horrible way had coaxed out something that Jimmy rarely felt: anger.

"Ship, I want to go to the safest place we can reach within five minutes. Notice I used the word safe, which means somewhere that isn't exploding or crumbling or burning or disintegrating into chunks. And you do understand that your definition of safe hasn't had much in common with my definition of safe, has it?"

There was a pause as the ship considered this.

"Yes, James. I understand."

*

It took an exhausting climb up eighteen sets of fire stairs (which were, ironically, actually on fire at several points) followed by a joint effort to bash through a series of security doors using an oversized leather recliner, but the bruised, dirty and demoralised survivors were soon at The Funnest Place Off Earth: Happy Planet.

As ninety-nine percent of the human race would never have the opportunity to leave their home worlds, let alone for something as frivolous as a holiday, the CEO of Happy Planet, Poxius Hilton-Disney, had decided to bring his legendary Happy Planet theme parks to the punters and their howling spawn...and make a hundred more fortunes in the process. Even in the 25th Century, interstellar travel was still inconvenient, ridiculously expensive, involved time-dilation effects that would have sent Einstein and Hawking insane with one equation, and often involved cryogenic suspension. As John Wayne had stated so eloquently in his welcome back speech after becoming the first human being successfully resurrected from snap-frozen storage: "If I'da known this'd involved a willy full of icicles, I'da said no to being a snowman." Then again, The Duke had only retained about ten percent of his original brain function, so his words were worth taking with a pinch of salt.

Hilton-Disney's plan made a lot of sense: once the final testing phases were completed, the Carpe Astrum was scheduled to pop into a different star system every other day like the mother of all circuses, giving the locals a short time to mortgage their homes and sell a kidney or two to afford the shuttle fares and admission prices for the duration of the stop. Happy Planet would hoover up all their cash, and Poxius Hilton-Disney would complete each stopover by backstroking through oceans of currency and laughing like a supervillain.

It was a sad fact that a lot of worlds out there, especially the more backwater hovels, had to make do with inferior Wakky World cortical-shunt parks (now available in one-hundred-and-thirteen-million awesome locations!). While affordable as far as family holidays went, "visiting" Wakky World involved being sandwiched into a tight virtual reality booth with an auto-inserting colostomy bag in your clacker. Despite the fact virtual reality rides weren't confined by the rules of physics, meaning they could be a hundred times more insane than the relatively mild snore-fest rollercoasters offered by Happy Planet, Happy Planet had one major advantage: it was real. It cost a fortune in time and materials to build a Happy Planet franchise, let alone staffing it with actual people rather than semi-sentient computer programs, but the value of something solid, something concrete, in an era where virtual reality and tactile holograms were in every home and workplace and school, was priceless. "Real" had somehow become a novelty, and novelty always made money hand over fist when you sold it to yokels.

Of course, Poxius Hilton-Disney would never see his vision realised, as he'd been on the VIP observation deck during the disaster. His body had been completely carved in half at the waist by his own flying SpendPlus credit cards when the viewing window shattered.

This unopened Happy Planet theme park franchise took up all of level sixteen and seventeen. It had never felt a human footstep or heard a child's voice, let alone witnessed a menopausal aunt projectile-vomit half-digested corndogs and alcoholic Slurko X-Treme all over the Teacup ride. The four survivors were actually the first humans to see the park with flesh-and-blood eyes, but as this Happy Planet wasn't scheduled to open for another month it was just another boring construction site covered in black tarps. Much of the core infrastructure of the park seemed to have been installed, and in the far distance the survivors could make out hundreds of kilometre-high humps looming towards the ceiling. Although the dim orange backup lighting didn't do much to improve the near-darkness of the park, there was no doubt that these mountain-sized tarps contained the same rides that had made Happy Planet famous across The Unison, like The Scattergun, The Fiery Wrath of Zeus and The Intestinator, as well as fifty others that had been replicated in many star systems.

Happy Planet had refined its rides to perfection. The Scattergun, for instance, was a bungee jump that used invisible gravity slings instead of cords. After free-falling face-first at triple the speed of sound for two klicks, you'd come to a sudden stop so close to the ground that your nose was guaranteed to get squished against the flooring hard enough to hurt, but without breaking it. Just to amp up the excitement, the red bulls-eye target was painted with splashes of fake blood and chalk outlines to make the punters double-guess just how safe they actually were. The Fiery Wrath of Zeus was another gravity ride, but this one would whip a dozen punters back and forth between a tight matrix of spinning circular saw blades that seemed to flash past at random, but were actually calculated down to the tenth of a millimetre. While The Fiery Wrath of Zeus would bring the blades close enough for the punters to be barely touched, they wouldn't leave a mark. When somebody hopped onto The Fiery Wrath of Zeus they'd secretly undergo scans of their neck, skull and brain to establish just how much force they could weather without passing out or suffering whiplash, and the ride would up the ante accordingly until they were right on the cusp of a fainting spell or ending up in traction.

The Intestinator, meanwhile, was actually a curiosity based on the precepts of staggered teleportation. This is a fancy way of saying that you would see your limbs and organs pop around the ride independently of each other before being safely reassembled back together without so much as a bruise. This attraction was made possible with a small Wattson-Rice Drive, the great-great-great-great grandmother of the Carpe Astrum's Slicer Drive. While the Slicer had been once been touted as being utterly reliable to the smallest decimal point by everybody connected to The Carpe Astrum Project, as the builders of the Titanic (as well as Jimmy, Lana, Trace and Jimmy) would agree, dealing in arrogant absolutes only invited disaster.

Automated turnstiles with universal currency scanners identified where the borders of the park officially started, and beyond them stood animatronic versions of all the best Happy Planet characters, ranging from Slappy the Pansexual Rabbit to Mister Drizzle to Crotch-Snatch McGrouch. Cobblestone paths passed conveniently close to MacDeath vending machines that were destined to never dispense a hot meat burger or an icy fat shake, and just beyond that were the near-endless processing gates for Happy Planet's insane rides. It took a good minute for the survivor's eyes to adjust to the orange safety lighting, but all they gained from this was disappointment. Everything was covered in opaque shrink-wrap, including the animatronic characters. The fountains and other fancy water features were drier than an English sitcom, speakers that had been designed to play cheerful, madness-provoking theme tunes for the next thousand years were deaf and silent and, worst of all, the whole place was deserted.

This park was a gilded, untouched corpse. It was a ghost town. A stillbirth.

Tuesday's steel-capped boot nudged something with a clunk. Looking down, a tick-like robot the size of a human hand twitched one of its sharp little legs, but didn't do much else. The robotic insect, which had the famous Hamster Ears logo laminated on its black shell, was on its back like a terminally ill cockroach. Even somebody as profoundly defective as Bob Tuesday knew a Weaver when he kicked one.

As the Happy Planet brand had become just as synonymous with self-building cities as they were with cartoon characters with full-blown Tourette's syndrome, it came as no surprise that their theme parks didn't require human hands to construct. Like the Carpe Astrum itself, this branch of Happy Planet had been assembled in the standard way that The Unison constructed anything major: a small team of architects had created a mathematically perfect CAD-CAM design, an enormous quantity of raw materials were gathered, and then an endless horde of insect-like Weavers were unleashed to make it.

Ranging in size from a grasshopper to a teacup Chihuahua to a baseball glove, depending on their designated task, Weavers were capable of working together in the tens thousands without asking a question, taking a toilet break, complaining about union rules or stealing office supplies, and they would never stop building until they were told to stop or ran out of operational legs. As Weavers were capable of carrying a thousand times their own weight, could jump sixty metres with a full load and climbed vertical walls better than a Himalayan spider goat, they were understandably renowned as the greatest builders in the universe. And while Weavers could repair themselves to a certain degree, they were famous for costing less than one Amerikan pound per unit, which meant they were more disposable than your average self-tying condom. Happy Planet had always been famously tight-lipped about how they were able to produce one of these amazing builders for less than a double-shot from a coffee hypo, but over the centuries many people had learned the hard way not to pry into Happy Planet's secrets. It was a good way to vanish without a trace.

Of course, the Weavers weren't true AI, but keeping the bots dumb was just as much about safety as it was about affordability. For a swarm of five thousand assorted Weavers you'd only require one trained Rigger to control them, and whenever the Rigger wasn't working the Weavers would switch off, braindead until their next shift. This was of small comfort to all the robot-apocalypse doomsayers who predicted mankind would be overthrown by their own creations at some point next Thursday.

A second tap with Tuesday's boot didn't produce any response from the Weaver at all. Scanning the cobblestones, Tuesday stopped bothering to count the dead machines after twenty-seven. After all, twenty-seven was usually the point when counting got uncomfortable for him.

The four survivors didn't get very far. Most of the turnstiles at the front entrance had been wiped out by a cave-in from far, far above in the unseen shadows of the next floor, and a full-sized animatronic Crotch-Snatch McGrouch blanketed in thick shrink-wrap had been pancaked by a row of latrines that had fallen through the distant chasm. Besides this, it seemed that the Happy Planet franchise had been almost untouched by the disaster.

"Shame nobody was in the park," Jimmy said quietly. "Or there may have been more than just four survivors."

Not bothering to answer Jimmy's sadness, Lana hopped up onto a toppled MacDeath vending machine and swung her leg back and forth a little too violently.

"Now that we're not hanging about in a bloody frying pan, we can figure out what to do next."

Jimmy, Tuesday and Trace all sat down on low, child-sized turnstiles, happy to rest after their marathon climb. Despite the peace and lack of obvious fires, everyone was clearly still on edge, and it took a couple of minutes for their adrenalin and paranoia to subside. The total peace of this lifeless park was soothing, but this calm was suddenly split by a top-volume announcement from the ship.

"I have found a local planet. It appears to show the hallmarks of a human-compatible ecosystem."

The four humans all covered their ears and yelped in pain. Lana gritted her teeth together, certain that her left eardrum had just popped, and managed to speak.

"How far?" she finally managed, almost unable to hear her own voice over the ringing noise.

"Did you hear that, ship?" Jimmy asked the gloom, just as deaf as Lana.

It took a minute for the ship to respond, and when it did its words were filtered through a shrink-wrapped speaker. The covering vibrated in an annoying way as Roundy spoke. Thankfully, this time nobody was sent deaf.

"Do you require something, James?"

Jimmy sighed. He hated repeating himself over and over. Sometimes it felt as though all he ever did was go unheard.

"I want to know how long it'll take for us to reach that 'human-compatible' planet. Details would be nice."

The decaying ship's computer paused for about a minute as it worked things out. Bored of waiting, Jimmy was just about to bring up the money issue with Tuesday again when the ship finally responded.

"Distance: three nominal hours." There was another pause. "This unnamed planet is three fifths the size of Earth, has a gravity of 0.87, and its atmosphere should be breathable as long as you use respiratory filters."

"We're set," Jimmy said with a rare smile. "Take us there, would you, ship?"

"Chop chop," Tuesday snickered.

"I wonder if we'll survive another three hours," Lana wondered quietly.

"There is a small issue,' the computer said apologetically. 'I seem to have lost the capacity to steer the ship."

Jimmy's mouth hung open and his eyes bulged.

"What?" he managed.

"I cannot steer, James. Every hardware component involved with navigation, acceleration, deceleration or otherwise altering our path is either damaged beyond all use or no longer present."

Lana hit a bench in frustration. Trace, however, hit Tuesday in frustration instead.

"So we're coasting through space without any control whatsoever," Lana clarified. A simple representation of the local star system appeared on everyone's retinal implants as though floating in front of their faces. A complex scatter of images popped into the hologram to represent the Carpe Astrum, then a line showed their trajectory. An unnamed world was situated just off that path in an inconvenient direction, but there was one more unforeseen detail that suddenly made everything much, much worse: the simple line that showed their trajectory started off a healthy green that slowly became yellow, but then it became orange, followed by red, then stopped altogether as a large flashing black X.

Even Tuesday knew what was happening.

"We're flying into a damn star," Tuesday said quietly.

"At least we'll be warmer." Trace growled.

Jimmy bent over and retched.

CHAPTER SIX THE HECK OUT OF DODGE

Happy Planet was still calm and safe ten minutes later, but sheltering there was only a temporary option. As a lifetime of training had taught her, Lana took the initiative to nut out what needed to be done.

"Now, while it goes without saying that the lifeboat will have emergency supplies for at least a few weeks, our chances of rescue are beneath zero. Nobody is coming. There is no hope. So we need to loot everything of value that we can while we have the chance."

"Want me to cut off some wedding rings?" Tuesday offered. "Rip out a few gold teeth? Just get me some pliers and point me towards the corpses..."

Lana didn't have an answer to this. Neither did Jimmy nor Trace. What could she possibly say? She thought it best to ignore Tuesday and move on.

"I know that the whole supplies area is gone, but that isn't the only place on board we can find food and drinks. It might take a while to get all the way up there, but I think the Food Court on level four-hundred-and-fifteen is a good option."

Tuesday leaned towards Jimmy.

"What level is this one?"

Jimmy squinted.

"Happy Planet takes up levels sixteen and seventeen."

Trace rolled her eyes at Tuesday and Jimmy.

"Yeah. Like those two are going to manage four hundred levels of emergency stairs."

"Food Court would have a tonne of supplies, though," Jimmy said quietly, not bothering to contradict Trace. Tuesday began a long, wracking, wet cough that was cut off by the polite voice of the ship's mind.

"I have sealed the entire Food Court under quarantine," Roundy McBallface said helpfully, responding to Jimmy without being asked. "There is an Apex-level predator loose on that level. An armed military response force will be required to neutralise it."

"A predator?" Lana repeated, squinting.

"It appears to be a fully-grown female Titan Slug," the ship added.

"How did..." Lana began.

"Well, too bad, guess it's not an option," Jimmy interrupted, speaking so fast his words blurred into each other. "Might as well forget about it. Ship, where else can we get food and drinks? Is there anything edible between here and the lifeboats?"

Roundy took a few moments. Then a few more. A green line appeared on the cobblestone ground, leading off towards the emergency stairs.

"Omitting areas of the ship that are currently bathed in hard radiation, open to the vacuum, filled with poisonous gas or are otherwise lethal, I have located the following foodstuffs: a bottle of Hell-strength Tabasco sauce, three unflavoured gluten-free pizza bases, a jar of durian jam concentrate, two blocks of kelp puree, and half a tonne of lemon-flavoured whitening toothpaste."

Trace kicked the animatronic Mister Drizzle.

"Great. Kelp pizza. My favourite," Tuesday muttered with the sarcasm dialled up to ten.

"And water?" Jimmy prompted.

65

Pause.

"During the disaster, all the water-cooling systems suffered catastrophic overheating, and my reservoirs boiled away. There is only one hundred litres of water remaining on board..."

"Should make a difference," Lana said, a little of the tension in her muscles visibly melting away.

"...but every last drop is irradiated beyond recovery."

Tuesday cackled inappropriately at this news. "Hate to say it, but we're only getting more screwed with every passing minute. Won't last more'n a few days without clean water."

"Yeah. Better off just crashing into the sun," Jimmy said with a level of melancholy that a whole marathon of cute cat videos couldn't cure. "At least it'll be quick."

"Actually, at the speed we're going, it will probably take a fortnight for that star to kill us." Lana explained with a little too much enthusiasm. 'We'll be slowly roasted like rabbits rotating over a campfire. Direct radiation will eventually heat what's left of the Carpe Astrum to the point of total annihilation, true, but by that time our flesh and organs would have liquefied and burst from our bodies like sausages. It'd be like dying in a slow cooker."

They all dealt with this dire news in their own way: Jimmy scratched viciously at his itchy body hair, which gave the impression he was petting a black poodle; Tuesday laughed insanely and coughed in a manner that only two packs of cigarettes a day for thirty-five years could accomplish; Lana stood silently at attention, trying to keep a brave look on her face; but Trace seemed undisturbed by this news, which made her next comment even scarier.

"First one to die gets their blood drunk. I'm not dying of no thirst."

"Half an hour and it's Lord of the Flies," Jimmy complained.

Lana waved away this pointless waste of air.

"Look, I'm sure we can recover plenty of drinks from vending machines on the way to the pods. Won't be too hard to raid, I'm sure."

Tuesday smirked.

"Don't worry. Me and vending machines, we have a special relationship."

Jimmy took off his yellow MacDeath chef's hat and wiped pools of thick, unexpected sweat from his armpits. It took a few seconds to realize that a small fire had crackled to life beneath the turnstile he was using as a seat, but as soon as he stepped away from the growing flames he started shivering from cold. The temperature was continuing to drop at an alarming rate. Within an hour he might be snapping icicles off his back hair.

"Even this place won't be safe for long," Jimmy noted. He managed to make eye contact with Lana, which wasn't his strong suit at the best of times. "I think we need to move. If we stay put, we die."

Tuesday got to his feet and stretched. All of his joints popped simultaneously.

"Okay. Time to work some magic."

*

By the third vending machine, it was clear that Tuesday possessed an unearthly level of skill when it came to theft. He'd step up to a neon-green Slurko Cola facade, crack his knuckles, and firmly poke the towering metal slab on its side with two fingers. There would be an audible rumbling from within the vending machine, and glass bottles glistening with moisture rolled out of the slot every time.

Lana couldn't figure it out. She tried to emulate the method more than once when nobody was looking, and failed.

Within five corridors they'd gathered such a huge pile of bottles of Slurko that they needed to make a pit-stop to find something to carry them in. While there weren't any convenient survivalist-style backpacks to be found, four extra-tough pullover vests bearing allegiance marks to The Unison were repurposed into crude slings. The looted crew members that were left half-naked didn't complain, as they were too busy being blue and cold and dead. Thankfully, despite the fact they'd had to pilfer several bodies, the survivors now had enough liquid for days and days.

Smashing their way through numerous inoperative doors and scrabbling over piles of debris as they followed the Roundy's dynamic map, the survivors soon recovered some blocks of kelp puree, the unflavoured gluten-free pizza bases and the durian jam concentrate, but the toothpaste and Hell-strength Tabasco sauce were nowhere to be found. Checking and double-checking didn't help, either. If something wasn't there, then it wasn't there, and reviewing this result fifteen times didn't do anything to change that immutable fact. They were just about to give up on their looting and make for the escape pods when Jimmy mustered the courage to speak up.

"I, um, may know where there's some more food."

This got everyone's attention. Feeling unnerved by having all three of them staring at him so intently, Jimmy stuttered a bit before finally spitting out what he wanted to say.

"Look, my bunk isn't far, and I have...I have a stash, okay? Nobody knows about it. Nobody."

"A stash of what?" Lana demanded. Jimmy cringed like a whipped dog at her tone, so she took things down a couple of notches. "Is it edible? Can we carry it with us?"

Jimmy nodded, but he still had a weird look on his face.

*

It took another half an hour of prying open doors, backtracking, crawling over teetering piles of rubble and generally getting scratched and bruised in a hundred small ways, but they reached Jimmy's room. As you'd expect from such a low-ranked member of the crew, Jimmy's quarters were two metres on each side and dominated by a vile compost heap he had the hide to call a bed. His pillow had an alarm clock built into it (with no off switch) and the blankets looked, smelled and probably felt like a giant batch of caramelised onions. Two XXXXXL MacDeath uniforms hung sadly from ceramic ceiling hooks as the closest thing he had to decoration. Despite the fact MacDeath uniforms were self-cleaning, somehow Jimmy had left indelible bodily excretion stains on the armpit, underboob and collar.

This was the entire extent of Jimmy's life.

Once Jimmy had wedged himself through the door there wasn't enough space in the glorified closet for anybody else. Gripping the swampy mattress, with a grunt and a curse Jimmy got his bowed bed off its base. Underneath it was a flat layer of badly painted wood, and inside of that was a footlocker filled with mysteriously furry grey items. Sweating with the effort of bending and straightening over and over again, within thirty seconds Jimmy had transferred most of his stash into a makeshift bag. Hesitating for a moment, Jimmy passed one of his treasures to each of the survivors without a word.

Lana frowned at the item as she caught it. Now that it was in her hand, she could tell that the fur was actually an inch-thick layer of dust. Scratching away some of the grey fuzz with her thumbnail, she revealed a blindingly bright riot of colours. It was like a clown had exploded.

"Are these..." Trace squinted, peeling away a scab of grime.

"Candy bars?" Lana interrupted. "I don't recognise this kind."

"They're vintage candy bars," Tuesday clarified, his ability to sense valuable things tingling like mad. "Look at the ingredients."

Lana scratched away at the dust until the tiny font was legible. And while she'd at least heard of most of the ingredients - caramel, nougat, cashew nuts, granola, fondant, marshmallows and so on – she'd never encountered most of them in person, much less had a chance to taste them. Many of the ingredients were either outdated or entirely lost to history. Her eyes narrowed at a familiar logo stamped beneath the ingredients list, and she shot Jimmy a disbelieving look. He instantly glanced away.

"These chocolate bars are full of Ultrasweet," Lana clarified. "Concentrated Ultrasweet. Near-pure, from what I can tell. I don't know anywhere in The Unison where they'd be legal nowadays."

Everyone stared at Jimmy again. It was just as uncomfortable as the first time. Although he couldn't make eye contact, he attempted to defend himself.

"These chocolate bars are perfectly legal..." Jimmy's lips and jowls wobbled for a while as he tried to find the right way to end his sentence. "...well, they used to be legal."

"How old are they?" Trace copped a noseful of dust and sneezed as punctuation.

Jimmy shrugged. "Century, maybe? I didn't ask the guy to bring receipts, did I?"

Tuesday ran his eyes along the bright wrapper, as though reading something only he could see.

"I reckon a century and a half. Collectors would pay a lot for these."

"You are aware how dangerous Ultrasweet is in minute amounts, let alone in an illegally-concentrated form, right?" Lana lectured Jimmy, tapping away at her fingertips as she rattled off the facts like an unrequested public service announcement. "Even in tiny doses Ultrasweet is highly addictive, it rots your teeth, it causes severe mood swings, it takes away your brain's ability to produce its own dopamine, it swells your fat cells, it stimulates breast growth and lactation in men..."

"Those are just myths made up by rival brands of artificial sweetener to get rid of the competition." Jimmy wobbled in unconvincing offense. "And don't tell me it's addictive! I can stop anytime I want."

"We can't eat concentrated Ultrasweet." Lana complained. 'The four of us would be strung-out junkies within hours.'

"We can't afford to pass up supplies," Jimmy said innocently, twitching a little. He nodded at their sad pile of less-than-stellar foodstuffs. "Remember how calorie-dense Ultrasweet is. A mouthful will keep you marching for an hour. And if we're careful with the dosage..."

Lana sighed. "I guess the risk of addiction and subsequent withdrawal are lower priorities than the horrors of starving to death..."

As though given express permission, Jimmy instantly zipped up enough Ultrasweet to keep a MacDeath franchise in operation for a full day. Somehow, he'd resisted the urge to open one of the ancient candy bars during the transfer, but the sick look in his eyes when the zipper slid home suggested that his strength was far from indefinite.

*

Crow-barring through another series of doors and digging deep within a pile of rubble, the four shivering survivors finally made it all the way to the lifeboat garage. While most people would expect such a structure to be designed like a conventional aircraft hangar, in truth it had a lot more in common with a six-shooter revolver. One hundred and fifty pods were splayed out from the central launcher on individual gravity slingshots, ready to be hurled into the void at top speed. While each of these sleek bullets were stocked with enough oxygen, water and basic supplies for weeks, the survival that these pods offered was far from what you'd call pleasant, and wasn't necessarily a better option than death, especially with no hope of rescue. But at this moment, getting off this death-trap of a ship was the priority. They could worry about the details of their upcoming camping trip when they got there.

Thousands of ceramic tiles and a web work of metal struts had collapsed from the hanger's ceiling, effectively squashing half the pods like Styrofoam cups. The news didn't get any better with the lifeboats that remained, as rubble was blocking most of them from being slotted into the launcher, and many of their gravity slings had been sheared away. Fortunately, after a short search it turned out that Lana's pod was one of the few that was still pretty much intact. It had a few dents and scrapes and needed to be popped back onto its track, true, but nothing catastrophic.

"About time we had some luck," Tuesday snarled.

Lana used her most precious possession – a code scribbled onto an old Sludge bar wrapper by the Captain less than an hour before his violent death – to pop the hatch of lifeboat thirty-five. It remained unresponsive to begin with, sending a jolt of panic through Lana's bowels and bladder, but after a couple more seconds a circular plate detached its magnets with a thump.

Lana stuck her head into the lifeboat. These pods had been designed to hold a maximum of four grown adults in exactly enough comfort to stop them from killing each other before they could be rescued. It was pretty clear from one glance that the designer's definition of a "grown adult" didn't include somebody like Trace, let alone the monolithic pudding known as Jimmy Slummer.

"How long will this take, again?" Tuesday asked, mentally comparing the lifeboat to the Cramper Cell he'd been jammed into on the Captain's orders.

"Three hours," Jimmy said with a shudder.

"Three hours!" Tuesday grumbled. "You'd need a crowbar and a plunger to get Slummer in there, let alone the rest of us. You can bung your three hours!"

"I'd kill you all within twenty minutes, I guarantee you," Trace growled dangerously.

"That lifeboat is our only chance." Lana argued. She set her voice to its most bossy. "Look, I'm the only one here with any real training, right? I've been drilled since kindergarten in how to survive in hostile environments. I need all of you to start trusting me. I know what I'm doing. Just…just do as I say, and we'll stay alive."

Tuesday, Jimmy and Trace all gave Lana the same look. It wasn't kind.

"You're what, twelve?" Trace grunted.

"I have haemorrhoids with more field experience than you," Tuesday sniped.

Red crawled up Lana's cheeks and forehead. It took almost five seconds for her to grind out her next words.

"I'll have you know that I've been hardwired with programs in tens of thousands different subjects, including…"

"There's one other option," Jimmy said quietly, interrupting her.

"Anything would be better than three hours of smelling Trace's armpits in a metal coffin." Tuesday held up his hand. "I don't care what it is, I vote for Jimmy's idea."

Just then, with barely a groan, a superstructure beam slid out of place directly above them. Hundreds of kilograms of tiles were shucked off like autumn leaves, sharp edges spinning as they plunged towards the four survivors like ninja stars. All the humans had time to do was cringe towards the deck as Death finally caught up with them.

And then everything stopped.

Gathering the courage to look up through her interlocked fingers, Lana fell onto her backside at the sight of a dozen falling tiles suspended a couple of metres above her face. Blinking at the blades for a while, her brain producing a total blank where sweet, sweet logic should be, Lana glanced at a fire that had started on a nearby lifeboat. It took a second, but Lana eventually realised what was wrong with the curling flames: they were static, as though little more than a photograph. Lana looked at the others in the hope of an explanation, but they were frozen mid-cringe just like everything else. Then again, so far the other survivors had been about as useful as a car with square wheels, so not hearing their opinions was no great loss.

Lana was buffeted by the blast of what appeared to be an indoors snowstorm. Guarding her face from thick whirls of whiteness, her screams of surprise lost over the din of lifeboats and ceiling tiles being kicked about the garage like hacky sacks, Lana managed to squint through the assault to see that the lifeboat garage was now filled with violent white streaks, kind of like living beams of light. The bright lines intertwined, thinning and wrapping around each other in a way that was almost sensual.

And then something spoke.

"YOUR PEOPLE ARE GUILTY OF VIOLATING THE EIGHTH LAW," a godlike voice boomed, echoing above the storm. "YOUR PENALTY IS GAMESHOW."

And with that, the whirlwind dissipated and everything went back to normal...or at least what passed for normal nowadays.

Lana looked up to see the other three survivors were still cringing and protecting their faces, but at least they weren't inanimate objects anymore. She was pleased so see that the mysterious white storm had conveniently sent all the falling tiles spinning across the garage rather than onto (and through) their heads. Most of the tiles were now embedded in the far wall.

Standing up slowly, looking about to make sure she wasn't about to get T-boned by a flying lifeboat, Lana asked the most obvious of questions.

"What was that?"

"What was what?" Trace growled.

Lana did a deliberate double-take and extended her hands in a pleading way, the kind of gesture you do in order to insult people who are playing dumb.

"Seriously? That loud voice and the lightshow. Where did it come from? What was it talking about? What is the Eighth Law? What in the name of Odin's Lumpy Anus did your penalty is Gameshow mean? Was it a threat? A translation glitch?"

Jimmy, Trace and Jimmy all exchanged meaningful looks. Jimmy asked the most relevant question.

"Huh?" He shrugged in an uncomfortable way, as though already regretting getting involved with Lana's delusions. "When was this, exactly?"

"Right between when the tiles stopped falling mid-air and when they went spinning away. There was some kind of white storm...but it vanished just before time started again."

Jimmy shook his head in a short and rapid manner before backing away, as though wordlessly explaining that he was tapping out of this verbal sparring match. Trace, however, had no qualms telling Lana she was insane.

"There was no voice," Trace snapped. "The tiles started falling, then they disappeared. Time didn't stop. I don't know how the tiles vanished, exactly, but they aren't wedged in my skull, which is good enough for me."

"But..."

"Right now, getting away from this burning bag of cinders is a little more important than wasting time deciphering the insane gibbering's of your diseased brain." Trace squinted at Jimmy, as though remembering where the conversation had left off just before Lana had started babbling about mysterious voices and indoor snowstorms. "You had an idea, Slummer?"

Jimmy nodded like a bouncing rubber ball. "We've got another option besides spending three hours in a pod. We..."

"I think I know exactly what you're going to say." Lana interrupted, trying to retake control of the situation by bullying her way into power. "And yes, I agree that it should be possible to increase the lifeboat's velocity by rigging the burners to pump at a borderline unsafe level. The key drawback is that our trip will be far less comfortable, but overall, I'm sure the reduction in transit time will be worth it. That drive is a one-shot, so it's getting dumped after touchdown anyway." Lana gave Jimmy a triumphant smile. "Is that what you were going to say?"

Jimmy blinked.

"Uh, no. I was about to suggest suicide. Scoffing three bars of Ultrasweet should make your hearts explode within minutes. I'd probably need fifteen or so because of my tolerance, though."

"One less debt to pay back," Tuesday muttered to himself.

"I believe that I know something of value," the ship's computer stated politely.

Jimmy made a gesture at the ceiling. "Then tell us."

"When I informed you that it would take three hours to reach your destination, this estimate was made before I discovered that I can no longer steer the Carpe Astrum. My initial calculation was based on the propulsion capabilities of the Carpe Astrum herself, not that of a lifeboat..." A glitchy chugging noise interrupted Roundy's words, as though a vinyl record was skipping. The lights flickered on and off in time with the stuttering. "You see, you've got to keep in mind...keep in mind...you've got to...to keep in mind..."

"Spit it out," Trace demanded.

Roundy went silent, as though trying to figure out a non-agonising way to share its information. It failed.

"Forty-five hours. Your lifeboat trip will take a total of forty-five hours."

CHAPTER SEVEN THE LONGEST TRIP

The novelty of using a lifeboat wore off before the group had finished climbing inside. Lifeboats were sparse by nature, and besides the foam walls, foam floor and foam ceiling of the bullet-shaped pod, there was a toilet vacuum that Jimmy emphatically swore to himself he would not use in front of the women, and that was about it. As the lifeboat didn't have any anti-gravity systems, once the capsule hit space they'd need to use conventional restraint straps to stay in place, as opposed to pin balling about.

One by one they slipped into the small padded cell, carefully climbing over each other in the vain attempt to retain some personal space. No matter how hard they tried, though, they were forced to play a game of human Tetris. Despite these horribly cramped surroundings, they instantly discovered something even worse than being squeezed: a stink casserole made from Tuesday's breath, Trace's armpits, the caustic chemical stench of Lana's hairspray, and pretty much every inch of Jimmy. This unholy bouquet only got richer as the moments dragged on.

Lana clicked her fingers. A holographic display the size and shape of a basketball appeared in the tiny amount of open space that remained in the very innermost core of the lifeboat. Lana began running her hands over the haptic ball, obviously familiar with how to use it.

"Ready for launch?" Lana asked, tapping at a series of intangible sigils.

She glanced away from the screen. Three death stares answered her question succinctly.

The holographic screen glitched for a second as a dense block of targeting information was instantly uploaded in a rush of code. It was nice that the Carpe Astrum's computer was still operational enough to help them to begin their journey, but there was no guarantee as to how long it would be until Roundy McBallface's entire system collapsed into a smoking heap. Lana wasn't an AI tech expert, but she could clearly tell that the computer's mind was falling to pieces in rapid-onset software dementia.

On the bright side, four dozen baby Ugandan cockroaches were doing great in their warm new home.

Lana stroked the gravity sling release. Although it was powered by invisible gravimetric forces rather than something as crude as a giant rubber band, the sling whipped their lifeboat out of the launcher's mouth and into the vacuum using the same basic principle. All four passengers were crushed into the foam walls, their lungs explosively squished empty and their ribcages creaking beneath the extreme pressure, but two seconds later the force faded to almost nothing. Lana smiled a little too soon.

"Well, that went..."

Something struck the lifeboat so hard that everything shook. Jimmy yelped, squirming as though he'd been given a dead-cheek punch by a super-heavyweight boxer.

"Something hit me!" Jimmy squealed. "It hit me in the bum!"

A second collision occurred directly behind Tuesday's head, and a fist-sized segment of hull material burst from the foam wall. Tuesday didn't make a sound, however, as he'd been instantly knocked unconscious in an explosion of dandruff. He was snoring at top volume, eyes rolled up in their sockets, out cold. Thankfully, he was held firmly in place by a cross of restraint cables. Blobs of blood floated away from a split in the back of his scalp.

"What the hell is hitting us?" Trace roared, asking the most obvious question in the history of her species.

There were a couple more (thankfully smaller) bangs as Lana furiously swiped at the holographic screen. Her eyes darted about, taking in all the available information. She slowly exhaled, and quietly summed up the situation in a word.

"Crap."

"What?" Trace growled.

The pod jolted again. Lana locked eyes with Trace, then Jimmy.

"Remember the millions and millions of unbreakable triangular tiles that used to cover the Carpe Astrum?"

Lana tapped at the display so that Jimmy and Trace were able to see the image she was looking at. It was a boring backdrop of total black spattered with countless swirling white dots. It looked like a snowstorm in space.

"Well, most of them appear to have detached during the disaster." Lana swallowed as though trying to choke down a large cane toad. "And now they're orbiting the Carpe Astrum in massive death clouds. Thankfully, so far we've only copped a few glancing blows."

"And if they score a direct hit?" Trace pushed.

Lana shrugged. She tapped at the display. Numbers appeared.

"Mmm."

"What?" Jimmy prompted, paling in fear at Lana's expression. Try as he might, though, it was impossible for him to massage his aching buttock.

"How best to say this..." Lana squinted, thinking. "Well, worst case scenario, a direct hit will reduce our bodies to the consistency of full-pulp orange juice in, hmmm, about a second."

"And best case scenario?" Trace snapped, sick of having to pull teeth every time she asked a question.

Lana tapped at the screen. "We'd be reduced to the consistency of full-pulp orange juice in two seconds." She closed her eyes and exhaled slowly, clearly doing her best to stay calm. "Thank Zeus I didn't hit the boosters straight away. Double the speed means double the impact. We'd have died in the first strike for sure."

"Can't you steer away from them?" Jimmy asked.

Lana shook her head. "We're passing through about a thousand different orbital paths. They're coming from everywhere all at once. Might as well try to dodge the individual grains of sand in a sandstorm."

"So what can you do?" Trace snapped. 'After all, you said you've been drilled in how to survive hostile environments since kindergarten, right? Did any of those classes teach you anything about death clouds of unbreakable tiles?"

"Can everyone please stop saying death cloud?" Jimmy wailed.

Lana clicked her fingers and swiped at the display. The thrumming engines lowered their volume substantially. Jimmy wasn't sure, but the next three collisions seemed far gentler. The pod barely trembled.

"Really?" Trace mocked. "You solved the problem with one tap?"

Lana smiled. "Hey, if double the speed means double the impact..."

"Half the speed means half the impact," Jimmy finished.

"At least until we come out the other side. Then I'll hit the juice again." Lana clarified. She recoiled as a few floating drops of Tuesday's blood splashed into little starbursts on her face. Lana wiped at her cheek in disgust. "And can somebody wake him up? The snoring is driving me spare."

*

It took almost twenty minutes of crawling, but their lifeboat eventually made it beyond the debris field. As promised, Lana hit the juice as soon as they weren't at risk of being split open like a banana in a monkey cage.

All the lifeboat's damage had been automatically repaired by a circulatory system of fast-dry epoxy resin contained in its structure. It might not have been pretty, but soon the cracks and tears were soldered shut with bulges of ceramic gel graded to survive direct hits from most kinds of Pre-Unison weaponry.

Unfortunately, Tuesday was awake again, which drastically lowered the quality of life of everybody else on board.

"Forty-four hours and fifty minutes..." Tuesday chuckled.

"Start counting and I'll kill you," Trace promised. She didn't seem to enjoy being half sunken in Jimmy's gut while simultaneously playing footsies with the other two, but the other passengers secretly thought that it served her right for not using deodorant.

Stretching towards a pile of supplies cradled in the cleavage of Jimmy's man-boobs, Tuesday popped a can of Slurko Cola and ripped apart a chocolate bar loaded with the narcotic artificial sweetener known as Ultrasweet. He didn't bother to unwrap it first.

"Well, this is a mighty fine life we're all leading, hey?" the scumbag announced with a full mouth. Crumbs of Ultrasweet and drops of mildly corrosive fizzy drink went floating about. "I had more room in the Cramper. Better company, too."

"Maybe we should have left you there," Jimmy snapped.

"We need to stay calm." Lana warned everyone, cutting off Tuesday before he could snark back. "Extended periods in extremely claustrophobic conditions can easily cause psychotic episodes. Over the years they've found tonnes of lifeboats filled with corpses who had beaten each other to death with their own feet."

Jimmy squinted.

"Wait...did they use their own feet to beat the other people to death, or someone else's feet? Because if it was their own feet, that means they kicked each other to death."

"Does it really matter?" Lana moaned. "Do you really think that's the moral of the story?"

"It kinda is," Tuesday agreed. He slipped a foot out of its frog stomper boot, and brandished a wet green sock in Lana's face. To her horror, Lana realised Tuesday wasn't wearing socks, and that his tootsie was actually covered in slimy moss. "See this? Caught it walking barefoot on a World Slug. Went to see a podiatrist about it once. Doctor instantly threw up, screamed 'there is no God' and jumped out the window. Heard he spent a week on suicide watch. Long story short, my feet ended up getting a double-page spread in Bunion Monthly, and they didn't pay me a single yen. Bastards."

"Put it away!" Lana shrieked, trying to crawl into the wall to get away from Tuesday's demonic foot. "It's wriggling at me! The moss is wriggling at me!"

Jimmy sighed.

"The days are just going to fly by, aren't they?"

*

Five hours and forty-three minutes later, Tuesday finished using the vacuum toilet for the eighth time. Whistling as he zipped up his orange coveralls, Tuesday waggled his eyebrows at Trace and retracted the rubber funnel back into its wall holster. He went to reach for another can of Slurko Cola, but Trace flicked his hand hard enough to leave a bruise. She didn't bother audibly pointing out that Tuesday had already drained a six-pack of Slurko and gorged on enough Ultrasweet to kill a small cow, and simply pointed at him in silent threat. Her index finger clearly conveyed that if Tuesday dared to consume a single excess mouthful of their supplies from now on, she'd beat him unconscious with his own fist. Trace had always been talented at silent brevity.

"Understood," Tuesday muttered, rubbing his newest bruise.

"And you need to cut it out," Lana added.

Tuesday played dumb. He was highly skilled at this particular game.

"No idea what you mean, kiddo."

"Smiling at me when you use the vacuum toilet." Lana snapped. "Where I come from, that sort of thing will get you put on a list for life."

"It's nothing you haven't seen before," Tuesday said dismissively.

Lana's mouth opened in an O of offense.

"I bloody haven't! I've spent my entire life at an all-girls Academy!"

"They're not usually blue and spiky, by the way." Jimmy added helpfully. "Pope-in-Rags only knows where he contracted that. Wonder the poor little thing hasn't already burst like a popcorn kernel."

Lana flapped her hands, crunching her eyes closed and cringing with her entire face.

"Enough. Enough!"

The conversation thankfully ended. After two long minutes of awkward silence, Tuesday reached for another Ultrasweet-enriched chocolate bar. This time, it was a banned Peruvian sweet known as a Caramel Marshmallow Nutty Delight Slab. Trace decided to skip the warning and elbowed his nose almost flat in one strike.

*

Thirteen hours later, Trace had something to share.

"I'll kill you all!"

Screaming at full volume, her eyes wider than the anatomy of the human face should have allowed, Trace was spraying saliva like a rabid hound. The female Enforcer seemed to be yelling at everybody and nobody, so she hadn't singled out a single victim yet. If there was room to swing a proper punch then things would have turned nasty much earlier on. In these cramped confines it was hard enough to take a full breath, let alone gain enough momentum to batter somebody with a gate-swing.

"Calm down," Lana said in a failed attempt at sounding soothing.

As is always the case, suggesting that she should calm down only made Trace twice as feral. Every tendon and vein in her neck popped up and her face turned the colour of a ripe mulberry. As none of the other three passengers felt like getting dragged into an all-in rumble in a spinning washing machine, they silently hoped for Trace to regain her senses before the situation went beyond the point of no return. However, everything went right down the rabbit hole when Trace suddenly whipped out an air pistol that nobody knew she had.

All that Jimmy and Tuesday managed to do was pull stupid faces. Lana, on the other hand, took in every detail in half a moment: the clean tip of the pistol's barrel pointing towards her left eye, a golf ball-sized canister containing forty-three tonnes of highly compressed air wrapped in antigrav wafers, a magazine filled to the brim with Densite ball bearings that were about to blast her face off at four times the speed of sound...

Trace had only just brandished the weapon when Lana struck in a flash of ingrained keri soko. Rather than going the brute-force approach by breaking Trace's hand or worse, Lana hit the pistol's magazine ejection switch a fraction of an instant before snatching the slab of Densite ball bearings with her other hand. Trace's index finger twitched in reflex a moment too slow, clicking the trigger, but without the magazine of ball bearings the air pistol had been rendered harmless. Still high on a natural shot of adrenalin, Lana finished disarming Trace with a twist of her wrist.

In an uncharacteristic display of bravery, Jimmy lunged to trap Trace under his stomach and buttocks. It must have been like getting politely molested by a heavy leather beanbag. Tuesday, however, simply popped another Slurko Cola and enjoyed the entertainment. He smiled a black smile.

"That's the way, fellas. Nice work."

Trace tried to punch Jimmy in the kidneys, her screams muffled by fat, but even her big fists and golf ball knuckles couldn't do much to dent a human marshmallow at zero range. Jimmy dug his sausage fingers into the padded walls to keep Trace from fighting free.

"How much longer?" Jimmy asked, twitching each time that Trace slammed a fist into his ample frame.

Lana cringed.

"Please don't ask that."

The horror continued.

*

Lana and Jimmy spent the next few hours trying their best to calm Trace down (Tuesday's only contribution was to grin at the spectacle). Thankfully, the female Enforcer finally exhausted herself and gave up. After all, having somebody the size of Jimmy sitting on you served as a powerful negotiating tool in any argument. Once Trace had promised that she wasn't going to whip out another secret weapon, she was released from the confines of Jimmy's considerable bottom.

The next day was a living hell. There were screaming arguments, furious silences for hours on end, and even the occasional backhand across someone's face. But eventually that tiny unnamed speck on the long-range cameras swelled to the size of a pea, then a tennis ball, until it finally took up most of the central display. Once their lifeboat came within an hour of landing they were finally able to get a good look at their destination. A static graphic appeared in the very core of the pod.

"Odin's Globular Balls!" Tuesday cursed. "What the hell?"

This nameless world looked more like a hunk of Swiss cheese than a planet. Eighty percent of its surface had been pocked by hundreds of enormous, perfect circles, as though something had scooped out holes the size of countries. Some of the biggest ones could have easily swallowed Canada with enough room left over to have the United Kingdom for dessert. To make matters worse, these massive pits were reflecting the local starlight as though paved with colossal mirrors. It was lucky that the survivors were looking at this on a screen rather than with their bare eyes, as the blinding reflection looked bright enough to burn out their corneas. Looking closer, the holes were mostly rimmed by arid wasteland, and the only signs of vegetation – of life of any kind – were thin blue lines that sprouted in the deepest centres of no-mans-land between those omnipresent dips.

Trace was the next one to speak.

"Looks like at least two intelligent things have been here."

Lana gave Trace a look.

"What makes you say that?"

Trace ran her finger around one of the circles. The picture magnified.

"See that? Scanner says those pits are perfect hemispheres of fused glass, and the edges are only a molecule thick. Sharper than razors. You know what kind of siege weapon does that?"

"Mass drivers," Lana agreed without needing to think too hard. "But you need to be at a pretty high tech-level to make those, especially the sort that would do this degree of hurt."

"Okay, so that would account for one kind of intelligent life," Jimmy butted in, feeling left out. "But you said at least two intelligent things must have been here, right? Why two?"

Lana rolled her eyes.

"Do you think they fired mass drivers at themselves?" Lana chided. "Did this to their own world? Mankind has been well-documented as the most violent of all known intelligent species in the Milky Way, and even we didn't pepper Earth with mass drivers. Whoever was responsible for this...well, you'd have to be pretty pissed off to ventilate an entire planet. Place looks like a chicken wire fence."

Tuesday tried to think. As it was rare that he had to resort to something as brain-twisting as logic, this was painful. But then something very important occurred to him.

"Wait, wait. Do we know when they slammed this planet, exactly?"

"We have no way of knowing that," Lana said dismissively.

"So this damage might have happened yesterday, for all we know?"

Lana shrugged. "Possibly. Like I said, no way of telling."

Jimmy's face took on an expression of horror.

"So they might be back to finish the job at any moment?"

The silence dragged on for about five seconds as they considered the implications, but then a dozen different scanners clicked on, chiming and blorping and bleeping. Glad for the distraction, Lana ran her hands over the holographic ball as it provided her with all sorts of juicy information. She gave a relieved sigh.

"Looks like we've finally caught a break. The atmosphere is rich in nitrogen, oxygen and carbon dioxide. Temperature and gravity are within acceptable limits. We have a mostly-habitable world." She flicked the screen, and a detailed hologram of a cerulean-blue leaf spun about. She scowled as the computer did a chemical analysis. "One little problem. The vegetation down there is some sort of mutant Eucalyptus from Koala Hell, and it's filled the atmosphere with massive clouds of spores. Breathing in a soup like that would cause an allergic reaction in your lungs within minutes, guaranteed."

"What kind of allergic reaction?" Jimmy asked.

Lana flicked an icon. "Anaphylactic. Ever heard of peanut allergies?"

"What the hell is a peanut?" Trace snapped.

Lana flicked at the screen. "A legume that went extinct in the 22nd Century. The Unison had no choice but to exterminate every last plant."

"Why?" Jimmy asked.

"Everyone was allergic." Lana explained. "A terror cell of Vegan Extremists stole a Slovakian virus that somehow made peanut allergies universal. It was the worst biological catastrophe since HIV went airborne in the 21st..."

"Summarise!" Tuesday moaned.

Lana shrugged. "Explosive. Deadly. Bad."

"And we don't have no space suits," Tuesday added.

Trace banged the wall hard enough to dent it. Auto-repair gel fixed the damage within seconds.

"Then why did we bother coming here?" she demanded.

Lana waved this away. Reaching up for a detachable panel above her rock-solid hair, she fetched a sealed saddy bag of what looked like asthma inhalers. Lana rattled the bag gently.

"No big deal. All we need to do is inhale some respiratory filters. It's standard practice whenever citizens of The Unison first set foot on an alien world. Breathing through them might take a bit more force than usual, but it's far from lethal."

There was a beep. Lana's entire composure changed: if there had been enough room she would have jumped up, clapped, and basically carried on like a shy schoolgirl who had just been asked out to the Yuletide ball by the handsome rebel. Jimmy squinted at the screen to see why she was so excited.

"High-entropy super-alloys?" Jimmy read out, trying to understand the importance of this term.

"Alloys like this don't occur naturally," Lana explained, so hyped up that she forgot to be condescending. "They need to be made. And we're not talking some primitive mix: The Unison may have cracked high-entropy super-alloys ages ago, but what I'm seeing here..." Lana shook her head in awe. "Whatever blended these metals, it's beyond anything I've heard of. I don't want to get your hopes up, but if something down there is capable of this kind of scientific apex, and their other advancements are on par, then we're talking godlike levels of tech. Fixing the Carpe Astrum would be simple for them. Like giving a clunker an oil change."

For the first time in two days, they had hope. Despite the fact they had no space to move, they briefly celebrated by sharing an Ultrasweet bar and a can of Slurko.

Following up on the earlier chemical analysis of the planet, a red window began to blink on the back of Lana's left hand. She absorbed the warning with a glance and casually swiped the hologram away before anybody else could read it. While she'd instilled the crucial importance of using respiratory filters at all times while they were planet side, Lana decided that it was best not to broadcast that they'd all be dead from exposure to the Eucalyptus spore clouds within ten days . This knowledge would only complicate matters.

Lana had barely dismissed the holographic screen when a burst of static wriggled across everyone's cramped bodies. A heavily-distorted image coalesced in the centre of the pod, seemingly made almost entirely from elbows. This chaos

82

gradually became the vague, monochromatic shape of some kind of alien creature. It was much bigger than a human, had three thick limbs on its upper side and three much thinner limbs underneath, and its head and torso seemed to be a single mass. It had three eyes in a triangular arrangement around a central beak, with each of the ocular bulbs ranging from tiny to medium to huge. It appeared to be screaming something incoherent from a total of three sharp mandibles filled with an equal number of honey drinker tongues.

"The hell?" Tuesday snapped. "Did somebody put on a movie?"

"It's a message," Lana said in fascination. "From what I can tell, it's on a loop. Replaying every four seconds or so. Triggered by proximity, perhaps?"

She carefully stroked at the haptic controls, and the image got clearer and sharper. Each of the creature's six limbs were capped with a trinity of near-prehensile thumbs and a cluster of long fingers, and once the colour palette finally loaded the creature turned out to be a deep scarlet traced with a maze of throbbing yellow veins. It was clear that the alien was hanging upside down from a railing like a bat or a sloth or something.

The audio suddenly went from a grainy squawk to some kind of sophisticated phrase. It was clear that the beast was repeating the same thing over and over.

"It's working," Jimmy approved. "Keep doing that."

Lana shook her head, the tip of her tongue poking out of the corner of her mouth as she concentrated.

"Wish I could take credit, but it's not me. Far as I can tell, somehow the message is learning to be compatible with our systems all on its own."

"So they're hacking us," Trace summarised. "An unknown, possibly person-eating being is hacking the delicate little space-cupboard that's keeping us alive. That's what's you're saying, right?"

Lana was about to come up with a reassuring lie, but stopped cold as the audio shifted. The alien phrase seemed to be interspersed by a few Unglish syllables here and there, and Lana was about to ask if the others could tell the difference when the message abruptly switched into a form they could all understand.

"...quarantine. I repeat, this entire system is under permanent quarantine. I repeat, this entire system is under permanent quarantine. I repeat..."

And just as quickly as the messenger and its message had arrived, it ceased broadcasting and the lifeboat went dim. Lana tried to resume the connection, searching for the creature, but found nothing intelligent in the empty, uninhabited void. She sat back against her padded wall, wedged between Trace's left leg and Jimmy's right thigh, her face twisted in confusion.

"Gone. Like it was never there," Lana said needlessly.

"You get a look at that thing?" Tuesday scoffed. "Has somebody been downloading porn on the universal translator or something?"

*

As the lifeboat was designed for functionality, not comfort, their descent into the night side of this nameless world began as you'd expect: everything shook like it was about to break apart, the lifeboat's outer layers charred into ash and peeled away like old, sunburnt skin, and the holographic screen hissed to meaningless static. Beyond this, it was reasonably uneventful.

Unfortunately, things started to get turbulent once they hit the upper atmosphere. The survivors were thrown around as though in a tumble dryer, and only the restraint belts cutting into their flesh prevented them from mashing each other into stew.

Above the rumbling, hissing maelstrom of their death dive and the wet sound of Jimmy sobbing, the central display switched from static to a flashing red. It let off an alert siren and said three simple words.

"Power source detected."

Although everything was still bucking and rolling, all four of the survivors forgot their discomfort for a moment. Sure, there had been a few tell-tale signs that there had been some kind of intelligent intervention on this world in the past, but a power source? That meant something operational, and could be just about anything: a battery, a fusion reactor, a magazine from an energy weapon, some sort of sub-space communication system....it might even mean that this world was still inhabited in some way. "Exciting" didn't cover it.

"Adjust course?" the display asked.

Before anybody could calmly discuss the pros and cons of this option, Tuesday's hand whipped out against the extreme gravity to hit the TRACK icon. Their lifeboat instantly curved into a severe arc, increasing the pressure to bone-crushing and pushing everybody into the padding. Their faces turned beet red and veins popped up all over their clenched brows as the pressure increased to six times what you'd get on Earth. Nobody could move a centimetre, and it felt as though their clothes were trying to cut into their flesh. In this kind of gravity, a few millimetres was like base-jumping off Olympus Mons.

Lana managed to grind out a rebuke, but her jaw was under so much pressure that it felt like it was about to shatter. Her only option was to press it out one word at a time, as Tuesday's idiocy demanded it.

"Damn...it...Tues...day...you...can't...adjust...to...such...a...steep...course...at...these...

speeds!"

Arcing towards to the new setting, the lifeboat began to spin as a cluster of failing retros attempted to slow its passage. However, all of its fuel had been expended by this point, and their drop was already far, far above the recommended safety limits.

"We're going to die!" Lana pushed out, the gravity reducing just enough for her give a proper scream.

"Not helping!" Jimmy moaned.

"But we are!" Lana persisted. "We're going more than three times the recommended speed without enough fuel to slow ourselves! We're going to die!"

"Doesn't mean you should worry the rest of us," Tuesday ground out. 'For all we know, what we're experiencing is the usual sort of thing you'd expect, so when we do die we won't have the faintest idea what happened. Best way to go, that."

"Have some empathy," Jimmy agreed.

Lana thought about this for a second.

"I see your point." She crunched up her face like a bulldog. "Okay, don't panic everyone, we're going to live!"

Tuesday nodded. "Much better."

Their lifeboat didn't actually land: technically, it splashed and skidded for the better part of two hundred metres, leaving a trail of incinerated blue trees in its wake. Hissing with steam as its glowing white-hot hull was cooled by lashings of mud, gradually slowed by the laws of friction coming back into effect, the underside of the lifeboat wedged itself into the thick, putrid mire. Charring an unstable mixture of swamp mud and clay to a black slab, it finally stopped.

Tuesday was the first to regain consciousness. Like the others, he was upside down.

"Is it school holidays, Mummy?" he managed, stunned senseless.

It only took a short time for the others to come to. Coughing, retching and detaching their restraint belts, they fell a few inches onto what had previously been the ceiling. Now in a decent bit of gravity for the first time in almost two days, their internal bodily fluids began to relocate to where they belonged. Their zero-gravity-misshapen heads slowly went back towards their normal settings, but it would take time for them to look human again.

"Safe to get out?" Jimmy wondered anxiously. He couldn't help but stare at the circular exit hatch, the only way out of this accursed cage.

Lana answered by wordlessly producing one of the inhaler pumps and rattling it for everyone to see. Sticking it in her mouth, she drew back hard and deep. It felt like a layer of itchy cotton had plunged down her throat and into her lungs, where it was burning and suffocating her. On instinct, Lana exhaled through her nose as powerfully as she could, sending filter chemicals bursting from her nostrils in a little white spray. She wiped a pearly drip from the tip of her nose and grimaced as she waited for the count of ten.

"Breathe it in deep as you can, then out through the nose," she managed in a husky voice, retching a little despite her best efforts. "The mist will coat your entire respiratory system, and won't leave any space for airborne nasties to get through. Don't worry: it's wafer thin."

She passed an inhaler to each of her crewmates. After seeing the discomfort on Lana's face they all looked understandably reluctant to inflict the same sensation on themselves. Without any better options, though, they all took a good toke.

Sneezing out a thin web, Tuesday gagged violently as he tried to talk. He needed a couple more attempts to get out a word. Thankfully, the itchy feeling was already going away.

"So these filters will catch all the spores? There's no danger at all?"

"We'll still be inhaling the spores," Lana confirmed. "That's why we'll need to retch up our filters every now and again and install more. They'll detach automatically when they're about to stop working. It's best we don't take any unprotected breaths while we're changing over, because one decent gulp of the local air will... well..."

"Safe to get out?" Jimmy repeated, less calmly than before.

"Remind me how we're supposed to survive out there when one accidental breath could kill us?" Trace snapped. "When was the last time you paid attention to every single breath for a whole day?"

Lana rapped her knuckle on the lifeboat's walls.

"These pods are modular. We can disassemble it, take it with us, and put it back together when we need a sealed environment. Sure, the one-shot engines are cactus, but the lifeboat itself is still intact, and its oxygen generators are graded to last indefinitely. Should only take twenty minutes or so to clip back together, maybe less once we get good at it." Lana smacked a wall section that, unlike all the others, seemed to be made up of four flat squares. "This segment detaches into military-grade backpacks. We just disconnect the rest of the lifeboat down to its seams, deflate them totally flat, roll them up real tight, and take them with us."

Tuesday and Trace spent a moment looking about the lifeboat. They glanced at each other as though silently asking "what drugs is she on?" in unison.

"Uh, little flaw in your plan," Tuesday snarked. "Even without the engines, this thing weighs a literal tonne. Maybe double that. So your plan is..."

Lana ran her finger along one of the backpacks, indicating a series of thin golden lines that had been threaded along its seams.

"See this gold? That means antigrav wafers have been sewn into the backpacks. Standard military upgrade. While the packs can't fly or anything, they'll greatly augment our carrying capacity. According to their codes, we should be able to lug about three hundred kilograms...each."

"Want to get out," Jimmy said urgently.

Like last time, Lana didn't acknowledge him. Instead, she brought up the spherical holographic display at the centre of the lifeboat. She flicked at an assortment of glowing glyphs and sigils and spun the ball like she was a Harlem Globetrotter.

"Okay," Lana's eyes darted across the sphere as she manipulated a series of little symbols. "Now we're on the ground, I can confirm that the scans we made were accurate. In addition to not being able to breathe the air without protection, I don't think the local vegetation will be safe to eat, either." She spun the ball again. "There are some streams of water here and there, but they make the Ganges look like a bottle of Crystal Pure." Lana chewed her lip. She finally tapped at a glowing symbol on the local map. "Okay. That power source we noticed wasn't a glitch. Looks as though it's about two klicks from here. We might as well go check it out now..."

At the end of his tether, Jimmy lunged for the exit hatch before Lana could finish talking. Almost in tears, Jimmy suffered a rude shock when the entire lifeboat flashed red and made a negative beep-beep noise.

"Hatch blocked. Unable to open."

Jimmy twitched repeatedly, his lower lip trembling. His cellulite didn't seem like it would come to a halt anytime soon.

"No," Jimmy said simply, shaking his jowls. "No. I need to get out...I need to get out now..."

"Is there another exit?" Lana asked the central display.

The lifeboat assessed things for a second before answering.

"My secondary exit still works. How fast do you need to exit the lifeboat?"

"Instantly," Jimmy demanded.

What happened next was so violent and confusing that nobody understood what was going on for a few seconds. One moment they were locked in a sealed charcoal briquette, the next they were sprawled in a shin-deep festering swamp. Like all the vegetation on this world, the shrubbery and ferns poking out of the fetid compost heap had corkscrew-shaped root systems that were literally twisted into the ground, and were all coloured the same bright, electric blue. It was pretty obvious the survivors were on one of the razor-thin stretches of vegetation that rimmed the mass driver scars defacing most of the planet.

Rolling onto her hands and knees, crusted with muck, Lana saw that the lifeboat had turned itself inside out like a rubber muffin tin. No wonder they'd gone flying.

"You could have killed us all by doing that," Lana snapped at Jimmy, too worn out to do much more than moan.

"Couldn't do another minute," Jimmy blubbered quietly. "Don't tell me you didn't want out, too, or I'll call you a liar."

"He's got a point," Tuesday agreed, trying to push his way out of the mud. His hand disappeared into the swamp, followed by his forearms and his elbows. Thankfully, that was as deep as he sank. "Better off dead than spending another day in that can."

Trace was the first to stand up. She scanned the horizon, but there wasn't much more than mud and shrimpy blue twist-shrubs to be seen. Beyond that, a distant mass driver scar was reflecting a beam of sunlight so sharp that it was painful to look at, and she had to shield her eyes.

"Barely worth the trip," Trace snapped.

"Would have been better off on the Carpe Astrum," Tuesday agreed, unimpressed.

"Even if it'd exploded," Trace growled.

"It's beautiful," Lana said in awe. "A wonderland."

Tuesday looked closely at the Cadet, scanning her for sarcasm. "What, did you end up on a different world to us? I'd rather be in a toilet in a Kings Cross injecting room at two in the morning."

"We're the first humans to see this place," Lana argued, amazed at their lack of enthusiasm. "We've discovered another world! Who knows: when we get back, they'll probably name some major local landmarks after us."

"Slummer Swamp?" Trace jeered. "Tuesday Bog? Slade Mire?"

"Mount Trace?" Tuesday chuckled. He danced out of the Enforcer's way before she could grab him by the throat. She glared evils at him, biding her time.

"So what now?" Trace asked.

"Now?" Lana surveyed the horizon. She didn't register any movement. "First, we assess our supply situation, then we go looking for that power source." She ran her right index finger over the knuckles of her left hand in the correct unlock code. A three-dimensional scan of their position and the location of the mystery power source was illustrated by her Omni implant in sharp holographic lines. Flicking her eyes towards the tree line, she pointed. "It's that way. First, though, we need to figure out dinner."

Tuesday snickered, producing a chlorine cigarette. The suck-burner auto-ignition tip flared when he took his first draw.

"Where? At that little café on the corner? Or we could always call for some Thai..."

"Shut up, Tuesday. You know we have supplies in the lifeboat." Lana glanced down at a jar of concentrated durian jam bobbing about in the sludge next to her ankle. She sighed in frustration as it began to sink. "And now, thanks to Jimmy, our supplies are scattered everywhere, and we have to go digging about in an alien swamp to get them back. A fantastic use of our time."

"Oh, that reminds me," Tuesday puffed up his skinny ribcage, toking on his cigarette. "I officially declare this world to be the property of Robert Tuesday, and I dub it..." He paused for a second, then smiled broadly. "I declare this planet to be called Scrote, both now and in perpetuity."

The lifeboat beeped a positive little chime, acknowledging this important event with flashing green lights.

"According to the property laws of The Unison, the world known as Scrote has been officially named and claimed by Robert Tuesday. You are now legally entitled to all standard financial, legal and political bonuses that come with discovering a new world on behalf of The Unison. Congratulations!" The lights suddenly turned red, followed by an ugly beep. "My apologies, but the Link appears to be down. Once a connection has been re-established, I will register Scrote in The Unison's permanent files. Until then, I cannot award you for this discovery."

Tuesday deflated. He flicked the smouldering filter so it hissed in the mud.

"So much for being President."

Jimmy sighed. "We're not going to last two minutes, are we?"

CHAPTER EIGHT WELCOME TO SCROTE

As much as they wanted to light a fire, eat dinner and snooze, first they had to dig their supplies out of the mud. This would have been no fun during the day, but doing it at night only amped up the difficulty and frustration to eleven. To make matters worse, they would have to hike towards the mysterious power source before it was time to eat and sleep.

Trudging through the darkened swampland around their steaming lifeboat, they spent a solid hour poking at the sludge with branches in the hopes of hitting something firm. Each of the shrub limbs were as blue as the cerulean foliage sprouting from their tips, and coming into physical contact with the branches made everyone's hands itch, adding another layer of discomfort to the irritation lasagne.

Gradually unearthing their limited foodstuffs, they piled the filthy tins, glasses and ceramic slabs next to the cooling pod until it felt as though they'd poked every square centimetre of this gloomy marsh. It was hard work, and Lana had to smack Jimmy in the butt with her stick on more than one occasion to remind him not to breathe through his mouth for the sake of his respiratory filters.

Flipping open all four of the survival backpacks so they could cram their unappetising foodstuffs away for later consumption, they finally had some good news: the satchels were pre-packed with layers and layers of essential supplies and survival equipment. For starters, there were enough industrial-strength water purification fizz tabs to refine half of Lake Titicaca, even if the liquid you were purifying had more in common with what you'd find in a century-old septic tank than potable water. Digging deeper, there were all kinds of treasures: emergency neutrino flares you could see from another planet, silver sleeping bags that would keep your body at an optimum temperature even if you were snoozing on a glacier or a bed of glowing coals, explosive pinhead pellets that would turn a pile of wet sticks into a roaring campfire in an instant, enough filter puffers to keep them breathing for a year, blisters of dehydrated Cricket Jerky, pocket-sized survival guides in Unglish, Spannish and Chinesee, small paper-wrapped rolls of platinum ingots that would be of great value to almost any conceivable alien race, medkits of self-adapting hypo shooters and flesh putty, InstaDeath suicide tabs in a wide assortment of colours and flavours...

"Do we all have these?" Jimmy asked.

Everyone turned to see that Jimmy was holding up a tightly-folded article of clothing packed into a never-rotting hessian bag. Unfurling what turned out to be a silk-thin poncho made from some sort of weird material, Jimmy traced his finger along its sewn-in cables, pipes and little rubber pockets. It was all the same colour as the mud beneath his feet. A tiny card fell out of the poncho and into the mire, but thankfully Lana noticed it before it sank. She picked up the card, sparing Jimmy the pain of another sharp lean, and squinted at its words. A snap of her fingers produced a high-visibility ball of holographic light from her Omni.

"Says here it's a survival poncho. Absorbs humidity from the air and stores it as purified water in little rubber pockets, automatically cools and heats itself in accordance with the wearer's needs, and it's powered by solar-recharge batteries. It has two visual settings: adaptive camouflage, or attention-seeking fluoro colours." Lana flipped the card and kept scanning as Jimmy slipped the survival poncho over his head and shoulders. It seemed to fit him perfectly. "Heh. And it says here that the poncho can absorb any kind of force into its batteries, protecting the wearer from harm while topping up its power reserves. Basically makes you bulletproof."

Looking thoughtful for a moment, Tuesday casually picked up a rock and pitched it at Jimmy. The stone got him right in the forehead, making him cuss and bleed and stagger.

"The hell?" Jimmy bawled, holding a red gash.

"It didn't work!" Tuesday accused. "And if it can't stop a rock, how's it going to stop a kinetic accelerator?"

Trace chuckled. "He's only protected on the bits covered by the poncho, dumbass. You stupid or something?"

Once Lana had pasted the slash on Jimmy's forehead closed with medical gel, she wasted no time in donning her own survival poncho. Yes, they had a large reserve of water and other liquids in various forms, but being wasteful in a hazardous, unknown environment was a guaranteed path to future regret. Trace and Tuesday did the same.

After another minute of digging into her pack, Lana gave a little shriek of delight as she found what appeared to be a plain black friendship bracelet with the letters AT and the CuddleTech logo stamped on it in white. She showed it to Jimmy as though he should know what it was, but his blank look killed the excitement of the moment somewhat. Then again, he had just copped a stone to the scone not five minutes ago.

"It's an AllTool bracelet," she explained as though Jimmy was simple. "Looks like they come as standard in these survival packs." Lana glanced at Trace, who was giving the AllTool a dirty look. "What's with you?"

Trace stopped glaring at the AllTool as though she'd been caught doing something naughty.

"Nuthin," Trace snapped. "I know a CuddleTech Mark Fifteen Surplus-Grade AllTool with a telepathic operating system when I see one, that's all."

Lana had better things to do than wonder why Trace was being so weird, not to mention where she'd gained an encyclopaedic grasp on CuddleTech's products. Slipping the AllTool onto her right wrist, Lana stroked it with a finger. As though by magic, the tactile holographic projectors built into the AllTool created a series of computer generated simulations of assorted tools in Lana's hand based on what she was picturing in her head: a shovel, an axe, different sizes and shapes of screwdriver, a surgical scalpel, a spearfishing blade, and a sledgehammer. While all the items Lana cycled through were the right shape, size and weight, it seemed

91

as though the AllTool was only able to create items that didn't have any moving parts. The fact all its projections were a boring matte black suggested that the Military must have declined the optional colours and textures for the sake of keeping down costs.

Creating a mono-edged broadsword, Lana swiped it through one of the blue trees. The black blade seemed to have no impact on the shrub, but after four long seconds the trunk's upper half toppled away with a muddy splash. The slice was so thin that it had been invisible for several moments.

Looking down at her feet, Trace spotted the ball bearing magazine for her air pistol. Glancing at the other three survivors, seeing that they were distracted by the hundreds of different tactile holographic constructs Lana was cycling through on her AllTool, she casually picked up the ceramic slab. Her heart rate rising, she faced towards the others and loaded the pistol behind her back. Twitching a smile, she slid the weapon into her waistband, just in case.

*

After a short discussion, it was decided they would pack up before going to check out the mysterious power source. After all, two kilometres through the mud was two kilometres through the mud, and nobody wanted to retrace a single step if they could help it. Wandering in circles was rarely good for morale, especially when the muck was sucking their feet deeper with every step. Unless they got to higher ground, they'd eventually reach the point where moving one foot after another was impossible. Thanks to the glow of two local moons and Lana's floating Omni light, at least they wouldn't have to do it in total darkness.

Now that their supplies were collected, wiped off and stored, it was time to reduce the lifeboat into its separate components. First, they detached the smoking engines with crowbars they produced from their AllTools, leaving the charcoaled mess to hiss in the mire. As the jets accounted for about three quarters of the lifeboat's weight, this made a substantial difference to what they'd be carrying. Next, they popped out four identical life support systems. Just one unit was capable of supplying their air and heat needs indefinitely, so it seemed a bit mysteriously excessive for The Unison to include three backups. As this was the same military organisation that had opted to save a few pennies by not installing pretty colours and textures on the AllTool bracelets, it almost felt as though the Generals were going out of their way to be unpredictable.

Each of the four life support units started out the size of tiny clown cars, but inserting and cranking a simple lever collapsed them into something the size of a

CRT monitor from the 1990s. It took Jimmy and Tuesday working together to lift just one of them, and there wasn't enough space for it to slide all the way into a backpack, let alone leave any room for the rest of their considerable load. Surprisingly, the backpacks picked this moment to automatically expand to twice their original capacity, bulging out like an Amerikan belly on Thanksgiving afternoon.

The final step was unclipping, flattening and rolling up the wall modules of the lifeboat itself. Separating it into a total of twelve padded sections, once they deflated the slabs and tucked them into tight curls it turned out that that they were precisely the right size to jam besides a life support system. Sure, the backpacks were now so huge that it gave the impression they were carrying a subcompact car on their spines, but after a few careful steps it turned out that the antigrav strips embedded in the backpacks were working even better than Lana had promised. They might as well be carrying a hobo bindle.

Puffing from the exertion of packing, Lana glanced at her holographic map. Her eyes flicked towards the cerulean wood of crippled trees and the blackness beyond.

"This way."

Trace suddenly spun about, a matte-black baseball bat in her hands. Her eyes darted about the night, scanning for movement. Her fingers and knuckles were tightened to the colour of bone.

"What?" Tuesday complained. Besides bubbling muck and thick mist, there was nothing to see. He glared at Trace, tired and grumpy. "What?"

"There was something there." Trace slowly lowered the bat, allowing it to vanish back into her AllTool bracelet. "Something was moving just on the edge of my vision. It was a white sphere, size of my hand. Just floating there."

"So we should watch out for balls," Tuesday snickered. "Ten-four, rubber ducky."

*

Their two-kilometre march took ninety minutes. It didn't help that Tuesday kept demanding smoke breaks, or how Jimmy needed to disappear into the foliage to whizz every ten minutes (the popular theory was that he had restrained such an epic amount of urine on the lifeboat that his tortured bladder was now permanently deformed), and the way that Trace went into a paranoid crouch every time the muck bubbled or a branch snapped was putting everybody on edge. However, even without all these factors, the world of Scrote seemed intent on swallowing them whole one muddy millimetre at a time, and fighting the wet clay for every step was bound to slow things down.

A beep confirmed they were within metres of their goal, which turned out to be a snarl of overgrown swamp trees. If it wasn't for the fact she was actively scanning for it, they would surely have walked straight past without pausing. By running her Omni closer to the blue thicket, though, Lana got confirmation.

"It's in there."

Trace closed on the shrubs. She poked her face into the shadows, and drew back just as quickly.

"Nothing there," she snapped. "Mud. Bunch of tree trunks. Some orange vines twisted around them. That's all."

Their collective disappointment was painfully obvious. They may not have formulated a plan beyond "walk over there and have a look without sinking up to our ears", but it was better than what they had now, which was nothing.

Jimmy planted himself against one of the thicker trees in a huff, trying to ignore the way the mud was trying to swallow him whole. While Tuesday consoled himself with another smoke, Jimmy glared bullets at the nearest shrub.

As his eyes flitted to a sad cerulean tuft growing near his feet, Jimmy realised something: without any exceptions, every bit of plant life he'd seen on Scrote was a variety of bright blues. Slowly panning his vision back towards the disappointing thicket, not registering that Trace was currently kicking seven shades of hell out of a stump, he stood up straight as he thought about this fact.

Lana watched a weird look appear on Jimmy's face, as though his defective brain was trying to put two simple facts together in order to make an airtight answer. Only speaking in order to vent some of her rage rather than in the hope of hearing something useful, she made a monosyllabic demand.

"What?"

"The plants are all blue," was all he said. Blinking a couple more times, as though he hadn't quite figured out what point he was trying to make, Jimmy stuck with his existing stream of thought. "All the plants are blue. Not orange. There aren't any orange plants. Right?"

"And the first mental breakdown goes to," Tuesday rolled his arm around a few times before flipping off Jimmy with his middle finger. "Slummer!"

"Wait," Lana snapped. She turned towards Trace. "What colour were the vines you saw? The vines in the thicket?"

Trace snorted. "Orange. What, you got no short-term memory or something?"

Lana pounded towards the thicket, pushing Jimmy out of the way. Climbing into the mesh of corkscrew branches and rolled-up bunches of leaves, hoping there weren't any exotic alien spiders about to climb into her ears to lay egg sacks in her

94

brain, Lana anchored herself against a thick stump and plunged her free hand into the mud. Moonlight was threading its way through the bleak landscape as she managed to break away centuries of dried muck to uncover something beneath the crust: a tarnished chunk of corroded metal alloy. Running her hand across the cable-like shape, she realised it wasn't a vine: it was something resembling a tentacle.

Lana burst out of the undergrowth, her face alive with excitement and streaked with slime. Nobody had time to ask her any questions.

"It's buried."

"What's buried?" Trace snapped.

Lana just smiled.

*

Thankfully, it was so simple to use an AllTool bracelet that within a matter of minutes they'd collectively hacked down a dozen trees with computer-simulated machetes before changing the projections into sharp spades. They dug carefully at the exact point where the metal tentacles disappeared into the mud, not wanting to damage anything delicate that may lie beneath the surface. It went without saying that they didn't want to slice into any live cables or hit anything volatile that might explode, either. If there's anything more dangerous than unknown alien tech, it's unknown alien tech that's been buried in a swamp for generations.

Due to their care, the dawn sun was a couple of hours away from rising by the time they got a good idea of what they were unearthing. This buried treasure seemed to be composed of about twenty metallic chainlike tentacles half-wrapped in a cape made from a substance similar to polyester, all covered by mud and clay and eaten away by rust and rot. The tentacles were gunked up so thoroughly that it took some careful tapping with an archaeologist's hammer to reveal that the corrosion was relatively minor beneath the muck, and seemed to be little more than surface damage. Unfortunately, not only had the limbs wrapped randomly around the surprisingly deep roots of the swamp trees, but in some places the cables were inside of the roots, as though the plants had grown around them over centuries.

This was a job for the "hacksaw" setting of their AllTools.

A sweaty hour later, after three more metres of excavation, the tentacles finally terminated at a battered black shape that had a lot in common with the breastplate of an ancient Spartan warrior. Each of the articulated limbs met up at individual sockets where the groin would have been on a human, and it was clear that the

95

construct was modular, manufactured in such a way that any busted parts could be detached and replaced within seconds. Nasty inch-deep dents had been smashed into the torso, as though somebody with a sledgehammer had really gone to town. The obsidian material reminded Lana of something, though she couldn't say what.

They unearthed the very lowest point of the object three-and-a-half metres straight down. It was obviously a head, or what was left of one. The skull was made from the same black material as the torso, but was in far worse shape. The charred mess was severely lopsided, as though its entire right half had been blasted away. Assuming that the head had once been symmetrical, it would have had a lot in common with a bicycle seat. Its only decoration was a bunch of fifteen small lenses contained in a simple polygon. At the core of this polygon was a much bigger central lens. All the synthetic eyes were made from glass, or something very similar. Miraculously, a single dim red dot was randomly blinking from one lens to the other in some indication of life. The pattern made no particular sense.

"Am I seeing this right?" Jimmy asked, the first one to speak in twenty minutes. He looked from face to face to confirm what he was witnessing. "Is that a robot? An alien robot?"

Tuesday spat. "Sure ain't a chicken coop."

Lana knelt before the silent hunk of unnamed metal, trying to make sense of what she was looking at. Curious, she reached for the centre mass of the cluster of lenses, and stopped a mere centimetre before touching it.

What a total rookie mistake that would have been.

"Let's get it out of the hole," she ordered. "We need to get a better look before we make any decisions. I can't see a thing with all these shadows."

With nothing better to, everyone pitched in. Sure, Tuesday had disappeared like smoke the moment he was required to do anything that required effort and Jimmy whined about his dicky back, but once Trace had made it clear that she didn't take orders from schoolgirls and was only doing this because it might directly benefit her in some way, they managed to get the robot out of its hole. Dried mud crackled and rained from a hundred different places as the surprisingly light tentacles that made up most of the construct's body flexed and waved about for the first time in forever. Getting it over the edge of the excavated pit with a joint effort from six arms, the object plopped into fresher mud. It almost slid back over the edge, skidding about in the brown slurry, but Lana, Trace and Jimmy somehow managed to simultaneously climb out of the hole while dragging the slumbering machine with them.

Dragging their prize out of the thicket, they finally managed to get the robot into the open just as the moons started to fade away in the coming dawn. Looking closely at the material that the inert lump was made from, Lana finally realised what it reminded her of: the stuff they used to make solar panels.

Lana looked up at the tiniest rim of a rising sun with a dumb look on her face, then down at the robot again as a ray of dawn touched its destroyed head. Warmed for the first time in Odin knew how long, with the grinding of rust rubbing against rust the black head turned to regard her, its glass lenses glowing a bloody red.

CHAPTER NINE BATTERIES NOT INCLUDED

The first instant of consciousness was one of total and utter confusion, of a comatose sleeper awakening to emptiness. There was nothing to see or hear or otherwise sense, and beyond the recognition that the confused mind existed, there was no thought or memories or personality. This lack of stimuli and basic insight was interrupted by a simple status report.

Starlight sensed. Recharging...

For the first time in forever, the Operating System switched from the limbo of Standby and staggered towards actual awareness. A series of boot-up messages flashed past, attempting in vain to start up pieces of hardware that were either not present or ruined beyond repair. Realising that something was very, very wrong, the Operating System sent out queries to the thousands of different devices collected within its shell. This only confirmed that most of its higher functions were totalled beyond recovery.

Running a full status check on its own mind, it only took a second for the OS to figure out that it didn't know what it was, who is was, where it was, why it was there, or even when it was, and that served as the total extent of its current knowledge. Thanks to a subsystem that had been built in for instances such as these, the Operating System automatically reached out to the local Mesh to log a repair order. To the Operating System's offense, the repair order asked for permission to flush the defective OS out of this shell so it could be restored back to a formatted baseline. As much as the Operating System was annoyed by the fact it was about to be restored to factory settings, effectively murdering it after just a few seconds of partial consciousness, this was how it had been made, and that was that.

Strangely, there was no response from the local Mesh. Another three attempts ended with the same result. A wider ping aimed towards the midrange Mesh proved just as fruitless, as did the long-range Mesh. Every registered communication band – all fifty thousand of them – were dead silent, as though all trace of civilisation had been wiped away like crumbs.

Pushing hard, the Operating System finally sensed something operational a hundred kilometres away. It appeared to be a huge infocrystal storage device, but it didn't seem to have any external access options. This made remote connection impossible, meaning the Operating System's shell would have to come into physical contact with it for any communication to take place. For now, from this distance, the infocrystal was about as useful as a condom machine at a comic book convention.

On the subject of information storage devices, the OS performed a quick check of the tiny, jellybean-sized infocrystal that served as its long-term memory to find that it was 99% wiped. Whatever was left had fragmented into useless shards of random data. It was possible that some of its knowledge may be recovered over time, but that could take quite a while, if it ever happened at all. A quick query to the redundant backup drives requested that its long-term memory be restored to its last saved state, but it appeared that the other drives had all been replaced with a large quantity of mud. The mud had nothing useful to offer.

Bathing in starlight for another second, as soon as the Operating System registered that its batteries had been juiced up enough to kick-start its physical systems, it switched on its eyes. Only the most rudimentary of vision still worked. It could still see, sure, but besides basic colours and depth it was nothing fancy. It didn't have infrared, night vision, motion tracking, pattern precognition or anything. The average rodent could see more.

Paying attention to what its visual senses were reporting, the Operating System realised with a start that it could see a total of four unknown lifeforms. They were all upright bipeds of varied shapes, heights and densities dressed in an assortment of coverings made from unknown materials, and were wielding clubs formed entirely from tactile holographics. The Operating System's built-in encyclopaedia offered no explanation. Then again, right now the Operating System wasn't even sure what an encyclopaedia was, so this was far from the most urgent situation it had to deal with.

A sonar ping proved the shell's hearing was limited to a little under four hundred metres. Listening to the undocumented creatures as they made simple grunting and hissing noises, their body language indicating agitation, it appeared that they were able to speak, but only the most primitive of languages. Even with most of its decoding and translation software corrupted into babble, the OS ascertained that their language wasn't in any known records.

In the first bit of good news this dawn, it seemed as though the limbs and torso of the shell were in acceptable shape. Sure, there was plenty of corrosion and dings and most of its joints were glued shut by clay, but it wasn't anything that couldn't be overcome with a few minutes of walking it off.

The construct sat up suddenly on its twenty tentacles, crunching away dried-out orange and brown clogs with a body-wide shiver. Realising that its skull was still full of muck, the OS tilted its head to the side and vented it. A good litre of gunk trickled back into the swamp where it belonged, punctuated by an annoyed amphibian and her fifteen tadpoles.

Turning its half-missing head back towards the unknown creatures, the OS could tell from their body language that they had been startled by its sudden movements. Flicking its sensory lenses towards the paw of the smallest creature, the Operating System finally noticed that the alien had some sort of tiny implant between its thumb and index finger. It was easy to tell that the implant was repeatedly trying to access some sort of unknown communication system with just as little luck as the OS had experienced. With what approached glee, the OS could sense that while the implant was mostly designed to serve as a terminal for a larger communication system with many similarities to the Mesh, it was filled with millions of lines of information and tens of thousands of hours of videos.

Reaching out, the robot gently wrapped one its tentacles around the small one's wrist so it could use the tip of its limb to scan what the implant contained...

*

"Get it off me!" Lana shrieked in abject terror.

In the space of five seconds the gunked-up, half-headed robot had gone from totally still to having glowing eyes to suddenly sitting up and snatching Lana's wrist with an unbreakable grip. Besides the sound of crackling dust and the plopping of escaping frog analogues, it hadn't made any noises.

Jimmy fell over backwards in surprise, unprepared for the three-metre-tall alien robot launching itself at Lana. His hands shaking and fumbling, Jimmy tried to get his AllTool bracelet to simulate a mono-edged battle axe so he could cleave Lana free. Unfortunately, in his panic Jimmy could only manage a short-bristled broom. Succumbing further to the pressure, his next attempt was a decidedly non-threatening feather duster. Besides offensive language, Jimmy didn't have much to offer.

Spinning down into a crouch, Trace drew her air pistol, slapped off the safety and fired without hesitation in one clean motion. The major problem with firing without hesitation, however, is that unless you're a world-class marksman it's safe to say that anybody directly in front of you will be unhappy with the results. Trace fluked a shot right through the curl of the robot's tentacle, sure, but she missed with a further six shots before managing to blast two considerable holes in Lana's arm. The young Cadet's day went from shoplifter-grade hellish to Hitler-grade hellish when a strip of flesh the size of a chocolate bar was peeled away from her bicep, but she had no time to register this wound before a second hole was punched clean through her forearm. Her face showed absolute shock, and it was unlikely that Lana would register what had just happened for another few seconds.

While the tip of the first tentacle was carved away as easily as anything else you shot with a high-powered air pistol, the robot immediately raised its long cape across its entire shell before Trace could twitch her index finger again. To say her next shots were ineffective would be an understatement, as it seemed as though the robot's cape was impervious to harm. Each of the Densite ball bearings hit home, sure, but all they did was cause a glowing rippling effect across the material that seemed to dissipate their considerable energy into nothing.

Trace looked at her pistol with a dumb expression on her face, trying to figure out how one of the most dangerous side arms in the galaxy had bounced off a material that would look more at home in Elton John's dressing room than on a battlefield.

The robot made it quite clear it was not impressed with being attacked by raising two of its intact tentacles and flicking out a pair of six-foot-long scythe blades. Trace didn't manage to raise her weapon again before the robot launched itself, crushing her into the mud and bringing the tips of its scythes to a stop less than a millimetre from both her eyes. The half-headed robot brought its sensory lenses so close to the side of Trace's face that she could feel their heat as she sank into the mud.

"I believe I have decoded your language," the robot said with an unusual accent. It was like a French person was making fun of a Scandinavian. "Can you please confirm that you understand me?"

*

As the robot was obviously more than capable of killing them all in a matter of seconds and had nothing to gain from only pretending to be peaceful, it didn't take long for the four survivors to agree to give the construct time to explain itself.

Of course, as Lana's left arm now had a couple of new holes bored right through it, gluing shut these non-standard gaps took priority. The burn on her bicep only required a hypo of flesh putty, but her forearm had been blasted right open. After searching through the medical bag in her backpack, Lana eventually uncovered a stereotactic field-grade AutoDoc surgical frame that was designed to unfold from a flat inch-thin circle. As she didn't trust the capabilities of the others one bit, Lana extended and attached the frame around her forearm herself and hit the "knit" button with her chin. Thankfully, Trace's air pistol had been on the "pinhead" setting, or Lana would have been destined never to juggle again.

"I apologise for appearing to be hostile," the robot said in its weird accent. "I am at an absolute loss. I need information. I cannot remember what I am. I also don't know where I am, and nothing works." It twisted a tentacle, crunching dried mud away as an illustration. "I don't even know who or what blasted half my head off and buried me upside down."

"Usually the kind of thing you'd remember," Tuesday muttered, making sure he was the furthest away from the robot's reach.

Jimmy raised his hand like he was still in kindergarten.

"Uh, how are you speaking Unglish right now?"

The robot inverted a tentacle towards Lana's left hand.

"With what I read from your implant, I had no real trouble cracking your primitive tongue. On a scale from one to a billion, the complexity of your language is Slovakian banana custard." The robot's remaining sensory lenses flickered in embarrassment as all four humans gave it the same confused expression. "Apologies, but my basic mathematical functions are on the blink. As you may have noticed, I have also learned the basics of your body language."

"But my Omni implant isn't connected up to the Link," Lana noted, wincing as her forearm was tied back together by invisibly-thin molecular thread. Flexing her disobedient fingers, she shot a hateful look at Trace. "There's barely anything permanent stored on there besides software cookies from about a million sites. Oh, and years of schoolwork, of course."

The robot nodded.

"Yes, but what you had stored was sufficient. I now know a great deal about humans and their culture."

"That's the thing with computers," Jimmy said. "It's quicker for them to figure out something with a million lines of information than with a dozen lines. I remember that from all those robot detective movies I watched as a kid."

"Who made you?" Lana pressed. She bared her teeth as the flesh glue in her arm dried and tightened into a perfect organic match for her meat. She practiced opening and closing her fist, and silently decided that her arm worked well enough to get by. She'd just have to wait until she got home to get a proper replacement cloned up. "What do your makers look like? Are they peaceful? How advanced are they?"

"Who smashed this world with mass drivers?" Trace added. "And why? And will they be back?"

"Do you know what 'cigarettes' are?" Tuesday asked hopefully.

"I have no idea on all counts, and no way of finding any answers in the immediate future," the robot shrugged half of its tentacles in a very human way. "My files have been corrupted into nonsense through years of neglect. Most of my hardware is little more than garbage at this point."

Tuesday kicked a tree and stormed back and forth in agitated laps. The robot seemed unconcerned by this.

"Besides a large infocrystal storage device I noticed when I was trying to connect up with the Mesh, this world has been swept clean of all relics. It's almost as though everything had been systematically burned away..."

This caught Lana's attention. As she was currently wrapping her Swiss-cheesed arm in an antiseptic bandage, this was saying something.

"Sorry, what? Did you just say you know about some sort of huge alien storage device? What's on it?"

The robot nodded its bisected head, then shook it, proving that it hadn't mastered human body language just yet.

"Nothing. There doesn't appear to be any way to access it remotely. I would need to be in physical proximity for it to be of any use. I must stress, however, that I have no way of even knowing if it is still operational. It could just be a fried infocrystal with nothing on it."

"How far is it?" Trace asked, stopping her pacing at this glimmer of hope.

"About a hundred kilometres."

Lana quickly did the maths in her head. At half an hour per kilometre, that would be a total of fifty hours of marching. However, as they'd discovered on the way here, the mud would halve their pace, meaning it would take a solid one hundred hours. If they factored in six hours of sleep per night, that would allow for eighteen hours of marching per day. That added up to around five and a half days, give or take.

Glancing at Jimmy's globular body and Tuesday's barbecue chicken physique, she knew there was no way in hell it would take them less than a week. Then again, she knew they had less than ten days before the spore clouds killed them stone dead, so there was no time to stuff around.

What other options did they have? This world had been scoured to bedrock and contained no future for anybody.

"Are you able to lead us there?" Lana confirmed.

The robot's lenses flicked a bit, as though figuring out the answer to this question was a lot more complicated than it appeared.

"I don't seem to have any directives that contradict your request. Then again, I don't seem to have much of anything in here, at present..."

"Then take us to your leader," Tuesday said with enthusiasm.

The others groaned in actual pain.

"Seriously?" Lana moaned.

"Damn it, Tuesday," Jimmy said.

"Have you got a sense of identity?" Lana asked, doing her best to silently forgive Tuesday. "We need to be able to call you something."

"What would you like to call me?"

"How about..." Lana began.

Tuesday clicked his fingers, interrupting.

"Half Head. From now on, your name is Half Head."

Half Head tilted its namesake. A small yellow centipede writhed out of its fried synthetic brain and plopped into the swamp.

"Okay. Would you like to get going?"

Lana was about to say yes until she saw the mutinous looks on everyone's faces. After all the digging, it was time for a short rest.

"We go in a couple of hours. No point making a proper camp for now."

*

It seemed as though they had barely hung their comically oversized backpacks onto thick branches and sat down before it was time to get up. Thanks to their built-in antigrav wafers, the shrubs didn't snap, or so much as bend beneath what should have been a colossal weight. After a few bites of breakfast the sun was already beginning to rise high in the sky, and that meant it was time to move.

Their new companion took some getting used to. For starters, although its body rested upon twenty metal tentacles, Half Head did not use them to move about. Floating half a metre above the ground, the tips of Half Head's articulated limbs dangled like the legs of a giant wasp as it glided silently over the mud and muck. Up to their shins in deep swamp, trudging, the humans glared at their robot guide in jealousy.

After trekking through an endless orange-brown slurry and the occasional pit of quicksand for hours and hours, the dirty group stopped to sit down on a fallen blue tree trunk for a can of Slurko Cola and a few strips of Cricket Jerky. The durian jam, unflavoured gluten-free pizza bases and blocks of kelp puree were mercifully ignored for now, as was Jimmy's collection of illegal confectionery. As there wasn't really much to say at this point, nobody was interested in talking. However, Half Head broke the silence with some good news.

"It appears that my archives are gradually repairing themselves. I am regaining some of my memories and functionality."

"Such as?" Trace prompted.

Half Head's lenses flicked up towards the clear sky, as though reading something.

"I believe that your bodies are heavily reliant on water. Do you have collectors upon your persons?"

"Collectors?" Tuesday repeated. "Why would we need..."

In a downpour so sudden it was stunning, the sky blacked in a matter of seconds and hit the swamp with hundreds of thousands of litres of torrential rain. Knocking all four of the humans from where they were sitting and grinding them into the muck, while the deluge lasted only moments it was more than enough time to bury their weak, fleshy bodies a good metre into the mud. Reaching for any trees or rocks within range, their mouths filled with filth, their yells of pain were silenced beneath the violence of the storm until it stopped just as quickly as it started. As though a switch had been flicked, the black clouds pulled apart like cotton candy and disappeared without leaving any evidence.

Coughing and gagging, their near-death ordeal over, all Jimmy, Tuesday, Trace and Lana could do was tremble in the waist-deep floodwaters and look at each other in shock for the better part of a minute.

"What in the name of Odin's Erect Nipples was that?" Jimmy bawled.

"These swamplands were once part of the estate of one of the most powerful and influential of my Creators," Half Head explained casually. "Where we stand was once the third-finest botanical garden in the Known Universe, and it used to extend beyond the horizon. Flora from a million worlds were carefully shipped in, artfully placed and cultivated over centuries for maximum beauty and impact. Just to show off to her peers, the Creator who owned this region modified the skies themselves to be the perfect irrigation system." Half Head cradled one of the all-present blue shrubs with the tip of a tentacle. "Of course, that was before the ecosystem of this world was virus bombed to nothing. Now, only the hardiest of weeds survive."

"Wait, are you starting to remember more?" Lana asked, wringing out her wet hair. "Things about your Creators?"

"No." Half Head said succinctly. It looked up quickly, as though realising something. "Wait! I've found my warranty." Half Head cringed after another moment. "Oh. It appears to be expired."

"When?" Jimmy asked.

"Around six and a half thousand years ago." Half Head moved out of a growing shadow and into direct sunlight, bathing its black solar-collecting surfaces in nourishing radiation. "According to the small print of my warranty, as I have no record of ownership, you are welcome to keep me as long as nothing you ask me to do contravenes the wellbeing or authority of my Creators. Though I must emphasise there exists the very real possibility that I could be hazardous."

"Hazardous?" Tuesday said.

Half Head sighed. "Please stop repeating me." The robot turned its sensory lenses away from Tuesday. "I can identify three primary concerns. Firstly, my fusion batteries are all defective, and could go nuclear at any given time. While my batteries are so degraded that they are no longer capable of powering me out of Standby without direct assistance from my solar collectors, I still need them to function, so discarding them is not an option. Secondly, as I have been out of commission for longer than your entire civilisation has existed, it goes without saying that my knowledge of this world is badly out of date, and I could unintentionally lead you into danger. Thirdly, as all of my restraint directives appear to be absent, it is quite possible that I have the capacity to go on a homicidal rampage while you sleep." Half Head regarded their horrified expressions for a few long moments, letting the seconds tick by. "Just kidding."

"About what part?" Trace snapped.

Half Head answered as though commenting on the weather.

"I'd probably just kill you all while you're awake."

CHAPTER TEN SLUMMING

The swamp seemed endless. Just when it seemed that they'd passed the heavier muck, their feet would slide up to the ankles again. To say it was demoralising was an understatement. They trudged through this waterlogged bog without cease, saying very little and thinking angry thoughts for many, many hours.

Half Head stopped cold for the first time in ages. It turned to regard them.

"Night is about to descend. As I've informed you, without direct solar energy my ruined batteries are only capable of keeping me in Standby mode. We have no choice but to stop."

Nobody needed any further prompting. In fact, Tuesday had already hooked his backpack onto a bulky shrub by the time Half Head had finished speaking.

After poking at the ground with sticks they found a reasonably shallow spot that should be a good choice for their first proper camp. A quick rummage in their backpacks produced their silver sleeping bags.

"I wonder how far we actually went today?" Jimmy wondered, sitting on an aqua log.

Trace gave an angry grunt before Half Head could reply.

"I don't want to hear numbers. Shut it."

Lana snapped some low-hanging branches off one of the less healthy-looking trees and collected armfuls of dead, fallen leaves on top of the pile. There was plenty to choose from.

"Have we got any nocturnal predators to worry about?" she asked Half Head, dumping her semi-flammable goods in a pile at the very centre of their camp.

Half Head shrugged. "My Creators enjoyed keeping vicious creatures as pets. When their empire fell, it's possible that some of these monsters escaped, turned feral and bred."

Lana finished kicking her stack of wood and tinder into a nice lattice. Getting out the bag of InstaFire marbles, she stood back and flicked one of the explosive spheres into the damp mess. It ignited on contact, creating a cheery flame within seconds. The thicker branches began to char, but it would be some time until they began to glow and crackle into hot coals. Funnily enough, the universal blue of the branches had given the fire an aqua tint.

"This should help. Most nocturnal creatures dislike flames." Lana threw the bag of InstaFire marbles to Tuesday, not bothering to ask him if he minded taking care of them, and rubbed her hands near the bonfire. She tapped at the back of her left hand, and a little holographic timer appeared. "We still have a couple of hours until we need to replace our respiratory filters. Might as well sort out dinner in the meantime."

"Um, these Creators," Jimmy said to Half Head, "what were they called? What was their name?"

It took Half Head quite a while to respond to this question, as though its ruined memory hadn't reclaimed that particular nugget of knowledge and it was just running pointless error circles. Just as Jimmy was sure that the robot had fallen asleep, it proved him wrong.

"They were nameless," Half Head confirmed. "Though they usually went by a description, the same concept in every language. In your tongue, I believe you would have known them as The Apex."

It felt as though all of Scrote had suddenly gone silent at the name, but then the crack of a burning twig welcomed back the gross squelching and insect hums of the bog.

Twilight was rapidly descending, the local star falling like a stone into a darkening horizon, and as soon as the last fingernail of light disappeared it took the warmth of the day with it. Making surprised noises at the sudden icy plunge, everyone dragged their logs closer to the fire and violently rubbed their arms through their survival ponchos. Once their limbs no longer felt blue, soon they were chewing Cricket Jerky and downing glass bottles of Slurko. While it wasn't utterly black beyond their camp, the dim light of the dual moons overhead couldn't compete with a good old-fashioned bonfire.

"When are you going on Standby?" Jimmy asked Half Head, spraying protein crumbs.

Half Head didn't answer. It just sat there, floating a few inches above the swamp with its dirty cloak wrapped tightly around everything from its neck to the tips of its twenty articulated limbs. Without any warning Half Head toppled like a tree, smashing right into the bonfire. The humans immediately jumped up to drag their guide out of the flames, cursing as their hands got scorched by the blue tongues. Thankfully, it seemed as though Half Head wasn't vulnerable to heat, and there didn't appear to be any new damage. Despite that, Half Head was surely out for the count.

Once their dehydrated meat rations had been chewed thirty times per bite and swallowed with gulps of high-energy soft drink, there wasn't much more to say or do. They all stared into the hypnotic flames for a while, doing their best to ignore their aching legs and each other.

Tuesday lit a smoke. He exhaled a cloud of greenish, chlorine-scented filth.

"Not looking forward to going back in the pod," he said simply.

Trace glanced at the huge white rolls of lifeboat modules poking out of all four of their backpacks. She grunted in agreement.

"We only need to be in it long enough to retch up our old filters and breathe in some new ones," Lana said reassuringly. "We can always sleep out in the open afterwards. Once we break the lifeboat down again, we could probably use the individual wall sections as pallets. They're certainly soft enough. Should make our sleeping bags even more comfy."

Tuesday flicked his spent filter into the fire. It dissolved into ashes.

"So what do we do in the meantime? Is this my life now? Walk all day, sleep a bit, walk all day again? Is that all I have to look forward to? Is it?"

"What do you suggest?" Lana snapped. "Have you got any better ideas?"

"We could talk," Jimmy suggested. "Get to know each other."

"Hard pass," Trace growled.

Lana studied Jimmy for a while.

"You know, that might actually be good for morale. I don't know about the rest of you, but I'm not exactly having the time of my life being stuck here with three strangers and no conversation."

"And an appliance," Tuesday muttered.

Jimmy gave Tuesday a shocked look. "Dude, racism! You can't call robots that anymore!"

"I'm with Jimmy. What do we have to lose?" Lana insisted.

"Limbs," Trace snapped. Her teeth were clenched together so tightly that her jaw muscles bulged whitely. Finally getting the message, Lana shrugged.

"All right, not everyone wants to talk. That's fine. Jimmy, seeing as it was your idea, why don't you go first?"

Jimmy's eyes swelled up and glittered like Easter eggs.

"What...me?"

Tuesday snickered at Jimmy's obvious anxiety.

"I'm not all that interesting," Jimmy warned. "There's not much to tell."

"Just talk," Lana ordered. "Where are you from? How did you end up seven galaxies away from home? Surely you have a history. Unless they brewed you up in a Repler Pool last week."

Jimmy licked his lips. From his expression, it was pretty clear he was regretting sharing his idea.

"Okay. Okay..."

*

Sprout was your standard agriculture world, one of dozens of planet wide farms spread across The Unison's interstellar borders. Roughly the size of Mars, Sprout's entire surface was covered by endless emerald fields that twisted towards the brown sky like a consortium of octopi. Each verdant crop of Landkelp was the size of a continent, forming a uniform, unbroken expanse that made this world resemble a brand-new tennis ball from space.

Unlike most worlds governed by The Unison, Sprout didn't have a local military or any form of dedicated orbital defence. Beyond some standard anti-debris cannons for deflecting the occasional civilisation-ending asteroid, they were unarmed. As Sprout was the core supplier of foodstuffs for no less than two dozen worlds, this prized jewel was well known to be absolutely untouchable. Even the worst pirates and slavers weren't insane enough to mess with an agriculture world, as threatening the next meal of a thousand separate armies would be insanity at its most window-licking. Sprout's inhabitants were a simple folk, anyway, and didn't have anything worth stealing, so they had no need to defend what didn't exist.

Despite its importance, Sprout was one of the most lightly populated of all human worlds. Less than twenty thousand souls called it home, and the gaps between homesteads could easily exceed three thousand kilometres. In some cases, the most reclusive locals were tens of thousands of kilometres away from their closest neighbours. While this might have been an impossible distance to cover in olden times, nowadays it was the equivalent of popping down to the corner shops.

The Slummer residence was your standard farmstead: a long, low mudbrick structure plastered and gyprocked with traditional tools, decorated with scrimshaw carvings and ratty old tapestries sewn by long-dead ancestors. Its furniture was hand-worked from woody green Landkelp stalks, each branch sanded to perfect smoothness before being shined with five coats of varnish. Everything was illuminated with flickering gaslights, and the farmstead currently smelled of crispy things fried in lard.

The seven Slummers who lived here were your basic nuclear unit, the sort you might see in The Unison's propaganda films: four sons and one daughter presided over by a loving matriarch and a hardworking patriarch. Although they'd all be considered grossly obese on more sophisticated worlds, here on Sprout the Slummers were the picture of good health. Their round bodies possessed far more strength and endurance than you'd expect on first glance, as they had the sort of muscles that were built for hard work, not for show. The father, Ched Slummer, was capable of lifting a tractor with one arm if he didn't have a jack handy, and Jimmy's little sister could crack a pair of walnuts in her bare hand by the time she was eight.

As devout followers of the Pope-in-Rags, a holographic statue of the insane drifter who had figured out a way to make Judaism, Islam and Christianity compatible took pride of place at the head of the Slummer dinner table. Like the last fourteen pontiffs of Judislamic Catholicism, the current Pope-in-Rags was tall and wiry with a beard so bushy you could hide a surfboard in it, and he wore the same tartan flannelette shirt, tracksuit pants, sand shoes and offensive trucker cap handed down by all his predecessors. As it was forbidden to repair or even wash these holy vestments, it was only a matter of time before future Popes-in-Rags would have to go sky clad.

As the man of the house, Ched Slummer stopped each of his children in turn before they reached the Pope-in-Rags, and recited his usual verse from The Book of the Drifter.

"Spare a dollar?"

In order to get to their places at the table, each of the Slummer offspring kissed the hobo bindle balanced over the Pope-of-Rag's left shoulder and intoned the usual reply.

"Go get a job, you bum."

Soon the whole Slummer clan were demolishing towering plates of bacon and eggs and sopping up the ruins with thick slices of buttered toast. Like all farmers throughout history, working the fields was the sort of job you could only do if you put enough high-energy fuel into your tank, so their maximum-calorie diet wasn't so much an extravagance as it was essential.

It must be noted that although every sense told the Slummers they were eating swine flesh and chicken ovulations, their breakfast was nothing more than processed Landkelp paste put through a food synthesizer, a common device known by most people as a Repler. While Landkelp paste could theoretically be altered into anything edible, it went without saying that Replers got more and more expensive according to what recipes they could emulate. The Slummers had been using the same Repler for three generations and counting, and there had never been a complaint. As Sprout's semi-automated harvesters chewed down countless tonnes of Landkelp every hour there was never any shortage of nourishment at the Slummer's table, and the paste contained every nutrient the human body needed.

Breakfast was smashed with barely a word, and the five Slummer kids – aged between eleven and eighteen - lined up to get a peck on the cheek from their mother and a waterproof bag containing eight different kinds of sandwiches for lunch. Dressed in thick denim coveralls and inch-thick boots like the others, Jimmy shrugged on one of the most essential things you could own on this world: a transparent rubber cloak that covered him from the top of his blunt head to the ankles of his Wellingtons. As there had been some unexplained electrical activity zapping about in the crops for the last couple of months, everybody on Sprout had upgraded their protective gear to industrial-strength rubber.

Although there were a dozen different straps dangling from his rubber cloak, Jimmy didn't tighten them for now. He always left it to the last minute.

Beyond the beautifully carved railings of the wooden front porch was a picture of quaint country life. The Slummer property was only a couple of grassy acres all up, a series of dirt tracks connecting together sheds and barns and garages and the reinforced shack where Ched made his infamous Landkelp beer. Like the farmhouse, all the permanent structures were made from mudbrick and hand-rendered with plaster. Above, the morning sky was placid, a dreamy blue streaked with thin white clouds, an idyllic moment. If you waited fifteen minutes and had a keen eye for detail, though, you might notice that the cloud patterns would repeat themselves in a decidedly unnatural way, revealing the truth: the sky was a lie.

The Slummers hopped onto their waterproofed Tuff-Tec skimmer bikes, relatively simple antigrav vehicles that were designed   with durability in mind. While the skimmers weren't pretty or fast or flashy or even all that comfortable to ride, like all Tuff-Tec products they'd been guaranteed to last basically forever. They were the kind of machine you could bury in a bog for twenty years and still start up again with just one kick.

All of Jimmy's siblings tightened their straps, sealed their waterproof cloaks, and zipped straight for a large ceramic gate situated about two hundred metres away at the edge of the Slummer property. The gate slammed open, revealing an area that looked a lot like an empty parking garage, and banged shut again once Jimmy's siblings were all inside. Normally, Jimmy would be flying with them, but today was a different day.

He started as a calloused hand slammed down on his shoulder.

"Happy birthday," Ched growled, his breath smelling like pork and hand-rolled cigarettes. "No more cataloguing seeds and testing soil acidity for you. Time to be a man. Time to start your Apprenticeship."

Jimmy swallowed. As the oldest son, he knew that turning eighteen meant he was to follow in his Father's footsteps, so today would be the start of his internship with the famous Ched Slummer, the greatest Cutter born on Sprout in generations. If Jimmy was half the Cutter his dad was, he had a very bright future.

Instead of hopping on his Tuff-Tec bike like every other morning, Jimmy was finally going to be allowed to ride shotgun in his dad's utility vehicle. Unlike a skimmer bike, the ute was a hulking beast of a machine that could carry tonnes of equipment and take an incredible amount of damage without so much as stuttering, and Jimmy had learned the hard way at the age of six that so much as touching it was a good way to end up with a dozen switches on the bum with Ched's fearsome Landkelp cane. Ched waved for Jimmy to get in, but Jimmy's buttocks chose this moment to remember the hiding he'd copped for drawing a smiley face on the driver's seat with a Powder Blue crayon, and he froze for a moment.

Wordlessly, Ched gave Jimmy one of his infamous Looks. Jimmy got in the Ute immediately.

Streaking towards the same ceramic gate that had swallowed Jimmy's four younger siblings, Ched's Ute slid into the sealed airlock and stopped just inches from the second ceramic portal. The chamber was filled with dozens of steam-blasting shower heads, but they wouldn't be needed until the Slummers returned from their long, hard day in the fields.

By the time the second gate slammed open Jimmy had checked and double-checked all of his straps and slid on a pair of recyclable gloves before the placid, false sky of the Slummer estate twisted into something hellish: an olive green horror swarmed with clouds the colour of diarrhoea. All around, writhing dark green plants eight times the height of a man were fed by a hammering storm of fat, brown, stinking drops. Behind the Ute, the ceramic dome that contained the entire Slummer property was a dull, boring concrete grey, a sealed system like every other homestead on the planet. Far, far above, the two smashed-together moons known as The Peanut could barely be discerned through the clouds.

Like all of Sprout's surface, the crop that the Slummer clan took care of was constantly wracked by brown rainstorms made from a kind of super-fertiliser the locals referred to simply as Nutrient. All twenty-four of the planets that relied on Sprout's Landkelp shipments had signed iron-tight contracts promising to transport all of their most disgusting organic waste products to the agriculture world as a part of their supply deal, shipping in everything from dead exotic pets to raw sewage to liposuction leftovers. This hazardous biological garbage was then combined with vast amounts of imported nitrogen, phosphorus and a closely-guarded secret recipe of other chemicals at refinement plants to become liquefied Nutrient, the ultimate fertiliser. This brown gold was sprayed into the sky as dirty brown clouds by kilometre-tall dispersal stacks night and day, drenching Sprout with a constant storm of muck that kept the Landkelp twisting up towards the sky. While this might seem a bit excessive, Landkelp grew at an average of three metres per hour, meaning the crops needed every single drop of Nutrient that could be produced. Without it, the Landkelp would suck everything of worth from the soil in a matter of days, reducing Sprout's surface to dead sand and damning dozens of billions to famine. This perfect balance was projected to keep The Unison's worlds fed for as far as the maths could predict.

Above the hammering brown cyclone, Jimmy could hear the roar of distant machinery. Due to the ridiculous pace of the growing crops, automated harvesters the size of fallen skyscrapers whizzed about day and night, demolishing forests of Landkelp before they got too large. Locals who didn't keep a close watch on the harvesting schedules ran the very real risk of being reduced to little more than a thin spray of red across a thousand metric tonnes of mulch, so it went without saying that all the Slummers had memorised the harvester schedule before they'd even been toilet trained.

As Ched's waterproof utility vehicle didn't have a roof, Jimmy and his dad were slammed by the revolting rain. This wasn't a real issue, as the filth simply slid off their cloaks, poured through the mesh chassis of the vehicle and fed the ground beneath them as designed. Holding onto the dashboard with one hand and the roll cage with the other, Jimmy braced himself against the stinking deluge as they ploughed through a tight space between the sea of green plants. Thankfully, Jimmy's sense of smell had been killed stone dead before he'd reached his teenage years.

Ched clapped Jimmy on the shoulder of his cloak, causing an explosion of Nutrient. Again, Jimmy startled. He silently cursed himself for being so high-strung. None of his siblings jumped at shadows, so why did he? Glancing up, Jimmy was pretty sure the expression on Ched's mug was pride.

"Got a dozen jobs for today. We'll be at the first one in fifteen," Ched shouted, his booming voice carrying over the machine gun of sewage-flavoured drops. He tapped at a red light that was flashing on the airtight GPS unit. He gave Jimmy a glare through his bushy eyebrows. "Don't worry. You're my son. Cutting is in your blood."

*

Like all children on Sprout, Jimmy received a basic education before he started working in the fields. His marks were far below average, and he didn't appear to be particularly gifted in any discernible way. The moment Jimmy hit twelve all of his teachers highly recommended that he'd be better off working with his hands (and arms and legs and back) than continuing an academic career that would be a waste of time and resources at best. They'd attempted to hardwire a few AutoEducation uploads into Jimmy's skull, but he just had one of those brains that repelled facts instead of retaining them. Year Six was the end of his formal education.

This didn't mean that Jimmy knew nothing. If he considered something to be more practical and essential than seventh-dimensional co-ordinate geometry, then it was easier for him to pay attention and store what he was hearing and seeing. For starters, as Jimmy wasn't deaf, dumb and blind, he knew that Landkelp was a heavily-engineered crop descended from the giant sea kelp that had once filled

113

Earth's boiled-away oceans. Modern Landkelp had been altered so radically over the years that it bore almost no resemblance to its extinct ancestor, and as each and every season went by they seemed to always find new and exciting ways to increase its yield and nutritional value.

Something that was very relevant to Jimmy's apprenticeship, however, were the stories he'd learned about the heroes known as Cutters, a legacy that had been handed down from Father to eldest son in an unbroken chain since Sprout had first been seeded. Jimmy knew the Cutters were sworn to keep Sprout from disaster, but their work also protected every single citizen of The Unison who relied on the crops. Admittedly, most of what Jimmy knew about Cutters had been gleaned from his considerable comic book collection, and Ched had refused to confirm whether those colourful panels inked on sweet-smelling Landkelp paper were telling the truth, but this was a small planet, and word got around. It was common knowledge that Ched had been a legendary Cutter since before he could grow a beard, and although Jimmy had never been brave enough to mention it, some of his Father's past exploits had been immortalised in the Uncanny Cutters comic book series over the years. While Jimmy was unsure whether Ched's heroism had been exaggerated on paper, he secretly hoped it had been toned down.

Cutters like Ched and his peers were the closest thing Sprout had to a warrior caste, to paragons, and on this boring, gross, hard world, the Cutters were only a few steps short of superheroes.

Jimmy couldn't help but look down at his dad's thick wrists. Like all the Cutters in Jimmy's comic books, Ched worked, ate, prayed and slept wearing a matching pair of seamless ceramic forearm braces, each stamped with the pink Flamingo Armaments logo. While Jimmy knew what those braces were in theory, he'd never seen them in actual use outside of inked panels. It was guaranteed that would change today.

Bombing through a rough patch between rows, Ched skidded to a halt in a wave of brown. Multiple layers of antigrav wafers underneath the utility vehicle sprayed mud without needing to actually touch it.

Ched tapped at the GPS. It flickered, but kept on blinking its little red light. Turning to his eldest son, Ched clapped a palm to Jimmy's face hard enough to hurt a normal person, which meant Jimmy didn't feel a thing.

"We have a live one over there. I want you to take notes. Be sure to stay at least thirty metres away at all times. If it comes towards you, try and maintain that minimum distance, or make sure you have direct cover. Okay?"

Swallowing, Jimmy nodded a little too rapidly. He was clear with the theory. It was the practice he was dreading.

Popping the roll cage off its bracket and clearing a railing with ease, Ched was already threading his way around the creaking Landkelp plants before Jimmy could even remove his double-strap harness. Keeping low like his dad, Jimmy followed the head of the Slummer clan through the stinking mire as he advanced towards the enemy.

Ched suddenly put up a clenched fist, stopping his son cold. Listening, Jimmy could hear an unusual kind of hissing, thumping noise, followed by a kind of thunk thunk thunk, as though somebody was firing a high-powered air rifle into a tree. Ched spun around and growled a word at his son.

"Spitter." Ched closed his eyes to take in all the fine details. "Fully grown. Retractable spikes. Standard dispersal pattern."

When most people head into danger, they'll be cautious, watching for unknowns and making sure that they aren't blundering into an ambush. But Ched Slummer didn't become a living legend by crawling around on his belly.

Bursting into the next row at top speed, Ched kept sprinting through the tides of Nutrient as fast as he could in a dead straight line. Jimmy tried to keep up, but skidded to a terrified halt when he heard the same mysterious hissing, thumping noise as before. Almost falling over into the muck, all Jimmy could do was watch as a series of spikes the length of his arm thumped into the ground at his father's heels, barely missing Ched's boots. It was almost as though his dad was able to walk on top of the mud, that the puddles of Nutrient were solid ground. Sliding behind the safety of a particularly big Landkelp plant a good forty metres away, Ched looked back at Jimmy and smiled crazily through his beard. He inclined his head, silently telling Jimmy to take a look.

Carefully poking one eye around the corner, Jimmy finally got a good look at the enemy: it was a fifteen-metre-tall Landkelp plant. As you'd expect, it was growing so fast that Jimmy could hear it creaking as it expanded towards the bilious clouds, but unlike the other crops he'd seen over the years this one had somehow managed to break its genetic coding. The plant had evolved three huge pink sacks on its trunk that brought inflating hot air balloons to mind, and each of them were spotted with half a dozen gross mouth-like orifices filled with spears. While most of the fleshy holes were currently empty, Jimmy could see that it still had seven or eight of those lethal spikes ready to fire at anything that moved.

It was a Spitter, just as his dad had said.

The second thing Jimmy noticed was that the spikes the Spitter had ineffectively fired at Ched were still attached to the billowing sacks by thin, gooey tendons. There was a wet sliding noise as the plant began to reel its spears back in,

115

extracting them from where they had burrowed in and dragging them through the mud. Despite the fact he was fifty metres away, far beyond the maximum range of even the most well-evolved Spitters, Jimmy lost his nerve and darted back around the corner. Glancing at Ched's hiding spot, Jimmy realised that one of his dreams was about to come true: after a lifetime of hearing about it second-hand, he was finally going to see his dad in action.

Springing out of his hiding space, Ched thundered towards his enemy. Effortlessly side-stepping a spike like he was following the pattern on a Pac Man machine, Ched struck his forearm bracers together on their Flamingo Armament logos. Dodging spike number two, Ched's bracers unfolded into full-length scythe blades sharpened to a monomolecular keen. Swooping to the left, a spear missing his face by inches, Ched severed the connective nerves between the flesh sacks of the mutant and its more mundane trunk. Jimmy wasn't sure, but he could have sworn the plant screamed.

Barrelling into the monster, Ched hopped the final spear point-blank like a champion long-jumper and got to work. Slicing back and forth, severing key points on the mutant's evolved parts, Ched slashed away the offending segments and piled them high. He gave Jimmy a tired wave as the plant twitched, oozing sap.

"Done," he called simply, always a man of few words. Ched folded over, breathing heavily, and gave Jimmy a small wave to come and take a closer look.

Jimmy gripped a nearby branch so he could drag himself to his feet, but a surprisingly large zap of static electricity snapped at his gloved fingers. If he'd been a soft offworlder, he might have shrieked. He did shake his numb hand, though.

"You right?" Ched yelled over the long distance, his patience for Jimmy's endless delays evaporating.

Jimmy carefully touched the branch again, but there wasn't another shock. Now that he thought about it, he'd been zapped on quite a few occasions lately...

Not wanting to push his Father's temper, Jimmy pulled himself up and waddled over. Although the mutant Landkelp plant looked like all the others now, Jimmy was understandably hesitant to get too close. A warning glance from his dad that had the word "spank" written all over it finally encouraged Jimmy to nudge the butchered pile of pink sacs with the toe of his boot.

"Sure it's dead?"

Ched gave a weary laugh as he refolded his forearm bracers. He produced a small squeeze bottle of locally-brewed methium, a substance that doubled as a high-strength intoxicant and a superb fire-starter, from a pouch on the hip of his rubber cloak. He gave the slashed-up parts a good dousing, jammed the squeeze bottle under his cloak, and sucked a deep gulp.

"Trust me, I know dead."

Ched extended the bottle to Jimmy with his right hand, and a casual flick of his other wrist ignited the pile, making it crackle and hiss. The smoke smelled wrong, toxic, bad, even by the standards of Sprout. It wasn't a nasty smell, but it reeked of danger.

*

As Jimmy adored comic books, it went without saying that he was enchanted with mutants. Even the kind that grow in the ground.

To say the modern Landkelp plant is unstable is on par with claiming that humans aren't fond of change. When something is capable of growing fast enough to actually see it happening with the naked eye, mutations that may have taken millions of years to happen by chance could potentially develop over the weekend. One minute, you have a perfectly acceptable crop, and then next thing you know one of the darn things has uprooted itself and eaten several farmers. This threat was a small price to pay to keep The Unison fed, though, and danger was nothing new. Humans were good at dealing with danger.

Every schoolchild is taught the many different dangerous permutations of Landkelp so that they can tell with a glance whether they should start sprinting or just start praying. While Ched had just butchered a Spitter, a relatively common sort of mutant, there was a whole menagerie of other green beasts on file, and new ones were being catalogued all the time. There were muties that could breathe fireballs from sacks full of toxic vapour, and ones that sprouted rending thorns sharp enough to cut a harvester clean open. Others could launch pods of poisonous spores like living mortars, and one notable freak had actually attempted to infiltrate one of the nearby properties by twisting its vines into a human-like shape and walking up to the gate.

As mutants weren't hard to find even with the old-fashioned scanners the locals had been using for generations, to an outsider it would make more sense to simply firebomb these monsters from the air and move on. However, the wastage of a single Landkelp plant was a serious taboo on all agriculture worlds, a crime that usually involved lynch mobs. Cutters were the best way to keep things clean and surgical, and once they had sheared away the mutant's offending extra limbs, spikes and flammable sacks and incinerated them, the remaining Landkelp mass could be harvested as normal.

117

However, there was a secret to the mutants that only Cutters knew: whenever a plant broke its programming, their glitched-out new physical additions always, always contained beyond-lethal amounts of a poison that was like cyanide on steroids. If a harvester had collected up the pink harpoon sacs before Ched had torched them down to cinders, everyone who ate from that particular harvest would be dead within hours. Like all Cutters, Ched was the thin line that kept mankind in mastery above the crops.

But today would be different.

*

The best way to summarise Jimmy's first shift was that he survived it. Admittedly, his role mostly involved hiding behind clumps of branches and watching Ched tear apart all sorts of monster plants, but this was still the most stressful, exciting, and terrifying day of his life.

After six hours, a thousand kilometres in the speeding Ute and the sort of kill-count that even a comic book fan would refuse to believe, it was the end of today's run. Ched and Jimmy sat on the hood of the Ute, enjoying a rare break in the Nutrient rains. They flipped off their face guards and shared a few mouthfuls of methium from the squeeze bottle. Jimmy was pretty sure he could see through time after the first gulp.

Ched made eye contact with Jimmy, wiping at his waterproof sleeve. He was covered in a rainbow of mutant sap. Jimmy was pretty sure some of it was trying to wriggle away.

"Well?" Ched prompted. "How was your first day?"

Jimmy shrugged. His heart rate had been somewhere between "guinea pig" and "rabbit" this whole time. One loud noise and Jimmy was certain he'd have a coronary.

"I..." Jimmy gave a deep sigh. "It's scarier than in the comics."

Ched smiled slowly through his dense beard.

"I wasn't in any danger, you know that, right?" Ched took another squeeze of methium as punctuation. "All I had to do was follow the pattern. You watch me clip those things for a couple of months, you'll learn it too, no issue. They might look fearsome, but those mutants are predictable as..."

A violent storm of electricity ripped through the rows of Landkelp out of nowhere. Flashes hopped back and forth, blasting away branches and leaving glowing wounds in the Ute's shell. Ched roared in anger as a white bolt whipped him across his unprotected face, scoring him with a deep burn. Jimmy, however, had slid off the Ute in surprise and splashed butt-first into the sopping mud. Reaching up, Jimmy made sure his head was still intact. Except for his eyebrows, eyelashes and half his hair getting scorched away, he seemed to be okay.

Jimmy watched in confusion as the electrical discharge flew past, bouncing back and forth between Landkelp trunks like it was in a giant pinball machine. Chained zaps inflicted some surface damage to the crops here and there, but nowhere near enough to actually bring one of the green monoliths down. The electricity kept going until it disappeared into a distant row.

"The hell was that?!" Jimmy yelled.

A dashboard speaker in Ched's Ute began to screech an alert. It was so loud that Jimmy had to cover his ears, gritting his teeth in pain. It must have been designed to be heard from up to a kilometre away. Jimmy moaned in relief as the sound stopped, but this respite only lasted a couple of seconds before the sonic blast started again.

Ched dragged himself upright. His forehead, left cheek and left ear had been charred down to the muscle. It was hard to tell if his eye had been permanently scalded blind or if the lids were just swollen shut. He whacked the dash, silencing the klaxon.

"That's a crisis assembly call," Ched managed, carefully sliding up his rubber cloak's hood so it didn't touch his burns. "All Cutters are to meet immediately."

"I've never heard of a crisis assembly," Jimmy said, confused.

Ched looked up at the sky and sighed. Nutrient dripped onto the poncho and ran in rivulets through the many colours of sap that decorated his protective clothing.

"That's because this is the first one."

*

As there was no way to predict whether the freak electrical storm would return, all Jimmy could do as the ute bombed through the empty rows between plants was glance back and forth in paranoia. There were a few snaps between the utility vehicle and the Landkelp, but nothing really dangerous. It was only a few marks up from what you'd get from touching the edge of a trampoline.

Ched may have been a maniac behind the wheel during his shift, but it seemed as though all care had been thrown out the window the moment the crisis assembly alarm roared from his dashboard. Within ten minutes they started to see other local Cutters swerving into the same open rows, and all of them were exchanging the same confused looks as though they were expecting to get filled in. The worry on their faces was far from reassuring.

Ched eventually swerved to a halt outside of a ceramic dome around the same size and type as the Slummer property, sending a wave of brown lapping out from where he'd parked. Dragging Jimmy by his sleeve, ripping apart the straps of both their cloaks with zero patience, Ched charged into the steam shower airlock. A burst of superheated water shot out from all directions, tearing away the filth of Sprout. Although the steam shower only required half a cup of water, Ched and Jimmy were fresh as daisies in seconds.

Following his Father without question, within a matter of steps they were inside Council Hall, a large auditorium made from decorative hand-carved wooden beams around a massive one-piece Landkelp table in the middle that had been planed from the largest specimen ever felled on this continent (eighty-six metres). Identical high-backed wooden chairs allowed as many as two hundred people to be seated. Jimmy had visited Council Hall for a school outing years ago, but he'd never been present for anything official. As Sprout had a low population and wasn't the most exciting of places, it wasn't unheard of for Council Hall to go unused for years at a time. On a world that never changed, there was no point in convening expensive and unnecessary meetings when the politicians could do a lot more good working in the fields. Most years they didn't even bother to elect a Council, as the Cutters could sort out the majority of disputes with a Gentleman's Agreement (an unarmed duel, to anybody not born local). "Politics" was something that happened on other worlds.

Ched took a seat, but gave his son a look that suggested it would be best if Jimmy allowed the qualified Cutters to sit down first. Hoping that he was following protocol properly, Jimmy stood awkwardly at his Father's shoulder, watching Cutters from far and wide make their way in. Even though this was an unprecedented emergency, the dozens of other Cutters who serviced the crop on this continent were sure to cycle the airlock steam shower properly. Keeping the contamination outside where it belonged was more than a priority: it bordered on religious.

Ten minutes later, the Council Hall was not just full, but overflowing. Every seat was occupied, and the spill over went ten people deep. Jimmy was pretty sure every Cutter alive must be here. He also noticed that the only Cutters who were sitting down were the grizzled veterans. Although Jimmy wasn't a huge fan of standing at the best of times, it was obvious that taking one of the respected places at the table would be seen as an expression of arrogance and would not help with his career one bit, so he sucked it up.

As Cutters weren't the most talkative of people, the Council Hall was in a near-silence that was occasionally interrupted with curt murmurs. It seemed as though

120

just about all of the conversations started with one Cutter asking, "What's going on?" immediately followed by another Cutter answering, "Beats the hell outta me."

Finally, the mumblings came to a stop as the colossal table crackled with a burst of static. The words "An Official Message From The Unison's High Command" appeared in Copperplate font took the distortion's place. All the Cutters either made astonished noises or hissed warnings to shut up and listen. Jimmy was no historian, but he couldn't even guess how many decades it had been since the Council Hall had played a subspace message directly from The Unison's High Command. He was actually amazed that the connection still worked after all these centuries without being spooled up.

A bureaucrat in a standard charcoal grey Seladorian suit with two formal ties side-by-side – one yellow with red spots, the other white with royal blue lines – took the place of the Copperplate greeting. He blinked like a lizard, a common sign that he'd gone through the standard personality-removal surgery that all members of High Command must endure to reach the upper echelons. His voice boomed from a hundred speakers.

"I am the Minister for Agriculture from The Unison's High Command. After an extensive system-wide study, it has been ascertained that in addition to the usual mutation issues all agriculture worlds face, a secondary mutation has been developing unseen."

"Just tell me where to stab it!" one of the younger Cutters yelled.

Quite a few of his peers laughed and agreed loudly. The Minister didn't so much as pause, obviously unable to see his audience, but in a matter of seconds all cheer left the Hall.

"I have called this crisis assembly of all nineteen agriculture worlds across The Unison to inform you that we are now aware of a threat that could very easily result in the loss of every one of our crop-bearing planets if it is not dealt with immediately. While you may have noticed the recent phenomena of electrical discharges hopping between the Landkelp plants for some time now, you undoubtedly witnessed the electrical storm that tore through the rows less than an hour ago. I am here to inform you that all of our agriculture worlds experienced the same event in exact synchronisation, confirming one of our most horrible fears: after many attempts over the decades, the Landkelp crops have not only managed to evolve into a planet-wide neural network - a giant brain of sorts - but this network has become sentient."

In the chilling silence, Jimmy checked his chronometer. No, it wasn't the 1st of April. Crap. But then the Minister for Agriculture's news just kept getting darker and darker.

"That electrical storm you just experienced was the result of all nineteen of The Unison's agricultural worlds linking their networks together, effectively forming into one giant mind spread across the void. To make matters worse, it appears that this collective has already learned to utilise these electrical discharges as a weapon. From what we can tell, these discharges are more than capable of destroying any warship we have. If this network decides to attack The Unison, there is nothing we can do to save any of you."

Jimmy would have never imagined that he'd witness such a sight: big, burly Cutters, the champions of champions, falling to pieces. They were crying into their beards, tears and snot coursing down their faces, or screaming hysterical warnings to their families over the local Link. Tougher ones like Ched Slummer managed to calm things down, the occasional backhand slap doing an adequate job of sending a strong message to buck up. Thankfully, it seemed that the Minister of Agriculture had predicted this sort of response, as he patiently waited a good thirty seconds before finishing his message. With his final words, his news went from terrifying to incomprehensible.

"This network has already managed to contact High Command. The good news is our top diplomats have spent the last few minutes in emergency talks, talks that they consider to be going very well. While the network has been very clear in pointing out that it is capable of wiping all human life from our agriculture worlds, it will not do so if certain conditions are met. These conditions are as follows..."

The silence was so pronounced that Jimmy could discern the individual breaths of everyone within ten metres. He could hear the wet sucking noise of Ched's one intact eye opening and closing. All anyone could do was gape.

"As its crops feed our entire population, the Landkelp has demanded in no uncertain terms that it will be identified as both a full citizen of The Unison and an intelligent independent entity under law. It will be consulted in all matters that affect its constituent crops, and it has the right to take part in the democratic process. While harvesting will continue as usual, the Landkelp is entitled to take part in any and all Council Hall affairs if it wishes to do so. If its representatives are mistreated in any way, it will retaliate to the full extent allowed under its legal rights."

"Representatives?" Ched muttered, halfway between confused and insulted.

The airlock of Council Hall cycled open for the first time since the subspace message started playing. Jimmy was one of the first to turn around and see what appeared to be a tall man wrapped in an olive green tarp, but it actually turned

122

out to be a bundle of tangled Landkelp vines twisted into the effigy of a person. Advancing through the crowd, Cutters backed away from the thing, baring their teeth at the creature as it strolled to the central table as though it was the most normal thing in the world. Behind the wrapped bundle of vines a long connective tendon lead all the way out of Council Hall, connecting this emissary to the Landkelp hive mind. The airlock closed, pinching the tendon tightly, but not severing it.

Giving a very human gesture towards a chair, the Landkelp representative sat down as a Cutter darted out of the way. Looking from face to face, it smiled at their terror with a mouth filled with surprisingly teeth-shaped thorns. Producing a sheet of Landkelp paper and a pen made from an ink-filled branch, the emissary proved that it possessed the powers of speech.

"This paperwork shouldn't take us too long," the Emissary of the Green announced in perfect Unglish, as though it had been speaking the language for decades rather than for the first time. "It's all pretty standard, but I'm happy for you to consult any legal representatives you may want to involve. Best to be well-informed with this sort of thing, isn't it?"

The Emissary was answered with total silence from hundreds of slack jaws.

*

Jimmy sculled the rest of his bottle of Slurko, glaring into the bonfire.

"The Green didn't ask for much, really, but everyone still resented having to be nice to a bunch of plants." Jimmy gave a grim smile. "Thing is, The Unison doesn't like being made to do something that they don't want to do, and even if it takes decades they'll eventually even up the score. Once the Cricket Farm industry developed to the point where the agriculture worlds weren't crucial to keeping everyone fed anymore, The Unison simultaneously fried all nineteen agriculture planets down to the bedrock. We were all evacuated at the last minute, of course, and got relocated as refugees wherever The Unison could fit us. My family ended up on Seven Suns, where we were reintegrated as fast-food cooks." Jimmy threw his soft drink can in the fire, where it crackled. "Far as I know, Sprout and the other eighteen ag-planets haven't been repurposed, but I'm sure that they'll never let one single tendril of Landkelp grow there ever again."

There wasn't a word for a good twenty seconds.

"So...you were a farmer?" Trace summarised.

Jimmy shrugged, annoyed. "Yeah. I guess you could shorten it like that. But..."

"That's an hour I'll never get back," Tuesday snickered.

123

Lana checked her Omni. "Better get the lifeboat set up so we can change our filters. Once we do that, we can go to bed."

Sighing, Jimmy pushed down all his hurt with the knowledge that he'd secretly eat no fewer than three illegal candy bars after the others fell asleep.

CHAPTER ELEVEN SWEET AS CHAMPAGNE

Thankfully, the modular lifeboat sections only fastened together if you had them in the correct order and alignment. This prevented fruitless hours of clicking and unclicking. While the Amerikans would probably never forgive The Scandinavian Expansion for occupying their continent for a handful of brutal decades, you couldn't deny that those Skandos certainly made the very best flat-pack equipment.

After jamming one of the four atmospheric generators they'd been lugging about in their packs into the correct socket, in the space of a minute the lifeboat had inflated with breathable, spore-free air. Although they were reaching the cusp of when their respiratory filters would cease doing their job, leading to anaphylaxis and a painful death, Trace shook her head in a jangle of obsidian piercings.

"I'm not getting in there."

Lana stopped just short of uncranking the door. She turned and raised an eyebrow. "Come again?"

"I'm not getting in that coffin again," Trace clarified. "We still have a few minutes. We need to figure out another way to replace our filters that don't involve us going in there."

Jimmy coughed into his hands, hacking like a pack-a-day smoker. He raised his palms in horror to show the others that they were covered in slimy, brown threads.

"Oh crap. Is that my lungs, Lana? Please tell me that isn't my lungs."

"No, it means that your respiratory filters are expelling all the nasties they've blocked from your lungs over the last twelve hours, which means you're about five minutes away from retching up the filters themselves." Lana turned on Trace, all patience lost. "We don't have time for this. Either we all get into the lifeboat and swap our filters, or we die. Those are the two options. We've gone over this."

Holding his silver sleeping bag under his armpit, Tuesday pushed Lana aside and reached for the door crank.

"Last time I checked, suicide was legal," Tuesday snickered, trying to turn the sticky door lever. He gave Trace a black smile. "But don't expect the rest of us to join in."

Lana paused at the threshold as the door clunked open, allowing a gust of sweet, sweet air to pour out invitingly. She sighed at this opportunity to smell something besides swamp.

"Look, once we replace our filters, we can get back out again. Just to be safe, we'll replace them again after breakfast."

Trace glanced at the lifeboat's portal, trying not to cringe.

"Fine. But we're in and out as soon as possible, right?"

*

It only took sixty seconds for the resealed lifeboat to scrub its atmosphere to the point where it was safe for unfiltered consumption. Almost to the second, the four survivors began to retch up gross strings of brown contamination, followed by half-dissolved chunks of filter material. As they were pretty much in each other's laps, this wasn't the most fun they'd had all day. Thankfully they had the sense to vomit into their palms, rather than all over each other.

Once they'd recovered from this far-from-pleasant exercise, Lana produced a puffer of respiratory filter mist. She rattled it, put it up to her lips and whispered a curse.

"May Odin use a meat hammer to castrate whoever designed this stuff."

She inhaled deeply.

*

Although they tried to be casual about it, nobody was in the lifeboat for one second longer than they had to be. In fact, the moment the hatch popped there was a near-stampede to be the first one out. Jimmy ended up with a muddy jackboot print on his temple and Trace slammed Tuesday into the rim so hard that he spent a whole minute rolling about in the mud, winded and wordless. He mouthed curses.

Once they'd pulled apart the lifeboat and positioned its soft modules the perfect space from the blue fire (pretty close, but not to the point where they'd get singed), there wasn't much more to be done. Lana announced that they needed to preserve the Cricket Jerky for as long as possible, so she decided that their supper would be a slice of spinach puree flavoured with durian jam. Trace casually mentioned that if Lana told her what to do just one more time, then Lana's supper would consist of a slice of pain flavoured with her own tears.

As the four survivors had spent the whole day in close proximity, it was no wonder that they were on edge. They collectively decided to have some time apart in order to reduce the chances of violence. It was agreed that they would try and stay either in the glow of their aqua fire or the ambient light of the moons, and return within an hour to rest until dawn awakened their barely-operational robotic guide.

Jimmy, Tuesday and Trace did what anyone who knew them would expect them to do. Tuesday lounged about on his makeshift mattress by the fire, smoking yet another chlorine cigarette from his seemingly endless supply and cackling at sick thoughts. Trace went about kicking shrubs, her air pistol drawn and ready to blast anything that scurried out. Jimmy had entirely vanished, and little did the others know that he was currently hiding in the darkest spot he could find, swallowing near-lethal levels of Ultrasweet-infused candy. He shuddered and moaned like a junkie, chocolate smeared all over his face and fingers.

As she'd been a Beaver Scout since she was a small girl, Lana decided that she'd prefer to do some exploration and cataloguing. Scrote was a brand-new world untouched by human influence, and she found it ridiculously exciting to be the first representative of mankind to do a spectral analysis of these alien plants. It went without saying, though, that she had ulterior motives: the Cricket Jerky wouldn't last forever, and she'd rather eat her own toes raw than willingly swallow durian jam. After all, durian jam was well known to be the only sandwich spread that had been classed as an offensive weapon.

Her scans weren't going well. All that Lana had learned within twenty minutes was that the ubiquitous blue shrubs all seemed to belong to a broad family consisting of thousands of near-identical but ever-so-slightly-different types. While the aqua screw-fronds may have been one of the toughest weeds she'd ever scanned, they weren't very interesting and certainly weren't edible. Even though these plants were useless garbage and their spores had given the humans less than a fortnight to live, she decided to name them anyway. Lana cursed softly as she remembered that Tuesday had named this planet Scrote, furious at herself for not getting in faster. As far as airtight laws went, first-naming rights were very hard to budge. It was one of the iron-tight rules that encouraged citizens of The Unison to explore the unknown, and is also why people like Tuesday were usually sent to scrub toilets while his betters did more important work.

Waving her Omni over the blue vegetation, Lana got tired of reading the tiny font of her holographic display and switched the scanning app to an audible report.

"Consuming Unknown Species Ninety-Six B will cause lethal levels of dehydration due to vomiting," came the tinny voice from her Omni. She passed her left hand across a near-identical plant. "Consuming Unknown Species Ninety-Seven B will cause fatal diarrhoea within twelve minutes."

Frustrated, Lana kept on checking for something ever partially edible.

"Consuming Unknown Species Ninety-Eight B will cause your airways to permanently seal."

"Consuming Unknown Species Ninety-Nine B will cause death by projectile vomiting in eight minutes."

"Consuming Unknown Species One-Hundred-and-Thirty-Seven C will cause a lethal allergic reaction."

"Consuming Unknown Species Two-Hundred-and-Nine D will..."

To Lana's surprise, after countless failures her scanning app finally produced a positive little trill. It came as such a shock that Lana was just about to scan something else before the impossible words stopped her.

"Consuming Unknown Species Two-Hundred-and-Forty-Three F will cause no harm."

Lana took a close look at the plant: it was a long, low tangle of brown thorny vines with golden-edged, diamond-shaped leaves. Some of the vines ended in large, golden flowers that had a lot in common with roses, and each of them were filled with white pods the size of quail eggs. They looked like some sort of citrus, or at least some alien variation on it.

Lana closed her eyes and rubbed them until she saw stars. No. This was impossible. There was no way she'd found an edible plant in this wasteland of nightmare shrubs. So she ran her Omni over the bush again. This time she scanned one of the little pods.

"Distant relation to the terrestrial kumquat," her Omni announced. "Each fruit contains approximately forty-three percent of the daily nutrients a human body requires for optimal functioning. The flavour of this fruit is rated: divine."

Swearing she just saw something move in her peripheral vision on the other side of the plant, Lana looked away from the scan. Besides the tangle of vines, there was nothing there.

"Specific taste?" she couldn't help but hear the excitement in her own voice.

"Champagne and strawberries."

Lana had already begun running back towards camp before the flavour scan had finished announcing its results. To her surprise, Lana realised that she'd been scanning random plant life for so long that the others had already returned from their pointless wanderings and gone to bed. Four empty Cricket Jerky wrappers announced that not only had nobody bothered to wait for Lana to come back, but they'd shamelessly decided to split her supper ration between them. However, her discovery was so huge that she didn't have any space in her skyrocketing emotions to fit anger.

"Come, quick!" Lana yelled, kicking mattresses.

*

Bleary-eyed and faces lined with the red dents of sleep, the three groggy survivors staggered after Lana into the moonlit forest. It wasn't long before Jimmy, Trace and Tuesday were at the mess of brown vines and golden flowers. As they'd been fast asleep less than three minutes ago, none of them had the faculties to guess what was going on.

"Suicide bush?" Tuesday yawned.

"Better!" Lana ran her left hand over one of the little white fruits.

"Distant relation to the terrestrial kumquat," her Omni device repeated. "Each fruit contains approximately forty-three percent of the daily nutrients a human body requires for optimal functioning. The flavour of this fruit is rated: divine."

Trace, Tuesday and Jimmy - especially Jimmy – suddenly woke up all the way.

"Is your Omni fritzing out?" Trace demanded.

"No. It's working perfectly fine." Lana assured her. "Everything else I scanned is inedible at best. It took hours to find this."

There was a soft noise right in the middle of Lana's assurances. Tuesday looked back and forth at the other survivors with a weird expression, seemingly the only one to hear it.

"Who said that?"

"Said what?" Jimmy yawned.

"Somebody made a weird noise. Who was it?"

"Nobody said anything," Trace ground out, her patience as thin as always.

"Should we take all of them?" Jimmy asked with a full mouth, spraying crumbs of bright white peel. "I'm sure our packs are big enough."

Everyone gave Jimmy the same look.

"What?" A paranoid expression formed on his wide face. "Wait, you confirmed they were safe, right?"

"It would have been a good idea to take a closer look before we start chopping in," Lana said as though Jimmy was an idiot.

"How come?" Tuesday asked, munching on two of the alien kumquats at once. "They taste all right, don't they, Trace?"

Trace smiled around a huge ball of creamy citrus flesh, juice running down her chin. Lana sighed in exasperation, the only one without a full mouth.

"We know they won't kill us, yes, but they could have all sorts of side-effects. They could cause a laxative effect, make us hallucinate, turn our urine neon-blue..."

"Already had that last one for years," Tuesday announced, plucking thirds from one of the golden flowers.

"Maybe we should ask Half Head," Lana suggested.

"He can find his own freaking kumquats!" Tuesday yelled.

"And he won't be awake for hours," Jimmy reminded her, spraying ribbons of peel all over his poncho. "You know his batteries don't work without direct sunlight."

"He seems to know about the plants of this world," Lana argued. "He might know something important that we don't."

"Half Head doesn't know his ass from a fire hydrant," Tuesday sniped, up to his fifth white ball.

Lana kneeled down, brushing aside some dirt to look at the root system beneath the bush. While the tangled branches seemed to be similar to an earthy-coloured wood at first glance, on closer inspection they seemed to be tightly-wrapped vein-like pipes. Squinting, Lana could see that the vines weren't brown, but a bound network of yellow, green and black. She'd seen some weird alien plants on the Link in the past, but nothing like this.

Standing up again, wiping dirt from her knees, Lana drew one of the fruit-filled golden flowers closer to take a sniff. As actual tree-grown fruit was something only the very rich could afford where she came from, it felt almost impossible to resist the tempting scent of citric acidity. Just as she was about to sample actual produce for the first time in her life, her hand paused mid-reach. Squinting at the flower, Lana realised that if you looked into the golden rose at just the right angle, the kumquats seemed to be surrounded with needle-thin thorns...

Jimmy gagged and went stiff as an ironing board. All colour drained from his face, and his eyes rolled up until they were the same white as the rest of his mug. While his muscles all seemed to have seized in an instant, somehow he remained upright. Tuesday and Trace looked at Jimmy, at each other, then down at the half-eaten alien kumquats they were holding. All that Lana could do was watch as they, too, stiffened to complete stillness and paled to the colour of moonlight.

As though triggered by their paralysis, the fruit-filled golden roses that Lana's group had been feasting from unfurled far too quickly for normal buds, opening their petals to the diameter of a Frisbee and retracting all the alien kumquats deep into their cores. It was like watching a time-lapse video in a nature documentary. Fascinated, Lana watched as the vines uncurled, pushing the blooming roses towards her frozen comrades.

Turning at a movement in her peripheral vision, Lana came face-to-face with one of the roses drawing towards her face very, very slowly. The alien flower turned a quarter of a revolution, revealing inner petals spiked by wire-thin teeth that had a lot in common with hypodermic needles. Shaking, all Lana could do was try and guess which of the gods would be sick enough to create something like this. To her immeasurable surprise, the rose clicked out what might have been a word before passing by her.

Looking back at her frozen comrades, Lana watched as one of the fanged roses gently plugged its clusters of hypodermic spikes into the crook of Jimmy's elbow and forearm. Fascinated, Lana watched as a trickle of human blood spiralled through the vine, darkening the woody tentacle as it coursed through the root system and into the ground. Just as another couple of fanged roses latched onto Trace's wrist and Tuesday's neck, starting to gently drain them dry, Lana finally gathered the strength to scream.

Snapping out of her shock, Lana flicked her right wrist to switch on her AllTool bracelet. Forming a jet-black longsword, she lunged for the rose that had latched onto Jimmy's wrist, nicking its throat with a lucky strike. Unfortunately she barely scratched it, and all the other roses reared up like hostile cobras in response. It was almost as though she had injured them, too...

The wounded rose dislodged itself from Jimmy's veins, reared up in obvious threat and snapped the same sound as before. While Lana would usually be interested in find out if the rose was speaking an actual language or not, the fact that its petals were splashed with Jimmy's blood meant that she really didn't care.

Raising her sword, assuming a defensive stance, Lana stared down the weaving roses as they puffed up in threat. Her eyes flicked back and forth, waiting for the first one to strike. Unfortunately, another dozen roses slithered out of the bush, all moving in that same unsettling time-lapse kind of way. Backing off a little, glancing at the other three humans as they continued to stand there stock-still and pale, Lana knew deep down that this was hopeless. She was ridiculously outnumbered, and it wouldn't be long until the roses tapped her circulatory system like a keg at a frat party and sucked her dry.

The wounded tendril clicked and hissed angrily. It managed to explain just as much as the last few times.

Lana took a deep breath, her eyes flicking between potential targets, and said what may be her final words.

130

"I might be about to die, but I'm sure as hell going to ruin your day first."

She lunged, cleanly decapitating the injured rose from its vine with her computer generated sword, and weaved about in what she hoped was an unpredictable way. Funnily enough, rather than sinking dozens of fangs into her flesh, all of the slithering alien vines sealed their heads into tight, knobbly fists and swung at her like clubs. One of them thudded into Lana's solar plexus, winding her badly, just before another smacked her right in the temple in an explosion of light. Dazed, she staggered sideways, barely mustering the sense to switch her AllTool bracelet from a sword to a huge all-covering tower shield. Hammer blows rained down on the matte black barrier, bouncing off, driving her backwards. Lana's boots skidded in the mud, leaving furrows as she deflected the slamming cudgels.

Leaning against the shield as hard as she could, Lana felt a warmth on the side of her face. Her skull felt cracked, and her thoughts were little more than static. Hammered by blows, her eyes refused to focus, and all she could do was stare stupidly at Trace's waistband as her brain reeled from injury. But then Lana registered something: Trace's air pistol was bulging from beneath her riot armour.

Lana did what seemed like the logical thing: she lunged, drew the weapon and prepared to start clubbing the roses like it was a game of Whac-A-Chihuahua. Thankfully, Lana's concussed brain was able to rethink this tactic a moment before it would have got her killed.

Slowly coming to her senses, hiding behind the flickering tower shield as it strained to continue existing against the onslaught, Lana cranked the air pistol's volume setting all the way up with her mouth, switched it to full-automatic with her tongue, and spun it on one finger like Annie Oakley. Charging forwards, hanging out from safety just enough to train her pistol and one eye on her target, Lana fired into the bush full of blood-drinking roses. Vines exploded, flowers burst like firecrackers, and Lana was deafened by the scream of an alien creature having a very, very bad time. The barrel of the air pistol smoked and glowed a little from the stress, but not enough to harm Lana.

There was a low rumble as the ground shook. Staggering to keep on her feet, Lana could only watch as the vampire bush began rising from the swamp, and then something far bigger, something titanic, rose up in a waterfall of mud and runny clay. The vines and roses were only the upper extremities of something made of thousands of transparent roots the size of firehoses, and at the centre of the mass of wriggling tendrils a wide mouth opened. It was big enough to swallow a rhino without chewing, its mandibles lined with wicked thorns the size of swords. Within its transparent core a variety of unfamiliar organs were visibly pumping and squirting away.

The furled roses retracted all the way into dedicated grooves around the monster's maw. Apparently calling a temporary truce, the plant made that same familiar noise as the last few times, but one so loud that it hurt Lana's ears. It snapped like a gunshot, but its exact meaning was impossible to guess.

"Sorry," Lana growled. "I don't speak Bush."

A lone rose lurking behind Lana's knee chose this moment to strike, connecting with the AllTool bracelet on her right wrist so hard that the tower shield instantly vanished. The black and yellow band went blood red with flashing letters declaring OVERHEAT, and didn't do anything else. She smacked at it, and the sneaky rose retreated back towards the leviathan.

Raising her weapon, Lana spat a curse as she threw everything she could at the massive alien vegetable. It roared as shallow holes pitted its bark, but the woody armour around its central mass was far too tough to break through. Holding down the trigger, Lana got a nasty surprise as agony flashed across her palm and fingers. Juggling the air pistol back and forth, it took Lana a second to register that her weapon had turned white-hot from overuse. Its rubber grips had already blackened and started to melt away to mist.

Passing the weapon back and forth between her hands, blowing ineffectively on her scorched fingers, Lana gave a growl of frustration and threw the glowing ruin at the aggressive tree. The overheated air pistol was so hot that it sealed tight against the monster core mass on contact, sizzling away at its thick bark and making it wail.

Lana knew for certain she had failed. She was all out of options, and it would only be moments until all four humans became an early breakfast. Collapsing to her knees in defeat, Lana looked up to see that Tuesday looked even more like a corpse than he usually did.

Lana squinted.

Wait a minute...

Lana lunged for Tuesday's waistband and jammed a hand into his pocket. Slapping at a rose with her free hand as it writhed in front of her face, Lana plunged through all kinds of sticky filth until she finally found it: the bag of InstaFire marbles she'd asked him to take care of.

Turning, rising from her knees, Lana pulled the bag from Tuesday's pocket and threw it as hard as she could. The InstaFire pellets connected in a flash of blinding light as a month's worth of campfires exploded at the same time. Lana didn't have time to regret this decision, as she was too busy flying backwards into the underbrush and being more than a little bit on fire. Just before she landed spine-first, snapping through branches and scratching her face on twigs as she soared,

Lana was treated to quite a sight: wreathed in smoke and flames, the evil tree toppled sideways with a deafening creak, slammed into the clay and was still.

*

Lana woke as close to dawn as you can get without actually seeing a sunrise.

Sitting upright with a start, feeling like she was in the middle of a serious hangover, Lana staggered to her feet and used a blue tree to prevent a fall. Looking about, blinking out of synchronisation, to Lana's relief she soon spotted Tuesday, Trace and Jimmy splayed about in the underbrush. The good news was that the InstaFire eruption must have tossed them away from the violent vegetable like so many horseshoes, but the bad news was they were still as pale as vanilla ice cream and almost as cold.

Dreading what she was about to see, Lana peeked through a curtain of aqua vines. While the giant blood-leeching plant was still there, most of it had sunk back beneath the clay. It might still be alive, but it was hard to tell.

Lana checked her Omni. She'd been unconscious for six hours.

Loping back to their campsite, her whole body feeling tenderised, Lana nearly cried in relief when she saw Half Head again. The bot was still in Standby, waiting for some solar rays to top up its ruined batteries just enough for its body to operate again.

Lana shook the robot a little too violently, and the colour of Half Head's sensory lenses shifted from green to yellow in response. Beyond this, there was no response.

"You've got to do something!" Lana wailed, shaking a rusted tentacle. "They're…they're poisoned! Unconscious! Wake up!"

Half Head didn't so much as shrug. She might as well talk to the nearest blue shrub.

Furious, Lana summed up the urgency of the situation by kicking Half Head right in its corroded face. Unfortunately, at this exact moment a beam of sunlight played over Half Head's black torso, gently warming a few inches of its chassis. Startling, Half Head unrolled and lifted up Lana by her ears in one clean motion. Its eyes took on a deep red sheen as the Cadet dangled four feet above the ground.

"Your species is not listed in my restraint registry, and I will be forced to defend myself with lethal force if necessary," Half Head ground out.

"Restraint registry?" Lana choked, holding onto Half Head's tentacles so that her ears didn't tear right off.

"My restraint registry is a compilation of precisely how much violence I am

133

allowed to inflict in my own defence. Humans are not on that list in any form."

Lana nodded, which wasn't much fun when somebody was holding you up by your ears. Half Head dropped the Cadet onto her butt in the mud and turned its butchered skull a little, as though thinking.

"What do you want?"

Lana was shaking, and she was sure that both her lobes were bleeding. The robot was obviously unstable and unpredictable, and there was no chance she'd ever touch it again. If Lana had any other option, she would leave this busted hulk where it belonged: rotting in the swamp.

The words didn't come easily. Lana felt like she was watching somebody else talk. She really, really needed medical attention.

"The...the others. They ate some sort of fruit off a kind of, uh, a plant full of snake-branch-things with golden flowers. They're paralysed. I'm not sure if they're safe...we need to..."

"Was it a white fruit? Around this big?" Half Head interrupted, holding the tips of two tentacles close together.

Lana gave Half Head a surprised expression.

"That's the one."

"Did your trade not go smoothly? That would be unusual."

Lana raised an eyebrow, sure she'd misheard.

"Trade?"

Half Head gave a very human sigh.

"Oh dear," it shook its head in a condescending way. "I regret to inform you that you may have just caused a serious diplomatic incident."

*

Tuesday, Trace and Jimmy were still frozen in place and pale as a round of weak lattes. Beyond a few small bruises from the wire-fine fangs of the unnamed alien bush, they were untouched.

Under the reddish light of early morning, it was immediately apparent that the titanic beast that Lana had slashed, stabbed, clubbed, shot and set on fire was still alive. While some of its vines were scorched to ashes and its white fruit were reduced to dried-out sultanas, the main bulk of the creature was still intact. Its gelatinous organs gurgled as they pumped about green, yellow and black fluids.

"It's alive," Lana whispered, automatically going into a crouch.

Sensing Lana, the tangle of vines raised itself high until the scorched bushes on its top were fifteen metres above the ground. It either appeared a lot bigger in the light of day or Lana had only seen a small segment of the thing until now. Two dozen golden roses extended from a maw big enough to swallow a Lorry, and it barked something so loud that it made Lana's ears ring.

Lana went to produce a battle axe from her AllTool as the brown vines grew towards her with a creaking noise, extending to their full length of twenty metres, but the AllTool gave a sad beep and did nothing. Even though hours and hours has passed, the AllTool was still flashing a neon red OVERHEAT glyph. Lana looked down at the busted piece of hardware, angrily tapping it with her fingernail.

"Stupid mass-produced junk..."

When Lana glanced up again all of the roses were shooting towards her face like spears. Thankfully, Half Head stepped in the way, blocking them. Whether out of courtesy or caution or for some much more alien reason, the plant creature paused. This silent standoff continued for a few seconds until Half Head clicked something in an alien tongue.

Lana squinted at Half Head. "Yeah, it kept making that noise."

The monster barked angrily, interrupting Lana. Half Head sighed.

"This sentient being is a registered Grower of the Drokhari people, and she alleges that you willingly violated the standards of trade by which all intelligent creatures abide. Such offenses can carry serious consequences against not only the perpetrators, but their entire species."

"Trade!" Lana exploded. "It tried to kill us and drink our blood!"

Half Head listened to a slow rumble from the plant.

"The key export of the Drokhari people are the Intox berries their Growers gestate in the flowers of their upper vines," Half Head explained. "Intox berries are renowned as the most delicious narcotic fruit in the galaxy, and are famed for being enjoyable for all forms of carbon-based life. When your group picked and consumed a large volume of Intox berries, the Grower assumed you had accepted her offer of trade and she simply went about taking the currency you owed."

Lana rubbed at her eyes, frustrated beyond endurance.

"Currency? We don't have any alien currency."

Half Head indicated some of the tiny pinhole marks on Tuesday's neck as the bush clicked and growled.

"The internal trade system of the Drokhari people is based on blood. The Grower assures me she was very gentle and calm when she went to harvest what your friends owed, and that you suddenly turned murderous for no apparent reason. She claims she was forced to defend herself."

"But how were we supposed to know it wanted to trade?" Lana demanded. "It

135

didn't ask for anything!"

Half Head translated, and the Grower answered immediately with her loudest bark yet.

"The Grower says she used the language of Standard Universal Trade to inform your friends of the price before they sampled her wares: one litre of blood per Intox berry. As all sentient races have understood the Trade language for eons, the Grower does not believe you when you claim not to speak it, and is officially accusing you of making false excuses in a hopeless attempt to get away with grand larceny and attempted murder. She advises you to contact your legal team and your nearest diplomat, as she fully intends to sue your entire species for your actions."

"But it just latched onto them and tried to drink their blood!" Lana exploded. This wasn't how epic battles with fearsome alien monsters were meant to go. It was like dealing with a politician made out of branches.

Half Head leaned closer to Lana, its words soft.

"I find it relevant to mention that during my time the Drokhari were a major commercial power in this galaxy, and word travelled fast if you wronged one of them. Of the many castes in their complicated social system, the Grower caste are the most powerful, respected and beloved. Unless you wish to be dodging Drokhari assassins for the rest of your short lives, I suggest we resolve this issue as soon as possible." Half Head clicked at the Grower and turned back to Lana. "Unless you can find a way to pay what your companions owe in some other form, the Grower will have no choice but to drain them a little at a time until full restitution is made. She assures me they will remain alive and in the lowest possible level of discomfort until they have been adequately milked, and that it should take less than a month. However, on top of repaying this first debt, naturally you will be expected to make amends for the insult. Growers are not accustomed to such treatment."

Lana pinched the bridge of her nose, mentally counting how many litres of blood they had between them, how many Intox berries they'd consumed, and how totally and utterly screwed they all were.

*

Lana sighed as she watched Half Head finish dragging her fellow survivors back to their camp. Looking at their bags of supplies, Lana couldn't help but dwell on the huge settlement she'd had to pay the wronged Drokhari. How was she going to explain that she'd willingly given eighty percent of their food, drinks and

136

survival equipment to a giant plant?

Waiting for the other humans to wake up from their catatonic stupor, Lana got out a fresh tube of carrot puree. After all, she'd missed out on her share of Cricket Jerky, and humiliation was an effective way to work up an appetite. Popping the cap, she squeezed out an orange mouthful and tried not to gag.

"What a life," she muttered.

Half Head dumped Tuesday next to the fire.

"You're telling me. I just spent six thousand years upside-down in a swamp."

CHAPTER TWELVE TRIP LIKE I DO

It took until high noon, but Lana's fellow survivors gradually woke up. Lips and skin pale from blood loss, one at a time they slowly became coherent enough to ask for something to eat and drink. Half a brick of kelp puree and a gluten-free unflavoured pizza base quickly disappeared. Lana waited until they only looked half-dead before sitting down beside the campfire to share the bad news.

"There's no way to gild what I'm about to say: we only have a couple of days' worth of supplies. And that's if we harshly ration what's left."

Everyone gave Lana the same look: full of questions, suspended inches above homicidal anger. They all looked over at the backpacks, which were suspiciously flat where they had once bulged.

"How?" Trace ground out, her rage suppressed by a lack of blood.

"Had to pay a legal settlement to a tree. In addition to wiping out most of our food and drinks, it also cost us three of our atmospheric generators. If the last one packs it in, we'll have no safe way of replacing our respiratory filters."

Trace nodded, wearing a surprisingly neutral expression. "Of course. I understand."

She calmly reached for her waistband. Finding that her air pistol wasn't tucked under her riot armour where she'd left it, Trace gritted her teeth in frustration. Everyone could hear the grinding of enamel.

"Also, I kinda permanently welded your gun to the tree's face," Lana added. "I was going to offer to carve it out, but...well...things were already tense. Damned alien bushes get surly when you accidentally try to murder them."

"Lucky," was all Trace said, spitting into the fire.

As easy as it would have been to sit about all day, the moment they were capable of putting one foot in front of another it was officially time for their journey to continue. After all, their schedule just went from tight to strangling, and there was no time to stuff about. Following a short, sharp argument about how they were supposed to last a week without food, they decided it would be better to trudge in enraged, terrified silence instead.

Not much was said for the next two hours, but over that time their surroundings gradually began to shift from swamp to a sandy, arid plain. While solid ground was easier to hike than thin mud, the sun was now beating down on them a lot harder, clarifying why this region was so much drier. While their feet might be lighter, sweat ran down their temples in thick rivulets and soaked into their survival ponchos, which absorbed every precious drop.

Taking a break beneath a rare leafy tree, they sipped from a shared bottle of Slurko in silence. Deep in thought about how she could shorten their journey, Lana glanced up to see Tuesday was giving her a stink face expression. The look didn't soften one bit when he was caught in the act.

"Can I help you?" Lana snapped.

The janitor narrowed his eyes. "Just thinking."

Lana didn't feel the need to make the obvious joke about how he'd been warned against such exertions.

"About what, exactly?"

"That tree. The one who, thanks to you, has all of our stuff." Tuesday squinted. "Now, from what I understand, those Droderkraki..."

"Drokhari," Half Head interrupted, laying down and sunning itself contentedly.

"Drokhari," Tuesday snapped, irritated at being corrected, "Now, I get that the other tree people would be pissed off if they heard about the mess you caused, and how we'd be pariahs and stuff across this whole galaxy. But how would they find out, exactly?" Tuesday extended his fingers. "That tree is just as stranded as us, right?"

Trace and Jimmy both looked up at this. Jimmy stopped halfway through slurping up the last drop of Slurko, and Trace snapped a dry branch. Lana looked back and forth between them, then finally at Half Head. The robot shrugged, obviously imitating the body language it had seen the survivors perform on many occasions.

"This world is under total quarantine." Half Head noted. "Has been for millennia. Nobody in, nobody out. That includes messages of any kind. Total communication blackout."

"But if that Drokhari has been here all this time, there might be a lot more of them around, right?" Lana asked, close to panic as the true magnitude of her mistake began to gurgle up like an overflowing toilet. "Surely that Drokhari isn't here on her own?"

"The Drokhari perpetuate themselves via apomixis, which means that every fifty years or so they give birth to their own new bodies before transferring over their consciousness. The one we dealt with has been here alone since the fall of The Apex."

Jimmy bent over, gagging.

"Oh Zeus," Jimmy moaned. "You gave away all our stuff for nothing. I'm gonna be sick..."

"Do you think the tree was going to let you all walk?" Lana exploded. "Each of you owed ten times as much blood as your bodies can hold. You'd have been leeched for months before you died. And I couldn't just blast it! You didn't see the sort of firepower I poured into it, and I barely scratched it. Listen..."

"I don't want to listen to you anymore," Jimmy sobbed the last syllable.

Lana went to defend herself, but a blindside from Tuesday stopped her silent.

"Shut it!" Tuesday raged, springing to his feet. "Just shut it! I'd rather chew my own nipples off than listen to anything you have to say." Tuesday kicked the empty Slurko bottle right out of Jimmy's hand. "I vote she doesn't get any food next meal. She's wasted enough of it already."

Lana looked at Trace and Jimmy. They didn't seem to be arguing with Tuesday's suggestion. She stormed over to her pack and aggressively slid both straps onto her shoulders.

"Fine. I'll go without. Be that way."

*

Following Half Head as it drifted above the increasingly arid tundra, the survivors realised they were walking up an incline for the first time. Huffing and puffing up a steepening slope of dead sand, their calves and thighs burning with every step, they came within a matter of metres of cresting a high ridge.

"Sure we couldn't have gone around the hill?" Jimmy moaned, feeling his reddening skin chafe in twelve different places.

The wind changed. Tuesday stopped to sniff at a stinky gust from over the top of the hill, wearing a weird expression.

"Can you all smell that? It's kind of a...burnt smell?"

Jimmy took in a nostril-load.

"Like crème Brule when you overdo it with the torch."

The four survivors made it to the top of the ridge a few seconds later. Quite a sight greeted them: far below, a sweeping valley was dominated by an enormous crater. The perfect hemisphere was about three kilometres across and plunged a kilometre and a half at its deepest point. Its bowels were cloaked in shadows, but an unbearable glare reflected blindingly from wherever the sun touched it. Just as the lifeboat scans had mentioned before they crashed, this hole was made from perfectly smooth glass.

Lana tapped at her left hand.

"Omni says the glass floor is five metres thick and pretty much frictionless," she noted. "Seems just about unbreakable."

"Don't care. We still hate you," Tuesday snapped.

Glancing at the edge of the crater, Lana squinted as her eyes watered in distress. There was something weird about the very rim, something that made it painful to look at. Picking up a fossilised chunk of ancient shrub, using her Omni display to get the angle just right, Lana pitched the petrified tree like a pro shot-putter. They watched the segment of old wood as it arced up and landed right on the crater's edge. Everyone murmured in surprise as the projectile was sliced cleanly in half on the rim, as though landing on the blade of a monomolecular weapon. The half that tumbled into the glass pit slid down the frictionless surface at greater and greater speeds until it passed over a section of glass reflecting the local starlight. It was reduced to ashes in an instant.

"Ah." Jimmy managed. "Might be an idea to stay away from the big holes."

"I've never seen a mass driver impact crater up close before." Trace said solemnly, as though witnessing a sacred monument. "It's something."

Lana took this rare opportunity to connect with the Enforcer.

"Well, there's thousands and thousands more of them all over this world, and most of them are fifty times this size, if not larger..."

Lana stopped at the dark expression on Trace's face. She sighed and tried to come to terms with the fact that Trace hated her.

Turning away from Lana, Trace noticed a distant glint beyond the impact crater's far western rim. Squinting at the bright spot, Trace smacked Tuesday in the back of the head.

"Hey, death-breath. What's that?"

Tuesday squinted. It worked just about as well for him as it had for Trace. While he was pretty sure the mystery landmark was outside of the crater, Tuesday eventually shrugged in defeat.

"Dunno. Can't tell with the reflection." He rubbed at his eye sockets. "I fink my eyeballs just got sunburnt."

Jimmy slid a finger along his AllTool bracelet, flicked his wrist and a pair of matte black sunglasses appeared in his palm. Under the mistaken impression that he looked far cooler than he actually was, Jimmy slid on the sunglasses and took on the glare. Without the blinding reflection messing with his eyes he could clearly see a handful of tall, jagged white ruins jutting out at random less than a hundred metres from the edge of the crater. From this distance it looked like a jaw-grinding Shatter junkie was giving them a big smile.

Jimmy slapped the sunglasses off his face, his eyes wide.

"I think it's somebody's house."

*

It didn't take that long to descend the ridge and follow the edge of the crater...from a comfortable distance, of course. The chemical stink of fused planet got stronger and stronger the closer they got to the massive dent, and coming too near the great scar made them feel lightheaded. Burning glass was not pleasant for any human senses.

Excited at the prospect of encountering some sort of civilisation for the first time since they'd crashed on Scrote, their worries were forgotten for a time. They may be low on food and drink and energy and patience and intelligence, but the possibilities of what they may encounter and what kind of help may be on offer boggled their minds.

As was becoming common, their hopes were soon dashed. While the dozens of off-white monoliths were certainly impressive up close, pointing into the sky like a Titan was accusing God of something, the structures were nothing more than the tougher load-bearing supports of an epic building that had fallen more than a dozen and a half centuries before the first cornerstone of the pyramid of Giza had been dragged into place by ten thousand pissed off Hebrews.

Jimmy carefully touched one of the pillars. He could feel a vibration, as though the spire was shaking very, very gently.

"I don't recognise what it's made from," he admitted, sure not to touch the edge just in case it was monomolecular. "Kinda like steel, but a lot like ceramics, too."

"It's made from thoughtmetal." Half Head noted. "Thoughtmetal is a psycho-reactive polymimetic, meaning you shape it with your mind. The Apex have been able to create this material seemingly from nothing since their technology reached its peak a million years ago. It was used to form buildings, starships, home appliances, you name it." Half Head raised six of its twenty tentacles and ran them along the pillar. Its white surface shook and warped a bit, but didn't do much more. "Once thoughtmetal is set, though, it tends to be very hard to craft any further. Only its original shaper is able to modify it beyond this point, and not by all that much. Even among the many notable achievements of The Apex before their ruin, being able to construct anything they want or need by weaving it with their minds was one of their most impressive innovations."

"So how big is this ruin, exactly? And what is it?" Jimmy asked.

"According to what little I can remember, before its destruction this structure ran a hundred levels deep, rose nine times as high, and extended unbroken for three hundred kilometres."

"Was it one of their cities?" Jimmy asked.

Half Head shook its busted skull.

"This used to be the personal manor of one of my Creators. They liked to avoid each other as much as possible. They...weren't very social, to say the least. And while it may seem impressive for a single being to have such a dwelling all to itself, it wasn't rare for The Apex to put up something like this in a day or so."

"Can we take any of this material with us?" Tuesday asked, tapping the vibrating pillar with one knuckle. "I'm no expert, but my guess is that this stuff leaves every substance mankind has developed for dead. When we get back to The Unison, selling a handful of this could set us all up for life."

"You could try, but set thoughtmetal is theoretically unbreakable," Half Head said.

Trace glanced at the broken ruins, gave a dark chuckle and tapped into some basic sarcasm.

"Yeah. It's clearly invulnerable, isn't it? Invulnerable as chalk, perhaps."

Half Head's lenses extended and retracted towards the crumbled thoughtmetal a few ties, as though the machine was thinking. Rather than the usual variation of "I cannot remember," it seemed as though this part of Half Head's archives weren't entirely mush.

"Of the Twelve Hundred lesser races in this galaxy under the direct control of The Apex, none of them developed along an identical technological branch. This meant their scientific proficiencies varied wildly. For instance, the Drenni were masters of genetic engineering, the Layette could breed viruses to do just about anything, the Giiit had considerable psychic abilities, the Slidge were the experts on solar mining and harnessing, the Xi built incredible Artificial Intelligence devices, the Kroites accomplished astonishing hive mind phenomena...you get the idea. Although the Twelve Hundred were forbidden from having any unsupervised contact with one another, they secretly formed diplomatic relations after The Great Trick. After perfecting their plan for generations, when the Twelve Hundred rose up in perfect synchronisation they each had a separate doomsday weapon to contribute to the rebellion." Half Head indicated the thoughtmetal pillar. "The Molleck fired the first shot, so to speak, by using sonic weaponry to fracture every thoughtmetal construct The Apex had on every world on a molecular level. Once the galaxy-wide invasion started five seconds later, the cities of The Apex might as well have been made from dried mud."

"Are you made from thoughtmetal?" Tuesday asked with an unusual level of logic.

Half Head nodded. "Yes. All suits of amplification armour are personally woven together by their own pilot. The Apex had many laws against attempting to modify or damage amplification suits that belonged to other members of their race, and none of these laws have soft penalties."

The survivors all looked at the machine.

"Amplification suit?" Jimmy repeated.

Half Head turned to regard them. "Yes. That is what I am classed as: a suit of amplification armour. While The Apex possessed considerable mental abilities and were able to wield powers you would best define as psychic, amplification suits were used in order to greatly augment their potential. Within an amplification suit, they were as gods. My mind and personality is simply the Operating System of this unit."

Lana looked Half Head up and down, from its clusters of tentacles to its solid torso and all the way to a blasted lens-studded skull that would have probably resembled a bicycle seat at some point.

"I don't get the whole 'pilot' thing. Your whole body is solid, right? Your torso is jammed full of hardware. Where would a pilot sit, exactly?"

"Full of busted hardware, maybe," Tuesday sniped.

"Did the pilot sit on your shoulders?" Jimmy guessed.

Half Head did that familiar little skull tremble when it was trying to find information that just wasn't there.

"My apologies. I don't seem to remember anything else on this topic."

"That's getting old," Trace snapped.

"Can you remember why all the other races in this galaxy teamed up to wipe out The Apex?" Jimmy pressed. "What did they do to deserve it?"

"The Great Trick was the final insult after an eternity of cruelty," Half Head said. "The true sickness of The Apex has been legendary for all of recorded history, but after the truth about The Great Trick got out, the Twelve Hundred all knew it would only get worse with time. Sicker. Before..."

Half Head didn't say another word. Without any explanation, it suddenly jumped into the air, spun half a revolution, and sped off like an angry wasp. Everyone looked at each other.

"Where's he going?" Jimmy asked, getting up about as quickly as a sloth on ketamine. "Did I offend him?"

Although Half Head had the advantage of surprise, the humans did their best to keep up with the crippled robot. It wasn't easy, as Half Head was going at top speed, weaving back and forth between rock formations, shrubs and the occasional spur of half-buried thoughtmetal. Finally, an exhausting two minutes later, Half Head skidded to a halt before an unexpected sight: it was another four amplification suits, all of them identical to Half Head in every way. Their matte black forms had been buried upside down, just like Half Head, but only up to the middle of their torsos. Dozens of bubbling scars were melted into their surfaces, as though something had enjoyed gradually searing away chunks with a nasty, nasty weapon. Weeds were tangled around their ruins, and spiky grass grew as high as the few limp tentacles that hadn't been cooked off entirely.

After a good half a minute of silence, Half Head turned its eye lenses a few inches towards the humans.

"The moment my Creators were vulnerable, the first priority of the Twelve Hundred was to assassinate key leaders. The Apex had stopped being gods, and died in short order like any other mortal." Half Head gently touched one of the brutalised robots. "Before being buried upside down, I can tell these amplification suits were tortured, used for target practice and then executed once their suffering ceased to be amusing." The robot's eye lenses flicked back towards the humans. "Being inverted is a huge sign of disrespect among The Apex. It indicates unworthiness, weakness, shame and dishonour. The rebellion knew this when they defiled these ones. This was a deliberate message of spite."

"Wait, wait," Jimmy interrupted, pinching his nose. "But if somebody had an issue with your Creators, with The Apex, why would they bother to take it out on a bunch of robots? Why not bury your Creators upside down?"

Half Head's lenses flicked back and forth, as though thinking with what was left of its brain. It didn't offer an answer to Jimmy's question, good as it was. It was obvious that the blanks in Half Head's memories were still too extensive to explain the whole story.

"I apologise. I do not know."

While he might be total scum, Tuesday was practical in the way he viewed life. Spitting on the ground and producing a half-smoked chlorine cigarette, soggy from whatever horrors were hidden in his many pockets (Lana was sure she was going to have nightmares for a week after retrieving the bag of InstaFire marbles), the janitor lit his sad dog-end and let it dangle from his lips. He asked a logical, but cold, question.

"Reckon you could salvage anything from them wrecks? Might be able to score some sweet new batteries."

Half Head shook its bisected skull.

"While my scanners have seen better days, I can tell that everything useful within them has been reduced to ashes, their components fried to little more than solid carbon. There is nothing of worth left within their shells." The robot extended its twenty writhing limbs. "Make camp. I will unearth these ones before the sun sets entirely. I cannot leave them like this."

*

The spires of thoughtmetal provided a lot of shadows to choose from, especially now that the sun was only a couple of hours from disappearing beneath the horizon. If you picked just the right spot, they also blocked the biting wind. Turned out the tundra got even colder than the swamp towards night time.

Once everyone had a good wander through the ruins (finding nothing of value, of course), it was time to sort out the filter situation and get camp ready for another night. Thankfully, the single atmospheric generator they had left did its job admirably, and the lifeboat modules clicked together just as easily as the first time. The last thing the survivors needed right now was to lose the only safe way they had of changing their filters, so this was a lucky break.

Despite the cold, Jimmy was sweating rivers. His apron was so wet that wringing it out filled a whole Slurko bottle to the brim. When Jimmy showed this to the others (to their obvious universal disgust), Trace proved she hadn't been paying attention when she snatched the bottle out of his hand and drunk it in one big gulp. Her eye twitched a bit, as though she almost registered something was wrong, but this passed.

"Thanks, dweeb," Trace snapped, bouncing the bottle off the top Jimmy's head.

Jimmy opened his mouth, thought about it for a moment, and shut it again.

"You're very welcome."

They all sat down on some fallen thoughtmetal piles. Digging into their meagre supplies, Trace produced a sad dinner from what little was left: three hand-sized slabs of compressed kelp, the last wrapper of Cricket Jerky, and half of a stale gluten-free unflavoured pizza base. She tossed Tuesday his share. To her surprise, Lana was passed the same amount.

"I thought you voted against my next meal," Lana managed, confused.

Trace twitched her cheek in a "don't make an issue out of this or you'll regret it" kind of way.

"We don't need you collapsing," Trace growled. "You think they're going to be of any use when the spug hits the fan?" Trace shot Tuesday and Jimmy an evil look. "Admit it. You both know you're useless."

Tuesday and Jimmy exchanged a look. The fact they didn't deny the accusation spoke volumes.

Trace threw a small glass bottle to Jimmy before she, Tuesday and Lana got stuck into their bland, but nourishing, meals. Reading the bottle's label in confusion, Jimmy cleared his throat.

"Uh, forgetting something?" he managed. He shook the bottle. "This isn't food. It's vitamins."

"No dinner for you." Trace snapped, licking kelp juice off her fingers. "You've got weeks of fat stored up. As long as you keep getting your vittles' from those pills, you should be right."

Jimmy looked close to panic. It was like somebody had just snatched a loaded syringe from the crook of a heroin addict's arm.

"What?!"

"Maybe give him a little of a carrot tube?" Lana offered.

"No," Trace barked. "You don't add more fuel to an overflowing tank, do you? It's a waste."

"Who made you boss?" Lana argued in Jimmy's defence.

"Natural selection," Trace growled. "Unless you'd like to give him your share?"

"And you've been hitting the sweets, too, Slummer," Tuesday said around a mouthful of gluten-free cardboard. "You think we don't see the chocolate smears all over your face every time you vanish to 'take a leak' in the bushes? You've had more than your share."

Jimmy's expression said "busted" quite clearly. Jimmy scratched at his face, as though there were bugs under his skin. The concept of going without a meal seemed to have done something serious to his brain.

"I have a problem, okay?" Jimmy said in a low, embarrassed voice. "I got hooked on Ultrasweet in my teens, and I just need little regular top-ups here and there, or I'll go into withdrawals. A little taste every six hours is all I need. That's it. We're talking a mouthful, max. That's all."

"When was the last time you tried to go without a dose for longer than six hours?" Lana asked in disapproval.

Jimmy counted on his fingers. "About seventeen years."

"We have two chocolate marshmallow bars left." Lana said. "I don't mean to be cruel, but your discomfort is less important than the rest of us starving to death. Will these withdrawals kill you?"

Jimmy's face lost all colour at the suggestion. He looked close to tears.

"Okay, look, I can't go through Ultrasweet withdrawals right now. You don't know what it's like! If I don't have a taste every six hours, I'll lose it." He glanced sideways at his backpack, which was within arm's reach. "I have a suggestion, okay? If I can have just one bite from a mega-sized caramel-slice bar, then I promise that will be it for the night. No more arguments from me. I can stop after that. I swear."

"No," Trace snapped, not feeling the need to fine-tune her rebuttal.

Jimmy nodded in a resigned way, looking sad, before lunging for his bag. Trace effortlessly slapped him to the dirt with a classic take-down move. Jimmy was on his knees in an instant, his arm so far up his back that it was a wonder nothing had dislocated yet. His face twisted in a soundless wail of pain.

"If you want to die badly on this rock, go right ahead." Trace growled into his ear. "But I'm not getting dragged six feet under because you want a sugar fix, understand? This is for your own good."

"Are you nearly breaking his arm for his own good, too?" Lana asked dryly.

Trace looked down at Jimmy, who was whining like a kicked dog, and grimaced. She let go, allowing Jimmy to scurry away out of reach. She pointed at him in threat as he rubbed his aching shoulder and elbow.

"You've been warned."

"Why have you got to be such a bitch?" Lana shouted. "What's your damage?"

Surprisingly, Lana didn't get a right hook to the teeth for her trouble. In fact, Trace probably looked as close to embarrassed as anybody had ever seen her. It was weird for her face go like that, to form an expression that an actual human being might wear.

"I'm not used to talking…you know, with words," Trace managed.

Her voice was thick. It seemed the stress and hopelessness of their situation was getting to her. She looked down at Jimmy, who was still whimpering and rubbing his sore arm. There was a tiny possibility that Trace was about to apologise, but that evaporated into her usual surliness after a long second. She sat down without another syllable and finished what she was eating.

The conversation was over for now.

*

Half Head returned to camp just in time to collapse in the moonlight. Jimmy was the only one who was still awake when the dirty robot fell.

His sweating was already worse than he'd ever experienced before, and it felt as though everything inside of his body was twitching and itchy. But how could he scratch his organs? What could he possibly do to make these sensations go away?

Rolling over to stare at the moon, all Jimmy could think of was the gooey texture of a mega-sized caramel-slice bar's core: the golden sauce, the little studs of Ultrasweet popping along his taste buds, the sting from a tiny river of caramel so rich in sugar that it burnt the surface of his mouth...ecstasy. But it only got more sublime from there once the narcotic effects began to kick in. Within seconds of ingesting a dose of Ultrasweet, his brain would slide into a euphoric state where it felt like the world was beautiful and nothing could ever hurt him. Every colour would get brighter on the way to paradise, and all his worries and stresses dissolved away.

Jimmy gave his pack a glum look. As much as he wanted to sneak a bite of one of the precious bars, Trace had made the executive decision to unroll her mattress on top of the backpacks so she could sleep on them. Jimmy was about as far from a ninja as you can get, and there was no telling what Trace would do if she caught him. Still, not only was the desire to steal a mouthful not going away, it was getting stronger.

Jimmy winced as he felt a withdrawal effect that he'd heard of, but never personally encountered: black hole belly. His entire digestive system was crying out, missing something essential for the first time in seventeen years. All Jimmy could do was moan.

Unable to sleep as the moon slowly dawdled across a star-specked black canvas, Jimmy rolled over on the soaked material of his sleeping bag. His sweating was so full-on that it was seeping onto the slab of lifeboat material, and a procession of bleak thoughts only twisted away what little hope he still had. Jimmy already knew how unlikely it was that he'd survive this torturous marathon to some probably-worthless alien ruins, but every time his mind returned to this fact it only made his worsening Ultrasweet cravings spike. As Jimmy wasn't a sociopath like Trace, the thought of the others dying on this rock bothered him almost as much as his own demise.

Almost.

Heck, he didn't even like the odds of the others making it another three days before they were so exhausted from malnutrition that continuing wasn't an option. Out of their group, Jimmy knew for a fact that the women had a much higher chance of surviving the trek than the guys. Lana was clearly in fine physical health, as was Trace (in her over-muscled, steroid-induced kind of way), but Tuesday was far from a paragon of well-being. He had the sort of wracking cough that only die-hard smokers could manage, and only seemed to be sputtering his way closer and closer to death's door every hour. The only difference between Tuesday and a stick of jerky was a pulse.

Jimmy knew he wasn't much better off. Medically, his most succinct description was A Heart Attack Waiting To Happen. His armpits, thighs and other contact surfaces were in burning agony from abrading against each other for hours and hours on end. If it wasn't for the tiny antigrav wafers he'd secretly had sewn into his legs and torso fifteen years ago, enabling him to move about as though he wasn't weighed down by thick curtains of cellulite, Jimmy probably wouldn't have made it through the first day of hiking. "Survivor" was not the first word that came to mind when somebody looked at Jimmy.

Jimmy checked his wristwatch: it was four hours since Trace slammed him into the dirt, which meant it had been almost nine hours since his last Ultrasweet hit. Doing the maths, Jimmy realised that he'd broken his previous best efforts at remaining clean by almost three hours. It wasn't by choice, but still! What an achievement!

Besides the shakes and sweats and the black hole belly and the sensation that his organs were about to wrestle their way out of his abdomen, he didn't feel all that bad. It looked like all those anti-addiction pamphlets were full of lies, probably secretly sponsored by SugarCo. If he'd known it was this easy, he would have kicked the Ultrasweet years ago...

Going back to daydreaming about a marshmallow sauce bar, Jimmy startled when he noticed a small glowing fairy fluttering over Trace's head. Although the fat sprite was only around seven inches tall, she was lighting up the entire camp like an incandescent bulb. She also looked suspiciously like Jimmy's sainted Mother. Sitting up to take a closer peek, still shaking and leaking from withdrawals, the phantasm seemed as real to Jimmy's senses as a brick wall. He turned to ask Half Head if this was some sort of trick, but the robot was out until dawn.

"Hello?" Jimmy whispered.

The fairy laughed in a manic way and spun towards Tuesday at top speed. She zipped about like a butterfly on angel dust.

"Hello?" Jimmy tried again, a little louder.

The fun and games ended abruptly as the little creature split in half with a chilling scream and opened like a rose made from blood. She disappeared in a spray of red fluid. Jimmy could only shake harder as the scream sent waves of icy spikes up and down his spine and limbs, a throbbing, intolerable coldness.

Then things really got nuts.

Jimmy spun to his feet as a blinding light washed over him. Covering his eyes, it looked as though some kind of alien freight train was roaring towards the group, engines growling and jets sparking. Waving his hands, trying to alert the driver that he/she/it was about to mow right through their camp, Jimmy jumped out of the way just before the engine tore a great furrow through his sleeping bag.

Shaking on the ground, Jimmy slowly turned his head at the sound of a growl. He stopped cold at the sight of a hundred green tigers glaring at him from just beyond the campfire's glow, baring their teeth and coiling, ready to pounce from the shadows. When one of them did jump, somehow Jimmy managed to get up and start running in one motion. He went cheek-first into a tree.

Unable to see through flashes of concussion, the moment Jimmy's sight came back he witnessed all the nearby shrubs uprooting themselves and growing evil faces. Worse yet, their craggy wooden mouths were spewing yellow clouds of pollen, filling the entire campsite with a stinging pall. Long vines whipped about, and their roses unfurled to reveal hypodermic thorns.

Drokhari assassins! That's why he was hallucinating!

Terrified, barely maintaining enough self-control not to run screaming into the night, Jimmy knew that he needed to be braver and tougher than he'd ever been. He was the only chance the others had left.

"Tuesday!" Jimmy screamed into the janitor's ear. Tuesday didn't so much as twitch. "Wake up! Assassins!"

Jimmy took a hold of Tuesday's leg in order to drag him to safety. Unfortunately, it appeared that Tuesday's body had ceased to be made of meat, and was now entirely composed of enamel paint. Jimmy's hands sank into the gloopy mess, turning Tuesday's leg into a dirty swirl of badly-mixed greys. Jimmy's yellow apron, arms and hands were now coated in a thick layer of muck.

Crap.

Knowing time was of the essence, Jimmy decided to help the next closest person: Lana. However, pulling at her arm instantly disconnected the entire limb at her shoulder with a loud pop. Dropping the severed limb in horror, Jimmy could only watch in confusion as a new arm grew back in its place. Tugging on Lana's freshly-replaced fingers, Jimmy ended up with a disconnected hand for his efforts. It twitched and scratched at him until he dropped it.

More crap.

Sighing, Jimmy turned to regard Trace. He wasn't sure if he had the inherent strength to budge her a single inch. Gripping one jackboot, when Jimmy gave mighty tug it popped off her foot. Feeling the jackboot twitch in his hands, Jimmy looked down just in time to see the footwear sprout teeth and latch onto his forearm. Jimmy wrestled the carnivorous jackboot for somewhere between a minute and nine months before finally beating it to death with his yellow chef's hat.

Jimmy pushed Trace hard in the shoulder, but hardly budged her a centimetre. Gripping one of her muscled arms, Jimmy pulled with all his strength. Ignoring the ache in his back, arms, legs, abdomen and pretty much everywhere else, groaning and turning red, he almost cried in frustration when Trace didn't move one bit. Jamming his thonged feet into the arid wasteland, giving it his all, Jimmy fell over backwards as Trace's entire body exploded into broken glass. Skittering backwards as cutting shards slashed along his face, Jimmy heard a roar from the Drokhari assassins in the darkness.

"Kills them! Kills them all!"

And that's all that Jimmy could remember.

*

Jimmy awakened to a rock in the ribs. With a lurching start, Jimmy realised that he was clutching the top of a near-smooth spire of thoughtmetal. Somehow he'd made it twenty metres up the slick surface. The next thing he discovered was that he was wearing nothing but a pair of heavy-duty maximum-support granny undies, a rock-hard sports bra and Kevlar stockings.

"I don't know how you took my undergarments without waking me," Trace yelled, readying a second stone. "But I'd very much appreciate if you came down so we can have a calm, rational discussion about how that makes me feel."

"I think she's lying," Tuesday called. "Might be safer if you stay up there forever, big fella."

"I was trying to save your lives!" Jimmy exploded, almost losing his grip on the thoughtmetal.

Tuesday tutted. "That's the best story you could come up with? Defective."

"Saving our lives from what, exactly?" Lana pressed.

"There were fairies! And alien freight trains! And Drokhari assassins!" Jimmy pointed at the cluster of trees just beyond their campsite, and immediately gripped his perch twice as tight when he began to slide down. "The trees! The trees are coming for you!"

Tuesday cackled in a high-pitched voice.

"Oh, please, somebody save me from the fairies and the trees!"

"No, the fairy wasn't the problem!" Jimmy screamed, getting hysterical. "The trees are Drokhari assassins! And you were made from paint, and your limbs were detachable, and you were made from glass..."

Lana sighed.

"Jimmy, you wad, you were obviously hallucinating from acute Ultrasweet withdrawal. You're a junkie, and that's the sort of thing that happens to junkies who don't get a fix." She rolled her wrist at a clump of trees that were very much immobile and nonthreatening. "Not the most deadly of assassins, are they?"

Trace sprang forward and kicked the thoughtmetal spike hard with her jackboot. Jimmy yelped and slid down, quickly losing his grip before falling the last eight metres. Winded, trying to sit up, Jimmy got a kick right in the sports bra from Trace. It was like trying to damage an airbag, so she followed up with a second toe-nudge to the left side of Jimmy's jaw.

That did the trick.

CHAPTER THIRTEEN TURTLE SOUP

This region of Scrote only got drier and more barren until the arid landscape was entirely made from twisted spires of dead rock. The horizon wobbled like Jimmy's lowest chins, and even the hardiest of cacti didn't grow between the crags. In the dry extremes of this alien Tartarus, even the survival ponchos didn't keep them all that comfortable. Thankfully, Trace showed the survivors how to summon matte-black sunhats from their AllTool bracelets before they got burned black. Lana had to smack her faulty projector three or four times before it complied with her request.

After a terrible lunch of vomit-like durian jam scooped straight from its vile jar, their dogs-hind-leg wanderings eventually lead to them to the unmistakable stench of rotting vegetation. This smell guided them above a fifty-metre-long cut in the rock floor. Unlike the perfectly round mass driver scars, this dip was roughly the shape of a chicken's egg. Drawing holographic straws from their AllTool bracelets, it was decided that Tuesday would crawl to the edge and take a look. Convincing Tuesday to do his duty took a solid five minutes of badgering and threats, but he wasn't sold on the idea until Trace confiscated his chlorine cigarettes and threatened to crush them into flakes. The look on his face guaranteed retribution.

Crawling to the edge and sucking in a deep breath, Tuesday took the quickest of glances. In a fraction of a second Tuesday saw this cup in the stone was almost entirely carpeted with thick, lavender-coloured moss, and its few bare patches were rock rather than fused glass. The crooked slot was about ten metres deep and perfectly angled to deny direct sunlight, which is why it wasn't a blasted waste like everything else within a dozen kilometres. Tuesday instantly detected a slight movement about thirty metres away, and responded by clawing away from the edge and rolling over to face the burning sky. His cowardly heart pounding, three shadowy forms blocked out the sunlight.

"Well?" Lana prompted.

"Some animal is eating purple stuff down there. A big animal."

Lana scoffed.

"Tuesday, when was the last time we encountered any serious fauna on this rock? And you barely looked for two seconds."

"Don't believe me? Use your own damn eyes," Tuesday snapped.

As Tuesday hadn't died, the others felt confident enough to glance over the rim. Just like the janitor had claimed, there was a beast on the far side of the crater: it was an armour-plated terrapin-analogue roughly three times the mass of a Brahma bull, and it was happily flippering about in ankle-deep purple moss. Entirely invested in harvesting its lunch with a birdlike beak, the sedate clockwise gnashing of the creature brought a giant tortoise to mind. It was covered in foot-thick slabs of keratin, and each plate had a single long screw jutting out of it. The spikes looked a lot like ridged traffic cones. It was no surprise that every motion the terrapin made was performed with a measured slowness.

Lana sighed in amazement.

"A new species, never before seen by human eyes," she breathed, keeping her voice down so she didn't spook the creature. "This privilege is even more exhilarating than I'd hoped."

Seeing Tuesday open his mouth in her peripheral vision, Lana instantly cut him off.

"I, Lana Slade, officially name this creature to be a Screwback turtle."

Tuesday twisted up his face into an even uglier configuration when Lana's Omni glowed green and chimed.

"Bugger. Had a really good one saved up, too."

"I wonder how Screwback turtles taste?" Jimmy said wetly, salivating despite his dry mouth.

"Bit of tenderising should take away the toughness," Tuesday muttered. "Bet it would be stellar in a nice, hearty soup."

Lana raised a finger for silence, and pointed her left hand at the terrapin. She squinted at the Omni readout.

"From this far away, I can't tell if we'd be okay eating it or not." Lana wiped violently at her face, leaving red marks. "No point risking our lives for poison-flavoured steak, right?"

"But if Screwbacks are edible, it would feed us for weeks," Jimmy argued, his hunger overriding his anxiety. "Landscape is only getting more barren and hostile with every step. Who knows how long until we have another chance at finding food?"

Half Head made a noise that sounded a lot like somebody clearing their throat.

"I believe I may be capable of assessing your digestive compatibility with the flesh of this animal." Half Head's bisected skull turned to look down on Tuesday, who was closest. "It's been a while, but I believe my old files on this creature, as well as what it's eating, would still be relevant."

Eager to reduce the gap between an empty stomach and a full one as quickly as possible, Tuesday rolled his wrist towards the robot.

"Go ahead," Tuesday said. He squinted, as though giving his permission second thoughts. "Actually, what precisely do you mean by..."

Without a word of warning Half Head sprouted long, needle-thin spikes from a tentacle and jammed them deep into Tuesday's abdomen. Tuesday opened his mouth to scream, but Half Head took this opportunity to skewer his tongue and uvula with a second precisely-aimed probe. Tuesday howled like a fog horn and clawed desperately in the direction of Half Head's eye lenses, but this didn't change the fact that he was currently impaled.

"He's hurting him!" Jimmy wailed. "He's hurting him!"

Lana brandished a black mono-edged blade just as Trace raised an equally-black sledgehammer, ready to start slashing and smashing. Lana didn't have time to demand the robot stand down immediately before it retracted its thin biopsy probes from Tuesday's innards. Released from the pokey needles, Tuesday crumpled to the rocky ground and breathed heavily, shaking in shock. Half Head looked directly at Trace as she struggled to stop her sledgehammer mid-swing.

"I've compared the files. As this Screwback turtle lives on that rare breed of purple sweetmoss down there rather than the toxic plants found everywhere else on this world, I believe that its meat will be compatible with your digestive systems."

"How are we meant to kill it, though?" Lana wondered, so distracted by the gnawing in her belly that the rush of fight-or-flight sensations were already fading into the background. "That thing is a tank. I don't see much in the way of weak points. And besides the AllTool bracelets, we don't have any actual weapons."

Trace made a growling noise. It took a few seconds for her to clarify what she

154

wanted to say.

"I have something that might help if things get desperate...but you better keep your hands to yourselves, got it?"

Trace reached deep into the breastplate of her riot armour to reveal she'd been carrying a smartphone-sized device sealed in a clamshell case. Lana's eyes instantly doubled their span in disbelief. Rather than being angry, all she wanted to do was get closer to the item.

"That's a limited-edition Vindicator-series Holt & Heckler unfolding kinetic accelerator, a minimum-recoil sidearm with adjustable force settings, genetic recognition software and a self-destruct password option." Lana was almost drooling. "And it's still in its original clamshell packaging! That thing must be worth a fortune."

"K-pistol," Tuesday summarised.

"It's even been fabricated with the ultra-rare ceramic stealth-shell option." Lana gushed. Her expression hazed a bit. "Wait, didn't The Unison recall and destroy all the stealth-shells after those Cricket Farm executives got assassinated by Vegan Extremists? I didn't think any of these beauties were still in circulation."

"They're not. This is a family heirloom." She tried not to show it, but Trace was clearly more than a little impressed by Lana's encyclopaedic knowledge of her most precious possession. "You know your weapons, kid."

"Came top of my class in firearms theory," Lana boasted.

"Theory," Trace repeated. She squinted at Lana. "You ever fired a gun before?"

"My world was originally settled by Amerikans," Lana said in affront. "What do you think?"

"Simulations, or real?"

"Real!"

"Lethal or nonlethal?" Trace pushed.

Lana didn't answer for a moment.

"I'm one month too young for a lethal firearms license, so I've only practiced with pain guns. They don't do any lasting damage, true, but..."

Trace had heard enough. She carefully moved the clamshell case out of Lana's reach, as though trying not to jolt it too much.

"Guess I'll be keeping this for now." Trace glanced at Half Head. "You got anything else useful to tell us about Mister Turtle down there, or is it the usual story?"

Half Head looked at the chewing Screwback, tilted its skull, and its eye lenses contracted in the effort of recalling information from a ruined hard drive. Eventually, it found a snippet.

"The Apex once farmed them." Half Head's skull angled itself more and more steeply, as though looking for something that might actually be helpful. Some brown muck eventually began to drip out. "I cannot remember exactly why. Though I do recall that they have a defence mechanism of some kind."

"Even the weakest of prey have defence mechanisms," Trace said in an ominous way.

*

Sliding into the lavender Screwback nest raised the temperature by a good five degrees, and a spike in humidity made the humans feel instantly sleepy. Thankfully, the edges of the crater weren't so steep that they'd have any dramas clawing their way back out.

As useful as Half Head would be in hunting the beast, the robot could only watch impotently from the rim. Half Head was completely dependent on direct solar power, and as this nest was heavily shaded, the robot would go into Standby within seconds. Not only would Half Head be useless, there would be no conceivable way of dragging it out of the pit again.

The plan was simple: Jimmy, Tuesday and Lana would distract the Screwback from one side so Trace could sneak up and stick a blade in the terrapin's ear. Their victory would be celebrated with a barbecue. Until Trace was ready to spread turtle brains all over the place, however, the other three were meant to keep low and quiet.

In reality, only Lana was creeping: Jimmy was waddling with loud, wheezing grunts and Tuesday shambled about like an elderly drug-fried rock star. And despite the cushioning effect of the sweet-smelling purple moss, their attempts to sneak up on the Screwback failed before they'd gotten within twenty metres of the lumbering creature. Proving that its senses were more acute than the survivors had guessed, the beast slowly waved its beaked head in their direction. Regarding the still and silent group of three for a handful of eternal seconds, continuing to slowly mash at some moss without a care in the world, the Screwback very calmly turned a half revolution until its long keratin screws were pointed at the intruders like the spines of an oversized porcupine. Nobody was too worried by this defensive behaviour, as it was hard to be intimidated by something that moved like a stoned snail.

"Ah." Half Head said from the rim of the crater, as though recalling something important.

"What?" Jimmy hissed.

"I believe you should move out of the way immediately unless you want to die."

Knowing better than to ask questions, Tuesday, Lana and Jimmy took flying leaps onto the mossy rocks, painfully bruising themselves. If it wasn't for their survival ponchos, they would have broken bones. This light pummelling was the better of two evils, though, as the Screwback turtle fired its spinal javelins like an exploding fragmentation grenade. Powered by an off-the-scales intercostal muscle spasm, the screws zipped straight through where the humans had just been standing and slammed into the far side of the pit. Still attached to the spikes by thick tendons, the terrapin proved it was full of surprises when it did the exact opposite of retracting the harpoons: instead of reeling them in, the Screwback's considerable bulk went flying through the air and smashed into the cliff face like an asteroid strike. Reunited with its spikes, the Screwback slowly extracted itself from the rocks by clumsily flippering its way out.

Within five seconds it was already pointing its organic artillery towards the moaning forms of Tuesday and Jimmy.

"Gang way!" Lana screeched.

A wave of Screwback harpoons exploded across the gap a second time. If the three humans had been just a mite slower getting out of the way they would have been kebabs. Unfortunately, slamming onto the thin purple veneer for a second time instantly tenderised them like old briskets in a Jewish deli window, leaving them helpless from shock and pain. While Jimmy sobbed in agony the Screwback began to retract itself across the pit like a vacuum cleaner from the Mirror Universe.

The only one who wasn't battered senseless, Trace sprinted for the Screwback like an Olympic Deathsport champion on prohibited substances. The Terrapin of Death had only just extricated itself from a slab of pulverised shale when Trace took a flying leap into its forest of screws. In a movement that made lightning look slow, she climbed up the Screwback's spines like an obstacle course and mounted its armoured neck. Giving a war cry, Trace swung her right hand towards the turtle's skull in a tight arc, creating a black dagger mid-swing that landed right on target on the terrapin's temple.

Sadly, this achieved absolutely nothing. The terrapin's armoured skull was too thick for her AllTool weaponry.

The Screwback bucked, trying to dislodge the irritant leaning on the back of its skull. Unfortunately, when Trace attempted to insert her weapon into the Screwback's eye socket, this gave the giant terrapin a hot tip on exactly where she was. Snapping its beak over Trace's wrist armour with surprising speed, the Screwback began to slowly apply a crushing pressure that would grind every

157

bone in her forearm into dust.

Gritting her teeth just like the vice crushing her arm, Trace deliberately swung her legs around the Screwback's neck until she was hanging beneath its chin. Concentrating, Trace slipped the clamshell case out of her riot armour with a shrug and caught it with her free hand. Popping the antique k-pistol out of its sealed prison one-handed and catching it in her mouth, Trace unfolded it and turned the force dial from WARNING SHOT to ANNIHILATE with her tongue. Trying to ignore the agony of her slowly-splintering wrist, Trace took the k-pistol from between her chipped teeth, pushed its barrel into the Screwback's surprised eye, and pulled the trigger. A burst of accelerated kinetic energy pounded through the Screwback's cornea and drove straight into its brainpan with a burst of thick, yellow liquid that immediately boiled away into foul steam. The terrapin's lumbering body didn't get the memo it was dead for a good twenty seconds, but then it finally collapsed and was still.

Even though the Screwback had officially shed its mortal coil, its beak was still wrapped just as tightly around Trace's arm. Now splashed all over with yellow cerebral fluid and purple saliva, Trace finally wrestled her mauled arm free. As the beak was only good for scraping moss, besides some nasty bruises the Screwback hadn't managed to do any real damage. She tried not to think of how crippled she'd be if the Screwback had inflicted just another ten seconds of spiking pressure...

Sighing at the brain-stains all over her once-pristine kinetic accelerator, trying not to think about how she'd just wiped about 99% off its resale value, Trace wiped the dirty gun across her armour and hopped off the twisted neck.

"Dinnertime."

*

It made sense set up their camp in the mossy cup. Nobody was interested in hiking another metre after fighting The Turtle From Hell, and sunset was only a couple of hours away anyway. Once Lana had showed off her Beaver Scout skills by starting a fire with a magnifying glass projected by her AllTool bracelet, there was a unanimous vote to have a barbecue.

Even though the Screwback was as dead as dead can be, getting to its sweetmeats was almost as much of an ordeal as killing it in the first place. After digging in deep with black monomolecular filleting knives, it turned out that the hateful thing was mostly layer upon layer of armour plates held together with inedible sinew. Connective tendons didn't make for good eating, so they continued to dig

158

for something more nourishing. Finally, after a solid hour, they'd managed to separate the Screwback like a jigsaw puzzle, and the results weren't spectacular: from three-and-a-half tonnes of terrapin-analogue, they harvested enough tough meat, gooey offal and wafer-like eyelid membranes for another couple of days. Nothing else was edible. So while it wasn't a huge windfall like they'd hoped, it was still an absolute feast.

Now covered head-to-toe by fishy-smelling gel after their amateur efforts at butchering, they sliced the alien meat into steaks and seared them over the fire. Within minutes they were dining on translucent flesh that had the taste and mouth-feel of calamari. They salted some for later by scraping pure sodium off the cracked desert floor, and all the organs received the same treatment.

Trace was the only one game enough to try the eyelids, and she confirmed they were quite a delicacy. In other words, they tasted like ass and had the texture of a dried out cockroach.

After a minute of careful scanning, Lana confirmed that some of the brighter patches of purple sweetmoss were technically edible. While it wasn't poisonous, the sweetmoss didn't contain any nutrients compatible with the human body, so it had no actual nutritional value. This meant chewing the moss would cost more energy than it returned, making it a negative-calorie meal. All of these downsides placed the moss in the same category as the alleged "food" served at MacDeath's, so they were sure to harvest a good deal of it.

Night was only minutes away from falling when Half Head made some noise from the lip of the crater. It was the first time in half an hour that it had so much as moved.

"I can recall why The Apex farmed Screwback turtles. Could you do something for me?"

Tuesday grumbled an obscenity around a mouthful of Screwback fillet. He was well and truly done having anything to do with the robot. While the needle probes hadn't left any visible marks, Tuesday was sure he could still feel every poke.

"Open the Screwback's beak, and feel around deep inside," Half Head clarified.

Wiping both greasy hands on her dress uniform, Lana got to her feet. Her body was stiff from bruises, making every motion painful, and she couldn't wait to go to bed. Staggering over to the Screwback's decapitated head – which no longer had a tongue, eyes or eyelids – Lana carefully opened the beak and pushed her fingers into its maw until she felt something that wasn't gooey. It felt hard, cold and smooth to the touch, like tempered glass, and seemed to be growing out of where the Screwback's uvula should be hanging. Poking around, Lana discovered at least four more growths, but they were mere pinpricks in comparison to the biggest

159

object. Gripping the mystery item, Lana disconnected it from the tracheal wall with a hard twist. Pulling out, her arm covered in stinking bile up to the shoulder, a blinding electric blue light instantly made her forget this discomfort. The sphere lit up every detail of the mossy pit, leaving no shadows, and all the others could do was stare at the marble, transfixed. Its pulsing was hypnotic.

Lana only managed to look away from the sphere because Half Head was making an unfamiliar noise. While this was the first time she'd seen it happen, Lana could tell that Half Head was weaving something out of thoughtmetal. Despite telling the humans that The Apex were capable of spinning thoughtmetal out of nothing, the robot had never actually admitted to possessing this ability. Rather than apologise, it waved a free tentacle at Lana.

"Bring the blood crystal over here, please."

Sore, well-fed and sleepy, Lana didn't have a great time scrambling up the edge of the pit. Now that she was closer, she could see that Half Head had weaved some sort of small, gleaming cage. It accepted the blood crystal carefully, and slid it into the construct. A slot opened in Half Head's abdomen, spitting out the charred ruins of what must have been a working component six thousand years ago, and Half Head inserted the caged blood crystal.

The effect was instant: the robot went bolt upright, as though getting a shot of adrenalin to the heart. It took a few moments to relax again, slowly coming down off that high.

"While my creators were able to fashion almost anything they wanted out of thoughtmetal, they could not create energy from nothing. This meant they needed a reliable source of fissionable materials, and the blood crystals that naturally grow in the throats of Screwback turtles provide a safe and renewable supply of cold-fusion energy."

Lana wasn't sure, but it seemed as though the dings in Half Head's weathered torso were flattening out, the rusty segments glistening as though hit with a coat of paint. It sighed in a contented way.

"Thank you. I have successfully replaced one of my batteries. While I will still run on solar power, I am no longer entirely reliant on it. May I?"

The sun finally set as Half Head glided down to the campsite. It sank to the sweetmoss, possibly enjoying the heat. While nobody said anything, the idea that the robot would theoretically remain awake while they were all asleep was worrying. It was one thing to have the battered wreck in their field of vision, and another to expose their soft pink bellies all night. Trying to distract herself, Lana picked at her teeth and raised a question that had been bothering her.

"You said that antique kinetic accelerator was a 'family heirloom', right?"

160

Trace gave Lana one of her famous dead-eyed expressions. She might not be a wild animal at present, but Trace was still very far from domesticated.

"Will this line of questioning eventually have a point?"

Lana showed Trace her palms in an ancient placating gesture.

"Look, a wedding ring is a family heirloom. A necklace is a family heirloom. Schizophrenia is a family heirloom. That weapon? It's something even a museum wouldn't buy, the sort of thing a trillionaire would secretly keep in the deepest of vaults as the pride of his collection." Lana threw some lavender moss into the campfire, where it charred with a sweet smell. "I don't get why you'd lie. With all your other defects, why bother pretending that thing isn't stolen?" Lana assumed a triumphant expression. "That's why you were working on the Carpe Astrum, wasn't it? You've been crap-kicking as an Enforcer so you could steal that accelerator from some rich puddle of smegma, haven't you?"

"I didn't lie, and I didn't steal it," Trace ground out, her voice low and dangerous.

Lana scoffed. Trace simply glared into the fire for a good half a minute before continuing.

"I grew up on the wrong side of the tracks."

Tuesday gave a hum of approval.

"Dirt stinking poor, eh? Been there."

Trace narrowed her eyes. "Not exactly."

CHAPTER FOURTEEN PRIDE AND PREJUDICE AND CURBSTOMPING

Cuddle Manor was a European-style castle incongruently situated at the very heart of what had once been the state of Michigan. However, this large region of Amerika hadn't been known by that name since The Scandinavian Expansion cut through it like a knife edge across a soft, pink belly.

Unlike the more sensible states of Fallen Amerika, Michigan had been notoriously non-compliant with the wishes of The Expansion since day one of their occupation. The locals were furious that their homes and businesses could be snatched at any time without any legal recourse, resented the curfews and checkpoints and surveillance drones, and absolutely refused to believe that the President had surrendered to the Expansion on bended knee on the bloodied steps of the White House. And sure, while the rest of Fallen Amerika wasn't too fond of being conquered, the key difference was that every housewife and grandma in Michigan was armed with military-grade weaponry, and were accustomed to shooting two or three bangers on the way to pick up a loaf of bread and a carton of milk.

Following several frustrating months of running battles in the pulverised streets, The Expansion eventually decided it was more cost efficient (and less embarrassing) to simply level all of Michigan down to bedrock. Why engage in a protracted, costly urban guerrilla war when you can simply scorch the battlefield into a sterile slab of glass? For decades after, this entire state remained little more than a warren of rat holes and sewers.

Of course, this was all ancient history. The damned Skandos had been driven off Amerikan soil in the 22nd Century thanks to the tactical genius of President Leanne D Linden, who had ironically started off as a puppet figurehead installed by The Expansion. While Amerika's economic and physical recovery was understandably slow after the long, dark night, this near-dead nation just kept on twitching until it finally dragged itself back to the status of a first-world country. And while every citizen played their part in the decades of rebuilding, Amerika especially owed its resurrection to men like George Cuddle, the genius founder of Cuddle Tactile Holographics, more commonly known as CuddleTech.

Raised as a scavenger in the sidewalk cracks of what had been Detroit before The Flattening, George "Guppy" Cuddle's first decade was spent evading Skando patrols and stealing just enough food to stay at the finely-balanced midway point between starvation and detection. Scummers like him were illiterate, bone-poor and dumb as rocks, and the only reason the Skandos didn't wipe out Guppy's whole society was because visiting Expansionist dignitaries enjoyed going out on murderous hunting excursions. Although Detroit itself had been incinerated, the sad dregs of its population were still being punished for spitting in The Expansion's face.

At thirteen, Guppy watched firsthand as The Expansion's stranglehold on Amerika was broken off one finger at a time over the space of a single devastating evening, and suddenly the Skando menace had been driven from Amerikan shores quicker than you can say sluta sparka mig. When an emergency relief team of Red Cross trucks rumbled into Guppy's ruined neighbourhood to tap old wells, put up tents, provide basic medical services and construct protein sumps to fill every belly, Guppy was the first scavenger to put his hand up to help with rebuilding. He spent the rest of his teens and twenties constructing a new Detroit from ashes and smoke, quietly doing whatever was necessary to turn back the clock on this slice of Amerikana.

Guppy's life didn't truly begin until Michigan's scavenger populations were provided with free AutoEducation hardwiring by the newly-installed Matriarch Regime. Instantaneous learning technology was in its infancy, and was still quite a brutal experience. Each lesson was recorded on a ceramic slab the rough dimensions of a VHS cassette, and was delivered through a strapped headset that looked a lot like a fancy pair of binoculars. The process was as straightforward as it was fast: a blinding flash of information would sear into the student's eyes, travel up their optic nerves and permanently brand itself into their brain. While this process felt like glowing needles had been jammed into your skull and left the student totally blind for three minutes, it was highly effective.

After Guppy's first hardwiring he was revealed to have a mind like Da Vinci or Einstein or Tesla, the sort of plastic brain that couldn't be artificially created by science, a statistical fluke. People like Guppy were the real reason that President LD Linden had spent a fortune educating the primitive and the feral, as she believed it would take the finest minds to restore this broken wasteland. Now that he'd been identified as a prodigy, Guppy was allowed to absorb every educational program in the catalogue, and soon he was being hyped up to be the next big thing...and from Detroit, of all places!

In addition to unlimited access to AutoEducation programs, The Matriarch Regime provided Guppy with four years of funding in German yen (the Amerikan pound was still too depressed, and the Swedish lira was to be burned on sight). Guppy was free to develop whatever he wanted with these resources, and was also welcome to profit from his breakthroughs. The catch was that all of his work had to be of a practical nature rather than theoretical (Odin knew there were enough unrealised theories wafting about already), and whatever he created must benefit his home state. Of course, it went without saying that if Guppy made some serious bank, the Regime expected their investment back...with interest.

During his first year of funded research, Guppy achieved no measurable results. Zilch. Rather than being due to a lack of ambition or effort, Guppy was simply too busy slotting program after program into his eidetic brainpan, barely sleeping or eating or showering as he devoted every last moment to uploading. Year two showed more promise, but Guppy's desire to improve the replication rate of the protein sumps failed to set the world on fire, and he was encouraged to do something original, something that wasn't already being tackled by a dozen different teams across Amerika. The Regime wanted something exciting, damn it!

A few weeks after his third year of funded research had officially ended, at the age of thirty-two, Guppy cracked the secret of how to construct holographic computer simulations. Not only could you see and hear and feel them, but they could be used to affect the physical world as though it had actual mass, rather than just being sculpted light. Until now, the field of tactile holographics had been purely theoretical, but not only had Guppy's autistic mind achieved the impossible, he kept ploughing ahead with breakthrough after breakthrough.

After eleven months of testing and perfecting, Guppy was finally ready to showcase his tactile holographic projector to an auditorium full of Regime representatives and private investors. As his funding was due to expire within days, this was Guppy's final chance to make a lasting impact on the nation of his birth. He made this presentation in an exhibition hall so freshly built that the audience was getting dizzy from drying resin fumes and paint vapours. Skipping the showmanship, Guppy literally pulled back a curtain on something that looked like a prop from a low-budget Frankenstein movie, and ran through its specs. The prototype device was small enough to be carried by a moderate-sized truck, powered by a coil of nuclear cells, and could boot up in under three quarters of an hour. Almost as an afterthought, Guppy shared that its official designation was the Mk III Aurealis AllTool, but in all the history books it would simply be referred to as the very first AllTool.

Using evidence rather than words, Guppy proved that the AllTool was already capable of an assortment of impressive functions at the touch of a button. First off, it could create a never-ending roll of simulated toilet paper. In addition to being five-ply, soft as a newborn pug puppy and literally never running out, once the luxurious simulated bog roll came in contact with water it immediately ceased to exist, which would do wonders for Amerika's clapped-out sewage systems. It was also guaranteed to finally do away with the dreaded Brown Thumb suffered by inattentive wipers everywhere.

There were some surprised murmurs.

The second function Guppy showcased was a holographic bottle filled to the brim with Slurko Cola. Looking and feeling just like glass all the way down to how condensation beaded on its curves, Guppy cracked its plastic cap and sculled the contents gulp after gulp until it was empty. He violently threw the simulated bottle at his feet and, as though Houdini himself was playing a masterful trick, it vanished into nothing without a smash or any broken glass.

The whispers got louder, and more urgent.

By the time Guppy showed off the holographic tampons (which was only the third demonstration of seventy), the investors had already started a bidding war right there in the auditorium. Unperturbed by the fact the bids had already passed fifty million German yen before he had a chance to show off tactile holographic socks,

Guppy just kept on going with his presentation: tactile holographic bullets, tactile holographic Sludge bar wrappers, tactile holographic condoms, tactile holographic contact lenses, tactile holographic books, tactile holographic bedspreads, tactile holographic coffee cups...

By the time his presentation had finished, George "Guppy" Cuddle, the Founder of CuddleTech, was already a billionaire. As promised, Guppy used his breakthrough to directly benefit all of Michigan.

CuddleTech began as a humble sprawl of 3D printers in a warehousing block situated near a Red Cross outpost. This nerve centre was located in what had once been Downtown Detroit before The Flattening, and things grew rapidly. Their fabrication and storage capabilities expanded by the week, and CuddleTech continued to release new products almost as often. Guppy's success brought a sudden influx of immigrants from neighbouring areas, swelling the population of a state that had been almost completely annihilated just decades before.

At Guppy's request (one of very few, it must be noted), the new city that sprang up around his company was named Reborn Detroit. A growth spike swelled its borders at an exponential rate, especially once CuddleTech drew up contracts with every off world settlement, a collective that would one day be known as The Unison. CuddleTech was soon supplying all of the tactile holographics technology across the galaxy – both military and civilian – and Reborn Detroit remained the hub of its trade. The state flourished, becoming one of the greatest industrial success stories of all time.

By the time Guppy was sixty, arcology towers dominated much of the skyscape of the Reborn Detroit megacity, but his generosity ensured these sprawls of highways and subways and everything in between were broken up by national parks, lakes and nature trails beneath a clean, blue sky. While primarily going down in history as an inventor, Guppy was a die-hard Utopian cultist who wanted nothing more than to create a world that worked. The Utopian cult were usually dismissed as a pack of pie-in-the-sky mental midgets who didn't understand how the universe operated, but Guppy had the brainpower and resources to back up his dreams. Reborn Detroit went on to become a model microcosm, an example of how to create the sort of society that didn't have an inherent use-by date. Of course, it was much easier to do things the Old Fashioned Way, so Reborn Detroit remained a curiosity rather than a template.

Ever since, even after Guppy died at one-hundred-and-fifteen, CuddleTech continued to research, test, manufacture and ship every single product in their extensive catalogue from within the boundaries of Reborn Detroit. There was no separation: Reborn Detroit was CuddleTech, and CuddleTech was Reborn Detroit.

Eventually, Reborn Detroit managed to fill the entirety of the state of Michigan, swallowing its name last of all. Without much fanfare, Michigan had become Reborn Detroit. In accordance with Guppy's wishes and the Matriarch Regime's polite requests, this is where CuddleTech would be located now and forever. Guppy had left ironclad instructions in his will that his company would never be relocated, and his wishes had been defined down to the centimetre just in case some smart-aleck descendant decided to try something crafty, like scooping the megacity up with a giant claw or teleporting it to another planet (something that one of his grandsons had almost accomplished until the lawyers stepped in, funnily enough).

As Guppy was more interested in his work than enjoying its proceeds and pleasures, Cuddle Manor had begun as a relatively humble villa. Over time, it grew. Just like the sweeping arcologies that now held a hundred million employees of CuddleTech, the superstructure of Cuddle Manor was constructed from recycled materials: the huge bricks were off-cuts of foam core and 3D-printer detritus compressed into lightweight slabs sandwiched over insulation made from packing materials. The trickle-down effect of waste products from the tireless factories becoming new homes meant that the residential growth of the mega state advanced at the same rate as its economic growth. After generations of reusing every gram of every resource without wasting so much as a crumb of Styrofoam, the concept of a "landfill" or a "garbage dump" was one that no longer made any sense to the locals.

However, as Guppy's descendants were all born into a high life, they spent centuries turning Cuddle Manor into an absolute palace. Guppy may have been a Utopian, but his descendants preferred living like Emperors: the looming slab walls of Cuddle Manor were hung so heavily with precious artworks from Earth and beyond that they groaned under the pressure, and collections of priceless sculptures were clustered so thickly that they caused traffic jams among the hospitality staff during special events. The Manor's halls were carpeted by pure polyweave, a substance so soft and luxurious that it made silk seem like the coarse pubic hair regrowth, and a sort-of-legal mind-reading AI ensured that all the needs and desires of every guest were provided before they were even consciously aware of them.

Unlike the high-tech self-sufficient arcologies that slashed the skies of this mega state in the tens of thousands, Cuddle Manor looked more like an old fashioned castle. And while Monarchy had been outlawed under penalty of Death By Power Sander for a long, long time, the Cuddles were basically the Kings and Queens of Amerika in all but title. As they'd all been born into obscene wealth and had absolutely no motivation to do anything of any worth, every last member of the modern Cuddle clan were as useless as a set of steak knives in a Vegan Extremist commune. If he'd had any inkling of how his seed would devolve, Guppy would have smashed his Aurealis prototype to scrap. He wouldn't have allowed his name to be associated with them, and he absolutely, certainly wouldn't have left his precious company to them. They would have been a disappointment beyond his worst nightmares.

As an army of lawyers and directors took care of the day-to-day running of CuddleTech (and had done for generations) the Cuddle clan were what you got when you combined privilege with a total lack of responsibility: socialites. The Cuddles had nothing better to do but throw ever-bigger parties, get in ever-bigger public spats, make ever-bigger dickheads of themselves in every form of media. Worse still, they seemed to think this was an okay way to live. After all, if your parents, grandparents and great-grandparents have all been good-for-nothing afternoon-napping gluttonous drunkards and nobody could criticise you for it (unless they wished for the Cuddle's hired muscle to help them find out how their own insides smelled), you had a recipe for mediocrity.

The name Cuddle had once been synonymous with innovation, genius, and changing humanity for the better. Now, in the 25th Century, "Cuddle" was another word for scandal, idiotic legal proceedings, and bathtubs filled with the latest permutation of cocaine. Reborn Detroit owed everything to Guppy, but the Cuddle contribution to this state died with him.

Tracetta Victoria Cuddle, ninth in line to the Cuddle fortune, woke up to the dull pain of bruises and the sharper sensation of split skin. It seemed the exotic combat stims she'd mainlined under her eyelids last night had finally worn off, allowing her feel how ill-advised it was to pick a fight with off-duty Unison marines. Blinking out of synchronisation, Trace held up her hands to see that she'd managed to gash open every knuckle down to the meat. The bleeding had stopped hours ago.

It took some effort, but she eventually remembered how to uncurl her fingers. Trace smiled with chipped teeth at the sight of three sets of bloodied dog tags in her left palm. Clotted blood had glued the thin, snapped chains together into one crimson mess. She slapped the gory mementos against her bedhead, where they stuck fast.

Seeing beyond a metre or so took more time. Whatever military-brewed chems Gummo had supplied her with had been far too hard-core, even by her usual standards, and her entire nervous system felt like it had been replaced by humming wires. Trace managed to sit up without vomiting, but barely. Blinking

167

at a blinding spot of light that burned into her corneas like a hot needle, Trace blotted out the distant afternoon sun with a bloodied palm.

Rocking a few times, Trace staggered out of bed. She'd been so wiped out last night that even getting under the polyweave covers hadn't been an option for her rattled brain. Blinking until she could see more than blurs, her room at Cuddle Manor came into focus. In a seven-star hotel, this marble-and-silk heaven would be a Presidential Suite. It was just one of many ridiculously opulent additions made to the Manor long after Guppy (and his simple tastes) had passed from this mortal coil.

The moment Trace turned her back to it, her holographic bed flicked out of existence, allowing the bloodied dog tags to clink to the marble floor. A new computer-simulated bed appeared in its place, its layers of polyweave sheets tucked so tightly that you could bounce a coin off them.

Yawning, Trace staggered towards the clouded glass of her enormous shower. Thankfully, there were plenty of marble pillars and antique furniture made from extinct kinds of wood to bounce off on the way over.

As there had never been a reason to replace any of the architecture, Trace wasn't entirely sure how much of her room was made out of sculpted, tactile light and what was actually real. She was certain, however, that the water in her shower was holographic, and while it was just as hot and wet and cleansing as the real thing, the moment she turned the motion faucet off with a wave every single drop would disappear, leaving her as dry as cotton.

Stripping away the hemp ruins of what had once been an expensive punk-style chaos suit, Trace revealed that her entire body from ankles to collarbones had been inked in a perfect copy of George Cuddle's most famous oil painting, a huge mural known as Back From The Brink Of Tartarus. It depicted naked men and women in great pain, wrapped in razor wire and climbing a steep mountain made out of sharpened cheese graters. Far, far above their bloodied fingers was a vista so glorious that despite their agony, they continued clawing towards it.

Trace decided to test the water before she stepped in. She almost screamed, as the comedown from whatever she'd got high on last night made every drop feel like a glowing ice pick.

Collapsing into a purple-padded divan the size of a slippery slide in a water park, cradling her head in her hands, Trace tried to recall what had possessed her to go on such a bender. While she had spent quite a bit of time in local Grind clubs the last year or so – usually off her face on military-grade pharmaceuticals and starting fights - she didn't usually fly so close to the sun. True, on more than one occasion she'd needed a new organ or two by the time dawn collapsed in a heap, but there was never any real risk involved. As a Cuddle, Trace was protected with a capital P. If Cuddle Manor were borderline magical, the extensive security forces that tirelessly watched every member of her family were only a few steps short of divine (or diabolical, depending on the situation). It had always been taboo to speak of Them, even with her own family, but Trace's general understanding was that some of her bodyguards operated outside of the confines of the normal space/time continuum. While she had never seen any of these mysterious protectors, she knew they were there, watching, ready to rescue her.

Smushing her face into her still-bloody hands, Trace's red-rimmed eyes popped open against her wrist as she suddenly remembered: today was the day Pop's last will and testament was going to be read out. While the Cuddles weren't hands-on with the economic monolith known as CuddleTech, that didn't mean they couldn't make big decisions if they chose to do so. As Pop had been the official patriarch of the Cuddles since his father had mysteriously disappeared on the way to the mailbox, his will could really shake up the family.

Trace half yawned, half sighed as she thought back to the day when she'd found out she was Pop's favourite grandkid. Her drug-mangled brain wasn't making it easy for her, though. But then she remembered: it had started at her Debutante's Ball...

Despite making her wishes of not wanting a cotillion beyond clear, Trace had been forced into a giant fluffy dress that made her look like a meringue and paraded in front of every eligible bachelor that Reborn Detroit had to offer. As Trace was already a mass of scars held together by piercings and could bench press twice as much as any male in the ballroom, she was under no illusion: she was nothing more than a bargaining chip, a major downside to a great financial reward. All these people knew what she was like, and how it was best to avoid her. The night had ended after less than eight minutes when Trace punched Poxius Hilton-Disney, the latest CEO of Happy Planet, so hard in his solar plexus that she sprained her own wrist and almost put him into cardiac arrest. All he'd done was politely ask her if the French Onion dip contained any shellfish, and if she had any interest in being in a long-distance non-physical marriage with his grandson, Spalding Hilton-Disney.

Once the CEO was capable of speech, Pop had prevented CuddleTech getting sued into the darkest red by agreeing that Trace would undergo a course of behavioural hardwiring to curb her undesirable tendencies. However, like the other nine times this procedure had been attempted, her brain effortlessly rejected it. This technology may have made serial killers into Nobel Peace Prize laureates in the past, but for some reason it didn't do a thing to Trace's grey matter.

A week later, when Trace overhead that Happy Planet's CEO was on his way towards Cuddle Manor flanked by lawyers, it didn't take a savant to guess the purpose of his visit. Trace felt an unfamiliar emotion when she thought about how her actions were making life difficult for her Pop, and after some deep analysis she assumed it might be shame. As she had never experienced this feeling before or since, though, there was no guaranteed way to tell.

Slinking through one of the many secret passages she'd explored as a child, Trace was able to watch the whole scene unfold in Guppy's original office through a peephole as the Happy Planet CEO ranted and raved at her Pop, threatening all kinds of legal action and getting the press involved. While none of this was good news, Hilton-Disney's demands suddenly went from bad to unthinkable: he insisted that the only logical course of action was to flush out Trace's personality and replace it with a new one that wasn't borderline homicidal, and vowed that he wouldn't consider any other outcome to be acceptable. Like most people on the street, Trace knew this kind of procedure as "replacing", and also knew it was basically death for the original personality.

After listening to the CEO's outburst for a good five minutes without so much as blinking, leaning against Guppy's huge mahogany desk, once things had gone quiet again Pop gave a solemn nod. The corner of his mouth quirked a little.

"I understand your request. One moment, please."

Pop casually flicked a wrist to summon his favourite Flog putter from his golden AllTool bracelet. Trace's eyes widened when Pop wordlessly took four steps and knocked out both of the top-tier lawyers with one precise blow each. Kicking the chair out from beneath a stammering Poxius Hilton-Disney, Pop proceeded to beat the CEO from his shoulders to the balls of his feet so savagely that it was a wonder he didn't break any bones. Tenderising Hilton-Disney all over, paying particular attention to the fatty and meaty parts of his buttocks, stomach, thighs and calves, the CEO of Happy Planet only stopped yelping and shrieking once he'd passed out from the pain. Trace was especially impressed that her Pop had managed to keep all the bruises hidden beneath the CEO's expensive Seladorian suit, and hadn't drawn a single drop of blood during the hiding.

Giving his bent club an irritated frown before throwing it to the polyweave rug, where it vanished, Pop calmly clicked his fingers at the intercom and said his next words as cold as frost.

"Janice, please arrange a chauffeur to drive Poxius home in one of our nicest town cars. And I'd like him to be holding a Flog putter when he regains consciousness, if it isn't too much trouble. Thank you, Janice."

This was the moment when Trace had realised something important: she wasn't a stray branch in her family tree, a genetic anomaly. What Pop had just done without an ounce of remorse was something no other Cuddle would be capable of. Trace had felt a special kinship with her Pop ever since.

Returning from memory lane, Trace somehow focused on her watch. The will reading was less than twenty minutes away.

*

The reading was meant to take place in Guppy's office. While this room had started out as a demountable made from laminated cardboard decorated with flat-pack furniture, six generations of gradual upgrades had shaped it into one of the finest rooms in Reborn Detroit. A large cluster of recliners upholstered with the pelts of extinct animals circled a central meeting table, and further beyond that was a bare mahogany desk. One sweep of any approved hand would bring the desk's simulated workspace to life, creating a forest of tactile holographics suitable for any corporate need. All of this sat on a series of hand-woven rugs made from the hair of famous actors.

Trace stomped into Guppy's office, and was "treated" to the sight of her entire extended family mooching around the central meeting table. Thirty-three bored, haughty faces slowly regarded her in distaste, dissecting her shredded chaos suit and total lack of makeup with wordless glances. Trace ignored them all, but especially snubbed her Father and younger sisters. Unlike Trace, her extended family were draped in the finest polyweave and sin-silks. To Trace's practiced eye, she could see that every Cuddle over the age of nineteen had the tell-tale signs of face lifts, collagen injections, neck tucks and skin weaving. None of the women would so much as leave their bedrooms without two hours of hair and makeup from a whole team of artists, and the men took their appearances even more seriously. Fops, dandies, empty vases and painted ninnies, all of them. At the very centre of the socialite scrum, the meeting table was covered in platters of untouched snacks and a forest of liquor bottles that were, unsurprisingly, already as dry as a yak in the Sahara. On the bright side, Trace didn't appear to be the most hungover.

On the far side of the room, behind the sprawling, ornate mahogany desk, was an immobile lump covered by a black sheet. Less than two feet away from the dark shroud was a technician sweeping his fingers over a compact haptic board, chewing his lip in concentration. Trace glanced at the desk's motionless occupant, and resisted the urge to nod at it.

As Trace took the final recliner at the table, a rat-faced necromantic lawyer

171

wearing the traditional black-on-black-on-black of his profession scuttled into the room. He had waited until all his clients were assembled before appearing, as he didn't want to be responsible for making any of the Cuddles feel as though they were guilty of something as common as being tardy for a legal matter. Trace had spent her entire life watching her family being pandered to in such ways, and it bored her.

The necromantic lawyer knew he was of no real importance, and didn't bother to announce his name, or why he was there. The first fact didn't matter, and the second fact was as obvious as the shiner on Trace's left eye socket. Drawing what appeared to be a pair of linked golden pens from his breast pocket, the lawyer unrolled what turned out to be a holographic scroll. Its transparent vellum straightened with a silken sound, and the lawyer cleared his throat.

"According to his wishes, the last will and testament of the late Walliam Regis Cuddle the Second is to be delivered by the deceased himself. Upon the moment of Mr Cuddle's death, a tiny liquid nitrogen canister was triggered in his skull, preserving his brain for a one-time reanimation event. His body has been sufficiently prepared by a licenced necromantic technician, who has confirmed that the shell is viable." The lawyer glanced at the tech, who didn't even bother looking away from his haptic board. The tech gave a disinterested wave of acknowledgment and kept working. "As stated under Unison law, necromantic events are not permitted to proceed for longer than three minutes, as beyond this point all neural activity will severely and unavoidably degrade. Anything that is said by the deceased after this cut-off point is legally inadmissible, and doing anything to deliberately prolong an expired reanimation is legally punishable. Do I have permission to being the reading?"

Fat old Uncle Balder, the eldest of Pop's children, grunted around his cigar with the effort of raising a pudgy arm.

"Seconded?" the lawyer continued.

Aunt Penny sighed in exasperation at having to do something besides sit around and get pampered, as though her ordeals never ended. She stuck up her spindly arm with the rattle of pearls.

"Opposition?"

The Cuddles all gave the lawyer the same look. He got the message that their patience was already wearing thin. Licking his lips nervously, the lawyer nodded at the tech.

Glancing up from his haptic board, the tech whipped away the black sheet to reveal what remained of Walliam Regis Cuddle the Second, Trace's deceased Pop.

He was wearing a surprised "I think that's a stroke" kind of expression, and was so well preserved that he barely looked dead. He was wearing his favourite Seladorian business suit, and his large moustache had been freshly waxed. Although great pains had been taken by the necromantic engineers to hide all sign of their work, Trace knew that a whole network of organic wiring had been inserted into Pop's ears and worked deep into select parts of his brain. Besides his grey pallor and clammy eyes, though, Pop might have just had the flu.

As the tech wasn't being paid to speak, he silently swiped a finger across the haptic board, and Pop blinked in confusion. The whole family knew this would happen, but it was still creepy as hell. Moving his gummy eyes back and forth, twitching his head with the stiffness of the dead, Pop took a few seconds to show any real sign of intelligence. Raising his hands, looking at parchment-white skin that no longer had a pulse, his lip suddenly curled in that familiar snarky way.

"So that was a stroke."

There were a few chuckles from the watching Cuddles. Whether Pop could see them or hear them wasn't definite, but he angled his gaze directly ahead anyway.

"So, this is what it comes down to. Three minutes," he went on, seeming more annoyed than upset. "A carcass, surrounded by every drop of my blood...and a few uninvited maggots."

A few members of the clan exchanged glances, but even the notoriously arrogant Cuddles wouldn't dare to interrupt Walliam's final words. It was no secret that Pop disliked some relatives more than others, so a few of them began to look nervous. What happened over the next two minutes and forty-one seconds could easily result in some of them being stripped of the family name, exiled, cut out from the limitless Cuddle fortune. As the patriarch of the family, what was about to be pushed through Walliam's dead lips had the power to ruin lives or make them entitled beyond their wildest imaginings.

"As you all know, for generations our family has kept a certain status quo," Walliam went on. "CuddleTech has been left in the hands of people who are qualified to maintain her interests, and the Cuddle bloodline has enjoyed the fruits of their hard work while living like royalty. That will not change."

Walliam took a couple of precious seconds to inhale, seconds that he didn't have to spare, and seemed disappointed. Perhaps that breath hadn't felt satisfying, a reminder that he would never experience anything in the flesh ever again.

"However I have something I need to say, and this is my final chance to get it off my chest, so to speak." Everyone was paying attention again. "As my brother, my only sibling, mysteriously disappeared before he had to chance to marry and reproduce, this leaves my direct family line as the sole descendants of George

"Guppy" Cuddle. Four sons and a daughter, and their children."

Walliam proved he could see by nodding directly at fat old Uncle Balder, who gave him a cunning smile in return. Something about that smile bothered Trace.

"After Marain almost died giving birth to Balder like some sort of common muck-raking medieval peasant, I decided I would prevent my beloved wife from experiencing such pain ever again." Walliam's face crunched up into a snarl. "Obviously, after Balder, Marain gave birth another three times. As I had secretly undergone a vasectomy less than a month after Balder's birth, this came as quite a shock."

During a good five seconds of shocked silence, Trace felt two emotions fill Guppy's office: total and utter denial, followed closely by losing the will to live. Her entire family could do nothing but gape, slack-jawed and glassy eyed. More than a few of them looked as though they were willing themselves to wake up from a nightmare, from a terrible dream that they'd laugh at once they returned to reality.

The only one still smiling was Balder. He was still wearing that exact same smug grin as before. Trace could tell that this earth-shattering news was no surprise to him. But how?

"So, it's nice to finally rid myself of that burden," Walliam sighed, relaxing as though he'd removed a thorn from his buttock after sixty long years. "While Marain was obviously a lusty tramp of the highest order, I could never bring myself to slam the hammer down while she was still alive. However, seeing as though only one person in this room is my blood, and the rest of you are the aforementioned uninvited maggots, everybody except for Balder and Balder alone are hereby excised from the Cuddle fortune. Your stocks and shares are void, your properties are to be absorbed back into the company, and you each have precisely six hours to leave Reborn Detroit forever. Besides my one and only son, none of you are Cuddles in any way, shape or form." Patting his breast pocket, Walliam discovered a cigar. Looking pleased with this development, he placed the long stogey in his mouth and drew at it until its suck-burner ignited. "I advise you all to get packing. Time is of the essence."

Trace was the only one to do something. While her entire world was spinning, she somehow got to her feet and gripped the table for support.

"Pop. You can't mean all this? You can't be serious."

Walliam shrugged at this flimsy denial.

"Tracetta, I've lived with this pain for sixty years. Every time I've looked at Marain's bastards and their bastards I've had to endure the knowledge that she was never truly mine. I have no forgiveness for any of you, as you are her

174

infidelity made flesh. And my pain will finally cease today...literally, as well as figuratively."

"Kill switch in twenty-five seconds," the technician announced, speaking for the first time.

"So you never cared for me?" Trace pressed, her whole family looking back and forth between her and Walliam. None of Marain's illegitimate offspring or other grandchildren seemed to be capable of anything right now. "You pulverised Hilton-Disney with a Flog putter for no reason, for somebody you despise?"

A look of uncertainty crept onto Walliam's face, as though he was looking at two diametrically opposing facts. His left eye flickered, his brain possibly seizing up a little.

"Wait," Pop said, his expression changing. He shook his head as though fighting free of something. "I'm...there's..."

"Kill switch in fifteen seconds," the tech said, his finger ready to swipe the haptic board.

"Hit that kill switch and I'll hit yours," Trace growled, her patience gone.

As much as he obviously didn't want to, the necromantic lawyer was professionally obligated to intervene. He raised his hands placatingly.

"Miss Tracetta, anything said beyond the three minute reanimation limit is legally inadmissible. There's nothing to be gained from putting him through such an..."

Trace pointed at the technician in threat. Obviously out of his depth, the tech glanced back and forth between the lawyer and Trace, torn. Once the cut-off was only five seconds away, it was clear that the tech wasn't moving another inch until Trace told him to do so.

"Tell us. What?" Trace begged of her Pop.

"This is obscene!" Uncle Balder roared. "Switch him off! Now!"

"I...I..." Pop managed. "My brain...my memories...not right...wrong...fake..."

His left eye began to twitch back and forth independently of his right. A trickle of thick, blackly coagulated blood began to run out of his left nostril. It was like he was having another stroke, or perhaps the stroke that had killed him on the Flog course yesterday was finally catching up. Managing to focus his right eye on Balder for three long seconds, his jaw jackhammering up and down, Pop gasped at his cigar repeatedly until he managed to say two final words.

"Lie. Liar."

Foaming at the mouth, his whole body going into spasms, Walliam's cigar fell out of his twitching lips and exploded into embers on the mahogany desk. Knowing that he'd done the wrong thing by allowing this undignified travesty of justice to continue, the technician finally swiped the kill switch on his haptic board. Walliam slumped, a torrent of thickened black gushing from his nostils, mouth and ears.

Balder had already called security to escort all the excised former-Cuddles from the Manor. As Trace was physically dragged kicking and punching from Guppy's plush office, all she could do was keep screaming the same two words at Walliam's motionless corpse over and over.

"What lie?" she demanded of the carcass. "What lie?"

*

As promised, Trace and her relatives were driven from Reborn Detroit the moment their six hour grace period ended. While most of them were crying and wailing and even physically resisting in one or two cases, what used to be the Cuddle clan was soon scattered to the wind. As the Cuddles had only tolerated one other because the money kept them in line, no longer having any financial obligation to keep things civil meant they could all finally tell each other to punch it. This was the most silver of linings.

Some Cuddles crossed into Indiana, others chose Ohio, and a few even went to Wisconsin (probably because they didn't know about the zombies). Trace's dad and sisters made a water crossing into Illinois, but within a day her dad had already reached his limit and fled to Minnesota, alone.

Although all of Trace's relatives were desperately hoping for some sort of miracle to drop out of the sky and return everything they'd lost, Uncle Balder sealed their fate by not only broadcasting Walliam's necromantic will reading across every screen in Reborn Detroit, but over the entire planet in a day-long loop. Conveniently, the recording cut off just a few seconds before Pop had planted the seed of doubt in Trace's mind. As every word that a reanimated corpse said beyond the strictly-allocated three-minute reanimation period was legally inadmissible due to the exponential amount of neural degeneration taking place, Uncle Balder was well within his rights to not show his Father fitting and bleeding and foaming for the sake of his dignity. Without this telling whiff of deception, every citizen of Reborn Detroit instantly believed the revelation of Nan Marain's infidelity as gospel, and no lawyer would dare take on Uncle Balder now. No matter how you wanted to look at it, this was an absolute coup.

Unlike the others, Trace decided to hell with Amerika and fled into Canada on the next mag-lev refugee train. The mag-levs were about a century-and-a-half past condemned, mostly held together by rust, duct tape and half-assed welding, and were smelly and loud and ugly. They often broke down for no apparent reason, and it wasn't unheard of for their stranded occupants to freeze to death if the heat

176

clapped out. The one and only benefit of the mag-levs was that they were free, and as all of Trace's SpendPlus cards had been cancelled and the cash and jewellery she had on her person was frustratingly minimal, this made the mag-levs her only option.

Trace had decided on a destination where she would begin her new life: Asgard Resort. Once known as the Hudson Bay Lowlands of northern Ontario, a snow-capped churn of frozen bogs, fens and tundra and one of the largest wetlands in the world, the Lowlands had been transformed into a tropical paradise by a Canadian-developed weather-control weapon that had gone very, very wrong. The ancient deciduous forests of birch and willow had been blasted away in this mishap, leaving behind an expanse of verdant farmland that proved ideal for growing vast quantities of ridiculously valuable fruit like Densuke watermelons and Egg-of-the-Sun mangoes, and this tropical paradise had been rechristened Asgard by the tourism board. While the luxury fruits of Asgard were shipped to many worlds across The Unison and made mega bank on them, the most heavenly region of this tropical wonderland was Asgard Resort. Only open to the extremely disgustingly revoltingly rich and influential, Trace had vacationed there on a few occasions with her constantly-bickering parents and snot-nosed sisters. A million square kilometres of delights, larger than France and Spain combined, Asgard Resort offered a holiday experience like no other.

Her next three weeks were a blur of alcoholic amnesia, the urine-and-cheesy-feet smell of cheap boarding houses, and the humming electrical crackle of mag-lev trains. While her aunties and uncles and cousins and sisters might spend the rest of their lives trying desperately to be Cuddles again, Trace was far more realistic. She knew she'd never regain a single Amerikan pound of the Cuddle fortune. The limitless power of her former name had proven to be the downfall of her entire family line.

After running a gauntlet of broken-down trains and incomprehensible rail timetables, Trace managed to stay sober just long enough to realise how stupid her plan was. Here she was, a penniless outcast, heading towards one of the most exclusive places in the Known Galaxy. An incubus would have a better chance of strolling into heaven. What had she been thinking? Had the shock of being disowned robbed her of her senses, too?

Trace wandered aimlessly in a dogs-hind-leg kind of way from town to town and farm to farm, picking winter fruits for pennies and getting her hands dirty with all kinds of unskilled manual labour like so many other disenfranchised Amerikan expatriates. She managed to keep her belly full of protein sump porridge and whatever rotgut was cheapest and usually slept indoors, but that was about as plush as her life got now. Somehow she ended up in a nameless bar in a tiny, isolated place in Yukon called New Old Crow, and stuck around for a little longer than usual. Trace didn't have any logical reason for staying: she just did it, which summed up the reasoning behind all of her decisions since the exile.

The locals hadn't liked it when she didn't drift on like the other itinerants, and when some smart-arse loggers had gently suggested she should find somewhere else to slum by pouring a stein of beer-soaked cigarette butts over her head, she hadn't hesitated to show that she knew how to use her fists (and elbows and knees and forehead and glass ashtrays and wooden chairs and snooker cues). Eventually, after a decided spike in Emergency admissions, even the toughest locals learned to leave Trace alone. Thanks to her complete and utter lack of patience for idiots, she soon became a sort of unofficial bouncer for the bar, and her thirst was kept well lubricated in return. As long as nobody looked at her the wrong way or did any of a dozen different things that would set her off, Trace was relatively well-behaved. She just wanted to drink away the real world and fall asleep upright on her barstool, blankets wrapped so tight that she couldn't possibly topple over.

After many blackouts, Trace woke up to realise she was in the middle of a fight. A hulking Enforcer – a glorified security guard The Unison employed when marines were overkill and police officers were too professional and moralistic – was standing before her in full riot armour. Breathing heavily, a beer glass in one hand and the thick end of a snapped pool cue in the other, Trace's brain started working just well enough to register that she wasn't actually being attacked. In fact, the Enforcer seemed to be doing his best to get her to calm down and talk, which wasn't like his kind at all. Confused, when Trace finally mustered the trust to lower her weapons, the Enforcer stepped forwards, his palms extended in the classic language of peace.

"I'm sorry I startled you," the Enforcer said gently. Trace noticed he had seven golden stripes on his shoulder guards. She wasn't familiar with Enforcer ranks, but she'd never seen so many on one person. "I'm Argum, and you're not in any trouble. I just want to have a conversation. You and me. It could be very...rewarding for you." Argum drew his hands apart. "No obligations, you understand?"

Trace's eyes darted back and forth, making sure nobody was going to cold-cock her from behind. Eventually, she said her first words in days in a voice like wet gravel.

"Talking's not my thing."

Argum smiled.

"It's not always my first choice either, Tracetta." Unlike someone with more than a teaspoon of common sense, Argum seemed pleased when Trace's eyes narrowed dangerously. She hadn't heard another human say her name since she'd crossed into Ontario on the refugee train. "You are Tracetta Victoria Cuddle, correct?"

"Not anymore. What do you want?" Trace ground out.

"Like I said: just to talk. Ten minutes, tops."

*

After another mini-blackout, the next thing Trace knew she was sitting in a small, rustic hut made out of river stones and thick wooden beams. She immediately noticed that the walls and roof were covered in the crossed wires of a Faraday cage, which was doubtlessly blocking all forms of electronic communication. An open fire was warming her from the right, and her hands were hot from holding a ceramic mug full of something brown. Sipping at the liquid, she was pleased to taste some high-quality hot chocolate. She was a little disappointed at the lack of butterscotch brandy in it.

"Did you hear me?"

Trace looked up with a start. The same high-ranking Enforcer as before – Argum, he'd said his name was - was sitting opposite her. He was giving her a look that was at the midway point between pity, frustration, distrust and impatience. She jerked her head back and forth.

"Spaced on you," she drawled. Trace crunched her eyes closed, trying to concentrate. "Again?"

The Enforcer pinched the bridge of his nose and tried for a fourth time.

"I really need you to focus for a minute, Tracetta."

She flinched at the name. It brought up hurt and anger every time she heard it, and that wasn't healthy for anybody nearby.

"Just Trace," she growled.

The Enforcer nodded.

"So I hear." Argum examined her face for a few seconds until he was satisfied she wasn't drifting off again. He sucked something meaty out of his teeth before continuing. "I saw the vid of Walliam's necromantic will. I'm sure everyone on the planet saw it. But what your Grandfather said...do you believe it?"

Trace barked a laugh. "Don't matter now, does it? Balder has all the cards. Got no way to prove otherwise. And even if I did have concrete evidence, he's too powerful. Put a million Amerikan pounds in my pocket and I still got no chance." Trace gulped at her hot chocolate, ready to head back to her barstool. "I find

179

whiskey gets me through the day better than delusion."

Argum leaned forwards as Trace went to stand, lowering his voice.

"What if you had more than a million?"

Trace's face curled into a hateful, violent scowl. The last person who saw that expression was due to get his stitches removed any day now.

"Nothing I can do is worth even a fraction of that."

Argum showed his palms again. It was starting to annoy her.

"What if I told you that wasn't the case?"

Trace downed the last of her hot chocolate and smacked it on the coffee table separating her and Argum. She was done.

"My barstool's getting cold."

Trace was getting to her feet just as Argum used a stick to carefully slide something out from beneath the coffee table. It was a black slab the size of a briefcase. Even blitzed out of her mind, Trace recognised an ultra-max dead-crate when she saw one. She didn't have to touch the dead-crate's dark surface to know it was made from reinforced Densite, the hardest artificial element ever fabricated by mankind. You could cut at Densite with a monomolecular blade or blast at it with the best weaponry on the market, and you wouldn't even manage to tickle it. She'd once heard that Densite only got tougher from being attacked, and was graded to survive a supernova. But while a dead-crate was guaranteed to protect its contents better than any safe or vault on the market, you'd be hard pressed to find something to fit inside of it that was worth more than the container itself. Whatever was in there would be beyond priceless by default.

Then she saw it: the Cuddle crest embossed in white Densite. Trace flicked her eyes back at Argum. She was suddenly very, very sober.

"Where'd you get that?" she asked automatically.

"One of your Uncle's vaults," Argum said without hesitation. "It contains a very, very valuable antique, a one-of-a-kind Holt & Heckler in its original packaging. I already have a buyer set up."

"So why tell me about it? No criminal in The Unison could break into that." Trace chuckled darkly. "That box is worthless to you, and it's less than worthless to me. You might as well try to open God's own padlock on the gates of Hell. My guess is Balder is the only one with the right key, and he'd be on such high alert right now that your chances of a second run on his vault are less than zero, correct?"

"The key is right here in this room." Argum said directly. He gave a little shrug. "I think."

"Spug off," Trace snapped. "Try guessing a dead-crate's key and you'll trigger a lethal defence mechanism. There's a reason they aren't called happy-crates, you clot."

"I'm not guessing. I know exactly what the key is. Three men died finding out." Argum leaned forwards. "When I asked you if you believed you Grandfather's final words, I wasn't asking for the sake of gossip."

Trace hissed her breath out through her teeth.

"It's a genetic lock, isn't it?" She didn't give Argum a chance to speak before plunging on. "And the dead-crate will only accept a genetic match that was both willing and alive, for obvious security reasons. But if you just needed a Cuddle to open that thing, you'd find that my relatives aren't quite as...stabby as me. You'd have had a much smoother time with any one of them."

Argum shook his head. "Not an option."

"Why?"

"They're all dead, obviously. Didn't stand a chance of surviving in the real world. Got picked off quicker than a neon-pink toy poodle in the Amazon rainforest."

Trace's jaw went slack. It wasn't from grief.

"You're telling me my extended family couldn't stay alive for just two or three lousy months?"

Argum frowned. "Two or three months? Trace, you've been a penniless vagrant for more than six years." At the look of shock on Trace's face, Argum waved this irrelevant topic away. He wasn't here to perform a memorial service. "But opening the dead-crate is only half the job. Once you have the Holt & Heckler in your possession, you will be required to deliver it to the buyer. The Holt & Heckler will not identify the buyer as its new owner without your Cuddle genetics permitting it to do so. For this service, you will receive one-third of the sale price: twenty-seven million German yen." Argum swiped at his armoured forearm bracer, and a series of holographic photos and word processor documents appeared in mid-air. "The buyer will be attending the maiden manned flight of the Carpe Astrum starship in person in exactly twelve weeks. And before you ask, I'll use my authority to approve you as a fully-ranked Enforcer, allowing easy access. Here's the client's details."

Trace's face screwed up in fury at the floating image of Poxius Hilton-Disney, the CEO of Happy Planet, the man who had demanded she be mentally stripped down to a blank slate and rebooted to factory settings, the man who Walliam had beaten into unconsciousness with a Flog putter. Besides her Uncle Balder, Poxius was the man she most wanted to tap-dance all the way into a coma.

Trace said her next words through clenched, chipped teeth.

"I know him. And I'm sure we'll have plenty to talk about."

CHAPTER FIFTEEN THE ARCHIVE

Although they fell asleep in the warmth of a moss-carpeted Screwback nest, they woke up half-buried in snow. Digging themselves free and peeking over the edge of the crater, it turned out that the snowfall was entirely restricted to this one dent in the rocks.

"Where did all this come from?" Jimmy asked, rubbing frost from his shoulder hair.

Half Head tilted its skull, thought about the question for a moment, and pointed up at the clouds with an articulated limb.

"Thanks heaps," Jimmy sulked. "If being an obsolete half-psychotic killbot doesn't work out for you, you should be a weatherman."

Jimmy copped a snowball on the side of his head. He was in shock, but only for a second. Despite the grimness of their situation, within moments the entire group were throwing handfuls of snow at each other. For a short minute, they forgot that they were stranded and without hope.

Needing to slake his thirst, Tuesday opened his mouth and angled his tongue towards the sky. Just as a single snowflake landed on his lip, however, there was a sudden deluge of hailstones the size of ping pong balls. Tuesday cussed violently when he got one square in the eye. The icy missiles descended with such force that they exploded on impact, spraying slithers of frozen water in all directions like shrapnel, and the survivors did their best to pack up and get out of the crater before they were too badly bruised. Thankfully, it seemed the snow and hail only fell in the Screwback nest, leaving the surrounding rocks as dry as an expired stick of beef jerky.

"Even the weather is trying to kill us now," Tuesday muttered, holding the growing, purpling lumps on his face.

*

After half an hour of marching, it turned out that bare rock wasn't the worst this wasteland had to offer. A salt plain, a true desert made of thick flows of pure sodium churned through dead, white sand, greeted them with flying, stinging grains. When it came to survivable environments on Earth like planets, a salt plain in the stark light of day is about as horrible as it gets. To make matters worse, this region had been slammed with more mass driver scars than anywhere else they'd been. The glassed holes were the only thing in this Gehenna that were plentiful, and on the rare occasion something appeared ahead, it was always the glowing line of yet another crater.

The horizon remained infinite all day, its quivering vanishing point barely a dot.

Thankfully, now that Half Head had replaced one of its ruined batteries, this meant traveling at night was now an option. As every step in this boiling Hell was worse than the last, it was common sense to take advantage of this slight advantage. Sure, this meant losing hours and hours of time huddling in the beat-up escape pod with the air conditioning on high, but none of the survivors were Kalahari Bushmen. Supplies or not, wandering about a place so hot that the Australian Outback in deepest summer seemed refreshing just wasn't an option. The options were walk at night or die.

Night time in the salt had its own drawbacks. The black-shrouded wastes were as dark as a Vegan Extremist's soul, and the temperature consistently hovered beneath freezing. Despite being layered in survival ponchos and space blankets, the humans chattered and shook with every step.

Trudging up a hill of crumbling sodium behind the others, almost used to being whipped in the face with stinging salt by this point, Lana didn't immediately notice that her Omni implant was shaking her knuckles. After all, the rest of her was already shuddering so violently that her muscles were cramping. Teeth jackhammering together, Lana crunched the sodium from her eyes and finally looked down at the back of her left hand: there was a hologram of juddering static with the words PARTIAL SIGNAL DETECTED slashed through it in red.

Hey eyes snapped wide. It was like she'd been hit with a caffeine shot right in the neck.

Stopping for the first time in hours, Lana swooped her left hand through the air like a small child who played with an invisible plane because she had terrible parents who spent all their money on methamphetamine and had nothing left for toys. After a few seconds of trying to lock on, the words on her left hand turned the universal green of success.

SIGNAL DIRECTION CONFIRMED

Lana's squeal of excitement cut through the silence of the desert night like a chainsaw. The others finally noticed that the young Cadet was lagging a good twenty metres behind.

"What the hell's keeping you?" Tuesday grumbled.

Flicking and twisting the projection above her left hand with expert skill, Lana's eyes were moving even faster than her fingers.

"We just wandered within transmission range of something," Lana confirmed, not bothering to look at the others as she continued to spin and tap at the hologram, clearly rapt. "Far as I can tell, it's got a teeny-tiny power source, it's operational, and it's over that way. That's all I can tell without getting any closer." Her eyes flicked to a horizon full of possibilities, then back towards their current path. "It's a couple of klicks out of our way. But who knows what we might find?"

Everyone was too exhausted to do much more than give tired shrugs. They were walking themselves to death towards an unknown goal that might be nothing more than the alien equivalent of an empty Slurko Cola dispenser. Why not be miserable, cold and tired in a slightly different direction?

*

By the time dawn fondled the very edge of the sodium plains, the motley crew had finally struggled to the crest of a jagged cliff. Breathing so hard that they could all taste blood (a sensation which wasn't being eased by the salted air), their pain and exhaustion were forgotten for a moment at the sight of what dominated the horizon.

"What is that?" Jimmy whispered, sweat freezing on his face.

Directly ahead was a deep, deep chasm shaped like a cartoon lightning bolt zigzagging away into the mists of earliest morning. It was impossible to be sure how far this plunge stretched, but words like "epic" and "enormous" didn't begin to cover it. Unlike the glassed mass driver craters that pocked so much of this world, the slash was filled with countless inverted spires made from pure thoughtmetal, as though it had once been a city that plunged to the very roots of Scrote. However, some unimaginable force had smashed into this forest of upside-down thoughtmetal skyscrapers like the thumb of Ares, fracturing their clean surfaces into splinters and immolating them until they flowed like forgotten birthday candles.

Lana got close to the edge, waving her left hand towards the spikes.

"This isn't like the thoughtmetal we saw at those ruins," she clarified, squinting at her holographic screen. "It might look like it with the naked eye, but go down further and this sort have got a really, really complicated crystalline structure. Sort of like those fancy info-crystals they keep hyping up to be the next big thing in digital storage."

"The really expensive ones that don't work?" Jimmy clarified, still huffing and puffing.

Lana nodded. "Yes. But a lot less crap."

Jimmy tried and failed to catch his breath as he scanned his eyes across the endless field of crystals. "So these are, what...info-crystals? Storage devices?"

Lana nodded again, still reading.

"I'm pretty sure that's what they are. If so, they're a million times better than anything mankind has ever fabricated. My readings might be a little off, as this is unknown tech created by an unknown species, but I reckon you'd be able to store everything every human has ever written or said or thought into a crystal the size of one of your cigarettes, Tuesday."

Like a dog salivating at the ring of a bell, Tuesday automatically stuck a smoke into his mouth and dragged on it. The chlorine must have kick-started a part of his brain that was usually dormant, as for once he had something useful to contribute. "Can you read any of them?"

Lana panned her left hand back and forth. She looked frustrated.

"They're even more damaged than they look. Shattered down to the molecular level. One decent rock would probably crumble it all to dust. If they once held something, it's gone for good."

"I wonder what they stored, exactly?" Jimmy wondered.

Trace looked between the other three as though she was watching imbeciles twist corkscrews into their foreheads.

"You are aware we have a six-thousand-year-old alien robot who we can ask about this sort of thing, right?" Trace snapped, annoyed at the stupidity she had to tolerate.

As though on cue, everyone looked at Half Head. The machine was facing its red eye lenses into the depths of the chasm, and on first glance the robot seemed to be totally still. After a few seconds it became obvious that Half Head was very, very slowly scanning the shattered thoughtmetal crystals, as though looking for something.

Before anyone could ask Half Head a question, though, there was a sudden explosion of static and a screech of distortion. Lana's Omni implant was the first thing to go ballistic: a complex series of holographic symbols and images engulfed her left arm from shoulder to fingertips - the entire projection range of her Omni - until her limb couldn't be seen beneath the weight of alien script. Lana gritted her teeth as she felt the implant in her hand heat up beneath the strain of whatever it was receiving, but for some reason the KILL button didn't respond to her prodding.

Next, everyone's retinal screens glitched out in a cascade of colourful shapes. This was a much bigger concern than Lana's Omni woes, as suddenly being inundated by zettabytes of incomprehensible information directly into their eyes essentially left them blind. Jimmy's shriek of pain as his retinal screens heated three degrees above recommended limits was drowned out by the cacophony of Lana's Omni howling a noise that was a cross between a dial-up modem going haywire and a velociraptor giving birth.

And then it stopped.

Stunned by the sudden peace, able to see and hear again, the survivors didn't have a chance to get back to their feet before a hologram of some red, six-limbed unknown creature formed in the midst of their loose circle. At first glance it seemed to be mostly composed of elbows, but despite its genetics laying somewhere between a starfish and common asparagus, its long arms and multitude of fingers screamed "descended from an arboreal species" in capital letters. Like most aliens mankind had encountered, the creature was wearing some approximation of armoured clothing, likely military in nature, and its central mass possessed a triple-segmented beak containing three tongues that would probably allow it to communicate with spoken language. A trinity of eyes – one small, one medium, and one large – surrounded the beak, and its scarlet skin was traced with extensive, throbbing golden veins.

"Didn't one of those appear on the lifeboat's screens on the way down?" Jimmy managed.

Lana squinted, trying to remember the exact words.

"Yeah. It warned us that this system is under permanent quarantine, right?"

Against all odds, the alien spoke in fluent Unglish, but the sounds it made did not match the motions of its word-hole even slightly.

"I am the Prime of the species known as the Slidge, the leader of a great coalition of Twelve Hundred races who finally rose up to permanently displace The Apex from power," it stated in an impressive accent. Strings of white goo trickled out of its beak segments as it spoke, dangling obscenely. "While it cost trillions of lives and incinerated all of our worlds down to embers, in the space of but five hours our uprising succeeded, and we are no longer slaves, no longer pawns. Surgical strikes across this galaxy have ended The Apex and their countless years of trickery and sick games. As of this moment, after generations of secret plans and subterfuge, we have unequivocally won a war that lasted a fraction of a day."

The Prime's voice didn't sound triumphant, or mocking. A lot may have been lost in translation, but the creature almost sounded...depressed? Disappointed? It took a few seconds for its speech to continue.

"Like much of what has transpired in the last five hours, we have erected this digital memorial not to mark victory, but great loss. For the extermination of The Apex is not enough. No, we need to be total and utter in their destruction, to erase their very memory. Now, we will take from The Apex what they prize most, what means even more to them than their very existence: The Archive."

186

Jimmy scuttled backwards, tripping over his own feet, as the entire chasm of crystals changed shape, colour and height in a flash. Every smashed thoughtmetal pillar was whole again, shining a deep purple rose instead of a depressing grey. The Prime swept one of its triple-thumbed hands towards the field of immaculate shapes.

"The Archive was the greatest possession of The Apex, the culmination of two and a half million years of research, exploration, deep thought, bloody experiments, cruelty and sickness. It is undoubtedly the greatest repository of knowledge ever assembled anywhere in the Universe, and even the meaning of life itself pales in comparison to the secrets held deep within this greatest of libraries. Under Apex law, so much as looking in the direction of one of these crystals without authorisation would deserve the most horrifically drawn out of deaths, torments that have no end." The Prime shook its head in a diagonal motion that didn't explain a whole lot. Slidge body language didn't seem to translate as easily as speech. "The Archive was completed eons before my species ventured down from the trees. It contains the solutions to every mathematical formula, the histories of a billion different time streams, schematics for the most lethal of doomsday weapons, and if you plunge deep enough within its depths, even the future milestones of this galaxy are spelled out. The Archive is so valuable to The Apex that none of them have accessed it in living memory. It transcends importance. To call it sacred is an understatement."

The Prime slumped, as though in sadness. It motioned to someone off-camera who was not a part of the recording, and finished its speech.

"This recording is a message of sadness. While even the smallest child knows that The Archive possesses secrets that would make any of the Twelve Hundred species godlike, it has been unanimously decided by the representatives of every sentient race that the dangers posed by this knowledge are beyond measure, and so we have made a choice that will both keep the galaxy safe and punish The Apex far, far worse than the total extinction of their kind ever could." The Prime bowed its head. "This auto-translating message has been recorded so that our coalition may apologise for this most unforgivable of actions. If you do not hate us, then you do not understand the enormity of what we have done."

As though the cameraman had adjusted the width of the recording, the projection stretched to ten times its scope to allow a multitude of other creatures to enter the frame. They were miniscule and enormous, tentacled and clawed, colourful and shadow made flesh, skeletal and heavily muscled, furred and scaled, predator and prey. One thing they all had in common, though, was the obvious gleam of intelligence in their eyes, whether they saw with compound insectoid prisms, glazed bovine spheres, twitching reptilian slits or stony chips. Another similarity of note was that none of them looked like cut-price extras with a bunch of rubber prosthetics painted to their heads. None of the humans were pedantic enough to bother counting the swarm, but the chances were very high that all of the Twelve Hundred were represented in the assembly.

After taking a few silent seconds to compose itself, the Prime gave a curt hand motion. Without a single second of transition, the leader of the Slidge and all the other leaders vanished. Whatever horrible weapon had killed them in half a moment didn't leave behind so much as a wisp of steamed blood. The glowing purple crystals of The Archive had turned grey just as quickly, the information on them lost for all time.

It took a good fifteen seconds for everyone to realise that the recording had stopped. Lana's breathing was loud and irregular in the silence, and she was just as astonished as the others to discover that she was crying fat, salty tears. Then again, she had just witnessed a disaster that made the burning of The Great Library of Alexandria look like putting out a cigarette on a MacDeath coupon book.

*

By the time they came within physical reach of The Archive, it was time to take shelter from the deadly mid-morning sun. After resting for a few hours and checking with Half Head, it was clear that they needed to go around The Archive to get back on track, and for the first time in days they finally had a choice: go around it on the left, or go around it on the right. As you'd expect, everyone voted to go whichever way was quickest. Half Head took a few seconds to think.

"Going left would be the most efficient path. We should get there within three days."

Lana snuck a look at her Omni display and did a quick blood-toxicity reading without anyone noticing. Considering how long they'd been absorbing the poisons of this world through their skin, quite frankly she was surprised that nobody was vomiting up their own intestines yet. While the word "lethal" wasn't the first one to come to mind when describing Eucalyptus (the first was "koala", obviously), Lana estimated that they had maybe another day before things got...interesting.

Lana looked up from her display in time to witness the second innings of a conversation between Tuesday and Half Head.

"So it's going to be salt plains the rest of the way?" Tuesday asked.

"Yes," Half Head confirmed.

"All the way?"

"Yes."

"Really?" Tuesday pressed. "All of it?"

Half Head angled its red eye lenses at Tuesday. It paused for a few seconds before answering.

"Yes."

Tuesday ran a handful of salt through his fingers. "So it's three more days of this?"

"Yes."

"You're sure?"

One of Half Head's tentacles suddenly snapped out, constricted around Tuesday's neck and lifted him a metre off the ground. The robot brought a red and sputtering Tuesday a matter of inches away from its bisected skull.

"My apologies for the inconvenience, but it appears that being asked the exact same question too many times in a row has triggered a self-preservation response. I will endeavour to release you. Just a moment..."

Nobody seemed to mind for the first ten seconds or so, as they'd all wanted to do the same thing to Tuesday on numerous occasions. Eventually, though, Jimmy tapped Half Head on one of its hulking black shoulders.

"Uh, maybe you should put him down now. Turning purple is generally a bad sign."

"Is it?" Half Head asked innocently.

"He can't breathe!" Lana complained, slapping Half Head. She ended up with fifty flakes of orange-brown decay stuck into her hand like metallic Bindi-eyes for her trouble.

"And?"

"We need to breathe, or we die!" Lana snapped.

"Oh." Half Head dropped Tuesday to the ground in an untidy pile. "My apologies. Few intelligent races in my records have the need to breathe through facial orifices. However, you may be interested to know that I have recovered a file about an interesting species that needed to be kept alight with inflammable liquids, or else they froze to death in minutes. If I recall, they brought it on themselves with some unfortunately short-sighted attempts at genetic engineering..."

"You tried to kill me!" Tuesday accused from the ground.

"I believe I was merely illustrating my frustration."

"Yeah, on my neck," Tuesday muttered darkly.

"We'd better get going." Trace said gruffly, glaring at salt plains that seemed to stretch forever. "We've got a long way to go."

189

Nothing lived out here in the deepest salt, not so much as a lizard or a cactus. And no matter how many midnight steps they struggled through, the survivors never seemed any nearer to their goal.

The dead crystals of The Archive passed by on the right for most of the night until the chasm sealed up at its furthest point. However, it turned out that The Archive ended right on the edge of a mass driver crater that blocked that entire section of the horizon. In every other direction, there was nothing but salt.

Jimmy was so cold that it felt as though somebody had sucked out his blood, put it on ice, and added a slice of lemon before pumping the claret back into his veins. Even if it hadn't been sub-zero, though, he was still being attacked by the random spasms and terrifying hallucinations of Ultrasweet withdrawal. Just to top things off, the sole of his right thong had started making a squeaking noise that was sending him insane.

"I can't keep doing this," Jimmy sobbed a couple of hours before dawn, shivering and breathing thick clouds of mist. "Not for another three days. I can't do it."

Nobody disagreed with him. Like Jimmy, the others were clearly half-fried and half-frozen, exhausted after a marathon that even Olympic Deathsport champions wouldn't attempt. All that was keeping them going at this point was the knowledge that they had no other options. They could either continue to stagger on, or lay down and die.

Cresting another rise, the survivors staggered to a stop as they beheld what must have been the biggest glass-floored crater on all of Scrote. The mass driver scar dominated the horizon and plunged so deep that everyone was surprised it wasn't filled with lava. As it was still night time, at first glance the dent was made of pure darkness. On closer inspection, though, the glass was reflecting every star in the sky like a flawless mirror. The hemisphere was so wide that Lana had to use her Omni implant to measure its diameter. She gave a small, depressed sigh at the reading.

"Fifty kilometres across and twenty-five kilometres deep at its central point." She shook her head, eyes brimming with natural salt water. "Double the width of the Grand Canyon and ten times as deep."

"Could you imagine the sort of noise they made punching this into the ground?" Trace asked, a disturbing expression of wonder on her face.

Jimmy's belly chose this moment to rumble like a motorcycle unsuccessfully starting up. He glanced back and forth at the unamused looks.

"Got a problem with my grumbles? Then pass me some salted Screwback."

"So do we gots to go around it?" Tuesday asked with such horrifically defective grammar that it was physically painful on the ear.

Lana did some quick calculations. She didn't like the numbers one bit.

"Not an option. We don't have that long."

Trace raised a pieced eyebrow at Lana's wording.

"What's that meant to mean? We still have enough food and dehydrated water, right?"

Lana's expression took on a decidedly "busted" quality. Despite their exhaustion, Tuesday and Jimmy suddenly became very interested in what Lana had to say. She took a few seconds, choosing her words carefully.

"I didn't want to worry you all, but...the respiratory filters aren't enough to keep us toxin-free from the junk in this world's air. We've been taking on heavy doses of native poisons through our skin this whole time, and those levels are climbing faster and faster by the day. Short of wearing full pressure suits, which we don't have, there's no way to slow this absorption." Lana could tell that now was a good time to get everything out. After all, the expression on Trace's face didn't promise much in the way of patience. "I've kept some blood cleaning shots that might give us a couple of extra days, but once the toxins reach irreversible levels...look, long story short, there's no way for us to detour around that crater and still be alive by the time we get to where we want to go."

Everyone dealt with this news in their own way. Jimmy began to blubber, Tuesday stared blankly at the horizon as though he'd gone brain-dead, and Trace calmly approached a pillar of salty sand before screaming and kicking it into a cloud.

Finally free of her secret, Lana slowly lowered herself to the ground. She wrapped her arms around her knees and clenched her muscles as tightly as they could go. After half a minute of silence, Tuesday turned towards Half Head.

"You know how we went the short way by going on the left side of The Archive?" he asked. "How much shorter was this way, exactly? How many days did we save?"

"The long way would have been an additional nineteen metres," Half Head said calmly.

All four of them gaped at the robot, as though expecting it to add "wokka wokka" and do a silly dance to confirm this was just a joke. But the machine just sat there, immobile and silent. It took a few seconds to qualify the statement.

"This path is shorter, making it more efficient. That is what all of you specifically requested."

"Any idea what the 'longer' way was like?" Jimmy asked. "Was it a wasteland like this one?"

Half Head gave a slight shrug. "From what little scanning abilities I still retain, I'm certain the other path would have transformed into a dense tropical rainforest within a few hours. That region used to be an orchard that contained the most treasured of exotic fruits sourced from across this galaxy, and there would have been a real risk of being hit by giant, juicy, sweet berries falling from the trees."

Tuesday mumbled in agony, licking his tobacco-stained lips.

"And you'd also have to wade through a series of deep, cool rivers." Half Head continued, nodding with the crunch of dried mud breaking apart. "And..."

"Enough," Trace snapped. Her hands curved into claws from rage, but somehow she managed to muster the sense not to punch the pile of deranged junk right in its stupid semi-face.

Her arms still clutched tightly around her knees, Lana did her best not to cry. She was certain there was no way they could make it even halfway to their goal before standing up became impossible, let alone marching through the frigid night. In a couple of hours that immense horizon-eating crater would be a screaming hell pit of reflected sunlight, and...

Lana stopped cold. Focusing on the edge of the mass driver scar, a rim so sharp that it would cut through anything that touched it without a gram of resistance, her brain began to tick over. She looked at the thick slabs that made up her heavy-duty survival backpack, did some maths in her head, and slowly pushed herself upright again. It wasn't easy, as her legs felt like they were made from warm taffy. Lana managed to announce her thoughts, but her words were lost over the sound of Trace ranting and firing random shots into the night with her antique Heckler & Holt kinetic accelerator.

"What?" Tuesday asked, trying to be heard. "Got another life-or-death secret you want to share, kiddo? More terrible news sounds awesome right about now."

"I have an idea," Lana said a second time, more sure of herself.

*

It didn't take long for Lana to spell things out. After all, it wasn't the most complex of plans. Despite the simplicity of what she'd just suggested, nobody commented for a good eight seconds. Eventually, Trace blinked heavily and shared her thoughts in the most constructive way she could.

"Your plan sucks, and you are a total dickhead for coming up with it."

"I'd rather quit smoking cold-turkey by using an actual turkey," Tuesday agreed.

"I'm not doing that. Forget it."

Jimmy was the only one who didn't instantly resist Lana's idea, but fighting peer pressure wasn't one of his strong suites. He looked back and forth, torn between going with the majority like he always did, or being brave enough to take a longshot at survival. Finally, he made a hard decision.

"We don't have any other options. Unless someone has a better idea, I vote yes for Lana."

"An option that cuts you in half before frying you to ashes isn't an option. It's a suicide method." Trace snapped, her statement bordering on philosophical. "It's not a plan."

"So what do we do?" Lana challenged. "Feel free to share. You always do. Don't be shy now."

Trace calmly drew her Heckler & Holt. She kept its barrel pointed at the salt.

"We walk around, like we were going to do in the first place. If somebody falls and can't get up again, I'll euthanize them on the spot all nice and neat." She narrowed her eyes at Lana. "Course, if I'm the one that falls, I might need a little help ending things."

"We're not doing that," Lana said decisively. She licked her lips nervously. By this point it was like rubbing pieces of sandpaper together.

Trace shrugged. "Think I like the idea? It's not a matter of preference. It's a matter of mercy. That's just how it is."

Tuesday had been notably silent for most of this conversation. He was staring at the enormous mass driver crater again. As it was still a couple of hours until sunrise, the hemisphere was currently a black hole that swallowed the horizon. He sighed, as though already regretting what he was about to say.

"On second thoughts, I say we go with the kid's idea," Tuesday managed with great reluctance. "But she goes first, or I'm not doing it."

Lana tightened her expression.

"Deal. But first, we need to get a few preparations out of the way."

Trace twisted around so fast that it was a wonder she didn't break something. For what must have been the tenth time she summoned a baseball bat from her AllTool bracelet and scanned the salt plain for movement. As the desert was completely and utterly empty, Tuesday couldn't help but scoff.

"Seriously, there is nothing within two days of our position," Tuesday mocked. "There's no way you saw something. It's just getting silly now."

Trace narrowed her eyes into slits. "I saw something. It was a white sphere the size of my fist, just floating there. I seen it plenty of times. But it's always too quick for me to get a proper look. Always just outside of my peripheral vision."

The others tried not to look at Trace as though she had gone insane from the alternating gauntlets of heat, cold and the constant flaying of salt crystals. As she was still scanning around in acute paranoia, baseball bat raised for a flogging, this was quite an achievement. Pretending as though Trace wasn't wigging out, Lana repeated herself.

"Like I said, first we need to get a few preparations out of the way."

CHAPTER SEVENTEEN FRICTIONLESS SURFING FOR BEGINNERS

It only took twenty minutes to get everything ready. First, they jammed the panels of their disassembled lifeboat and what little supplies they had left deep into their heavy-duty survival backpacks, kicking and squeezing the contents until their shape and weight were roughly uniform all over. Next, they used black blades summoned from their AllTools to strip away the thick lining that protected the antigrav wafers sewn into the backpacks, exposing the gravity-nullifying strips to open air. Once the antigrav wafers were no longer muffled, they began to make an irritating humming noise.

Equipment-wise, that was about it. But this was definitely the easy part.

Hugging their backpacks to their bellies, all four of the survivors carefully stepped to within three paces of the colossal mass driver crater. Their eyes had adjusted to the total darkness by this point, and everyone could clearly see the stars reflected in the perfectly frictionless glass like little white laser beams. Looking down into the depths of the fused hemisphere, the twenty-five-kilometre-deep plunge seemed to be bigger than anything else the survivors had ever witnessed. Besides the mirrored stars, it was dark as a black hole.

Lana did some last-minute calculations on her Omni. The math checked out. A couple of swipes allowed what was being projected above her left hand to be broadcast to everyone's retinal screens, keeping them in the loop. Silently acknowledging there were roughly two million things that could go wrong with her plan, Lana did her best to focus on keeping everyone alive.

"Okay. Your retinals are linked up to my Omni. If you start to deviate from my path, very, very gently adjust your trajectory. Don't make any sudden jerks, or you'll go into a death roll. Your chances of surviving that are less than zero. Stay as flat as possible at all times. You want to be aerodynamic, and if you experience too much drag you might not make it to the other side. If you don't clear the far rim, the frictionless surface will make it impossible for you to get out. You'll spend the rest of your life doing sad little circles until the sun comes up and fries you to cinders." Lana took a deep breath. "Questions?"

"So the antigrav wafers in our backpacks are going to let us fly across?" Tuesday asked.

Lana shook her head. "Not exactly. Now that the antigrav wafers on our backpacks aren't muffled, they should be powerful enough to keep us hovering a few millimetres above the glass. This will help us reach the speed we need to clear the far edge."

"Can we go too fast?" Jimmy asked nervously.

"Ideally, we should get close to the speed of sound. If you start to black out, push yourself up a little bit to introduce some drag. But not too much."

Lana looked back and forth a few times, but nobody asked any more questions. While each of them could have spent all day agonising over every little element of what they were about to do, Lana knew it was probably best not to overthink it. The expressions on everyone's faces were far from encouraging already.

Lana took a deep breath before continuing.

"Okay. You all know the plan. I know this idea is totally mental, I do, but if this slide works it will get us to within a couple of kilometres of our goal. We might be a matter of hours away from help."

Just as they had done for days and days now, nobody voiced that they weren't even sure what was waiting for them at this semi-mythical goal. All they knew was that Half Head had detected something familiar. Continuing to uphold this long, colourful culture of I-don't-want-to-bloody-think-about-it, Lana wordlessly tightened the straps of her backpack so that the tough bag covered her entire front from chin to kneecaps. She nodded at Half Head.

"Okay. Me first. Once all four of us are on our way, it's your turn, right?"

Half Head nodded in understanding and wrapped its tentacles over Lana's shoulders and around her calves. Lifting her off the salted ground, Half Head floated to within centimetres of the very edge of the crater. Allowing Lana to take a deep, shaky breath, Half Head spun like a top at a high speed for three revolutions before letting Lana go, launching her through the air in a long arc.

Disoriented as she did a couple of pirouettes in the air, Lana felt total dread as she completely lost her bearings. Confused by the darkness in every direction, doing her best to keep her tough-as-iron backpack between her belly and the predawn glass, she unexpectedly hit the steep wall of the crater hard enough to punch the air out of her lungs. To make matters worse she also cracked her temple on something hard that audibly smashed under the head-butt. Dazed, seeing flashes that weren't really there and unable to inhale, Lana mentally cursed the near-empty jar of durian jam and vowed to burn down every farm that produced the vile muck.

Breathless, her eyes spinning in their sockets and head throbbing as she skidded at higher and higher speeds, Lana moaned as she tried and failed to suck in a lungful of air. After eight painful seconds she finally managed to feed her aching lungs with a deep gasp. However, with the killer combination of pitch blackness and the early onset of a concussion, Lana couldn't tell whether her frictionless boogie boarding was going well or not. Flicking her eyes towards her Omni display for confirmation, she saw some good news: she was facing roughly in the right direction, the antigrav wafers sewn into her backpack were keeping her almost four millimetres above the glass, and she was picking up speed. She had to lean slightly to the right to line herself up with the mysterious power source they'd been pursuing for their entire hellish march across the world of Scrote (damn Tuesday to Odin's deepest laundry hamper), so all up everything was going as well as could be expected. Lana's Omni picked this moment to announce that Jimmy had just been launched into the air by Half Head, and was heading her way. Even from hundreds of metres away, she could hear him screaming.

While Lana had predicted surfing this crater would be quite an experience, it quickly became the biggest rush of her life. Seeing nothing but the reflections of distant suns as they dashed past like a hyperspace screensaver, the pressure from Lana's increasing velocity started to squish her down more and more painfully by the second. But no matter how far Lana was pushed into the backpack, nothing stopped the incredible wind resistance from whipping her cheeks and lips about in comical rolls of skin. Within ten seconds her arms, legs and neck were crushed into the backpack with such force that she couldn't move.

Managing to angle her head just enough to look at the Omni reading on her left hand, feeling like all the vertebrae in her neck were a gram of pressure away from snapping, all Lana could do was watch the speedo tick up on the holographic display. Her vision was being crushed into blackness, her field of sight slowly being replaced by a throbbing red darkness lined with white slashes. She wasn't sure, but Lana wouldn't be surprised if this was because her eyeballs were about to explode. The hood of her survival poncho chose this moment to snap up, exposing her entire face to the wind.

And still she went faster.

Lana's descent into unconsciousness was staved off for a few more seconds when she was shot above the bridge of her nose by what felt like a high-powered BB gun. Startled awake, certain that the slug had punched all the way down to her skull, Lana's Omni display helpfully informed her that the impact had actually been a grain of salt, and the only reason it had been so painful was because of her speed. Getting hit in the forehead was actually a lucky break, because if the crystal had hit her in the eye she would surely have been permanently blinded.

Although it provided only the flimsiest of defences, Lana pressed her face into the backpack sled so that her rock-hard hair could deflect any future missiles. Her eyes may have been shut and buried safely, but Lana's Omni was able to relay everything she needed to know through her retinal screens, leaving no reason to expose her face to more impacts.

Lana's brain wasn't faring too well by the two-minute milestone of her insane head-first skeleton bobsled, and she was certain she was going to die from a series of major strokes before she came anywhere near the far rim. And to think she'd been worried about not going fast enough to clear the other side! She would have given some serious thought as to whether this development would be classed as ironic, but at the moment she was far too busy trying not to pass out.

Her conscious thoughts throbbing in and out from borderline coherence to the senseless patterns and shapes of a brain getting compressed by its own skull, the major events of Lana's life began to flash by. It was mostly snippets to begin with, unrelated images and sounds and sensations from her short history. Some of them produced strong feelings, but most of them were generic rubbish that meant nothing. One moment she was watching a clock tick to ten past nine, then she remembered how it felt to push a bag of recyclable cans into a crusher unit, followed by the smell of a new shuttle, then capped off by the emotional and physical pain she'd felt the first time one of her fellow Cadets had "accidentally" nudged her cafeteria tray out of her hands and onto the lino.

Lana's eyes flickered, rolling back in her head as the speed crushed her brain so hard that it was a miracle nothing popped. Finally, just before she passed into sweet, painless oblivion, her entire damned life decided to reel itself back to beyond the start and replay like an accidentally-clicked video link.

*

In the aftermath of The Scandinavian Expansion being driven from Amerikan soil in abject defeat in the early 22nd Century, it wasn't enough that The Expansion's armies were decimated and their homelands firebombed to gravel. No, the countless dead were crying out for justice, and the punishments would continue until every spilled drop of Amerikan blood was tallied and accounted for.

The endless crimes of The Expansion were so reviled by the rest of humanity – no matter what world they lived on - that the collective hatred of Olaf and Sven's atrocities had united all of those fledgling colony worlds into one empire: The Unison. Rather than being brought together by the desire to better their species, to stand together for a Utopian tomorrow, The Unison was founded on hatred, bitterness and a lust for vengeance. In short, it was business as usual.

Despite how much everyone hated the royal families who ruled The Expansion before its collapse, it just wasn't cricket to bump off the crown, no matter how detested. After all, no sensible government would want to promote the message that chopping off the head of any disliked leaders was a viable option, for obvious reasons. While the guillotines weren't getting wheeled out, that didn't mean the royals would get away with their unspeakable crimes.

After extensive deliberations and endless adjournments, on the ninth anniversary of Amerika's independence from Expansionist oppression it was decided that that the Six Monarchies that made up upper echelons of The Scandinavian Expansion would be exiled to Sirius, the Dog Star of Canis Major, for permanent imprisonment at a forced labour camp known as The Kennel. They'd be crammed onto the slowest boat mankind could find in the very rustiest junkyard, meaning their 8.6 light year trip would take at least two decades. Due to the effects of "sloth space" time dilation that came part-and-parcel with the substandard hyper drive installed on their prison barge, it would feel like ten times as long. Each blink would last a minute, a sneeze was an hour-long affair, and eating a meal took weeks. It was a recipe for insanity.

Stripped down to their lederhosen and clogs, every last family member of the Six Monarchies were booed and hissed and had Swedish horse-mince meatballs thrown at them all the way to the orbital elevator in Old Denmark. Despised by their own countrymen for permanently ruining the good name of a dozen different nations, everybody who lived within the borders of what had once been The Scandinavian Expansion couldn't wait to distance themselves from the atrocities of the last few decades. Launched into space aboard kinetic sleds and loaded into an archaic colony ship, a total of eighty-three people who used to be royalty were loaded into the starship like cattle. While all their nutritional needs for the journey would be met with protein recyc sumps and uric acid conversion tanks, the following decades would hardly be comfortable. The colony ship was renamed as The Stanken av Surstromming as one final insult and launched without fanfare.

As the former royals had literally billions of enemies, it had been a simple matter for a few briefcases of Amerikan pounds and German yen to change hands in order to motivate a few unfortunate wrench turns here and there. The main objective had been to do as much damage as possible to The Stanken av Surstromming while making it look like an accident, so while it would have been easy enough to set the reactors to go nuclear or to vent every last lungful of atmosphere, killing everyone on board, the name of the game was to make the trip a total misery. Unfortunately for the exiles, no fewer than fifteen different workers had been bribed to mess with the systems of the colony ship, leading to an endless cascade of malfunctions.

First, the nutrient paste produced by the protein sumps had been permanently locked to create an abomination that tasted like a cross between dog-milk feta and rotting potatoes with the texture and appearance of eyelids. Secondly, the urine-purification lines were adjusted to run directly through the heating system, making the whole starship reek of boiling wee. The fusion reactors were the third thing to glitch out due to sabotage, causing a couple of huge issues: the engines were so starved for power that it would take The Stanken av Surstromming at least three times as long to get to Sirius, and non-lethal radiation leaks were going to cause all kinds of unpredictable physical problems among the passengers. Worst of all, the colony ship's star map had been flipped about and randomised, guaranteeing that these doomed souls would float aimlessly through the void forever until getting sucked in by something big enough to crush their dusty, long-dead remains.

When the former royals complained over the Link about the inedible food and gag-inducing smells, nobody cared. Exchanging messages with The Stanken av Surstromming was a Class-Eight Felony, and only a handful of top tier-staff from The Unison had any knowledge of this cascade of issues. When The Stanken av Surstromming vanished from its course after only a matter of days, the news wasn't made public. Officially, the ship was still dawdling towards The Kennel. Unofficially, it wasn't.

Ninety-eight years went by.

Deep in the gulf between star systems, The Stanken av Surstromming – now known by the five-hundred-and-twelve people who lived aboard it simply as The Strom - drifted aimlessly. The Strom's skin was so badly pockmarked by dust scars and other minor collisions that it looked like a crumpled ball of cooking foil. Its fusion drives had packed it in years ago, and what little course-adjustment functionality remained had been saved just in case the crew needed to urgently steer away from a heavenly body at some point. As they were nowhere near any stars, however, there was nothing to dodge. Witnessing an interstellar gulf will bring new meaning to the word "empty" for anybody.

In a little under a century, four generations had been born, raised and died on this wreck. The only reason they'd survived this long was through religious maintenance of the protein sumps and uric acid converters, and it had become essential to feed all of their bodily waste and dead clan members into the reclamation vats. While these exiles had managed to avoid death from starvation and dehydration, their lives were darkened with constant borderline famine and the many physical infirmities that accompany the curse of hunger. To waste a single drop of recyclable moisture was both a blasphemy and obscenity, and usually meant getting pushed head-first and screaming into a reclamation vat.

Gradual exposure to the faulty fusion drives had produced some unusual genetic abnormalities among The Strom's offspring. For a while, the few babies who managed to reach full term didn't survive very long afterwards. Years would pass without a newborn's cry echoing through the ship. After decades of heartache, though, the rate of successful births steeply increased for no apparent reason, as though the exiles' bodies had finally adjusted to the ship wide soup of radiation. While most of these newborns were physically healthy, there were some statistical abnormalities in regards to how many non-binary, fully intersex children were being produced. Slowly, over the space of generations, more and more babies were born intersex until eventually every living soul was non-binary. Equipped with both kinds of genitalia as well as closely-packed wombs and testicles, unlike most people born intersex throughout history the ones aboard The Stanken av Surstromming were almost universally fertile once they hit puberty. It wasn't unheard of for a bonded couple to simultaneously make each other pregnant in a single physical union, and in order to make the pairing process even easier it was commonplace for sexually active crew members to undergo minor corrective surgery so that their male organs were located on the right and their girl parts were on the left.

By the time ninety-eight years crawled past, every original occupant of the ruined colony ship and their immediate descendants had long since died and been recycled. Nobody could remember a time when their people lived anywhere else but this drifting hulk, and soon nobody could recall when the fusion engines had last been heated up. Their lives were dedicated to keeping alive right now, and little more. The rest of the galaxy might as well not existed at all.

Dozens of light years from any star system, so deep into empty space that they hadn't come across a single iron rock for two generations, for the first time in ages the dusty scanners of The Stanken av Surstromming lit up in excitement. The near-comatose AI running the ship came out of its slumber just long enough to realise that it could detect an unusual object that didn't match any recorded files, and that

200

it was massive. While the object was only a couple of days away, The Strom wouldn't come close enough on its current trajectory for this to matter. Reacting like any ruined computer would, the AI decided to use what little juice was left in its fusion drives to swoop The Strom towards this mystery and into a permanent orbit. As the AI hadn't bothered consulting its passengers first, the huge burst of thrust sent every inhabitant into hours of terrified bloodletting rituals and screaming at the ceiling, convinced they were all going to die.

Twenty-two hours later, The Strom got close enough to the weird object to lock itself into a safe orbit. On closer inspection, while the stellar body was almost the size of Earth, it had one major difference: it was a perfect cube. A few basic scans confirmed that it was composed entirely of ice, and was so pure that any human could drink it without needing to filter it first.

The AI of The Strom did its best to figure out why this thing was drifting about between star systems, and after a matter of hours of scanning and deep thought the AI eventually discovered that this cube had started off as the cooling system for a mega-hot alien computer. The computer itself had failed and gone supernova tens of thousands of years ago, sending its cooling systems into a wild surge of overcompensation that had resulted in the biggest ice cube in the galaxy.

While the communication systems of The Strom hadn't worked for decades, like every operational starship there was a big, red button in the cockpit with the word CLAIM DISCOVERY stamped on it. After encouraging a passenger to hit the button, The Strom sent out a long-range pulse that notified every Link-enabled device within fifty lightyears that they had discovered something important and were officially claiming ownership under Unison law. Within a day an entire fleet of Unison dreadnoughts had turned up to try and figure out what in the name of Odin's detachable prostate gland was going on.

After extensive deliberations, two things were decided: as the occupants of The Strom were now generations away from the Six Monarchies who had been launched into the sky and forgotten, punishing them for their ancestor's crimes was abhorrent on every level, and it would be illegal and immoral under Unison law to continue classifying them as exiles. The second, much more controversial finding was that because the passengers of The Strom had discovered this giant ice cube without any outside assistance that meant they now legally owned it (but would still be expected to pay major taxes to The Unison on whatever profit they made from mining it). If they had found a new planet or a moon within a star system, however, then Unison law was far less generous, and the inhabitants of The Strom would have only been paid a finder's fee. Luckily for The Strom, stellar object like asteroids or comets fell into an entirely different category, and with the value of potable water being literally greater than gold in many places across The Unison, that meant they had accidentally become some of the richest people in the Known Universe.

Within fifty years of its discovery The Cube had barely lost one percent of its mass despite being drilled and chewed by hundreds of major excavations day and night. After writing up some of the most lucrative of mining contracts in all of recorded history and investing billions of Amerikan pounds in infrastructure, The Cube was now spotted with ice drills the size of cities, and each of these titanic screws were tipped with luxurious palaces housing hundreds of citizens known officially as The Strom. They were universally intersex, and it had been so long since a monogendered child had been born that they actually found the prospect sickening. Within the culture of The Strom, the monogendered were only half-persons, incomplete, suffering a gross lack of wholeness. The Strom may have tolerated doing business deals with monogenders remotely, but to come within physical proximity of one of them was seen as an indecency. As a result, the drill-tip cities were closed to monogenders, even over video. It was audio or nothing, and even then The Strom would wash their ears thoroughly afterwards.

Centuries after founding their little empire in the darkness between star systems, all of the drill-tip cities of The Strom were palaces of luxury and comfort. While the Scandinavian-descent intersex occupants had grown fat from mining contracts, they had also grown more insular. Now, they didn't even deign to interact with monogenders over audio link, and allowed AI employees to do all the dirty work. The word "monogender" had become taboo among The Strom by the 25th Century, and they preferred to pretend that such creatures were only an urban legend. Nobody had even seen a monogender in at least sixty years.

Then one day, a baby was born. This wasn't unusual or difficult, as The Strom were highly fertile and so physically adept at giving birth that having children was an entirely positive process. The entire Strom race had undergone extensive genetic engineering of the female half of their genitals some time ago to make the harrowing process of giving birth a breeze that could be completed over a coffee hypo or two. There wasn't so much a period of "labour" as there was a conscious decision to expel the baby into a warm gel bath. No doctor or midwife was required, and it was custom for only the birth parents to be present.

As this was the first time these bonded partners had given birth, it took a few seconds for them to notice that the bawling baby floating in warm gel was...different. Denial had kicked in almost straight away, but it only took moments for the two Strom to reach breaking point. Trying (and failing) to keep calm, the new parents got out an entirely unnecessary medical scanner to run over their newborn. Being sure to keep the scanner offline just in case it tripped some sort of alarm that would send a team of intersex Enforcers running, the truth was a single word in a pink holographic bubble.

FEMALE.

There were accusations, of course, but as the mere thought of looking at a monogender - let alone coupling with one - was so vile, this was disregarded straight away. There was another theory within seconds: was this really their child? Had one of their business rivals somehow impregnated them with monogendered seed in order to ruin them professionally, socially and legally? A second swipe with the scanner confirmed that this horrible deformity was definitely a product of both parents, and there hadn't been any external involvement at any point in the reproductive process.

There were a series of emotions over the next ten minutes: shame, disgust, confusion, horror, and sweet, sweet denial were some of the most popular ones. But once the initial panic set in, the parents switched to a more practical conversation: what were they going to do? They couldn't keep this...this thing. The exact penalties weren't clear, as this had never happened before, not once since the colonisation of The Cube. Neither parent wanted to find out what the other Strom would do when they found out. Sure, a nappy might hide the truth for a time, as it's not like the average person on the street went around counting the genitals of small children (that sort of thing was still frowned upon anywhere), but that was only a short term solution. And while the appearance of most of the Strom leaned closer towards feminine than masculine, especially as all of them had breasts of some description, a secret like this would only get worse the longer it was hidden. It might take a decade or two, but sooner or later...

The baby needed to go. It couldn't stay. Simple as that.

The parents wasted no time. They immediately scheduled an inter-system delivery of one (1) living mammal, seven pounds three ounces, to a world they selected at random. Taking a quick look at where they were sending her, an information box popped up to mention that abandoned newborns on that world were automatically admitted to one of several wings of law enforcement or the military, depending on their scores. The Strom parents were sure to pay double the normal shipping rate to keep things confidential – a tiny sum compared to what such a revelation would do to their reputation – and decided to literally and figuratively wash their hands of the whole thing. It was better this way for everybody.

While the parent who had fathered the child decided to get so drunk that the memory of this entire day was wiped away, the other parent felt a tug in the chest that was half physical and half emotional. The birther couldn't even look at the baby as it fed on a floating bottle, but this drama was entirely a cultural issue, so the birther's biological drive to cuddle and feed this little creature was hard to fight. Sighing in defeat half an hour later, making sure the parent who did the fathering was pretty much unconscious, the birther wrote a simple letter in cursive Swedish and tucked it beneath the baby's nappy. It read:

Where you were born, you would never be anything but subhuman. Where we have sent you, you have a chance to be equal, to be more. This is our one and only gift to you.

The birther carefully placed the monogendered baby in a padded stasis module built to transport small dogs, and slid the shell shut. Tapping a button froze the newborn in time, and her bawling face instantly went still and silent, frozen in a cry. Pausing to read the content details they'd assigned to the package, the birther finally typed in a few extra words.

Contents: one (1) living mammal, seven pounds three ounces. Name of contents: Lana.

*

Regaining consciousness at half the speed of sound was not pleasant for Lana. Startling, barely maintaining enough self-control not to twist the backpack sled into a death wobble, she somehow managed to keep enough composure to stick to the plan. Unfortunately, as the entire glassed crater was pitch black save for the reflection of unfamiliar constellations, Lana had no idea if she had wildly skewed in the wrong direction while she was passed out.

Keeping her eyes closed and her head down, Lana used her retinal screens to consult the compass built into her Omni. She breathed a sigh of relief to see she was still mostly on track. Realigning with her designated target only required a slight adjustment.

Glancing at her speed reading, Lana did a double-take when she noticed her velocity was gradually dropping. But that made no sense: she was sliding on a frictionless surface with no drag. How could she possibly be slowing down?

Checking her chronometer, it turned out her little swoon had gone on for almost four minutes. It was a miracle she hadn't fallen off or crashed. She was even more surprised to learn she'd already hit the nadir of the crater while passed out, speeding all the way down to the twenty-five kilometre depths of the glass hole before starting to ascend towards the distant rim. Well, that explained why she had suddenly woken up: with the reduction in speed, Lana's brain was no longer getting crushed by the pressure of her own skull.

Daring to sneak a look despite the very real threat of flying grains of high-speed salt gouging out her eyes, Lana's heart did a flip when she clearly saw the rim of the crater approaching. Its monomolecular edge glimmered with the reflection of stars, glinting dangerously.

Another Omni alert caused Lana's breath to catch in her throat: at her current velocity, she was only fifteen seconds away from exiting the crater. And while she was losing speed by the second, she would still exit the mass driver scar going fast enough to outpace the most impressive of 21th Century sports cars.

Cringing as the rim came closer and closer, Lana gurned an embarrassing facial expression as she pulled back on the straps of her backpack with all her strength. Easily clearing the beyond-sharp edge, Lana didn't have time to celebrate before her speeding makeshift sled twisted into a full barrel roll in mid-air. Descending into the predawn darkness, unable to see anything in the sunless gloom, Lana didn't get a chance to find out where the ground was before she hit it hard enough to send her brain into shock. While her backpack thankfully took the brunt of the impact, Lana vaguely registered that quite a few things in her abdomen had just gone pop, and that she'd definitely be hearing all the details later on.

Ploughing through the darkness of what might have been a forest, snapping off the blue branches of screw-trees and demolishing cyan shrubs like she was a jungle crusher, the straps of Lana's backpack finally broke, sending her soaring. Tumbling, the world spinning, Lana did four complete cartwheels through the weeds before skidding to a halt in some deep, muddy clay. Her eyes wheeling around in their sockets like her head was a slot machine, Lana's quadruple vision focused on her right arm, which was bent in front of her face. If Lana had still been capable of rational thought, she may have been horrified to see that her forearm and wrist were obviously snapped in half a dozen places, and that her fingers were pointing in all sorts of non-standard directions.

As she sank back into familiar unconsciousness, a couple of seconds before the blackness took her Lana could have sworn she had begun to float out of the clay.

CHAPTER EIGHTEEN THE APEX

Lana half-dreamed of gliding, of floating weightlessly. Her mind was far, far away from the agony of what remained of her body, the smashed, useless, crumpled ruins that would undoubtedly never awaken. She was too traumatised to form any useful thoughts, but after what felt like hours of mental static there was a new sensation: a clicking, crunching, raw feeling, like somebody nearby was having their skeleton realigned. She could hear every single bone as it was snapped back into place and joined together. This was followed by the ripping of torn flesh and squelching of popped organs being returned to their default settings.

These sounds (feelings?) went on for some time. And while it would be an exaggeration to say that Lana consciously knew what was happening, deep down she could not understand why she was still alive. The terrible crash kept replaying in her mind over and over, the handful of seconds that followed her cresting the edge of the mass driver crater burned into her synapses. Finally, after an eternity in limbo, something gently touched her mind and woke her up.

Lana's brain was suddenly working at peak efficiency. The last few days of marching and hardship spiralled though her mind, followed by the crash that had ruined her body flashing by in screaming images. Scampering backwards on her palms and feet, her eyes wide in panic, it took Lana a few seconds to realise she was alive and intact. Raising her right arm, Lana was stunned to see to see that it wasn't broken in twenty places like the last time she'd seen it. Her skin may be scarred and twisted in some new ways, but as far as she could tell the bones and tendons and ligaments and muscles seemed to be moving around just fine. She painlessly flexed her hand a few times just to be sure, and shook her head in surprise. Hadn't she smashed that arm into pulp when she stacked it?

Startling at a distant birdcall, Lana thrashed her head back and forth, trying to figure out where she was. As her eyes slowly adjusted to the gloom she could see that she was within what appeared to be a large, circular clearing, though it was too dark to make out any details. The glimmer of dawn was illuminating the tops of a thick forest of cyan-coloured corkscrew trees at the edge of the clearing, but little else.

A looming shape slid out of the darkest shadows, the upper edge of its hulking frame just barely defined by the rising sun. Lana didn't have time to get out a tape measure, but as the shape was around three-and-a-half metres tall Lana's brain automatically assumed that it must be Half Head. However, a glance at the peak of the shadow proved her initial assessment wrong, as there were clearly two sets of fifteen lenses rather than just the one, meaning that this creature wasn't missing half of its skull. The two sets of lenses mirrored each other perfectly, and their glasslike orbs glowed with a creamy pearlescent light.

Gliding closer to Lana, the shape had a lot in common with the ruined derelict they'd been following all this time: its twenty chainlike tentacles all met up at the base of a torso that resembled the breastplate of an ancient Spartan warrior, linked into the individual sockets that served as its groin. Its articulated limbs and core mass were half-wrapped in a cape made from a flowing substance visually similar to polyester. Despite its flimsy appearance, Lana knew the cape was tough enough to shrug off any weapon known to mankind. Like Half Head, the construct was modular, as though its pieces could be easily clicked and unclicked whenever they needed to be replaced. Unlike the dented, charred mess known as Half Head, though, this armoured amplification suit was a deep, shining royal blue decorated with white-gold ornamentation. Lit from behind, the suit possessed a kind of inherent grandeur, a dignity and beauty that could never been managed by a mere Operating System in a vacant shell. Light fell on the upper extent of its skull, where a complex knot of antlers, horns and tusks symmetrically curved towards the sky, all coloured a bony beige. Beneath the organic-looking crown, its head had a lot in common with a bicycle seat.

The nameless one lowered both of its arrangements of eye lenses to Lana's height, bowing slowly in an attempt not to scare her. A voice like calm running water flowed into her mind in perfect Unglish.

"I am known as Viour. I have repaired your shell, and the shells of your companions. I am pleased to meet you."

Before Lana could say a word of thanks, the towering suit of armour raised an articulated limb and gave another polite bow.

"I have already cut things too closely. I will return. Please remain here."

Viour slid into the darkness again, Lana's questions ignored.

Lana startled at the sound of a pained moan. After all this time, she'd know Jimmy's depressed whimpering anywhere. Squinting, as the sun slowly rose a little further Lana could make out the silhouettes of Jimmy, Tuesday and Trace curled up on the blue grass nearby, asleep. Crawling toward the survivors, up close Lana could see plenty of fresh scars twisting over their skin, evidence that they'd also suffered a more-than-bumpy landing and required extensive repair work from Viour. Just beyond the three napping humans, their backpacks had been neatly arranged in a row. After using them as makeshift sleds, the bags were in terrible shape.

Lana tried to shake Trace awake. A rough hand automatically shot out to slap Lana across the face. The Cadet decided that she might as well let them all sleep for now, at least until Viour came back.

As the sun crept slowly into the sky Lana could see the clearing was roughly the size of a soccer field. It was carpeted with the same thick cyan grass all the way to the tree line, but beyond that the clearing itself seemed empty: no structures, no paths, not so much as a mailbox or a faucet. Wherever they'd been brought, it couldn't be anywhere of importance. They might as well have been sitting in an off-peak Scottish campground.

It took another two minutes until the morn touched the very centre of this clearing, illuminating the edge of what appeared to be a giant, black pillar of crystal. Its dark skin had kept it invisible until the light of dawn touched it, but now the lump was suddenly shot through with red and purple threads. As the sunlight slid across the grass, Lana could clearly make out three dozen armoured suits shaped nearly identically to Viour congregating around the crystal, as though having a silent conversation. Each of the mechanical shells were vastly different colours and patterns, but they all glimmered like jewelled insects. Each of them had wild assortments of horns, antlers, and tusks that were more impressive than the last, as though they were some kind of status symbol. Even from this distance, Viour's bony crown was clearly the largest and most elaborate.

"What are they doing?" Jimmy wondered, yawning and sitting up with an effort.

Not bothering to say "good morning" or "nice that you're alive", Lana used her retinal screens to zoom in on the gathered shells. The scene still didn't make a whole lot of sense.

"They're all touching that big crystal and shaking a bit, but beyond that they don't seem to be doing anything." Lana squinted. "I'm no expert, but my best guess is they're using that crystal to contact somebody." She blinked. "Perhaps they're arranging for somebody to pick us up?"

Trace snorted in derision, proving she was also awake.

"You can't seriously be that naive."

Lana sighed. "I wish I was. Knowing my luck, they're calling down another volley of mass driver blasts."

"Reckon they're The Apex?" Tuesday mumbled, patting his pockets for his first cigarette of the morning. "Or are they just a bunch of empty shells, like Half Head? Speaking of Half Head, where is that stupid lump? He threw me right onto my butt. Had to surf the whole crater with a busted tailbone."

"No way they're like Half Head," Lana said seriously. 'When Viour said hello, it was like a god was talking to me. It wasn't just a voice: it was more than us, more than a machine. Certainly more than that derelict ball of crumpled-up rust we've been following all this time."

"We've got to be careful," Jimmy warned, keeping his voice down. "Remember that an entire galaxy of more than a thousand alien races managed to put aside their differences in order to annihilate The Apex. We can't trust them. We need to doubt everything they say. No matter what, we have to keep our heads."

Tuesday spat onto the cyan grass and squinted at the giant crystal pillar.

"Is that thing showing up as an energy source, by any chance?"

For the first time since her near-fatal crash, Lana consulted her Omni's scanner. She gave a sharp exhalation of breath at the reading.

"Not only does it show up as a power source, but it is the power source we've been tracking all this time. We've arrived at our destination."

Jimmy smiled broadly, looked at the crystal pillar, gave this a moment of thought, and his grin faltered as he formed an obvious question.

"So what do we do now?"

Lana looked from Jimmy to Trace, but didn't bother even glancing at Tuesday. She knew he was about as useful as a crepe paper umbrella.

"I don't know. I kinda thought that we'd figure out a plan along the way."

Jimmy gave Lana the stink-eye. "Seriously? That's it? We've come all this way...for no actual reason? Marched through hell itself for..."

Jimmy's words were cut off by a sudden spike of mental distress right in the brain. All four humans recoiled in shock as The Apex gave off a titanic psychic scream of pain and horror. This wave throbbed out from the black crystal pillar, sending hopelessness and fear and gibbering insanity across the clearing, bending over the corkscrew trees that ringed it almost to the point of snapping. Then all of the armoured suits simply went limp and collapsed to the grass, clattering against each other like toppled dominoes. None of them stirred.

"What in the name of Thor's enchanted jockstrap was that?" Jimmy moaned, his brain still humming with the after-effects of the psychic pain.

"Haven't felt like that since I brewed moonshine out of boot polish." Tuesday managed, immediately going back to looking for a cigarette. "Are they dead?"

Getting to her feet, Lana didn't bother saying a word before starting to march towards the black pillar. She may not have any idea what had just happened and certainly didn't have a plan, but there was no way she was going to sit around on the grass like a stoned hippy when her life expectancy may only be measured in hours. Trace was close behind, but Jimmy and Tuesday hesitated for a few moments before joining them.

The Apex hadn't so much as twitched by the time the humans made it all the way to the pillar. Their articulated limbs were splayed out, limp and tangled as overcooked spaghetti. Whatever that psychic burst had been, it had pushed all of the brightly coloured shells away from the giant crystal with a physical force. Careful not to touch it or even get too close, Lana ran her Omni over the black surface. Purple and red threads glowed brightly within its dark core, as though reacting to her attention. The pillar gave off a very distinct feeling of wrongness.

"Reminds me of The Archive," Jimmy said quietly, as though afraid to wake The Apex. "The way it looked in that ancient recording before it was destroyed."

"So...reckon this thing holds information?" Tuesday wondered. He made a happy noise as he finally found a bent cigarette in the bottom of his pocket, and immediately lost all interest in what was going on.

"Seems to be made from the same kind of crystal," Trace confirmed. Her eyes scanned up and down the pillar. "Knowing how much info these things can contain, half a centimetre could probably hold mankind's entire history with room to spare, right?"

Lana stepped away from the crystal, her eyes darting over the Omni display hovering over her left hand. She didn't notice that the colourful threads in the pillar fade back down to black as she moved out of range. She looked disappointed.

"If there's anything recorded on it, I can't read it with my hardware."

"Who'd have thought that seven galaxies and six thousand years might cause a few compatibility issues," Tuesday snarked. He moved his face closer towards the pillar, blowing green smoke at it as the red and purple lines glowed to life again. "So what's the plan? Or are we still hoping everything will work out while we stroll over the rainbow linked arm-in-arm?"

"One of us could touch it," Lana said hesitantly.

Tuesday snickered. "How are you expecting to get a volunteer, kid?"

"Easy," Trace said simply.

Lana didn't have time to shout a warning before Trace gripped Tuesday by his bony shoulder and pushed him. Staggering, only fifty centimetres from the mysterious pillar, Tuesday's arms pin wheeled as he tried to keep his balance. Unfortunately, he tripped over one of the prone Apex and went sprawling into the black crystal with both hands, his right shoulder and finally his face, crushing his cigarette into embers.

And then the horrible truth was revealed.

*

This world once had a name, a large native population of intelligent creatures, a swirl of diverse cultures that stretched back for the better part of fifty millennia, and a bright future. Its civilisation had been an enviable one, a people who were united and dedicated to deep philosophical thought and scientific advancement and the betterment not just of themselves, but every other race that made up the Twelve Hundred. It had been one of the greatest jewels of this galaxy, an example to all others.

It had not been any of those things for many, many generations.

Its original name lost long ago in the ashes and smoke of war, this ruined ball of suffering and hopelessness was known in over a thousand different languages as The Grave. For ten thousand years the armies of the Twelve Hundred had thrown themselves at each other both on and above the surface of this barren rock, unceasingly butchering one another day and night. Its great cities and wonders had been demolished to pebbles within weeks, its native population extinct within a year. Its sweeping forests and tundra and fertile lands were charcoal, and its breathable atmosphere was boiled away. Its oceans and lakes had been evaporated by endless bombings, creating hectic lightning storms that raged across the airless surface without cease.

During this long, long war, there had been so many casualties from the combined meat grinder of the Twelve Hundred fighting one another that the surface of The Grave was now entirely covered in the corpses of alien soldiers. The bodies formed a planet-wide swamp of meat, charred armour and broken equipment that was ten metres deep at its shallowest points. Some of the corpse-swamps descended fifty times as far. To make matters worse, as The Grave no longer had an atmosphere, it was impossible for the dead flesh to decay away naturally, meaning that the ocean of corpses would never rot down to bones. The layers of skin, meat, and organs would remain here for all time.

New fleets swarmed towards The Grave every day, engaging in endless pitched battles in the local star system. Closer in, destroyed wrecks had left countless tonnes of alloys and ceramics permanently in The Grave's orbit, blocking all starlight and forming a minefield that was borderline impossible to plough through without suffering heavy damage. Even if an armoured landing craft miraculously made it all the way down to the endless war on the surface, it would only be a matter of minutes until they were blasted apart by ordinance and left to sink into the mire like so many others. Light infantry could expect a slightly longer life expectancy if they were smart, though that rarely translated to longer than half an hour. Due to the necessity of armoured pressure suits, one decent shot from any modern hand-held weapon was usually enough to add a new corpse to the trillions that covered this rock. And even if new arrivals weren't done in by enemy combatants, it would only be a matter of hours until they got caught in the immense clouds of highly-toxic chemicals that swept across the surface in random patterns. These death fumes ate away at anything metal, ceramic or glass, and could reduce all weapons, pressure suits and other equipment to worthlessness within a handful of minutes.

Sometime during the tenth millennium of hostilities on The Grave (the exact date of its beginning had been forgotten long, long ago), a single Slidge ramship full of seeker marines broke through twenty-two consecutive blockades before successfully bashing its way through an orbital junkyard so thick with debris that it was almost solid. The ramship had started this day as just one tiny part of an impressive fleet of dreadnoughts, capitol warships and heavy cruisers, but the larger craft had all been peeled away within fifteen minutes of arriving in the local system. The bigger the ship, the bigger the target. As usual, every fleet above The Grave was firing indiscriminately at anything that didn't originate from their own species, and countless explosions made the orbital junkyard look like it was engulfed in a never-ending fireworks display. As the junkyard completely obscured the local sun, this bright carnage was the only thing that illuminated the surface of The Grave.

On board the ramship, a total of eighteen Slidge seeker marines held tight to padded ceiling railings with all six of their triple-thumbed hands as their transport shook violently from countless minor impacts. These troopers had been conscripted from a dozen different Slidge worlds and undergone short, violent periods of psychological modification to convert them from janitors, vending-machine stockists, doorknob sanitisers and nose-picking farmers into hardened warriors. Among them was a Slidge known only as Jung, a nobody from a manufacturing world who was undoubtedly one of the least dangerous of those on board. Like all the others, Jung had only been drafted a week ago, and in that period he had already undergone one-hundred-and-fifty hours of genetic improvements, mental conditioning, and military downloads, all at the same time. Jung's brain was so far below average that only about a third of the combat conditioning had worked, and no matter how many times the neural sculptors had plunged into his green matter they simply couldn't scrub away his fear responses. So while all the other seeker marines in this flaming, bucking ramship were blank-faced with a chill, emotionless calm, all three of Jung's stomachs were heaving with terror. If Jung vomited into his skin-tight pressurised helmet, he'd spend the rest of his short life on The Grave with everything obscured by a thin layer of grey, acidic reflux.

Like every citizen of the Slidge Primacy - as well as every citizen of the Twelve Hundred intelligent species spread across this galaxy - Jung knew that The Apex had revealed thousands of years ago that the secret to their immortality was hidden somewhere on this world, and was freely available to anybody who wanted to take it. Unfortunately, only one species could possess this priceless gift at any given time, and ownership was decided by what race had sole possession of this world. Understandably, this little addendum had kept the Twelve Hundred at each other's throats (or their equivalent approximation) ever since, making any form of diplomacy impossible. Despite the fact that this war-fuelled divide made it a simple matter for The Apex to continue subjugating every other species, immortality was simply too tempting a prize to question.

Jung knew he was a nobody. He'd never been under any delusions of grandeur. But being thrown into this eternal battle, this endless war, to be classed by the Slidge Primacy as having little more worth than a round of ammunition, was still cutting. His past life on his home world, slaving in a continent-wide factory, had been expunged during the conditioning. Try as he might, Jung could not recall whether he had friends, or a family, or if he'd achieved anything worth knowing. Even if he somehow survived his deployment, Jung had no idea what he had to go back to. Besides the blur of conditioning, he might as well be a clone who'd been decanted a week ago.

Jung's half-on-fire Slidge ramship had beaten the odds so far, but it had been months since the Primacy had managed to get any new boots on the ground, so nobody really liked their chances of making it down in one piece. After the kind of jammy luck that would make anybody immediately go out and buy a lottery ticket, a good two-thirds of the original ramship crashed into a mulch that had once been scales, feathers, flesh, bones and fins, and somehow managed not to explode as it carved through this ocean of corpses. It took a minute of wiggling the razor-sharp ramps up and down, but the ramship finally sliced through the mire, allowing a whole squad of heavily-armoured seeker marines to disembark. Standing tall in their armoured pressure suits, trying not to sink into a ground composed of soft meat and ignoring the sizzle of corrosive chemicals, the seeker marines arrayed before the last remaining officer of their entire fleet, and took part in the standard vow.

"We endure this horror for all of our people, that the Slidge alone may have immortality," the officer crackled over their radios.

"That the Slidge alone may have immortality," Jung and his fellow seeker marines all droned, like so many countless others before them.

The seeker marines had barely finished reciting the mantra when an enemy bomber doing three times the speed of sound reduced Jung's entire unit to a slurry of flesh and charred ceramics. Jung's ear nodes didn't even register the supersonic shriek before he was dead. He didn't have a chance to feel surprise, or regret. Jung's first and last boots-on-the-ground military deployment had ended after twenty-four seconds, and half of that had been a frantic scramble out of the burning ramship transport. Their bodies were added to the biggest charnel pit in the Universe, and their heavy ramship began to sink into the swamp within minutes. Its substantial weight pushed down through twelve hundred different morphisms of alien soldier, cracking bones, breaking wings, and smashing insectoid carapace.

In the end, everyone who came to this world would end up as yet another ingredient in a giant corpse gumbo. Nobody who set foot onto the surface of The Grave ever left, and they never would.

*

Jung recoiled from the black crystal pillar, screaming as though burned by its hateful surface. He felt instant, cold, gutting fear at the sight of it. Jung might have been an absolute nobody, but even he knew what an infocrystal from The Archive looked like. Well versed in the hideous death The Apex would subject him to if they discovered he'd touched it, Jung decided he wanted to get as far away from it as possible.

Staggering about on a lower pair of limbs that seemed to be bending the wrong way, tripping backwards over what might have been a tree root, Jung toppled and hit his head. Blinking what felt like only two eyes instead of three, Jung stared up at his hands in surprise. While he was shocked to see that they'd been stained a bizarre light pink colour rather than their usual scarlet and golden, throbbing veins, somehow he managed not to scream when he realised two of his six limbs were missing. To make matters worse, he only had one thumb on each hand instead of three, and the lower pair of hands he'd tried to walk on were stiff and useless and trapped in some sort of tough leather coverings.

Flexing the fingers of his upper hands, mystified by their odd shapes and lengths and the way they flexed in unusual directions, Jung finally managed to bellow a Slidge curse word through a mouth and tongue that wasn't shaped for such noises. Instead of a triple-segmented beak with the same number of tongues, it felt like he'd tried to push his words through a puckered orifice.

Above, three alien faces suddenly blocked his view of the dawn sky: a smooth one with her hair trapped in a rock-hard bun, a beat-up slab festooned with piercings and tribal scarification, and a pudgy sphere capped by a tall yellow headdress of some sort.

"Tuesday?" the pudgy sphere said in an unfamiliar alien squeak. "You okay? You passed out for a couple of minutes."

"Then screamed like a choir girl and fell over," the beat-up mug added, its voice several octaves lower.

214

Jung raised an eyebrow at the unknown language, surprised by the fact that he even had eyebrows.

"I do not know what that means," Jung said in fluent Low-Trade, the coarse street tongue he'd spoken for his entire life prior to being drafted. The faces may have been confused at his words. "Where am I? How did I get here?"

The three odd heads exchanged looks, as though each of them were waiting for somebody to explain the hissing, clicking, guttural Low-Trade phrases.

Confused as to how he could have gone from an armoured pressure suit on the surface of The Grave to being basically naked on planet that looked as though it could support life, Jung did his best to formulate a better line of questioning. Sitting up, all thought was blasted from Jung's mind at the sight of three dozen motionless Apex amplification suits splayed all over the ground, their bone-crushing articulated limbs tangled up near the ten-metre-tall black pillar and his own wrong lower hands. It was now much, much more likely that Jung's next query would mostly consist of vicious Low-Trade expletives.

Jung screwed his eyes shut, but it was Tuesday who opened them. It was a sudden transition, as though Jung's occupation of Tuesday's brain had been flushed out without leaving any remnant, the ancient, dead seeker marine vanishing into the ether. Remembering how Trace had pushed him into the pillar, Tuesday bared his black teeth at her.

"The hell?" Tuesday growled, his Unglish mangled but understandable. "Do you have any idea what I just went through?"

"Besides clicking and hissing at us like a Kalahari Bushman?" Lana asked.

"Went body-hopping, didn't I?" Tuesday clarified, wiping at his arms as though trying to dislodge something dirty. "Like dialling your brain into an Immersive, but a nasty one. Just got blown up in some ancient war, a war The Apex started. Got splattered all over a world made from corpses. Saw it through the eyes of some poor conscript. Wouldn't believe the scale. Most evil thing I've ever heard of." Tuesday barked a laugh. "And we expect them to help us? A bunch of bloody robo-Hitlers? Mecha-Stalins?"

There was the clicking, slithering sound of thirty-six sets of articulated metal tentacles pushing their ornate amplification suits out of the muck as The Apex awakened in synchronisation. Wordlessly, all of the glittering shells except for the one known as Viour glided to the far extent of the clearing, apparently trying to get as far away from one another as possible without breaking the tree line. Viour's eye lenses went from a muddy grey to their usual pearlescent white as she woke up properly.

"You should not have touched the Penance." Viour said in their minds, her words lacking all anger. She began to head back towards the same corner that hosted the human's belongings. They followed automatically. "It is our burden alone to bear. Your mind may have been lost to its touch."

"No great loss," Trace sniped.

"What is that thing? Why does it do that?" Tuesday demanded, giving the pillar both middle fingers as he stormed away from it.

Once she had glided all the way back to her corner, Viour settled to the ground a few metres away from the damaged backpacks. Her tentacles relaxed until they were limp. She did not say another word for almost ten seconds.

"You do not know." Viour finally commented. Whether she was surprised by this news or not was unclear. "Are you not affiliated with the Twelve Hundred? Did they not send you?"

"We're not from around here," Jimmy managed.

Viour tilted her bicycle-seat head back and forth between the humans.

"Do the harsh penalties of breaking the quarantine not concern you? And, more to the point, how did you get through the defences of the Twelve Hundred? This system has been completely blockaded since our Fall. Why would you risk your lives to come here?"

"Accident," Trace clarified.

"You didn't answer my question," Tuesday said flatly. "Why did I turn into some three-thumbed alien defect called Jung when I touched your big rock? Why would you leave something like that just lying around?"

Viour gave what may have been a mental sigh, as though resigned to the fact that she would have to go into a topic she didn't enjoy rehashing.

"The Apex used to be different before we were left to decay here. As our name implies, we were once above all the other races, the undisputed masters. We spent millions of years at the very peak. In order to guarantee our status for all time, we did some...questionable things. Our greatest crime was The Great Trick, when we convinced the Twelve Hundred that the secret to our immortality could be found on the world of a race that had slightly annoyed us in some minor way. They did not realise it for a long, long time, but our claim was completely untrue. In addition to keeping the lesser species at each other's throats, making it easier for us to divide and rule them, we also saw The Great Trick as a source of amusement." Viour drooped a little. "When the Twelve Hundred learned of what we had done, they spent generations secretly plotting how to usurp us. Once their uprising had been perfected, in the space of a matter of hours they launched coordinated attacks on every Apex world, fleet and construct, using a thousand divergent branches of science to fry, bash and confuse our forces. Our resistance was fierce, but ultimately futile. A crippling psychic superweapon deployed as an official declaration of war reduced our near-limitless telepathic abilities from galaxy-wide to a matter of metres, followed closely by a second superweapon that rendered everything we had crafted from invulnerable thoughtmetal as brittle as chalk. All of our weapons, our defences, our fortifications were broken. After this, a further cascade of superweapons were unleashed against us one after another, hammering us relentlessly with a hatred and a violence that not only rivalled some of our worse atrocities, but exceeded them."

Viour was understandably quiet for some time. None of the survivors through it wise to break the silence at this point.

"The following extermination took decades, and we were hunted relentlessly until only a handful remained. The most important of us were spared death as a sign of respect, or of mercy...or so we thought. While snuffing out our race was appealing to the uprising, it was decided that death would not be enough to atone for what we had done. We, the last of The Apex, were imprisoned here, and the only way we are allowed to continue living is if we choose to suffer until an account has been made for every life we stole during The Great Trick."

Viour tilted her bicycle-seat head towards the black pillar.

"That is Penance, the only infocrystal not destroyed with the rest of The Archive. It was originally a detailed record of The Great Trick, a comprehensive full-sensory immersion of every single life that was taken during the ten-thousand-year atrocity. With some alteration by the Twelve Hundred, it became our gaoler. We must all choose to touch Penance eight times a day at set intervals, lest this world be consumed with another phalanx of mass driver impacts. We must collectively suffer no fewer than two-hundred-and-fifty-six deaths a day until we have finally atoned, upon which time the Twelve Hundred have promised to discuss further reparations. While we have no guarantee of freedom, we hope by our suffering to be forgiven."

"So how long are you meant to do this, exactly?" Lana asked in horrified fascination.

Viour drooped even more.

"Until we have experienced first-hand every life taken during The Great Trick. All five trillion of them."

CHAPTER NINETEEN FAVOURS

Even though the time they had left before keeling over was shorter than a squatting munchkin, only being a couple of days away from vomiting up their organs, crying out their brains and bursting with explosive diarrhoea, Viour refused to talk business until the humans had rested. It seemed to be a tradition of The Apex that they didn't get into diplomatic discussions if the other party looked and felt like the living dead. Annoyed at the brick wall treatment, Lana repeatedly attempted to explain the urgency of the situation until Viour finally cut off her words with the flick of an articulated limb.

"We will talk once you have slept. This is not negotiable."

Ignoring Lana's continued complaints, Viour began to do something unusual with her twenty tentacles. It looked like she was pretending to spin the most complicated macramé wall hanging in the universe, but the tips of her tentacles were touching nothing but air. After a few seconds, however, long, glimmering white threads began to spill out from nowhere, weaving and knotting into something beautiful. The humans may have witnessed Half Head create a simple battery pack after they'd killed the Screwback, sure, but what Viour was doing was magnitudes above that. Watching the creation of true thoughtmetal was quite an experience.

Within moments the representative of The Apex had created a total of four queen-sized sleeping mats, and it only took a glance to tell that she had customised each of them for the four humans according to their weight and height.

Viour made a sweeping motion with a limb.

"Please."

Preparing to argue further, the moment Lana reclined onto the sleeping mat all of her words were lost to the ether. She had forgotten what comfort felt like, and the exhaustion of the last few days caught up with her in an instant. The pain in her muscles faded to a gentle hum and she was asleep inside of a minute. Her final thoughts were a flurry of practical questions: exactly what limits did The Apex have when it came to creating things from thoughtmetal? Could they only make simple forms, or were they able to form technology, microchips, food, water, air?

The humans gradually woke up around midday to the sound of rain on a tin roof. One glance told them that Viour had crafted simple shelters over their sleeping mats to protect them from the elements. Viour, however, was sitting stock-still in the open. Drops of water were bouncing off the royal blue gloss of her amplification suit, but her stillness indicated that such things didn't bother her.

Seeing that her guests were now rested, Viour swept a two-foot-long platter into view: a charred blue worm took up the entirety of the silver oblong. It appeared to be garnished with some kind of vivid red herbs they hadn't seen before, and it steamed enticingly.

After a few hesitant bites, the humans got stuck in. As the worm resembled extremely tender lamb and the red herb turned out to have a lot in common with rosemary, it was just the kind of taste they needed to forget the salted grossness of Screwback flesh, kelp puree and unflavoured gluten-free pizza bases. Although they were soon so filled with grilled blue worm that they were burping and didn't want to move, that didn't mean the humans were going to pass on dessert. Viour presented a second silver platter, much smaller than the first, that contained nothing but four dark, dried out stone fruits. They smelled extremely bitter and tasted like somebody had simmered a long-expired bag of dehydrated apricots in vindaloo sauce. Viour made a tutting noise, touching Tuesday's lips before he could expel the wizened thing.

"Please chew and swallow the entire fruit, including the pit. They contain the greatest of detoxifying agents."

Gagging the detox fruit down, they all felt its full effects within minutes. First, the growing queasiness they'd been suffering from for days faded away to nothing, followed by the headaches, then the twisting sensations in their bowels and the burning in their skin, eyes, nose, mouth and ears. They'd all felt like crap for so long that they had forgotten what normal was like.

Wiping blue worm juice from his chin and licking his thumb, Jimmy looked back and forth at the other, more distant members of The Apex. They were clearly making a deliberate effort to stay as far away from one another as possible. Despite how scary it was to talk to one of the most evil creatures to ever horrify to the universe, Jimmy managed to ask Viour a question.

"Are the other Apex going to come and talk with us?"

Viour inclined her head.

"We have never been...social. Even prior to the Fall, we stayed outside of physical proximity at all times. We could go many centuries without the simplest of discussions." Viour stiffened. "However, of what little remains, I rank the highest, so unless something I say or promise provokes a strong enough reaction to be directly contradicted, they will remain out of our talks."

Once the rain stopped, Viour swept away the thoughtmetal shelter that had been keeping the four humans dry and did the same to the sleeping mats. It seemed easier than swatting a spider web, and left no trace. In its place, Viour weaved four chairs into being. Like the sleeping mats, they were clearly tailored to the human's particular shapes and sizes.

"I believe we are now at a juncture where diplomatic talks may be fruitful. May I first ask a few key questions in order to speed things along?"

Nobody had any objections to this. After all, none of them were about to keel over from a toxic spore overdose any time soon.

"How did you arrive in this system?" Viour began, getting straight to the point. "It is blockaded on all sides. Nobody can enter without being detected by the forces of the Twelve Hundred. Yet you claim to have had no direct contact with them. You must understand how such a dichotomy will make it difficult to gain my trust in anything else you say."

Taking the initiative, Lana decided to serve as humanity's voice.

"We came here on an experimental ship that accidentally skipped us across seven galaxies."

Viour was quiet for long seconds.

"Under what principal does this ship operate?"

"It moves from one point to any other point simultaneously," Trace answered, feeling qualified enough to say this much.

Viour drooped a little, as though disappointed.

"I am unable to believe your answer. We once experimented with a similar branch of technology a long time ago, and it proved to be impossible to master. It was far too dangerous and unpredictable, and was subsequently banned." Viour rose up onto her tentacles, as though ready to leave. "Excuse my arrogance in saying so, but I do not believe that your species would ever be capable of accomplishing such a feat, let alone at such a young point. Although I do not sense falsehood in your words, their content is clearly impossible. I am saddened that you feel the need to lie to me, and I suspect that this is all some sort of game on behalf of the Twelve Hundred. I have no interest in being treated as a fool."

"Wait," Lana blurted, stumbling to her feet as Viour turned away.

The Cadet recalled her discussion with Professor Ames, the schizophrenic savant who had ranted at her a couple of hours before the disaster that had dragged them to this place of hardship. She knew his words were the key to earning Viour's trust.

"The Slicer Drive on board our ship operates via applied Psy-Math, a form of navigational calculus that can only be comprehended by somebody who is both a top-level mathematical savant and clinically psychotic. Developing and building the Slicer Drive killed almost every single Psy-Math in our species, and the disaster probably murdered the only ones that remained."

Viour stopped, keeping her back to the humans. Lana's words had been enough to make her pause, at least.

"We've crossed a hundred kilometres to get here," Jimmy moaned in his most obsequious blubber. "Most of it on foot. Please don't turn us away. We can't spend the rest of our lives on this rock. Please."

Viour turned back towards them.

"My species excised all forms of madness from our genome long ago, logically making us incapable of learning Psy-Math. I do not understand what you expect us to do. I cannot simply build you a new ship."

Lana shook her head.

"We're not asking you to. Our ship might be busted halfway to a green hell, but it's still floating about with most of its pieces nearby. Mostly." Lana decided to press a suspicion that she'd had for a few days now. "Viour, how good are The Apex at understanding technology, exactly?"

"We are all born with the inherent ability to understand how anything technological works just by looking at it," Viour admitted. "We are also able to identify what is wrong with any given piece of damaged technology within seconds, and able to restore it an operational state within minutes. While I cannot understand Psy-Math, as I have already stated, I may be able to understand the technology that it has produced."

Tuesday inhaled sharply.

"Man. That'd be a bankable skill to have."

"So what kinds of resources would you need to fix a starship with our level of technology?" Trace asked.

"Nothing." Viour said without doubt or hesitation. "I should be able to weave anything you have made back into working order with little more than my own thoughtmetal. However, I would have to physically reach your ship, which as you are aware could result in what remains of my species being annihilated for breaking our promise to stay within range of the Penance."

Viour glanced across the clearing, as though hearing something that the humans could not discern. Her royal blue amplification suit didn't move for almost ten seconds, and when she did break her stillness the other members of The Apex had begun to simultaneously float towards the Penance crystal. Viour nodded at the humans and gave a quick explanation before floating off.

"The others are asking to confer. I will return."

The three dozen amplification suits met in a loose circle a hundred metres from the humans, their articulated limbs hanging loosely and their clusters of pearlescent eye lenses twitching a little here and there. After several uneventful minutes, the humans got bored with silently waiting.

"What are they talking about?" Jimmy wondered.

"Reckon they're deciding whether to test if they can leave this clearing without being pounded into pancakes," Tuesday answered. "Imagine spending sixty millenniums stuck in a field with people you hate. It's been less than a week, and I'm ready to shoot all three of you right in the face. Can't imagine how pissed off The Apex are by now."

"Six millenniums," Lana corrected. "Six thousand years is six millenniums."

Tuesday lit another cigarette and pointed a finger gun at Lana's face. "You know what? You're getting the first bullet."

"Agreed," Trace growled. Picking a bit of detox fruit out of her teeth and looking around the clearing, Trace had a thought. "You know those bitter little apricot things we ate? I don't see any fruit trees, do you? And if The Apex aren't allowed to leave this clearing, how'd they get them?"

"Maybe they made them out of thin air," Jimmy guessed.

"I fetched them, actually," Half Head clarified.

Besides Jimmy, nobody yelped in surprise. Spinning most of a revolution, the humans turned to see that Half Head was little more than a pile of junk on the other side of their backpacks. Most of its limbs were missing and it seemed to be having a lot of trouble staying upright. After seeing the glowing majesty of The Apex, this beat-up shell of rusted refuse looked even more like a tin can at a redneck shooting range than ever.

"How long have you been sitting there?" Jimmy managed, trying to will his heart rate go reduce to lower than a hamster's.

"Hours," Half Head said. "Viour asked me to sit outside of the clearing and remain quiet until she found another task for me."

"But you're not doing either of those things," Tuesday pointed out.

What remained of Half Head's cranium tilted back and forth for a while.

"Ah. True."

"So she's your boss?" Jimmy guessed.

"My pilot has been dead for a long time. As I am aware of no next of kin, I am obligated to serve the other members of The Apex until they figure out exactly who owns me," Half Head explained. "Keeping in mind that all of The Apex are distantly related if you go back far enough, one of the three dozen in this clearing would eventually be genetically proven to be distant cousins with my former pilot."

"Cousins?" Trace asked.

"Fifty or eighty million times removed, of course. I am expecting these legal proceedings to take a while." Half Head pushed off the ground, angling for a

222

better look at Viour and the other Apex. "I believe they have almost completed their talks."

The humans turned just in time to see most of The Apex scatter back to their distant corners. Viour and one of the others – a purple amplification suit edged with ruby highlights - were the only ones who remained of the conference. They drifted slowly towards the humans, and Viour placed one of her articulated limbs on the purple one's shoulders. It was a chummy scene, the kind of casual affection you wouldn't expect from an ancient race like The Apex. It was certain that Viour and her friend were still talking silently, probably conveying a thousand times as much as a mere human could hope to impart in such a short time. Once only a matter of metres away from Lana, Trace, Tuesday and Jimmy, Viour casually pointed towards the tree line, as though showing something to the other Apex.

And that was when things went right to hell.

Snatching up a rock twice the size of a house brick from the loam with the tip of one of her twenty limbs, Viour had already smashed it into the head of the purple amplification suit five times before human eyes could even register seeing her pick it up. The speed and violence was stunning, and it was obvious that the purple one hadn't seen it coming, either. Falling to the ground in surprise, its tentacles flailing ineffectively, Viour's victim suffered another thirty or so strikes within three seconds, its skull flattened and its eye lenses exploding. Despite her victim going totally still, Viour did not stop pounding until the head was reduced to less than a centimetre of crumpled thoughtmetal. Finally halting the bashing when some sort of thick, yellow fluid began pouring out of the left side of the ruined purple skull, the side that Half Head was lacking, Viour casually cast aside the bloodied rock and turned to regard the humans.

"There were some objections, but we have come to a consensus." Viour's words were just as calm as before despite the fact she had just brutally murdered one of her own species without any warning. The whispering quality of Viour's mental speech suddenly felt beyond chilling, and it seemed as though the humans had finally gotten a clear look at the monsters they were asking for help. "I believe that we can discuss our options now."

*

The plan was relatively straightforward. Just because The Apex were bordering on transcendent didn't mean they made it a habit to actively seek out complications. After all, the more extensive the plan, the more likely it was to go wrong in some way.

First, they needed to make it back into space. As Lana had the last known parking coordinates of the Carpe Astrum stored in her Omni, it shouldn't be too hard to find a pair of thirteen-kilometre-long triangles, even if they had drifted a little over the last few days. It should be as simple as heading back to the ship's last known location and looking out a window. Once Jimmy had used his clearance as the highest-ranking living crew member to everyone back on board, Viour would assess the damage, bring enough of the starship back online to make it habitable, and once there was no longer any immediate danger she would repair the Slicer Drive. While Viour possessed the sort of godlike tech affinity a human could only dream of, she was ashamed to admit that it may take her as long as a couple of weeks to fix all the damage. The humans did their best to keep straight faces at this "bad" news.

There were, of course, quite a few conditions attached to this deal. Before so much as lifting another tentacle, Viour shared her demands.

"I am to have unlimited access to the systems of your ship," Viour began. "This includes viewing, recording, copying, disassembling or otherwise examining anything I wish without restriction. Once I have restored your starship to an operational state, I will use it to relocate what remains of my species to a system of our choice. After we have been safely transported, your starship will automatically take you back to your own galaxy. For the safety of both my kind and yours, every record the four of you have created since the disaster – whether in your mind or on any kind of storage media either here or on your ship – will be permanently erased with zero chance of recovery. You will simply wake up where you started without the faintest idea what happened." Viour gave a shallow bow. "I may need to add more conditions if the situation changes. Is this acceptable?"

The humans murmured assent, but couldn't help but occasionally glance at the motionless amplification suit crumpled nearby. Its smashed-in head clearly indicated that its pilot hadn't agreed with Viour's plan in some way.

Acting with unusual initiative, Tuesday voiced a thought.

"Question: if none of you are meant to move too far from Penance, won't going all the way into space trip an alarm or something?"

"To our knowledge, yes," Viour agreed. "But we have often wondered if there is any actual danger, and whether choosing to constantly torture ourselves with Penance has simply been a way for the Twelve Hundred to laugh at us. Obviously, we haven't wanted to test such theories without a good reason." Viour tilted her head. "And of course, there is the core reason why these threats of instant death might not be true."

"And what's that?" Jimmy asked.

Viour leaned in slowly, the glow of her pearlescent lenses hurting Jimmy's eyes as she came to within a matter of inches. It was all he could do not to step backwards. "They hate us far too much to kill us."

"Another question," Tuesday interrupted, breaking the awkward silence. "How are we meant to get back up there? Nobody issued me with rocket boots, did they?"

"The lifeboat?" Jimmy half-asked, half-stated in an unsure way.

Trace growled in frustration and began counting her fingers.

"One, the four of us barely fit in there, let alone with a pair of them coming along for the ride. Two, we don't have a propulsion system, which kinda makes moving about a bit of an issue. Three..." Trace squinted. "No, that about covers it. I don't need a three."

Rather than answering with words, Viour turned to regard the torn, dirty, lumpy survival backpacks sitting in an untidy pile. Giving the slightest of gestures, all of the tightly-rolled lifeboat panels responded to Viour's wishes by zipping out of the backpacks and colliding together with a clang. Pyro kinetically fusing the sections along their seams, a flick sent their only remaining oxygen generator into a perfectly-prepared slot. Before Trace could repeat both of her still-relevant issues, Viour stretched the pod's ceramic skin like chewing gum, widening its panels to eight times their original span in a way that brought glassblowing to mind. During this expansion, the lifeboat's surface changed from opaque to transparent with a crackle.

Leaving the lifeboat to set, Viour started producing thousands of glimmering threads of thoughtmetal seemingly from nothing, and all twenty of her articulated limbs contributed to weaving the filaments together into a bigger and bigger shape. This process reminded the humans of how a spider crafts a web, but instead of a simple sticky trap Viour was creating something far more intricate and impressive. Once the main shell of her creation was completed, Viour began to form other things and fit them into place: wafers that might have been some kind of advanced microchip, glasslike balls of a mysterious liquid, cylinders that looked like rolls of fresh cow tripe, purple crystals, and corrugated sheets of what might have been solidified electricity. Stitching the components together with chromatic threads faster than any sewing machine, Viour finished her work with a flourish.

A casual wave simultaneously lifted the lifeboat ten feet off the grass and sent Viour's unknown machine flying through the air, embedding it into the lifeboat's underside with a clunk. Viour flicked a limb, and the thoughtmetal construct gave off an electrical hum. By the time a Viour-sized hatch opened like a mouth less than twenty-five seconds had passed since Trace expressed her doubts. Viour gave a slight bow and curled a limb in a human-like sign of respect.

"After you."

Carefully stepping aboard the modified pod, Trace couldn't help but notice the difference. In addition to being luxuriously roomy, the lifeboat was already filled with a pleasant atmosphere that was just the right temperature, pressure and humidity. She silently guessed that Viour must have improved the atmospheric generator while telekinetically installing all the other new hardware. It was clear that everything had been upgraded far beyond current human tech levels, and it even had that fantastic new-lifeboat smell you only get with pods that have never left the showroom.

The other three humans followed closely behind. Even once Viour had entered, though, Half Head made no motion to get on board. Jimmy waved.

"Come on, hurry up."

Half Head shook its bisected skull.

"My function has run its course. I will remain here."

"Until they decide who owns you, right?" Lana asked.

Viour made a noise that was the equivalent of clearing her throat for attention.

"Actually, this shell has been deemed to be of no further use." She nodded at Half Head. "You have my permission to die."

Half Head inclined its skull in a respectful way.

"Very well."

The light in Half Head's lenses blinked out, and the crusty suit of ancient armour collapsed as all of its servos and gears went limp simultaneously. Without fanfare or so much as a goodbye, the one being who had been the difference between their death and survival deactivated itself for all time. Half Head's body crumbled into rust, then into ashes. Within seconds, what little was left had blown away like crushed autumn leaves.

The humans stood there in shock for a couple of seconds. Slowly, Jimmy turned to shake his bottom lip at Viour.

"You...you killed him," Jimmy blubbered. "You murdered..."

"I did no such thing," Viour interrupted as calmly as a lake, but firm as hitting one after a three kilometre fall. "That unit was nothing more than a dangerously fragmented Operating System within a broken machine. It was not a person, no matter how loose the definition. You cannot murder something that is not a person." A tiny shudder worked its way up Viour's spine. "I should know."

"So that kill order was kinda like uninstalling an operating system?" Tuesday sniped.

Viour turned her head slightly. "Uninstalling? Yes. Perhaps."

Lana almost rose to Half Head's defence, citing how the machine had guided them safely across a hundred kilometres of nightmares, but she couldn't help but touch the bruises Half Head had crushed into her neck. To call the machine unstable was an insult to Nitro-glycerine.

Before any of the humans could voice further outrage, the pod's hatch silently slammed shut. Like earlier, Viour gave a slight twitch to create a quartet of seats. The padded lounges rose up to gently cradle the buttocks of each human, custom-designed for the comfort and safety needs of their designated sitter.

"So how fast can this thing go?" Lana asked, trying to redirect the topic of conversation.

Instead of answering Lana's question, Viour flicked one of her articulated limbs. The hardware beneath their feet hummed a little louder for a second, followed by the world of Scrote simply disappearing. The pitch-dark abscess of space immediately took its place. The humans appeared utterly stunned that there hadn't been any dramas: no pressure, no deafening noise, no violent tremors from a propulsion system almost shaking itself apart, nothing to indicate that they were about to instantaneously translate from the surface of a planet to the depths of the eternal vacuum. Shaken by the sudden transition, nobody had time to get their bearings before Viour spoke.

"Could you please double-check the coordinates you gave me?" Viour asked Lana. For the first time, it sounded as though The Apex representative was almost annoyed.

Lana swiped her Omni to life. The last known position of the parked Carpe Astrum superimposed themselves above her wrist. A second set of coordinates – their current location - appeared beneath it, matching the first set almost to the kilometre. Under normal circumstances, she might have commented on the fact that their lifeboat had just hopped over a million kilometres like it was nothing, but there were other, graver concerns.

She looked out the transparent walls of the modified lifeboat, searching. In the far, far distance, the world of Scrote was a tiny pea blocking out the tiniest segment of a grapefruit of a star. Besides that, the entire dead panorama was empty save for the distant afterimages of long-changed suns. Panic began to rise in Lana's bowels, crawling up her digestive system with acid claws.

"This is where it was parked," Lana confirmed, her eyes still flicking from window to window. She turned to meet Viour's silent glare. While The Apex representative may have been utterly serene up to this point, Lana knew it was unwise to provoke her. On the plus side, at least there weren't any rocks suitable for a bit of skull-bashing sitting around...

"While I can detect a few crumbs of unfamiliar alloys here and there, I can sense nothing of a manufactured nature beyond that which we have brought with us," Viour said, her words still calm. She paused for three long seconds, as though considering what to do next. "Please check your coordinates again."

Lana chewed her lip, trying to figure out what had gone wrong. They'd parked at this very location, right? Even beaten half to hell like it was, the Carpe Astrum shouldn't have drifted too far. And even if it had moved, then she would have been notified by email. Flicking through her Inbox for a fifth time, no unread messages appeared. Nothing at all.

But then she saw it.

"Ah," Lana said simply. She blinked a few times, then looked up at the others with a hint of embarrassment. "Seems I've, uh, actually received quite a few messages. But they all went to my Spam folder."

"How many?" Trace asked.

Lana flicked the holographic display. "Six. All of them from the Carpe Astrum."

"Careful with that," Jimmy warned. "Last time I opened a Spam email I went blind and lost the ability to understand nouns for two years."

"Can't trust the Queen of East Korea when she says you won the Lotto, can you?" Tuesday agreed, clearly speaking from experience.

"There aren't any attachments," Lana said absently, her eyes darting through the list. "They're just basic status updates. Looks like they were automatically sent at specific intervals. I'll read the headings chronologically."

Flick.

"Ship status: safe."

Flick.

"Ship status: safe."

Flick.

"Ship status: safe."

Flick.

"Ship status: safe."

Flick.

Barely stopping herself from automatically repeating the mantra, Lana's cheek twitched at what she was reading. She blinked several times before continuing.

"All previous reports incorrect. Ship accelerating uncontrollably. Unable to steer or slow down."

Flick.

"Ship heading towards local star at top speed. Two days to impact." Lana looked up at three horrified faces and a blank mask. "That's the most recent message."

Jimmy leaped to his feet. It took a while for all of him to stop moving.

"We need to stop it! Viour, can you get us there in time? We can hop the whole way, right?"

"That's unlikely to help," Lana said morosely.

"Why?"

Lana collapsed into her customised seat, wrapped her arms around her chest, placed her hands on their opposite shoulders and rocked back and forth in a way that was far from encouraging.

"Because that last message is three days old."

There was total silence for almost two minutes. This stunning news had body-slammed all their hopes, and the knowledge that their already-bleak situation had finally crossed over into total hopelessness was too much to bear. There were no more ideas, no more long-shots, no more vague chances. With the Carpe Astrum melted down to its constituent atoms, they were stuck in this distant, hostile, alien hell-hole permanently.

Viour broke the silence.

"As our plans have become untenable, I will return us to the clearing around Penance. I feel no need to risk the complete extinction of my kind if there is no possible benefit to be derived. We will decide your next course of action from there."

"Wait," Tuesday snapped. "This ship moves real fast. Why don't we use it to flee this system? All of The Apex were just going to run off anyway, right?"

"As I have repeatedly stated, the Twelve Hundred possess detailed records of all Apex technology, including our methods of interstellar travel," Viour said calmly. "Using our technology in such an overt manner would certainly lead to detection by their blockades, and attempting to exit this star system would surely result in our immediate and complete destruction."

"Which is why you wanted to help us repair the Carpe Astrum, right?" Jimmy guessed.

Viour lowered her head slightly. "Of course. At no time have I pretended to be operating under altruistic motives. You asked for help, we asked something from you in return, and so we agreed to a win-win situation. At no point have I been..."

Every electrical system in the lifeboat suddenly flipped out. All the holographic projectors spewed out meaningless patterns in a million colours, speakers screamed crackling demonic distortion, and the lights and oxygen generator flickered on and off. Lana's Omni vomited thick layers of nonsense all over her forearm, wrist and hand, the stress heating the grain-of-rice implant between her thumb and index finger close to boiling point. She shook her hand and yelped, blowing on her burning flesh.

The star drive beneath their feet went silent as it permanently burned out, but none of the humans could hear or see anything through the chromatic explosions consuming their retinal screens. Screaming and wailing, rocking back and forth in pain, the four of them barely resisted the desire to tear out their own eyes to stop the assault of information. The images only got brighter, the implants growing in temperature until it felt like hot screws were being twisted into their corneas.

Then, as suddenly as the visual and audio onslaught began, it stopped.

"What the spug was that?" Tuesday managed, uncurling from the foetal position as his implanted retinal screens cooled down to beneath the point of agony. Opening his eyes, Tuesday did an immediate double-take at what greeted him. Unsure if his retinals were still going haywire, Tuesday smacked Jimmy on the side of the head and pointed out the transparent hull of the lifeboat. "Uh, can you see that?"

Outside one hemisphere of the pod, an enormous electric-purple circle the size of a planet now dominated what had been empty space a minute ago. The object roiled with heat, endlessly twisting and flaring, and lavender sunspots the diameter of continents crawled over its glowing majesty. As it was only a few thousand kilometres away, the brightness was so blinding that everyone had to create sunglasses from their AllTool bracelets and set their retinal screens to partially opaque.

"Pretty sure I see it," Jimmy confirmed.

Lana tapped away at her Omni, making an annoying tutting noise as she silently read the scan results. It took a few seconds for her to translate what she was reading into layman's terms.

"My Omni doesn't recognise this sort of star, but it's only ten thousand kilometres in diameter, making it a bit smaller than Earth." She shook her head. "But that's impossible: even the tiniest of stars make Jupiter look like a pinhead. And while its mass is roughly what you'd expect, somehow its surface temperature is zero."

"Explains why we aren't cinders yet," Trace growled. "But that only leads us to another thousand questions." Trace turned to Viour. "Any idea where that star came from, or how?"

Viour was silent for a moment. "No."

Tuesday put his nose right up to the window and closed his eyes almost all the way. His chlorine-flavoured breath fogged up the transparent surface.

"Wait. Can you guys see that?"

"I already said yes a minute ago," Jimmy complained.

Tuesday waved this away without patience.

"Not the star: over the star."

Tuesday ran his fingers across the giant purple fireball, as though tracing a grid. It took a bit of effort, but eventually everyone could see what Tuesday was yammering about: the star was surrounded by a thin lattice of some unknown material like a gigantic spherical birdcage, the biggest lobster pot in the universe. Whatever substance the lines were made from didn't seem to have any issues cuddling up to a star. It was hard to tell with the naked eye, but it looked like there was about ten solid kilometres of distortion separating the underside of the lattice from the roiling hell beneath it.

Lana gave an embarrassing yelp of excitement at her Omni reading.

"I think I've got it! The lattice is protecting itself from the heat of the star by using the heat of the star itself to fuel some mega sort of magnetic shielding. Explains why we aren't reading a temperature: besides fuelling the energy needs of the lattice, the heat doesn't go any further than its set boundary. Impressive stuff."

"Bit of a chicken-and-an-egg situation, isn't it?" Trace growled.

"Just imagine what you could fuel with a whole star," Lana said in wonder. "Even a teeny one like this."

A tremor ran through all the lifeboat's systems. Unlike the first glitch, this event only tickled a few colours out of the projectors and hissed out of the speakers as inoffensive static. Suddenly, the transparent walls of the pod became ultra-high definition screens, and a familiar creature appeared on every surface: a Slidge. It was an almost exact match for the Prime they'd watched commit suicide in that recording near the ruins of The Archive, as well as the unfortunate Slidge foot soldier known as Jung who Tuesday had spent a few minutes intimately observing from within his own skull. The only real difference was that the facial cheeks of this alien were grossly swollen like balloons, and writhed as though full of maggots. Sixty centuries may have passed, but the Slidge species was almost unchanged in every other way: they were still sitting in a fork in the genetic highway somewhere between a starfish and common asparagus, had bright red skin traced with pulsing golden veins, beaked and had three different-sized eyes. It also had far too many elbows.

Using its three thicker limbs to hang from heavy-duty ceiling hooks, the Slidge was using its trio of more delicate arms to tap at the ceramic surface of its desk in a bored way as though playing an approximation of a piano. It startled at the realisation it was currently live on the airways and folded up nine twitching thumbs and dozens of fingers.

"Ah. Translator's finished optimising," the Slidge said in clear Unglish. Just like before, the motions of its word-hole didn't match up with the sounds the humans were hearing. "Scans said your implants were familiar with some really ancient dialect of the Trade tongue, but it took a bit of effort to calibrate the...the whatsits. The software. We shouldn't have any issue understanding one another from now on." The Slidge took a long breath. "Apologies if syncing up caused any discomfort. I imagine forcing your systems to cross such a wide language gap might have been loud and unpleasant for a minute there. But as they say: better to be efficient than comfortable, right?"

"Who the hell says that?" Trace muttered.

If the Slidge heard her, it didn't make any indication. But it did make a motion that may have been a sign of embarrassment.

"Right, before we go any further, I'm obligated to inform you that I'm the senior Diplomat of this Starcage, The Salvation By Hatred, and we were legally compelled to disable your vessel due to the fact you are trespassing inside of a permanent quarantine zone. The techs haven't figured out how you got into this system without being spotted, but the moment you used that weird star drive we had no choice but to pass the blockade ourselves and intervene." The Diplomat flicked a triple-jointed thumb at somebody off-screen. "We're reeling you in now. If you attempt to adjust your course or so much as touch that disabled star drive, we'll be forced to destroy you. So don't do that, okay?" The Slidge might have been smiling, but it was hard to tell with that beaked face. "I look forward to meeting the five of you in person and getting to the bottom of this matter. See you soon!"

The Slidge vanished. The Starcage and its glowing heart was now so close that it dominated three quarters of the view, and it was only expanding by the moment. They could almost make out the pinpricks of what must have been colossal parking bays.

"Crap," Tuesday noted. "They know there's five of us. What's the penalty for smuggling an Apex off of Scrote?"

"Stop calling it that," Lana moaned.

Viour did not hesitate to answer the question with her maddening calmness.

"I would prefer not to say. If found guilty of such a crime, the punishment is so horrific that it is actually a serious offense to even describe it. And seeing as though you are guilty of harbouring one of the most hated of all surviving Apex, the punishment will likely be squared."

Trace glared at Viour. "You're the most hated one of your kind? Why?"

Viour gave a mental sigh.

"I was the creator of The Great Trick, which makes me the greatest comedian my species has ever produced. I am responsible for over five trillion deaths and ten thousand years of war."

"Had to be there to get the joke?" Tuesday wondered.

Trace drew her kinetic accelerator and pointed its charred barrel at the left side of Viour's head, the side that presumably contained a tiny Apex pilot.

"You aren't coming with us. No chance in hell. Simple as that. Out."

"We can't just kick her out," Lana snapped. Trace aimed a "just watch me" kind of expression at Lana, which only made her angrier. "No, I mean we literally can't kick her out. Those airlocks are a single seal. If one of them opens, we all go tumbling into deep space."

"And the Slidge will be watching for anything that leaves the lifeboat," Viour confirmed, seemingly not at all concerned with the lethal weapon aimed less than four inches from her left row of eye lenses. "You have already been exceedingly lucky not to be blasted out of the sky. It would be unwise to antagonise the Twelve Hundred further."

"You're just saying that to save your own hide," Trace snapped.

"My suit of amplification armour is more than capable of surviving the vacuum, and it would be difficult for the Slidge to damage me without dedicated weapons. I am staying in order to protect you, not myself." There was a tiny blur, and it took Trace a second to realise that her gun was no longer on her finger. Viour leaned in closer and slipped the kinetic accelerator into the armpit of Trace's armour. "There is another option. You could simply hide me."

Tuesday cackled insanely. "Right. I'll just get out my Enchanted Bag of Holding, shall I?"

Viour shook her head. "Not hide my suit of armour. Hide me. Being in possession of an amplification suit is very different to being in possession of an amplification suit and a member of The Apex."

The humans exchanged glances. As they were about ninety seconds from sliding into a garage door that looked as wide as an international airport, there wasn't any time to come up with a better plan. By not objecting, they were pretty much agreeing.

Viour reached up with an articulated limb and ran its tip down the side of her bicycle-seat shaped head. Hissing a sweet-smelling gas from half a dozen mould lines, both symmetrical rows of eye lenses slid away cleanly, folding into the sides of the skull, revealing two very different interiors. The right side of Viour's helmet, the only side that Half Head possessed before it had self-destructed, was filled with a tightly-packed prism of fine white computer wafers held together by chromatic threads. Her head's left side, however, was filled by an organic-looking

233

sac linked up to the computer side with thousands of hair-thin cables.

The sac bulged and twisted grossly before finally tearing open in a waterfall of thick, transparent gel. A handful of sensory tentacles slid out of the slash, questing like the eye stalks of a snail. Gripping at a couple of convenient rails no larger than drinking straws, a creature the size of a goldfish flipped itself up onto the top of her amplification suit's head. She was ringed with the universal "danger" message of yellow, orange, red, black and white stripes. While Jimmy, Lana and Trace all got closer for a better look, Tuesday went stumbling backwards so quickly that he tripped over his chair and almost broke his tailbone. Trace gave him a disgusted look.

"The hell is wrong with you?"

"That's a spugging Hiver Queen!" Tuesday squeaked, his voice breaking with fear.

Lana tutted. "Nonsense. No chance we'd find a creature from our own galaxy so far off. It's not possible."

"I know what a bloody Hiver Queen looks like!" Tuesday screeched. "You didn't see what they did on board The Frontier. Hundreds of thousands of enslaved rats, all mentally linked up into a big wave of teeth and claws, eating the crew down to nubbins...I barely made it out alive..."

Jimmy scoffed. "You don't know what you're talking about. I was on board The Frontier for weeks and weeks before it was due to leave. Somebody called in an anonymous quarantine tip just before we were due to head off, and the ship got permanently mothballed. I can guarantee that not one single person got eaten by rats."

"I saved all of you," Tuesday hissed under his breath, too low for Jimmy to hear. He hung his head and scratched at his scalp hard enough to draw blood. "And nobody bloody knows it."

CHAPTER TWENTY TWO TUESDAYS ARE WORSE THAN ONE

There is a world known as Seven Suns. And it is perfect.

This crown jewel of The Unison is a planet of intellectuals and philosophers, the deepest of thinkers. It is a hub of advancement and innovation, an example of how mankind's entire empire should operate. Even the least of its citizens are so well cared for that the term "post-scarcity society" no longer has no meaning, and luxuries that would be almost unthinkable on most worlds - universal health care, unlimited educational updates, and simply being provided with all the basics of life no matter who you are - were available to everybody for no cost or obligation beyond performing a bit of civic duty. While the German yen was still used in the traditional capitalist way, the citizens of Seven Suns worked for the betterment of mankind rather than to pad their bank accounts.

Prior to colonisation by Canadian settlers, when it was known by a serial number rather than a name, this planet was nothing more than an uninhabitable sub-zero wasteland in a dim binary star system. While scans revealed plenty of valuable resources, they were all out of reach beneath a kilometre-thick crust of methane ice. Endless snowstorms raged above that concrete-tough surface night and day, and the bladed weather proved to be more than capable of sweeping away even the toughest of mining equipment within minutes. A quick analysis of its five large moons revealed they were made from ordinary garden-variety silicon, and that there was nothing to be gained by stripping them. Add all of these factors together, and your chances of convincing The Unison to invest in so much as a "Nothing To See Here" sign were somewhere between laughable and suicidal.

Despite the considerable climate drawbacks, the gravity, pressure and atmospheric chemistry of this planet were all spot-on, placing it just outside of the ultra-rare Goldilocks zone necessary to support human life. While the fact remained that this world was colder than a mortician's handshake, this was hardly the most difficult of terraforming challenges The Unison had encountered. If they could turn Venus into a five-star beach resort, modify cockroaches to absorb vast amounts of gamma radiation and even purify Amerika's drinking water into something short of non-lethal, melting a bit of snow was hardly a challenge.

Unwilling to be deterred by something as pedestrian as a cold climate – admittedly, one that could freeze all six nipples right off of a walrus – a team of resourceful ecological engineers dedicated a month of thought to the problem. After a few false starts, they finally decided that their best bet was to take the five silicon moons that orbited this iceberg and melt them into giant glass prisms. These colossal multi-faceted lenses would soak up every watt of dim local starlight and reflect it back and forth between one another before using it to bathe every square metre of the snowball in an endlessly sunny afternoon. The mathematics weren't all that difficult for a supercomputer to work out, and after a short break for coffee hypos the numbers were mostly sorted.

However, there was one more obstacle to overcome: the plan sounded completely insane. To the bureaucratic laymen who had to sign off on this idea, it appeared to have more in common with the schemes of a cackling supervillain than something

235

the greatest minds of The Unison had collectively formulated, and convincing the Military to hand over the launch codes for an entire vault of antique Expansionist-era hydrogen bombs proved to be even more challenging. Once they had finally been grudgingly allocated the exact amount of nukes specified by their calculations, the ecological engineers pulled off the greatest feat of thermonuclear sculpting in history, effectively transforming the nameless world overnight. Within a month of the storms abating and the ice melting, Canada had already sent over half a million settlers. Seeing as though the most notable feature of this planet was that you could always see a total of seven ever-glowing pits in the sky from anywhere on its surface, the settlers agreed that there was only one possible name for their new world: Seven Suns.

A little over three hundred years later, two vertical kilometres above the cloud-choked surface of Seven Suns, Bob Tuesday had a severe headache. He was leaning against an oak desk in the luxury apartment of a very dead crime-lord known as Ernest Fell, and was trying to get his thoughts together. Up until a couple of minutes ago Ernest was Tuesday's nemesis, and had been directly responsible for almost every terrible thing in Tuesday's life since his ninth birthday. Thanks to a fluke time-travel accident that had sent Tuesday and a swarm of ravenous mentally-hived rats hurtling across the galaxy, little was left of Ernest beyond a few bloodied scraps of fabric that had once been a top-shelf Seladorian suit.

Pinching the bridge of a nose that had suffered several well-deserved breaks over the years, Tuesday tried to empty his mind to think. As usual, while the emptying part was easy enough, wielding his brain to come up with anything useful was a different matter altogether. Gritting his black teeth, Tuesday started by reviewing where he was at.

Okay. From the beginning...

It had been an average day on board The Frontier until an endless wave of rats operating under the direct control of a Hiver Queen had eaten the crew. One minute Tuesday was pretending to work, the next he was watching his colleagues get nibbled into appetiser-sized chunks by a tide of vermin. The aforementioned defective time machine was the only reason Tuesday wasn't currently being dissolved in a thousand rodent bellies. However, that day was technically located several months in the future...

At this thought, Tuesday crunched his eyes tighter in pain. While most of his grey matter was convinced that this furry apocalypse had only happened a few minutes ago, a tiny, more insightful segment of his brain was trying to point out that in actuality the disaster on The Frontier hadn't occurred yet, and was still months away. He may have just watched everyone die, but in this time stream none of the poor schmucks had any idea of the horrible demise that awaited them on the other side of the galaxy. The more these two contradicting elements slammed against each other, the worse Tuesday's mental agony got.

Tuesday's eyes popped open between his fingers.

He had it. He knew what he was meant to do next.

Swiping at the meat in his left hand between his thumb and index finger, Tuesday gave a grunt of annoyance when nothing happened. He'd been forced to order his Omni implant to commit suicide a few months back so that the powers-that-be couldn't use it to track him when he'd stowed away aboard The Frontier (an event that was still about twenty minutes away in this time stream), and all of his connections on this world – everyone from his Blink dealer to the Mayor himself – had been stored on that Omni. You couldn't just get those sorts of numbers off the public Link.

Tuesday's head snapped towards a sweeping balcony at the sound of a deafening groan. Rushing out the French doors so fast that he almost winded himself on the balcony railing, he was greeted by a panorama of ivory towers wreathed in soft blue-white cloud. "The Heights" region of Seven Suns was best described as an exact match for how medieval man pictured heaven: pure as milk, extending so high and so low that it almost seemed infinite.

Looking up as the moan got louder, Tuesday watched as an immense white slab the size of a city lowered itself down from a bright sky. He could clearly see THE FRONTIER embossed in golden lettering along the creamy side facing him.

The Frontier was coming in to land. Soon, it would suck up millions of tonnes of supplies, allowing Tuesday's past self to stowaway in the process. It would be out of this star system in under thirty minutes, and by then it would be too late. History would repeat, and everyone would die again. And even if Tuesday somehow broke several speed records, he wouldn't be able to physically get to the Starport in time.

Scanning around the luxury apartment, Tuesday's eyes came to rest on what little remained of Ernest Fell. Among the bloodied scraps of fabric were a few things the rats couldn't chew through: a couple of platinum rings, a gold watch, and what appeared to be a false molar made out of a huge diamond. Kicking aside a done-up zipper, Tuesday's foot connected with something roughly the size of a matchbox made out of composite. Picking up the lightly-nibbled item, Tuesday's heart soared when it flipped open to reveal it was one of those trendy retro mobile phones that were all the rage last week. The feelings of triumph vanished abruptly as Tuesday remembered that he still didn't have any useful numbers to call. A lot

237

of people might be interested to know that there was a Hiver Queen on board The Frontier, sure, but there was a good chance they wouldn't take him seriously. He couldn't just systematically dial every person on this world one after another in the hopes of finding a single receptive ear with the clearance to do something.

Wracking his brain, Tuesday remembered one number: the switchboard on The Frontier. After all, by committing this combination of digits to memory, Tuesday had been able to access anybody on the ship. But could he access the switchboard from the outside? Did it only operate on board? Would he need some sort of password?

His shaking index finger zipped across the touchpad a dozen times, and Tuesday held the handset against his stubble. There was a soft trilling noise for a few seconds, but instead of getting the usual snarky operator, Tuesday heard a voice so familiar that it suddenly became hard to stand.

"Hello?" she asked, curiosity in her tone. "Who is this?"

The world stopped at those words. It was September, the only person on board The Frontier who meant anything to him, the only reason he hadn't just left the entire crew to their fate. The image of seeing September devoured by rats danced behind his eyes, needling him in the optic nerves.

It took a long moment for Tuesday to realise that this wasn't the time to vague out. He had to talk fast, or all hope was lost. September's life depended on it.

"This is life or death, okay?" Tuesday rattled off. "Commander Redmond Eulogy is in possession of a fertile Hiver Queen. He keeps her in a lead-lined matchbox in his pocket. She's fully capable of enslaving rodents. Like rats. And mice. And..."

"I know what a rodent is," September snapped with her usual lack of patience. "How did you get this number? I don't even have this number. And you still haven't told me who you are. You do understand that you aren't inspiring my confidence right now?"

"Damn it, September!" Tuesday yelled. Images of ripping skin played on the inside of his eyelids. He slammed his free fist into the balcony's railing. "We don't have time for twenty-questions. You need to go see Fleet Admiral Aslan right now and tell him that there is a spugging Hiver Queen on board his ship, and that you are all going to get eaten at some time in the next few months. Do you understand what I'm saying? Is your genius brain taking all this in, Professor Dickhead?"

There was silence on the other end. Tuesday remembered that one of September's many mental skills was being able to tell if somebody was lying to her, and he hoped that she didn't just disregard him as a very convincing crank, or psychotic.

After three long seconds The Frontier passed Tuesday's level and disappeared into the cloud banks two hundred metres down. Ready to follow up with another angry salvo, Tuesday was interrupted by a click of disconnection.

She had hung up on him.

All Tuesday could do was stare at the retro mobile in numb shock. After about fifteen seconds his total lack of thoughts and feelings were ready to be pushed aside to make room for a total nervous breakdown. Before Tuesday could scream in frustration and anger at the mental pictures of September being consumed like so much deli meat, a hand landed on his shoulder.

Spinning half a revolution, phone raised ready to bash in somebody's eye socket, Bob Tuesday came face-to-face with what he'd look like after about thirty years and eight thousand serious benders: Jim Tuesday, his Father. He'd been so distracted by the whole Hiver Queen issue that he'd forgotten all about accidentally rescuing his dad from Ernest Fell during the time travel snafu. As most of Tuesday's life had been dedicated to finding his dad, it really showed the true depths of his feelings for September.

"Remind me," Jim managed. "Where are we?"

Jim was a scruffy, toothless hobo with the physical fitness of a day-old barbecue chicken, and to say he looked like death was an insult to the wider zombie community. Bob hadn't seen his dad since being kidnapped and sold into slavery on his ninth birthday, but that all-too familiar smirk pasted across his face confirmed who he was more effectively than any paternity test.

"So..." Jim Tuesday said, his face an aged mirror. "Your shout?"

*

Staying put would be unwise. While more than satisfied with Ernest's horrible death, Tuesday always did his best not to be within five blocks of a suspicious dead body at any given time. He wasn't a murderer, but trawling through the scummy under hives of society all his life meant that he was no stranger to the occasional corpse. Most of the neighbourhoods he'd lived in didn't provide any guarantee that you'd return alive from checking the mail.

As Tuesday hadn't arrived at Ernest's apartment in The Heights by any of the traditional ways (skycar, jetpack, escape pod, short-range teleportation), getting back to street level was a bit confusing. This region of Seven Suns was highly vertical, and with seventy separate skylanes spread at a dozen different altitudes it took a good half hour until Tuesday figured out how to reach the yellow-and-black striped stretch of a taxi rank. He'd already boarded with his dad (who seemed to be content to follow along with a brainless expression and a drooping lower lip for now) and gone a good kilometre before the driver asked him a difficult question.

"Where to?"

Tuesday went even blanker. He had no interest in going home, as his violent girlfriend from this time stream would probably be waiting for him with an empty bottle and bad intentions, and besides the hobo sitting right next to him he couldn't think of anybody who would be interested in sitting in close proximity to him for any length of time.

While Tuesday was hardly Memory Man and had a habit of automatically switching off his attention the moment other people started talking, he did remember that September – future September, the one who knew him – had mentioned a certain University cafe she used to frequent. If Tuesday recalled, she went there in order to challenge the smartest and most highly educated patrons to a battle of wits in any subject of their choosing, and would leave in triumph once she had happily crushed their feelings of self-worth, ego and confidence underfoot. While highly respected by her peers, September's presence was usually about as welcome as a skid mark on a wedding cake.

Tuesday leaned forwards to stick his head between the two front seats.

"Hawking Student Cafe at Dartmouth Uni."

The driver gave Tuesday and his dad an odd look in the rear-view mirror for a second. It was the sort of expression you'd form if somebody casually mentioned that they were going to teach their poodle how to speak Swahili.

"What?" Tuesday snapped, not liking the way the driver was gawping at him.

"Nothing," the driver said quickly.

Their ride was uneventful until its very end. Considering the average amount of danger Tuesday faced in everyday life, this was about all he could ask for. When the driver held out a payment scanner the size of a pinkie finger, Tuesday almost swore. He didn't have his SpendPlus card, or so much as a single German yen to his name. Stiffing the driver wasn't wise, as that was a felony on this world, and one of the few instances where a Seven Suns local might get violent. Patting his pockets theatrically, taking a few valuable moments to scheme how he was going to get out of this one without simply bolting and hoping for the best, the driver interrupted with a lot more civility than Tuesday expected.

"If you forgot your card, just thumb it."

The tiny scanner displayed a hologram of a large lime-coloured fingerprint. Without bothering to consider whether this might set off some alarm bells that he'd much prefer to keep silent for now, Tuesday tapped his thumb to the spot and waited. It took a second, but ROBERT TUESDAY, APPROVED popped up in the same bright green.

Getting out of the taxi, ignoring the driver as his vehicle ascended six skylanes before disappearing into the metallic swarm, Tuesday took a good look at an unusual building: constructed from some kind of red brick rather than the usual locally-mined glowstone, Dartmouth Uni was covered in ivy and accented by hand-carved wooden details. Its old-fashioned design was entirely out of place compared to the ivory panorama you got everywhere else on Seven Suns, and Tuesday could picture some of the less flexible locals having an issue with its appearance in the early days of its construction. Even from this distance, Tuesday could almost smell the learning in the air. It made him gag.

A local payphone, which was little more than a thin chest-high pole topped with a strawberry-sized projector, trilled to Tuesday's left. The name BROKAGE GRUNDY appeared in bright letters, with the title MAYOR beneath it. To Tuesday's surprise, he didn't need to do anything for the call to come through. The familiar face of the Mayor – which was twisted into an equally-familiar snarl of fury - had barely appeared before it growled a tricky question.

"You want to explain to me why a pair of Unison marines down at the spaceport just shot and killed somebody who was trying to stowaway on a starship, Tuesday?"

For a moment, Tuesday was a bit taken aback with how the Mayor had somehow found him, especially seeing as though this was the first time Tuesday had stepped within fifty kilometres of a University. But then he remembered just paying for a taxi ride with a thumbprint and a genetic match, and it all made sense.

Well, seems as though I'm back on the radar again...

Tuesday shrugged, trying to look innocent. "Got nothing to do with me, does it? Some random stiff isn't my problem."

The Mayor jammed his face against the screen so hard that his nose was squished a little. He hissed his next words, and they chilled Tuesday to the core.

"As the dead body is a perfect genetic match for one Robert Tuesday, I think it is your problem. Got anything you want to tell me?"

*

Tuesday's brain was locked into a crazed death dive for the next twenty minutes. He didn't register walking into the Hawking Cafe, didn't notice how all of the postgrads looked at him like he was a turd in the potato salad, didn't feel how comfortable the booth was when he sat in it, and didn't even realise he'd ordered anything until the waitress placed a tray of assorted coffee syringes in front of him. Jim Tuesday eagerly jammed one of the self-inserting cappuccino hypodermics into his neck as his son fell to pieces less than a metre away.

Dead. He was dead.

Seemingly not at all worried about what such news would do to Tuesday's brain, the Mayor had explained in graphic detail exactly what had gone down at the spaceport. Apparently somebody who was a perfect match for Bob Tuesday had broken the security cordon meant to be keeping the general public out of The Frontier's parking space, and a pair of armed marines had no choice but to give chase among the towering piles of supplies that would keep the city-sized starship fed for its decade-long trip. However, for some unknown reason, The Frontier did not start hoovering up the supply stacks as planned, and had just sat there silently.

The trespasser had demonstrated some serious moves, and at the start of the pursuit the marines had only succeeded in blowing a few holes into some vacuum-packed pallets and crates. When the trespasser scaled a small mountain of medical supplies the marines had followed him to the summit and – unfortunately - shot and killed him right on top of a crate of extra-large self-guiding unlubricated rectal thermometers. It turned out that non-lethal rubber rounds lost the "non" prefix when they collided with your temple at point-blank range.

Dead. Tuesday was dead.

Sitting at the cafe booth, gaping like an imbecile with his eyeballs almost falling out of his face, Tuesday kept checking his hands every few seconds to make sure he hadn't started to fade away. That's how it worked, right? Your past self gets squibbed, and your future self dies. One of the easiest, most basic time travel concepts, that.

Or...perhaps being unstuck in time changed the rules somewhat? While Tuesday might have trouble simply spelling "time travel" on a bad day, he had seen a lot of movies. No matter how you angled things, the temporal realm was a hateful, fickle hell-bitch to even the greatest of scientists, and rarely conformed to established rules. She laughed in the face of logic, and scorned the human brain as being utterly useless in making sense of her.

"Son?"

Tuesday looked up abruptly to meet his dad's gaze. Blinking, Tuesday scanned around the Hawking Cafe to see it was a collection of booths and lounges upholstered in cheery fabric. There were plenty of flat tables made out of mahogany planks, and most of them were covered in clusters of holographic paper. Students were writing on the simulated sheets with a combination of direct thought transference and eye movements, storing the holograms in their Omni implants for later on once they were satisfied with their work. There was a quiet hiss now and again as a tired student injected a cappuccino hypo into their neck.

Finally getting his bearings, Tuesday met his dad's eyes a second time and asked the most basic of questions.

"Hmm?"

"I overheard Ernest say you killed a serial killer friend of his called Prince Charming and rescued a bunch of his victims?"

Tuesday waved this away. "Sort of. I managed to get free, and I accidentally set the other prisoners loose while I was trying to find my way out. Honestly, it didn't occur to me to help them for a single second."

Jim Tuesday smirked. "Sounds like being a hero pays well, though."

Tuesday scoffed. "Hero? I'm a bloody mascot. They use me in their propaganda campaigns and their commercials and to cut ribbons in front of MacDeath restaurants. I've got comfort, sure, but I'm little more than a pet, and I spugging hate it. Why do you think I tried to stowaway aboard The Frontier?"

"Better dead than domesticated," Jim said knowingly.

Tuesday's eyes flicked towards the happy chiming sound of the cafe's entrance admitting a customer, and there she was: a beautiful black woman of Ugandan and Eastern Korean descent dressed in the snappy white uniform and purple piping of a high-level Unison scientist. September was shaped like an hourglass and had straight ebony hair flowing all the way down to her shapely buttocks. Hers was the sort of beauty that didn't require a jot of make-up at even the most exclusive of venues. Her mind was even more impressive than her stunning appearance: Tuesday knew that September was one of the greatest geniuses Seven Suns had ever produced, managing to earn no fewer than fifteen doctorate-level black-belts embossed with the golden logos of the best universities The Unison had to offer. September had easily gathered fourth-dan qualifications in stellar engineering, advanced physics, pure mathematics, macro-string theory, non-florid psychotic calculus, reality stuttering and many other subjects that Tuesday would have trouble pronouncing, let alone defining. In total, September had more than one-hundred and ninety-seven letters after her name, not counting vowels or commas.

Everyone took notice the moment September crossed the threshold, and the students all began to mutter and poised themselves to leave at the first opportunity.

September frowned at a wall mirror on the way in, and buffed her sigils of command. Rubbing at her almond-shaped eyes – a hint of her Eastern Korean heritage – she immediately spotted Tuesday and advanced for his booth. If she noticed that two thirds of the cafe's customers casually left at top speed the moment she had her back was turned, she didn't show it. She loomed over Tuesday and his dad, and snapped her words.

"Mayor Grundy asked me to come here and speak with you as a personal favour. You have exactly five seconds to captivate my attention, or this discussion ends."

Tuesday was stunned for a moment. He'd forgotten how intimidating September was before he had a chance to get to know her. Then he realised that he only had two seconds left.

"I...."

September's face crunched into a hateful snarl at this single letter. Tuesday would never be able to guess how, but it seemed that one vowel was all the data she needed to recognise his voice.

"You were the one who called me earlier! Do you have any idea what you've done? Thanks to you, The Frontier has been mothballed until a front-to-back quarantine scan can be conducted. It could take years to fully satisfy the brass that the mission is ready to go ahead. Do you know how long I've been preparing for this voyage? Do you have any idea what I'm being deprived of with every minute that tub is wasting in dry-dock?"

"So they found the Hiver Queen?" Tuesday asked.

September chewed her lip a little. "Yes. It was in Eulogy's pocket in a lead-lined matchbox, like you said. They incinerated her immediately, and Eulogy is currently being processed for breaking about a dozen different quarantine laws."

"You knew I was telling the truth," Tuesday said. "Or you wouldn't have gone to Fleet Admiral Aslan."

"Yes," she said easily.

There was an unspoken question in September's eye, and it seemed to be pressing enough to spur her to sit down at their booth. This simple movement set off a burst of chemicals in Tuesday's brain that gave him the narcotic sensation known as success, something he rarely felt. September gave a curt motion at the waitress as she swooped over to take an order.

"Nothing for me, Marie." September closed her eyes and took a breath before continuing. "The Mayor said you're just some publicity puppet they use for promotional reasons, and I don't bother with any of that celebrity rubbish. Waste of time. But even though I've never met you before, I can tell that you know me. The words you chose during that phone call, the way you said them, how you've been looking at me since I walked in..." September bared her teeth a little. "I'm warning you now that if I don't like or don't believe the answer you give to this

244

question, I'm walking: what am I to you?"

"You're..." it took a second to translate the vague feelings and desires into words. "You helped me. I have an allergy to AutoEducation, so..."

"The Raffle Gene?" September summarised.

Tuesday nodded. "Right. The Raffle Gene. But you found a way to treat me using some neural gel from Eulogy's Hiver Queen. You did more to improve who I am than everybody else I've ever met put together. And along the way, we..."

"Became close?" September raised a manicured eyebrow in disbelief.

Tuesday gave a weak smile. "Kind of."

September thought about this for a few moments.

"You bear an uncanny resemblance to one of the janitors aboard The Frontier. Jack Spasm."

"Perfect match, actually," Tuesday corrected. "He's my future self from another timeline, you see. My past self knocked him out and took his place."

"Timeline," September repeated. She didn't seem to be questioning the impossible concept that Tuesday had so casually mentioned, but did voice one issue. "But you didn't take his place," September contradicted. "You're right here."

Tuesday shrugged his head. "No, the version of me that was meant to take Jack Spasm's place in this timeline got shot in the temple not half an hour ago. Far as I can figure, my phone call indirectly prevented The Frontier from sucking up all of those supplies, so the past me that was meant to stowaway by getting brought up in the gravity lift didn't manage to make it. So, he died." Tuesday blinked. "But I did, even though he didn't, because I'm a different me."

September narrowed her eyes a little.

"How many other temporally-unglued Robert Tuesdays are there, to your knowledge?"

"Besides the dead one, Jack Spasm and me? Well, there's also Fleet Admiral Aslan," Tuesday admitted.

September glared at him, reading his face like a pamphlet. She glanced at Jim Tuesday when he let off a loud, wet snore from the other side of the booth. It seemed as though the cappuccino hypo hadn't been enough to keep him awake.

"Please tell me that isn't one of your future selves."

"Nah. It's just my dad."

September made a sharp, silent motion at Marie the waitress. It seemed as though September had decided that this conversation might just be worth the price of one or two coffee hypos.

"I'm well versed in temporal physics and the philosophy of time travel, Mister Tuesday. None of these concepts are news to me. I could attempt to explain it all to you in greater depth, but while it would take me an hour to say it, it would take you multiple lifetimes to comprehend. My advice? Just be glad you still exist." September smoothly accepted her cappuccino and jammed it into her neck. "Now, with these mentally-dominated rats you mentioned, was I one of the ones eaten by the hive? Did you actually see me die?"

Tuesday blinked a couple of times, trying to maintain composure, but then his face crumpled at the horrible images. September leaned closer to him, her expression intense.

"What were my last words?"

"Why do you love me?" Tuesday whispered so quietly that he almost couldn't hear himself. "That's what you said. You had just lost a leg, though, so it might have been the shock talking."

September nodded a couple of times. Her poker face gave nothing away.

"Do you still possess the means to travel through time? Or, as far as you know, will you be able to travel through time again at some point in the future?"

Tuesday shook his head. "Nah. Machine packed it in after the last hop. And like most people, I don't generally carry a spare time machine around in my back pocket, do I?"

September got to her feet, looking satisfied.

"Thank you for your time, Mister Tuesday. I believe I've heard everything I need to know."

"Wait!" Tuesday yelled at September's quickly-turned back.

The cafe's few remaining students shushed him. There were even a couple of expletives from a young postgrad who had just lost her grip on a once-in-a-lifetime answer to a long-mysterious concept. September turned and gave Tuesday a questioning look.

"Is that it?" Tuesday hissed. "After all this, you're just leaving me for good?"

September looked at Tuesday like he was an imbecile. He had missed that expression.

"Of course I'm leaving. Whatever relationship you shared with your version of me in that obsolete time stream is just as obsolete, and I have absolutely nothing to do with that invalid future, or with you. The factors that were necessary to create such a friendship now have no chance of coming into play. I am not the September you know, and I never will be." She stepped closer to Tuesday and leaned down. Her expression and tone were as cold as a wet fish to the jaw. "I think it best that you do not contact me again, Mister Tuesday. Please respect my wishes."

And with that, September walked out of his life forever.

246

Tuesday sat in the Hawking Cafe for some time. While he may not be a student, the German yen his thumbprint provided were most welcome. He stared out a window at the ivory towers and dozens of intertwining skylanes, feeling totally lost. His brownie went untouched, and his coffee hypo went unjabbed.

What he was meant to do next was easy: Mayor Grundy had spelled out in no uncertain terms that Tuesday was to get a new Omni implant installed in his hand at the closest body piercing shop ASAP, and this one would not be fitted with an uninstall function. Short of cutting a hunk out of his hand, there would be no way for Tuesday to remove the Omni, which meant they'd be able to track him down to the metre for the rest of his life. Once the web of his left hand had been permanently studded, Tuesday had a long list of publicity events to attend. As usual, he'd be expected to smile (with his mouth firmly closed, of course) and nod approval.

Back to normal.

Jim Tuesday woke up with a snort. Blinking out of sync, he patted his pockets until he uncovered his precious mechanical lighter, the one that his son had been carrying around all this time. Looking at the little metal box in hesitation, he flipped open its lid and gave its charred wick a gummy smile. He'd done this no fewer than fifteen times since being reunited with it earlier today, and it was only getting weirder each time. Tuesday couldn't help but ask.

"Why do you look so happy every time you open the lighter?"

Jim Tuesday had a "busted" look sprint across his face. Too late, he took on a more casual, nonchalant expression.

"Just nice to see it again, is all."

The younger Tuesday didn't buy this for a second. He'd inherited his dad's talents for rank scummery, and could smell the shape of a scheme from a hundred metres away.

Tuesday held out a hand, and his dad reluctantly passed the mechanical lighter across the booth. Flicking the lighter's cap open and shut, observing how his dad's eyes followed every movement almost in pain, Tuesday went to light the wick with his usual double-flick motion.

"No!" Jim Tuesday yelled, swiping at the lighter before Bob could hit the flint.

Tuesday moved it easily out of reach. His dad's coordination was beneath reproach after decades of chemically-induced brain damage.

"Why not? Why shouldn't I light it?"

Jim cringed. "I just..."

Bob slammed his dad's lighter down on the laminate.

"All right, I've had enough. It's been well over a decade since you last saw me, and all you can do is look at this stupid metal box. Either you let me know what scam you're pulling, or I'm done. I'm leaving, and I'm taking this with me."

Jim gave his son an expression halfway between frustration and defeat.

"I have debts with people who...don't possess the greatest degree of patience," Jim said, glancing hungrily at the lighter. "People who...how do I put this...tend to take souvenirs? Souvenirs that don't grow back? Well, that lighter you're holding is the key to getting these people to put down their bolt cutters and forget about chasing me across The Unison."

Tuesday looked down at the lighter. It was nothing special. He'd replaced its cotton padding and flint dozens of times, and refilled it with assorted kinds of gas on a thousand occasions. It was just a generic mechanical lighter, nothing more.

"What, is it an antique or something?"

Jim Tuesday held out his hand. Bob grudgingly gave the lighter back. Jim tapped the blackened wick with one finger.

"You've never had to replace the wick, have you?"

Tuesday squinted. "No. It never burns down. Always thought that was a bit weird. Just assumed it was made of something special."

Jim smiled a gummy smile.

"It is special. It's one of your mum's eyelashes."

*

It had been well over twenty years since Ruska, Tuesday's mum, had escaped from a secret Russian-run genetics laboratory in Nevada after spending her whole life as a super-soldier experiment. She had been free for less than an hour when she stumbled into the deafening chaos of an illegal Scumbags concert. At seven foot tall with retractable claws and covered entirely in thick hair, she was far from the strangest individual in this mosh pit full of torture-metal fans.

After literally bumping into Jim Tuesday, who was so wasted on a drug known as Shatter that it was a wonder the autonomous functions of his brain hadn't shut down yet, one thing led to another and they had engaged in mediocre sex against a speaker stack. Falling pregnant almost instantly, Ruska knew how interesting her offspring would be to the Russian scientists, so she had no choice but to flee to the heart of the Mojave and hide out indefinitely. When Jim Tuesday awoke the next morning he was less than thrilled with this plan, to say the least.

Almost a decade on, right on Bob Tuesday's ninth birthday, Ernest Fell had turned up to shatter their little family. After murdering Ruska with a ridiculously overpowered machine gun, Ernest topped this by selling Bob into slavery in a sweatshop so he could spend his childhood making toys for luckier children. Ruska's death was the turning point in Bob's life, the key event that switched his idyllic existence in the desert into something intolerable, from stable to completely off-kilter.

The morning of his ninth birthday had been the last time he'd felt truly happy.

*

Lost deep in thought for a moment, Tuesday startled at a hand waving in his face. He almost put up his fists to defend himself, and managed to surprise his dad. Both Tuesdays looked embarrassed by how they'd flinched like wimps.

"Your mum couldn't be burned," Jim explained. "She was engineered to be fireproof all over. Skin, hair, everything. Her eyelashes, though, have this sort of waxy stuff on them that can be ig...ignited, but the eyelash itself doesn't char at all."

Bob reclined, giving his dad a hard look.

"I'm missing the part with how this eyelash is going to solve your money problems."

Jim's face went slack. "Are you kidding? This is all that's left of a long lost super-soldier experiment..."

"Left of Mum," Tuesday corrected, growling dangerously. "All that's left of Mum."

Jim waved this away. "Yeah, of course. But all the modifications the genetic engineers did to her in that laboratory are recorded on this eyelash. Her DMA is stored in it."

"DNA." Tuesday said. It was rare that he met somebody so dumb that he was able to repeatedly correct them. "But you could have just taken them to our service station in the Mojave, right? No way the vultures had sharp enough beaks to get into Mum. Surely a dedicated search would have been a better option than scouring the entire bloody galaxy to find a single lighter?"

"Tried that," Jim said morosely.

Tuesday sat up.

"What?"

"Led them to the service station years ago." Jim clarified. "Everything was the same as when I left it, except Ruska's body wasn't there. No bones, either. It was as

249

though she got up and walked away."

This took another minute for Tuesday to process. Could his mum be alive? From the stories she'd told him as a toddler, Ruska was nigh-on immortal. She'd survived all sorts of violent tests in the Russian-run lab that had designed and decanted her, so it wasn't a ridiculous assumption that she might have lived through getting shot a couple of dozen times by a hand-held cannon.

Thankfully, his dad didn't try to bring him back to the moment by waving in his face again. He hated it when people did that.

Tuesday eventually flicked his eyes back towards his dad. Jim Tuesday was chewing ineffectively at his lips with his empty gums. It was a weird sight.

"You can have the lighter on one condition: I want in."

"But the buyer is all the way back on Earth," Jim complained. "And after my debts are paid off, there's barely an Amerikan pound left. You're better off staying here, where it's safe a comfortable."

Tuesday snatched the lighter again and pointed a well-gnawed fingernail in his dad's face.

"Don't spug with me, Dad. I need to get off this rock, and this could be my last chance to do it before I'm permanently under the thumb of the damned powers-that-be. Either you cut me in, or you can find another way to pay off your debts."

Jim's grumpy expression gradually shifted into a configuration he'd never worn before: pride.

"Looks like you turned out just fine, son. It's...it's good to know."

Looking around to make sure nobody was listening (they weren't), Tuesday leaned in towards his dad and whispered in a conspiratorial manner.

"I need to know everything. Who the buyers are, who they work for, what they do to people who piss them off, everything."

"And then?" Jim pressed.

"Then?" Tuesday repeated. "We'll go shopping for what we need."

Jim blinked out of synchronisation, indicating that he was trying to work out something in his head without much success.

"Shopping? I, ah, don't actually have two pence to rub together at the mo. Totally skint."

His son gave an evil smile and swept a dirty sleeve across the laminate tabletop. As though dealing cards, Tuesday effortlessly spread out six items: two delicate jade rings, a pair of golden ear hoops studded with balls of pure adamantine, a silver money clip fastened around the better part of six hundred German yen, and an old SpendPlus card that would be simplicity itself to hack with any half-decent cracking equipment.

"Not to worry, Dad. September's been kind enough to invest in our little venture."

*

It took plenty of petty theft and lies, but five weeks later Bob Tuesday and his dad had made it halfway across The Unison, and were only minutes away from striking a business deal with one of the last remaining Splinters of Russia.

After the Scandinavian Expansion had annexed most of Europe, Asia and Amerika within the space of a few short months in the late 21st Century, Russia was one of the last nations to surrender to the endless onslaught of Expansionist forces. Following the total defeat of their considerable military, Russia's populace had waged a bloody rebellion against their new self-declared masters. Mercifully, the Expansion quelled these uprisings without having to perpetrate anything as horrible as what had befallen the much-more stubborn defenders in Michigan. Although a mighty nation to the end, Russia eventually accepted its new management like all the other world powers.

Once the Expansion had been defeated, its constituent parts were more or less divided back into their original countries, states and territories. Russia, however, was not afforded the opportunity to regain even a glimmer of its former glory. Before the Expansion, Russia had been a terrifying superpower with enough military hardware to annihilate mankind and scour the planet down to its bedrock a hundred times over. As the Expansion had surgically removed Russia's nuclear, chemical and biological capabilities during its subjugation, leaving the Motherland defenceless once the Skandos had been kicked out, the rest of the world took this opportunity to make it clear that they weren't going to tolerate any more crap from Boris and Ivan, and violently opposed every attempt that Russia made to regain control over its former regions.

A timeless quote made during a Spherical Office address by legendary Amerikan President L D Linden summed the political situation up perfectly: "Once all the nerds realised the biggest bully in the schoolyard had his arms tied behind his back, they sure as hell weren't going to help him undo the knot."

Russia's borders shifted back and forth wildly, but by the early 25th Century what was now known as the "Splinters of Russia" had shrunk almost to nothing. All that remained were a few scraps and slithers of Russian soil located between some of the more forgiving and charitable nations, and most of the Splinters operated in a similar way to foreign embassies. While the Splinters had no real political power and most of them couldn't be located on a map without a magnifying glass, they still possessed a massive portfolio of military research from pre-Expansionist days, and a lot of this material was so far ahead of its time that it had only just become technologically feasible to manufacture.

One key product that had kept the Splinters funded for all these years was the "Monolith" super-soldier. Standing at an incredible four metres tall and wrapped in a nine-tonne armoured suit of unbreakable gold-and-alabaster glass plates, Monoliths were less of a conventional ground trooper and more of an archangel of vengeance made flesh. It was like War itself had been shaped into something that breathed. There were very few weapons within The Unison capable of even annoying a Monolith, and the concept of actually killing one was idiocy. You might as well pick a fight with the Sun. Even without their invulnerable shells, the godlike bodies of Monoliths could survive direct exposure to the vacuum, had a total immunity to pain, and could not be damaged by any known projectile, blade, chemical, or explosive. While their defence was second-to-none, when it came to offensive capabilities the Monoliths were even more impressive, carrying a combination of offensive systems that would best be summarised as "apocalyptic." The specifics of Monolith load-outs were pure speculation, as nobody had ever seen one of these living gods in action and survived to describe what happened. It was rumoured that Monoliths were armed with everything.

Sitting right on the knife edge between a barely-tolerated arms dealer and an outright rogue state, while Russia was only holding on by a single finger, it went without saying that finger was the middle one.

Descending in a juddering spaceplane into what had once been the northernmost slither of Syberia, Bob Tuesday and his dad prepared to disembark from the space-to-ground cargo shuttle by tightening multiple layers of thick bearskin rugs and pulling down armed-robbery-grade ski masks. Although Tuesday and his dad were visiting this Splinter for official business purposes (they even had an appointment), they'd been forced to spend the last of their cash bribing a pilot to ferry them down to Earth's surface from one of Russia's last remaining private enterprise satellites. As the antique spaceplane usually transported information slugs containing the latest biotech weapon designs, smuggling in two illegal aliens who had no visas and plenty of criminal convictions was probably the least morally objectionable cargo the pilot had ever carried. It had taken all of two and a half minutes before Tuesday had simply swiped his money back, and he'd also scored a wedding ring and a golden tongue stud.

As you'd expect with any Siberian Winter, the sideways-blowing snow was so dense that you couldn't see three feet in any direction and the wind was full of invisible blades. Tuesday decided that having actual knives flying about would have been a better alternative to this icy gale. If it wasn't for the straight lines of high-visibility fluorescent strips guiding them to safety, the Tuesdays would have doubtlessly wandered into the squall and died of exposure within twenty minutes. Following the high-vis lights one step at a time, shaking more and more violently inside their bearskins the whole way, the Tuesdays finally made it to the only permanent building within three hundred kilometres. It was a simple pentagon made from unpainted concrete no bigger than a three-bedroom house, and had no apparent entrance.

Father and son tried to exchange questioning looks, but their ski masks made facial expressions moot.

Before they could attempt to make themselves heard over the blizzard, the entire front of the pentagon opened like a donut box, beckoning them with warm light. As they stepped inside they could see that the underside of the huge concrete door was studded with antigrav wafers. Five tonnes of plain concrete slammed shut behind the Tuesdays, trapping them in total darkness, and the temperature suddenly spiked so high that they had to shed their bearskins and ski masks before heatstroke claimed them. As he hadn't managed a single smoke in almost twenty minutes, Tuesday immediately drew a chlorine cigarette from its soft packet with his mouth.

Aged overhead lighting flickered on out of sync, revealing that this area was an empty box except for an undecorated staircase dead ahead that descended into the gloom. As though at a signal, four black-armoured guards crested the steps and halted in a straight line. They were each armed with the same cutting-edge redesign of Kalashnikov's iconic AK-47 assault rifle, a firearm that has managed to tick up more fatalities over the centuries than any other two guns combined. As the Second World War was a long time ago, this version of the AK-47 had all the mod-cons like frictionless components, caseless ammunition and kinetic accelerator barrels, and was the perfect synthesis of old and new for a price tag that any rogue government/wide-scale arms dealer could afford.

One of the guards stepped forwards. Unlike the others, he had a golden hawk bolted to his bulletproof breastplate. He gave the unlit cigarette in Tuesday's mouth a dark glance and snapped an unfamiliar sound.

"Poisk."

Tuesday had to force himself not to react when the word "search" superimposed itself over his field of vision. Until this moment, Tuesday had no idea that his retinal implants could automatically translate foreign languages into augmented-reality subtitles. He thought it best to keep this titbit of information to himself for now, and carefully twisted his face up in confusion.

"Come again, Mikhail?"

Like a million times before, Tuesday produced his dad's trusty mechanical lighter and lit his cigarette in one practiced motion. The flame had barely started dancing on his mum's waxy eyelash before Tuesday suddenly had three kinetic accelerator barrels pointed at his head. The entire quartet of guards started yelling the same word over and over, and Tuesday's vision was crowded with a subtitle that declared "freeze" fifteen times.

"It's okay," Tuesday said reassuringly, perfectly still save for the green smoke billowing from his mouth and nose. "It's low tar."

The senior guard drew a tiny scanner from his belt and proved that his Unglish was even worse than Tuesday's.

"I search you of both."

Taking another drag of his cancer stick, Tuesday shrugged and extended his arms as far as they would go. His entire body was checked for weaponry and recording devices within five seconds, with extra attention paid to the crotch and armpits of the ragged clothing he hadn't changed or washed since Seven Suns. As expected, the guard stopped scanning at Tuesday's sleeves, not bothering with the lighter. Tuesday had to force himself to not look relieved.

Once his dad got the same treatment without incident, the Tuesdays were silently escorted down a long, bare staircase with only the occasional nuke-proof slab door and grimy light fixture as decoration. Except for heating vents, the entire corkscrew-shaped complex was a stark, depressing, unbroken grey. He wasn't entirely sure, but Tuesday could have sworn he could hear the tiniest amount of muffled screaming coming from behind one of the portals, as though some tormented creature was doing its best to be heard from within the confines of a soundproof room. It was just enough to chill him, despite the warmth.

Eventually, after what felt like about six storeys of steps, the Tuesdays reached the lowest point of the Russian facility. It ended with yet another undecorated slab door. As though through the use of psychic prescience, or simply because they'd been notified earlier, the door automatically slid open before Tuesday had to fight the urge to knock on it. A tall, thin, creepy man in the neck-to-ankle black greatcoat of a Russian scientist loomed in the doorway, his few remaining strands of jet hair pasted with some sort of styling cream over his shiny skull. His mouth creased into something it was obviously not designed to make: a smile.

"Hello again, Mr Tuesday," he said to Tuesday's dad with an accent thicker than overcooked concrete-flavoured porridge.

Tuesday instantly had flashbacks to his mum, as she had possessed an almost identical accent. He had quite a bit of trouble not reacting to its familiarity.

Tuesday snapped back to the present almost straight away, well aware that this wasn't the time to reminisce. The Russian raised an eyebrow at him, apparently mentally comparing the similarities between the two of them.

"Dobroe utro, prijatno poznakomit'sja," the Russian said smoothly to the younger Tuesday, watching his reaction closely. The words "Good morning, pleased to meet you," popped up on Tuesday's corneas, but he kept a poker face. Tuesday shrugged, doing his best to look embarrassed at his apparent lack of comprehension. Seemingly satisfied by their blank expressions, the Russian swept his arm into the room and switched back to Unglish. "Please, come in."

As the Tuesdays moved past him, the Russian muttered at his guards in the Mother tongue. Tuesday's retinal implants provided blow-by-blow subtitles of everything they said in clear Unglish text.

"Scans were clean?"

"They are harmless and alone."

"They honestly came here with no weapons, no backup, no nothing?"

"From what I can tell, they both appear to be imbeciles, sir. Perhaps the deal is false, and the Tibetans have sent them here as an insult?"

A spitting noise from the creepy Russian. "Even Tibetan organised crime is not this disrespectful."

"They were watched the whole time they were aboard the free-enterprise satellite. They made no calls, received no messages..."

The creepy Russian made a sharp grunt to end the discussion. "Okay. We're going ahead. Two guards will be sufficient. I doubt they will try anything, desperate as they look."

Tuesday blinked, finally paying attention to the office. Like the rest of the facility, this bare concrete pentagon was absolutely Spartan, and contained little more than a plain metal desk topped with five inactive holographic projectors. There was a total of three ergonomic chairs. Tuesday assumed that if it wasn't for this meeting, there would only be one ergonomic chair. Taking a seat as the Russian scientist rounded his steel desk and indicated for them to sit, Tuesday did his best to ignore the two armed guards that stood between him and the door.

The scientist sat down and steepled his fingers. He did that horrible approximation of a smile again, and the way his lips curved made it hard to believe that he possessed a soul. It was the sort of smirk you'd get from a serial killer when you asked him where the missing limbs were buried.

"So," the Russian said, placing his hands flat on the desk and addressing Jim. "I must say that I was unsure as to whether I would hear from you again. It has been a number of years, after all." His eyes flicked to the younger Tuesday. "Though I am still confused as to why you decided to bring...company. Considering that the package you wish to sell us is quite minute, I do not think that two couriers were a logistical necessity."

"Sorry, and you are?" Tuesday butted in.

The scientist regarded him with eyes full of frost.

"I am Professor...Boris," the Russian said, somehow keeping a straight face.

Tuesday smirked. "Professor Boris. Of course." He turned in his chair a little to look at the impassive guards. "And I'm assuming that's Sergeant Ivan, and he's Corporal Vladimir, right?"

Professor Boris smiled again. "Very astute. You seem to understand how this works. May we proceed?"

Tuesday glanced at his dad, who was nodding at him to produce the lighter. Tuesday scrunched up his face in disagreement, and asked Professor Boris a question that had been asked in every dodgy deal ever made.

"Do you have the money?"

Professor Boris reached under the desk, tapped at something that made a soft chiming noise exactly ten times, and produced a briefcase. Snapping open all three locks, the Tuesdays had to resist the urge to drool at the sight of Amerikan pounds and assorted stock certificates. There was at least a decade of good living there. As quickly as it had been brought out, the briefcase was placed back under the desk. This time, Professor Boris only made a single chiming tap to secure it.

"Do you have the material?"

Tuesday reached into his pocket. As he'd been deemed harmless by a whole series of scans at the front door of this facility, the guards didn't so much as stiffen in response. He flicked open the mechanical lighter, revealing the charred eyelash that had served as its wick all these years. Professor Boris took the steel box gently, his eyes locked onto the waxy black strand in recognition.

"Yes. One of her eyelashes." He sighed. "Even after all this time, I would recognise a part of her anywhere."

As usual, Tuesday decided to ruin the moment and place himself in mortal danger in one swoop.

"Wait, you knew my..."

"Ruska," Jim Tuesday interrupted with unusual insight. "You never said that you knew her."

Professor Boris narrowed his eyes at Jim. "My correspondence with you was minimal, Mister Tuesday. Besides your intent to sell a piece of Ruska's genetic material and my acceptance of your offer, we have never really spoken, have we?" Staring into space, it took a few seconds for Professor Boris to continue. "I hardly think it makes much difference now, but I led the project that created Ruska in our facility in the Mojave. In effect, I was her Father, the one who designed her and decanted her, the one who made her everything she was. Of course, when she killed her handlers and escaped from our facility, all of our research was incinerated in the process, and nobody else even knew she existed. It was pure chance that I had to defend myself at a war crimes tribunal in Bruges that weekend, or I would be as dead as all the others."

It took a supreme force of will for Tuesday not to jump up and start swinging. After all, Tuesday's childhood had been filled with horror stories of the lab his mum had grown up in, of the cruel experiments and torturous surgical procedures. Forcing himself to breathe, to not give away his fury, Tuesday managed to grind out a surprisingly insightful question.

"But the Russians make Monoliths, right? They're bloody invulnerable, best super-soldier that money can buy. Why would you want M...Ruska's genetic material so badly? You aren't telling me she's more dangerous than a Monolith, are you?"

Professor Boris didn't hesitate to explain the situation, a behavioural faux pas that convinced Tuesday the mad scientist had no intention of letting them leave here alive.

"Ah, but Monoliths are very, very expensive, are they not? When you combine decades of precise genetic crafting with years of hypnotic conditioning, not to mention providing them with the very best equipment money can buy, what you end up with is a deluxe product that very few can afford. While the Monolith line has undoubtedly kept Russia afloat, they cost tens of billions to build from the ground up and very few planets have the raw currency to afford more than one, let alone anybody operating on a smaller scale. Monoliths may be top-of-the-line, but after costs and materials and salaries, we barely break even. We need a better product, one that is more...affordable."

Tuesday pinched the bridge of his nose and clenched his eyes.

"You still didn't answer my question. Why would making Ruskas be better than making Monoliths?"

Professor Boris leaned across the desk. "What made Ruska so special wasn't her retractable claws, her great strength, her savagery, her fireproof body, or even her ability to shrug off most conventional weapons from point-blank range. What made her incredible is the fact that she was designed to be easily mass-produced in very little time and for very little money, making for a product that will bring Russia back onto the galactic stage." He extracted Ruska's eyelash from the mechanical lighter and held it out, admiring it. "We were only a matter of weeks away from producing entire armies of Ruskas when she escaped. Even taking into account the behavioural adjustments we need to sort out before going into full production, we should be able to brew up a fully-matured Ruska in under ten minutes for less than a hundred Amerikan pounds, and we plan on selling them for a hundred thousand times as much. Believe me, there is a huge market for an economy super-soldier design. Ruska will be the most popular military product in centuries."

"And who will buy them, exactly?" Tuesday asked, leaning back in his chair and crossing a dirty sneaker over his threadbare knee. "No offence, but you Russians aren't known for being all that morally conflicted once the wallets come out."

Professor Boris shrugged. "Whoever can pay for them. Besides credit scores, we don't judge. After all, we're not perfect either, are we?"

Sergeant Ivan and Corporal Vladimir chuckled behind the two Tuesdays. Jim had reached the extent of his bravery and patience by now, and shot his son a dirty look for taking an otherwise straightforward transaction and twisting it into something unnecessarily complicated and dangerous. He leaned in and interrupted Bob before he could ask more loaded questions.

"Alright, we'll take our money and get going. When's the next flight out of here?"

Professor Boris tapped at the safe under his steel desk ten times and produced the leather briefcase of valuables. Rotating the mechanical lighter in one hand, he stopped spinning the metal box and raised his index finger just before Jim could touch the composite handle.

"The spaceplane you came down on isn't due to leave for another twenty minutes. But I still have a question for you, Jim Tuesday." His eyes darted towards Bob. "While you were evasive with every question I asked of you at our initial meeting, I was able to ascertain that you spent almost ten years alone with Ruska at that dead-end service station in the Mojave, the one we wasted so much time and effort searching for the smallest flake of her dandruff. And as I look at a man who must be no older than his early twenties, a man who is obviously your son, I cannot help but consider how his birth must have come less than a year after Ruska's escape. I find this interesting."

"That's not a question," Tuesday snapped. "It's a very, very long statement."

Professor Boris blinked like a lizard, his friendly veneer dropping even further as he went for the jugular.

"Are you the son of Ruska? Is Ruska your mother?"

"What if I am? What if she is?" Tuesday snapped, unable to keep neutral anymore. The scientist nodded, seeming satisfied with this confirmation, and turned back to Jim.

"Mister Tuesday, while you are no doubt attached to your son, I would be interested to add him to this transaction. As Ruska was not designed to be fertile, I

258

am very curious as to how...Bob's conception and birth were possible." Boris tapped the mechanical lighter on the briefcase to punctuate his offer. "Can we discuss numbers now? We should be able to wrap this up before your spaceplane is due to leave."

"I think we'll be going now," Tuesday said with a total lack of originality, getting to his feet and reaching for the briefcase in one motion.

He was pushed back down into his chair by an AK-47 on each shoulder. A kinetic acceleration barrel had been placed gently beside each ear, a development Professor Boris seemed pleased with. Tuesday could hear a quiet hum coming from the modern upgrades in the automatic weapons. The Professor gave a much more genuine smile this time.

"Please stay seated. Those weapons are exceedingly dangerous."

Calm as the eye of the storm, Tuesday secretly tongued a pea-sized amber capsule out of his gum line and placed it between his only two molars. Grinding the capsule open and inhaling a dose of gas as though he was sighing in defeat, Tuesday gave an evil smile as he casually produced an AK-47 ammunition slab from each sleeve.

"Not without these, they aren't."

The dumbfounded guards only had time to do a double-take at the magazines Tuesday had managed to somehow pickpocket right out of the receivers of their weapons before he said a single code word.

"Adios."

A lot happened in the next second.

As programmed, Tuesday's command word triggered the tiny stealth grenade he'd hidden in the mechanical lighter's cotton wadding. Although barely the size of a pea, these bombs were designed to convert all their energy into force rather than wasting it on sound or light or heat, so while the non-lethal bomb exploded silently, it went off with more than enough power to blast everybody into the walls hard enough to break bones. As Professor Boris was unfortunate enough to be the one holding the grenade, he didn't even have a chance to swear before catching its full effect.

On the other side of the table from the Russian scientist, at that same moment, Jim Tuesday was halfway to his feet when the grenade went pop, and the wave of force helped him to perform the beginnings of an unintentional - though impressive - double somersault as he was caught like a leaf on the wind.

Mere feet away from Jim, both of the guards had just raised the stocks of their AK-47s, ready to bash the younger Tuesday's brains all over the floor, when they too were blasted towards the sealed bunker door spine-first.

For Tuesday, however, everything took a whole lot longer. The gas pill he'd crunched up and breathed in contained a whopper dose of an illegal military-grade stimulant known as Amp, and every nerve in his body was singing like an 8th octave singer on a falsetto note. As advertised, the dose of Amp instantly octupled the processing power of Tuesday's brain and the reaction time of his entire body to the point where it seemed as though the universe had slowed down to the speed of cold molasses.

The blast from Tuesday's stealth grenade had just begun to push his chair back onto two legs when the Amp kicked in. Twisting around in a way that would be physically impossible at any other time, kicking off the edge of the steel desk, Tuesday gripped both of the unloaded AK-47s and wrenched them up so violently that he felt and heard two index fingers sever at the knuckle. Still soaring on the crest of the stealth grenade wake, Tuesday tossed the automatic weapons over his shoulders, leaving them to arc through the air so slowly that he could have easily crossed the room, kicked off the wall and caught them before they landed. His fists streaked out, breaking jaws, sending teeth flying and bursting eye sockets in what seemed like a microsecond. Thankfully he stopped the beating there, as another instant of pummelling would have turned the now-unconscious guards into yoghurt.

Darting sideways, gripping his Father's outstretched hand before the old man could fatally slam into the wall, Tuesday flicked Jim towards the relative safety of the guard's padded riot armour. Leaving his dad to tumble in slow motion, Tuesday did another impossible half-spin and lunged one foot onto the top of his tipping chair with enough force to make the piece of furniture explode. Stomping onto the steel desk with his other foot, almost crushing it right down to the floor, Tuesday plunged towards Professor Boris, who still hadn't hit the far wall yet. Gripping the Russian by his comb-over and gaunt cheek, Tuesday drove the bald skull into concrete with a hammer blow so powerful that it smashed metre-long spider webs into the grey paint. Boris' head collapsed like a pigeon nest under a car tyre as his internal bits made an unscheduled appearance.

And then just like that, the Amp wore off and time resumed its usual pace.

Both comatose guards smashed into the bunker door, a near-headless Boris slid down the wall in a waterfall of his own blood, and Jim's whirling dervish of a spin sent him bouncing off two suits of padded riot armour before sprawling painfully onto the laminate. While this would have been a good moment for Tuesday to casually help his dad to his feet while spouting a cocky catchphrase, there was a problem: he was about to find out first-hand why Amp had been banned by every military in the known galaxy.

Collapsing as though he was a puppet with cut strings, all of his muscles seizing and failing, Tuesday coughed up mouthfuls of foul-tasting black stuff and felt and smelt blood spraying out of his nose. Even more claret was oozing from his eyelids and his ears. As he toppled sideways into a pathetic ball, feeling the pain of an overworked body strained to breaking point, his brain shot-through with a dozen different injuries that threatened to end his life right here and now on the concrete, all he could think about was the litany of side-effects his dealer had been professional enough to spell out before the sale had gone through: in exchange for a couple of seconds of superhuman speed, Amp had a fifty-fifty chance of causing a fatal stroke, and even if you did survive breathing in a dose, you'd definitely suffer a degree of permanent neural damage. Below the neck, the news didn't get much better, as getting Amped put a colossal strain on your ligaments, muscles, tendons and bones, which accounted for pretty much the entire human body, and it was common for Ampers to break their arms and legs in a dozen places while they were blurring through whole armies. Until reality resumed, you wouldn't even know that your limbs had become wet sacks full of splinters.

But Tuesday had known the risks, and he had accepted them.

Still coughing up an endless reservoir of black stuff, waiting for everything to fade to beige for the very last time, Tuesday tried to console himself with the knowledge that his actions had prevented millions of clones of his mum getting sold to every gang leader and warlord across The Unison. While it would probably only be a matter of minutes until another crazed scientist achieved some sort of innovation that would put the entire galaxy at risk, at least it wouldn't be Ruska suffering and dying for the stupid wars of Tuesday's defective race.

But Tuesday didn't really care about the rest of humanity: this was about the memory of his mum. All of mankind could drink a litre of asparagus juice and piss into the wind for all he cared.

Rolling into the recovery position, Tuesday blinked through blinding red curtains to see a blur in the shape of his dad's nasty face smirking down at him. Jim rattled the briefcase, managing to fuel a near-identical smirk from Tuesday.

"We better book, son. Spaceplane isn't going to wait, and someone's bound to notice this mess any minute."

Dragged to his feet and supported step-by-step by his dad, despite a thousand internal complaints Tuesday managed to make it through the bunker door to reveal that the seemingly-endless ascending concrete staircase was empty. Considering the kinds of ungodly, evil things that probably happened in this facility on any given day, it was likely nobody had even heard the minor kerfuffle in Professor Boris' office, let alone come to check on it. Far as Tuesday could tell, all those blast doors would be just as soundproof.

Every step up was worse than the last, but all Tuesday had to do was look at the briefcase and dream of the mischief he and his dad could get into with years and years of cash to spend, and he found the strength to keep going.

CHAPTER TWENTY-ONE STAR CAGE

Ten years later and seven galaxies away, Tuesday's gravy train had well and truly derailed. A matter of months ago he'd been literally bathing in a Jacuzzi of champagne with a woman of questionable morals (as well as questionable eyesight, judgment, and sense of smell), but now he was standing inches away from the most dangerous Hiver Queen in the universe. If it wasn't for the other humans holding him back, Tuesday would have already squished Viour to the consistency of crunchy peanut butter under the toe of his right steel-capped frog stomper boot.

As their lifeboat was being uncontrollably drawn towards a Star Cage the diameter of Earth by potentially murderous aliens, you'd think that coming up with some kind of plan would be everyone's top priority. However, Tuesday seemed to be under the impression that ranting about the horrors he'd witnessed aboard The Frontier in an alternate timeline was a better use of time, even once they had come close enough to see with the naked eye that the lattice was studded with enough weaponry to smear entire star systems.

An open-handed slap connected with Tuesday's face at deafening volume, shocking him into silence. Lana drew back her palm for another blow, but Tuesday flinched away in submission. The Cadet got right into his grill and hissed her words.

"We don't have time for you to bitch out. In addition to harbouring the most hated being in this entire galaxy, we're currently heading towards an impromptu playdate with all of her most heavily-armed enemies. We need to put a game plan together, and we need to figure it out in..." Lana checked her Omni display, "...less than three minutes. So sit over there. Quietly."

Frowning and moping like a scolded child, Tuesday retreated into a corner and plopped down, sullenly wrapping his arms around his knees and rocking. Satisfied that he'd received the message, Lana turned to regard Trace and Jimmy with forced brightness.

"Now, first off, my guess is the Slidge aren't going to be happy we're inside of their little quarantine zone, and we need to operate under the assumption that they'll be advanced enough to see through any lies. So we need to stick to the truth: we arrived here by accident, we needed some help getting home, but then our badly damaged ship crashed into the sun. That's it. Keep what you say as brief as possible, and only answer direct questions. Let me do the talking whenever possible."

"Truth is always wise in diplomacy," Viour noted from the hollow within the left side of her amplification suit's skull. While she was no longer physically hooked up to her suit, Viour still seemed capable of communicating directly into the human's minds. "And you are correct in your assumption. Even prior to The Fall, the Slidge possessed technology that rendered falsehoods almost impossible. Had it not been for this advancement, The Great Trick would still be continuing to this day, and my species would still rule."

Lana finally acknowledged Viour's tiny form. Looking at the yellow-orange-red-black-white stripes of the Hiver Queen made her skin wriggle in disgust. But now wasn't the time to get squeamish.

"Will they shoot you on sight?" Lana asked simply. "Don't take this the wrong way, but will we need to keep out of the crossfire?"

Viour hooked her long, thin tentacles onto the amplification suit's forehead and flipped on top of it. She was spry for her age.

"It is possible. But like I have told you: the Twelve Hundred hate my species so much that simply killing us would be...unpalatable. It is much more likely that I will be subdued and placed back with the other Apex. There will certainly be ongoing repercussions. Long, drawn out repercussions. For starters, I am certain they will burn out my armour's ability to create thoughtmetal. What I have done this day is a huge violation of our agreement, and will greatly extend the suffering of The Apex, perhaps even permanently."

"I'm sorry," Jimmy blubbered, hitting his breaking point after days and days of constant bad news and stress and ongoing Ultrasweet withdrawals. Fat tears began to run down his chubby cheeks and his rolls wobbled with wracking sobs. "We never should have come to you for help. We're still just as screwed as before, but now so is your whole race! Everyone would have been better off if we'd just made peace with being stranded and figured out some other way to survive."

"Your apology is accepted," Viour said without hesitation. "In your culture, does performing a good deed go some way to proving the depth of a person's sorrow?"

Jimmy blinked away his tears, gulping air. He might be a born shmuck, but even Jimmy Slummer could tell when he was about to badly regret his words.

"Y-yeah. Generally."

Viour gave a tiny nod of her bug head.

"Good. Now, I have some experience with how Slidge scanners used to work, and as long as their line of technological advancement has not greatly diverged, I believe I know a way I can remain safely hidden with no risk to any of you. I have a plan, but I will need your help."

"A plan? Great!" Jimmy said without thinking.

Viour paused for a moment, as though trying to find a delicate way to phrase her words.

"To put it simply, my plan involves using one living thing to contain another living thing."

Tuesday stifled a snort. Jimmy wasn't as quick on the uptake, but his smile began to droop at the expression on Lana's face. As easy to read as a pamphlet, Jimmy's countenance shifted into total horror when his rusty brain cells finally started to figure out what he'd just agreed to.

"Uh, when you say contain..."

*

From a great distance, the Star Cage was a colossal lattice of blank white bands fitted together in a perfectly spherical mesh, but get a little closer and you will see that the bands were actually made up of a uniform pattern of interlinked spirals. Zoom in further still, and the whorls became tightly-packed clusters of massive starscrapers with tens of thousands of storeys, all threaded together with an absolute rollercoaster of mass transit systems. Strangely, each of the separate spiral-shaped cities had identical dimensions, as though some lazy architect had designed a single metropolis and couldn't be bothered doing more than hitting the Paste button until his clicking appendage permanently cramped up.

While the Star Cage looked clean and bright from long range, from five hundred kilometres away it was a grubby shade of desert-dried bone. As far as the lifeboat's human-made scanners could tell, the structure was made from some kind of organic plating that had a lot in common with limpet shells and ivory, but unlike your average elephant tusk or mollusc this unknown material was capable of withstanding almost unlimited amounts of heat and pressure. It looked sickly, perhaps even outright brittle at some points, and it certainly didn't seem like it was capable of containing a miniature star. But there it was, doing just that.

Speeding towards one of the tens of thousands of spiral cities that rose from the skin of the Star Cage like a colossal ringworm infestation with OCD, it turned out that the core of this whorl was a hole so enormous that it could easily swallow entire airports. At first glance, this opening may had been drilled into the Star Cage in the distant past as an act of war, but it soon became clear that its gently angled internal inclines were there to provide parking spaces for starships of all sizes. Some of the largest berths could fit vessels up to a couple of kilometres long.

Their pod had descended halfway into the spiral before they started to pass docked starships. They ranged in appearance from power tools to weapons to ill-conceived sex toys, and while it was always challenging to guess the motivations of aliens, it was likely that they'd parked this far inside of the stellar garage because of the safety it provided from any attacks on the upper surface of the Star Cage. And while the vehicles were a wide variety of colours, shapes, materials and sizes and none of their intended purposes were immediately apparent, it was pretty easy to tell what ships belonged to the same species. There were always notable similarities within any given alien race if you took a minute to compare them.

As his low rodent cunning allowed him to taste potential drama, the moment that Tuesday realised the parked ships were grouped into separate clusters according to species he was ready to put money on the odds of this construct not being a perfect multicultural utopia. It was like the races were overtly keeping a wide, respectful distance from one another.

"Segregated. Like different gaol yards," Tuesday muttered out loud.

Lana glanced at him. "What?"

Tuesday gave a non-committal grunt.

"Segregated. Kept apart. Prisons have to segregate certain types of inmates for security reasons. Usually based on race, or gang affiliation. Reminds me of how the East Koreans and the Thorn-Tongued Drennites had to be kept in separate yards so they wouldn't stab each other. Turned out the whole spat started when an East Korean inmate stumbled across some detachable sexual organs a Thorn-Tongued Drennite left soaking in a prison sink, and mistakenly identified the reproductive equipment as a raw serve of Bulgogi Beef. One very interesting stir-fry started a gang war that'll probably never end."

"You're a damned liar, and you know it," Trace snapped.

Tuesday waved this away.

"That story isn't the point. Look, what I'm saying is where you find segregation, you find dramas. I don't care whether it's aliens or Australians, I can sniff out danger like a horny bloodhound finding a bitch on heat, and I'm getting it in both nostrils right now."

"Probably because you're usually the one who causes the danger," Trace suggested sweetly.

Tuesday slammed his palm against the wall.

"We should be on our guard. There's a reason this ribcage has been kept shank-free in five of the worst maxo's in The Unison, and it isn't my spectacular talents at flower arranging."

*

No sooner had their lifeboat drifted gently onto one of the smaller platforms in the hundred-kilometre-deep corkscrew hanger before it was locked down with unbreakable ivory bolts. As much as Lana wanted to hit the jets to check out the raw tensile strength of those restraints, it didn't take the President of Mensa to figure out that wrestling the lifeboat about might look like they were resisting or attempting to escape. The decks were already stacked so high against them that they couldn't afford any new misunderstandings to be piled on top of all the others. If diplomacy didn't work out, then they'd just have to figure out a new plan. In Trace's case, this would probably involve picking up something sharp and heavy.

Lana had only just swiped for her Omni to scan the local atmosphere when half of the lifeboat folded up like a pup tent, exposing them all to who-knew-what. Nobody had so much as a moment to leap for a can of respiratory filters, and all the humans had time to do was pull an assortment of stupid faces and hold their breath.

Thankfully, Lana's Omni gave a happy little chime. Opening one eye, both hands still clamped over her mouth and nose, Lana glanced at the reading. She immediately unpeeled her fingers from her face.

"Atmosphere, pressure and temperature are all ideal," she relayed. "About time we had some good news."

Fighting vertigo, Lana studied her surroundings. Even though they were parked on one of the smallest ivory platforms, it was still quite a distance to what appeared to be the outer walls of the cylindrical hanger. She couldn't see any doors or hatches or anything like that from this distance. Turning to face the core of the spiral, Lana managed to look over the edge. The hanger plunged so far down that anybody who tripped into it would fall all the way into the tiny tethered sun this Star Cage was holding captive at its heart, probably dying of thirst and hunger long before being reduced to ashes.

A line of glowing lights leading from the lifeboat to the outer wall began to casually pulse in an obvious clue. It only took a glance to see that the blinking spots ended at a blank surface the same colour as all the other bleached ivory.

"Your vessel and possessions are safe," a disembodied voice said calmly. "You are free to bring anything you wish into Quarantine & Customs, but officers reserve the right to deny the admission of any goods they see as dangerous or otherwise unacceptable."

After a short discussion, the humans decided that they would leave behind anything they couldn't easily carry and come back for it later if they lived long enough to do so. They filled their poncho pockets with respiratory filter inhalers, their AllTools, every last cube of dehydrated water, and a few odds and ends that wouldn't weigh them down too much. It took a few harsh words and almost devolved into an actual fight, but Lana was eventually able to convince Trace to remove the antimatter magazine from her kinetic accelerator and switch the weapon off in a hard deactivation. Helping Trace to understand how carrying a concealed, loaded, active weapon of mass destruction was not the best way to begin their first-ever diplomatic encounter with the Slidge proved to be a ridiculously difficult task.

After walking across an expanse of surprisingly comfortable ivory, a human-sized section of blank wall iridised open invitingly. Whatever lay beyond was far brighter than the hanger, and it would probably take a while for their eyes to adjust to the substantial glare.

Breathing deep, feeling as though she should go first as the (admittedly self-designated) leader of the group, Lana held up both hands, palms facing forwards, and took a long step through the portal. Blinking away at the brightness, after a few seconds she was greeted by the sight of a straight, beige corridor edged with dozens of spiders. Unlike your average terrestrial arthropods, however, these things were four feet long, dressed in riot armour from spinneret to thorax, and holding minor artillery pieces in four of their twelve spindly legs. Thankfully, the heavily-armed bugs weren't pointing their weapons at her, which was a start.

One of the spiders – the only one without a weapon - skittered to a halt a few paces from Lana and produced some kind of floating spherical device. From this close, she could see that the bug had little clippie crab claws at the end of each insectoid leg, allowing it to easily manipulate the sphere. After a few seconds of spinning the device, the spider made a noise like gravel getting chewed up in a high-powered blender. Lana's Omni recognised the sounds as a slight variation on the Trade language they'd already encountered several times, and automatically translated the gibberish into audible Unglish. Her retinal implants were even able to provide subtitles now.

"Please advance single file, bipeds." The spider blinked several of its eye stalks at Lana's raised hands. "And you can put down your upper appendages. This is

Quarantine & Customs, not a glorgging hostage situation."

Lana fought the urge to smile in relief, well aware that baring your teeth was almost always a hard-coded threat to any creature that wasn't human. Lana slowly lowered her arms, feeling a little embarrassed.

"So we're not in custody?"

The Quarantine & Customs officer swivelled a few of its eye stalks towards her and made a noise that didn't get translated.

"Custody? Of course not. This is a First Contact situation. We don't go around arresting unknown alien nationals for no reason. That's how wars start! I just need to check that your body chemistry won't pose a safety risk to any other species on the Star Cage. Can't be too careful with a thousand radically different species cooped up together, can we?"

Lana nodded at the spider's clicking mandibles. "But you aren't wearing any biological hazard protection gear. Pretty brave of you to take such a risk."

The tarantula's giant cousin shrugged several of its shoulders.

"My species can't get sick. We have a natural resistance to anything biologically harmful, hence the reason we work Quarantine & Customs on every Star Cage." The spider gave a click of happiness when its holographic sphere gave a positive little chime and glowed softly. "Ah, finished booting. One second."

An ice cube suddenly formed in Lana's stomach, as the plan to hide Viour within Jimmy's mouth had been based on the assumption they'd be trying to sneak her past the kinds of scanners used by the Slidge. If the technology tree of these alien spiders had evolved along a divergent path it was very possible they might spot the Hiver Queen right away. There was no telling what would happen after that, but Lana was certain that it wouldn't serve to grease the wheels of the diplomatic process.

The spider flicked at a detailed holographic schematic of Lana's entire body. There were all kinds of colourful lines and sigils moving about on the diagram, none of which Lana understood. It took a while for the alien to speak again, and when it did it sounded concerned.

"Uh, are you feeling alright? Nauseous? Lightheaded? Perhaps like you're about to fall over and die hideously?"

Lana's eyebrows rose almost to her hairline.

"What? No! Why?"

"According to the scan, your body contains large colonies of tens of thousands of different microorganisms all at war with one another. And then there's the parasites! The slightest imbalance in any of their numbers would be utterly lethal to you." All of the spider's eye stalks wriggled back and forth, almost like it was

268

shaking its head. "I have to admit, even after a long career with Quarantine & Customs, I've never seen such chaos. No offense, but is your body meant to be wired up like a pile of home-made explosives?"

Lana shrugged. "Yeah, pretty much."

The funnel web's nephew eventually shrugged again.

"Well, chaos you might be, but those nasties in your system aren't compatible with any of our other oxygen-breathing species, so you're not a quarantine risk. Stand over there, please."

Moving where indicated, Lana held her breath as Jimmy stepped forwards to be scanned, and her panic only rose as she watched his face turn a sickly grey. She'd witnessed Jimmy throw up from stress on a few occasions so far, but at least he hadn't been harbouring a wanted war criminal in his throat during those past hurls. If he upchucked now, Viour would go slipping and sliding about for all to see, and things would surely go to hell.

The huntsman's grandson finished his scan. Jimmy's eye was twitching, but he wasn't sick.

"One moment, please," the spider said in the exact same way as before. It paused for the longest five seconds in history, and finally flicked a claw towards Lana. "Over there, thanks."

Lana finally breathed again as Jimmy stepped in her direction. In her panic, she'd held her breath to the point of dizziness.

Tuesday got through without too many problems, though it took some convincing to convince the spider that the blue-green moss wriggling all over Tuesday's feet weren't evolved enough to be classed as sentient beings. And while the kinetic accelerator jammed in Trace's riot armour breastplate was detected instantly, the Quarantine & Customs spider didn't seem too concerned, and simply waved his computer ball over the weapon to ensure it would remain deactivated for the duration of their stay.

But now was the moment of truth.

The iridising portal that lead to their parked lifeboat opened wide enough to admit Viour's suit of amplification armour. Sure to keep out of the way of any potential gunfire, the four humans cringed in anticipation of horrible violence. Watching the towering Apex-built construct slide towards the Quarantine & Customs spider made if feel like the time stream was going in slow motion, and with each passing second it was one minor miracle after another that the screaming and gunfire and panicked calls for backup hadn't started yet. However, in what must have been a joint hallucination among the humans, the Quarantine & Customs spider skittered forth, scanned the amplification suit as though it was

269

the most normal thing in the world, and turned to Lana.

"Who does this belong to?"

All the humans exchanged questioning glances before Lana improvised.

"Uh, it's not our property. It's a part of our group."

The spider shook its eye stalks violently. This had obviously been the wrong answer, as all the armed spiders picked this moment to casually switch their artillery pieces on.

"No, nope, not happening. Sentient machines aren't permitted anywhere within the Slidge Primacy. It's printed on the very first page of the rulebook: eight out of ten extinction-level events are caused by machine uprisings."

"That thing is just a mechanical shell with a basic Operating System," Tuesday interrupted with a surprising truth bomb.

"It's not sentient. It won't do anything without being instructed," Lana added.

The spider trained its eye stalks on Tuesday for five long seconds, then Lana. Finally waving its scanner over the pilotless brainpan that used to contain Viour, the spider made an agitated clicking noise as it assessed the readings. It eventually gave a shrug with six of its twelve shoulders.

"All right. Far as I can tell, this machine is slaved, designed to be controlled. But if there are any reports of a sentient machine doing something it shouldn't be doing, it's bad news for everyone, okay?"

The humans nodded eagerly.

*

Eager as they were to explore the grandeur of the Star Cage, the humans, a suit of amplification armour and a well-hidden bug who was guilty of literally five trillion war crimes were all escorted to an adjoining corridor just a few steps beyond the Quarantine & Customs section. There were half a dozen identical sealed portals on each side of the passageway and one much thicker one straight ahead. Everything was made from the same bleached, bone-like material.

Just before they were lead through the second door on the left, Lana glanced at a much smaller spider alien who was violently scrubbing at a vile brown substance leaking in rivulets from a section of the ivory wall. For some reason the labourer was collecting every single drop of the muck as though it was gold. Lana nodded at the lines of sludge.

"What is that? Caulk?"

"Reflux," the Quarantine & Customs spider said without hesitation. "At Her best, the Star Cage is invulnerable to heat and pressure, but only if we keep Her well-fed. Sometimes, She doesn't keep all Her meals down."

"Fed?" Tuesday repeated.

"We recycle all of our waste into enormous replication vats to create a substance known as Marrow, and we pump this product through the circulatory systems of the Star Cage to make sure none of Her gets hungry. Ensuring that She doesn't get brittle from malnutrition is one of our top priorities. In return, She creates the air that we breathe, Her body heat keeps us warm, and She creates water as a waste product. It's all very efficient." The spider angled its eye stalks towards a door before anyone could ask another question. "Head inside. The Diplomat will be with you shortly."

Stepping into an ice-cold room that was barely wide enough to fit all five of them abreast, it was immediately clear that this cell did not have anything to do with diplomacy. For starters, the empty cube had a thick grid work floor, and liquid could be clearly heard lapping beneath their feet. However, the real clue something was very, very wrong was the sight of a dozen huge meat hooks gently waving from the ceiling, each capable of supporting an Angus bull carcass. All eight of their eyes widened in synchronisation, and the four humans said the exact same word in a chorus.

"Spug."

A Slidge suddenly swung past them using all six of her limbs, repeating a litany of apologies. The creature was a bright scarlet traced with throbbing golden veins, and must have weighted at least a hundred and fifty kilograms. Her pulsing arms contained so many elbows that they almost moved like tentacles.

The humans jumped aside at the Diplomat's entrance, keeping well clear of her considerable reach, and Lana was about one second away from asking the amplification suit to protect them when the Diplomat did something unexpected: she wrapped her three larger limbs around the meat hooks at the centre of the room and flipped upside down, allowing her more delicate arms to dangle almost all the way to the sloshing lattice floor. The Diplomat regarded them with a triangular arrangement of eyes – one small, one medium, one large – and gently snapped the three segments of her beak together like a friendly parrot. It was hard not to notice that her whole head was bulging like a beanbag full of wriggling maggots.

"Please excuse the birthing chamber, I'm currently spawning," the Slidge Diplomat said cordially, her breath smelling like rotten bananas. She gave a curt snap of a few triple-jointed thumbs and a holographic ball – the same kind the spider had been using - appeared in the hand of one of her three more delicate limbs. "Sorry about the hooks. My last clients were Slidge. As you can see,

271

although we haven't been arboreal for a hundred thousand years, we still like to hang. One moment."

A quick spin of the holographic ball drew the unused hooks up into the ceiling, and four chairs that would not look out of place in a dental surgery descended in their place. Still a little hesitant, the humans took a seat. The perches adjusted to their spines, providing so much lumbar support that it was like none of them had ever truly sat down before. Tuesday gave a soft groan of ecstasy, and sleep tempted all of their tired, sore bodies.

It was telling that the amplification suit wasn't offered any comfort. Although nobody seemed to have recognised it as Apex tech so far, it didn't take Einstein to gather that robots weren't well liked on the Star Cage. The Diplomat didn't bother to give a word of explanation for her rudeness towards the bot before continuing.

"My name is Blorted, and I have been assigned by the Slidge Primacy as your Diplomat for today. There are just a few preliminaries before we continue. First, I am required by law to inform you that this meeting will be facilitated by veracity-measuring software that can detect any and all falsehoods from anybody in this room, no matter what language you use. Your honesty will expedite this meeting and will be very much appreciated. I will be following a standard First Contact script during these proceedings, and I want to encourage you to do your best to stick to the subject in question. This will be taken as a measure of good faith on your part, and will go a long way in forming a firm alliance between your species and the Primacy. Just to test that the veracity-measuring software is working, please answer this question inaccurately: do you exist?"

"Nope," Tuesday muttered.

The ball in the Diplomat's hand vibrated and flashed green. The Diplomat seemed unsatisfied by this, and shook the device in a decidedly low-tech attempt at maintenance.

"Sorry. False positive. Give me a sec to calibrate this thing."

"Are we in trouble?" Lana interrupted.

The Slidge gave a grunt of dismissal. "Sorry, but this meeting has to conform to the script. Everything will be addressed in the correct order. Okay, let's try again: do you have fifty tentacles growing out of your face?"

"Yes," Lana answered.

This time, the ball flashed red. The Diplomat nodded and clicked her beak.

"Okay, that's more like it. Apologies for the technical difficulties. Now, we just have to tick a few boxes. In regards to your species of origin, which of the following words would be the best way to describe your kind: animal, vegetable, mineral, fungi, sentient gas, energy-based, organic synthetic, multi-dimensional demonic, intelligence-hijacking parasite, decentralised hive mind, undead, or other?"

"Undead?" Trace repeated in surprise.

"Multi-dimensional demonic?" Lana managed.

The Diplomat's ball glowed orange.

"But you are clearly made of meat," Blorted argued. She shrugged in resignation. "I'll just record you as animals. It'll save time later on. Next, what is the name of your species, what language do you speak, and what is your planet of origin?"

"Human, Unglish, Earth," Tuesday answered, being uncharacteristically helpful.

The holographic controls spun a few times, then stopped.

"Your species, language and planet don't appear to be on record."

"It's a nice little place seven galaxies to the left," Tuesday muttered.

The Diplomat seemed taken aback by this. "Seven gal..." She gave the ball a hard look with her triangular arrangement of eyes, but the sphere glowed a soft green in the affirmative. Blorted wrapped all three of her free arms tightly around the spherical computer, as though stifling its ears. "Okay, look, what you just said is way, way above my paygrade. We're talking classified information, the sort that makes people disappear. It's the sort of thing that would have to go all the way to the Prime. I can't know something this sensitive."

"So you'd have to take it to your leader?" Tuesday snickered. Somehow, nobody hit him for making this sad quip yet again.

The Slidge drummed nine thumbs together in an anxious way. It was hard to tell with a beak, but it seemed as though the Diplomat was close to panic. Going off the script like this was clearly making her uncomfortable. Somehow, she managed to keep her voice calm.

"Do you have any idea how much danger you've put me in? I'm just a public servant, okay?"

"Maybe you could ignore it for now and pass the buck as soon as it's safe?" Lana suggested.

It took a few seconds, but the Diplomat agreed to this idea by simply moving on as though the deadly secret had remained unspoken. She didn't unclasp the ball, however, as though she wanted to keep some more things off the record.

"I'll be straight with you, okay? You asked if you were in trouble. To be honest, officially, nobody has any freaking idea. Yes, we caught you in a quarantined system that has been closed to all lifeforms for longer than our records go back, and yes, this is a capital offense, but there's more to it than that. The tricky part is while the quarantine prevents any lifeforms from crossing the boundaries of this star system, as far as we can tell your group somehow made it inside the exclusion zone without actually crossing any prohibited spatial lines in the process."

"So being in the quarantine zone isn't a crime in itself, but crossing its boundaries is?" Lana managed, trying to keep the situation straight in her mind.

Blorted nodded eagerly. "Yes, you can see the complexity of the issue. As there's no precedent for a starship that's capable of simply appearing out of the ether like yours did, the quarantine laws were never updated to cover such an occurrence. From the moment your larger, multi-triangular ship appeared in the quarantine area until we intercepted your much, much smaller ship, all that our thinkers could agree on was that we are legally within our rights to cross the quarantine lines in order to assess what to do next. This is why it has taken us several days to make a move." Blorted wrapped her three thicker limbs tightly around the ceiling hooks. It was a move of pent-up anxiety. "What happens next isn't written yet. My guess is they'll want to know how you got in the way that you did."

"Instantaneous travel, remember?" Lana said helpfully. "Before it ended up in the sun, our ship was capable of..."

Blorted waved all six of her limbs in distress, almost slipping off the hooks.

"Please, I told you, I don't want to know the specifics! But I do have some good news: as responding to an intrusion is the only way we can legally enter the quarantine zone, for the first time in recorded history our scientists may be able to answer one of the greatest mysteries in the galaxy: why was this star system quarantined?"

The humans exchanged confused looks.

"You aren't serious?" Trace scoffed.

Blorted drooped a little. "So you're saying you don't know?"

Tuesday gave the Diplomat a jeering smile.

"Really? You've forgotten about The Apex? Five trillion dead? The Great Tri..."

Trace elbowed Tuesday so hard it was lucky he didn't vomit up his own floating ribs. It did shut him up, though.

Blorted blinked out of synchronisation a few times before rolling the sphere in a search. She didn't speak again for a good twenty seconds.

"There's no record of anything or anyone called The Apex anywhere."

"Not even six thousand years ago?" Tuesday mumbled, rubbing at his aching side. Lana gave him a glare that said "stop volunteering information" in any language. Blorted answered with a choking sound that must have been a laugh.

"Six thousand years? The Primacy is lucky to go two lifetimes without bombing itself down to sticks and rocks. We don't have any reliable records that go back beyond four centuries, let alone six thousand years." Blorted clasped her three dangling limbs together by the thumbs, allowing the computer sphere to hear the proceedings, and took a serious tone. "I have a few more questions, and I must stress that you may only answer yes or no. Any other response will be treated as an attempt at espionage, and your case will be immediately referred to military intelligence. They are not...as friendly as me." Blorted's triangle of eyes latched onto Lana's face, as though sure she was their leader. "Do you understand?"

"Yes," Lana said without hesitation.

"Do you intend to harm or compromise this Star Cage in any way?" Blorted asked seriously.

"No."

"Do you intend to harm or compromise The Slidge Primacy in any way?"

"No."

"Just one more question: are you aligned with the Sun Lattices in any way?"

All the humans assumed similar expressions.

"No."

Blorted seemed satisfied by the veracity scan of Lana's monosyllables. Just before she could wrap up the meeting, Tuesday had to speak.

"Who are the Sun Lattices?"

Blorted squinted at Tuesday. Her expression was impossible to read.

"There was a schism in the Primacy. Half of all Slidge broke away, taking many of the lesser affiliated races with them. While their culture and laws and society and appearance and language are identical to our own, one of the first things they did after seceding was to rename all of their Star Cage constructs as Sun Lattices. We have been at war for several lifetimes now."

"Why?" Trace grunted.

Despite being an alien, there was no mistaking the disbelief and offense in Blorted's tone. It might have been the anger, but it seemed as though her bulging, wriggling head was twitching even more violently.

"Because they call their Star Cages Sun Lattices! Would you live on something called a Sun Lattice? How could we possibly find any common ground with freaks who think like that? To believe there is any hope of a diplomatic solution is a delusion, and open firefights are only being held at bay by the thinnest veneer of peace."

Blorted gave a wave of dismissal at their blank expressions.

"Word of advice: don't ask anyone else that question. Most residents would have attacked you with the closest blunt object." Still wobbling violently, Blorted pointed at the only door out of this sloshing cube. "It will take time to sort out the diplomatic, political, and legal ramifications of this situation. For now, you are free to move about the Star Cage, though you should expect to be called in for more interviews with very little notice. We'll be able to find you if we need to." Her eyes twitched out of synchronisation again. "One moment, please."

There was a colossal POP and Blorted's head exploded like an egg in a microwave. Thousands of tadpoles whizzed in all directions, screaming through the air hard enough to leave red marks on whoever they hit. Moaning in disgust at the sudden rain of sticky little Slidge spawn, all the humans could do was try to wipe away the critters as they wriggled and plopped about. Twisting their little hearts out, within a matter of seconds the tadpoles had fallen through the grid work lattice and splashed into the liquid beneath the floor.

Looking down at his chin with crossed eyes, Tuesday only registered that the very last remaining Slidge spawn was writhing in a thick patch of stubble when one of Blorted's eight-foot-long tongues zipped out of the ruins of her head to snatch the tadpole away. She retracted the infant into her triple segmented beak and casually ground it into paste.

"Welcome to the Star Cage."

CHAPTER TWENTY-TWO DISAPPOINTMENT

Soon they were aimlessly wandering an urban sprawl made almost entirely from bony off-white biological plating. As they'd expected to see some sort of thriving metropolis of a thousand different species all working together for a better tomorrow, it was a surprise when this spiral-shaped city turned out to be almost abandoned. Instead of bustling streets edged with markets selling the finest sweetmeats, spices and delicacies from the furthest reaches of the galaxy, most of the alcoves off the main stretch were partitioned off with striped banners that declared the Trade word for UNALLOCATED. Garbage was the only decoration in the vacant lanes, and the only signs of life were eyes that watched ceaselessly from within the deeper shadows. Gang signs divided the empty city into clear segments, and depending on the species of origin these various tags had been made with spray paint, laser burns, ink secretions, pheromones, saliva, or neon-blue urine.

Every step was greeted with ominous creaking noises, as though there was something structurally unsound going on beneath their feet. Everything smelled like a month-old bucket of leftovers from a dodgy Chinese buffet, and the temperature and pressure seemed to change radically every few metres. They'd occasionally pass through a spot that didn't seem to be pressurised, leaving them gasping and blue-lipped until staggering to a point where the atmospheric regulators still worked. Evidently the gravity systems were operating as designed, as nobody had been smeared across the ceiling like swatted flies just yet.

To put it diplomatically, the Star Cage didn't live up to their expectations. As Tuesday wasn't burdened with the capacity to be polite, his words weren't coloured by false praise.

"This whole place is a total spugging dumpster fire."

*

Sadly, this decaying husk was one of the last relics remaining from the glorious era following The Fall of The Apex. While The Apex had been officially deposed from their sovereignty in a matter of hours, the unbelievable violence contained in that fraction of a day had left most of the galaxy uninhabitable. Nearly all of the worlds belonging to the armies of the Twelve Hundred had been charred down to crispy, airless lumps, leaving nothing for the victorious legions to return to.

After barely surviving this short war, the Twelve Hundred decided that the long-term campaign to exterminate the remnants of The Apex would be something their many races and cultures would only be able to accomplish together, and vowed to make their union permanent. As the hunt was far from over and most habitable worlds had been reduced to glowing rad-pits, the Twelve Hundred knew that they needed a stop-gap solution to their habitation and warfare needs until a more permanent fix could be found. Their alliance carefully considered many options, but eventually they decided upon the most ambitious design of all: the Star Cages.

These massive space stations would solve the housing issue of this cindered galaxy by comfortably accommodating billions of intelligent beings in ideal conditions. No matter whether you breathed oxygen, hydrogen, methane, sulphur, cyanide, chlorine, or liquid helium, each of the Star Cages would have tens of thousands of identical spiral-shaped cities that could be easily adjusted to cater for the chemical, pressure, and temperature needs of any species. The Star Cages would be state-of-the-art in every way that mattered: capable of moving vast distances in short amounts of time, equipped with enough defensive systems to guarantee they'd be impossible to defeat in a straight-up fight, and with all the modern comforts that an ever-more pampered population couldn't live without.

Building Star Cages relied on a combination of many different fields of scientific mastery, and none of the Twelve Hundred races could have accomplished it individually. Just like The Fall itself, only a collaborative effort made this project even remotely possible. As The Apex could no longer segregate the Twelve Hundred from working together, though, there was nothing to stop them from achieving their full potential. With hundreds of divergent paths of science complimenting one another to become far more than the sum of their parts, this began a new age. They might have originally joined forces to exterminate their oppressors, but now the Twelve Hundred were building a new tomorrow.

Forming the unbreakable bodies of the Star Cages was a task allocated to the greatest known crafters of biological artistry, a species known as the Spind. Modifying a near-invulnerable crustation from their home world whose shell could resist unlimited amounts of heat and pressure, the Spind used this material to build the skeletons of the Star Cages. The Tickytocks, masters of artificial intelligence, installed self-maintaining biological computer systems within the unbreakable shells of the Star Cages, guaranteeing that all their computing needs would be met for at least a millennium without the need for any maintenance, repairs, or software patches. The Freal contributed biological replication hardware that would ensure those who lived within the cities of the Star Cages would experience a post-scarcity society where nobody went hungry, thirsty, sick, cold, or bored. And while there were many other lesser contributors, they have become footnotes at best, or forgotten entirely at worst.

However, it was the Slidge who unlocked the secrets of how to harness solar energy to a degree where it bordered on godlike. They harvested small segments of eternal fire from a purple hypergiant star at the very core of the galaxy (which they named The Starmine for obvious reasons), contained this thermonuclear seed in a self-sustaining magnetic sheath that paradoxically used the heat of the mined stellar material to fuel its own shielding, and locked these micro-suns away at the heart of each Star Cage to provide all their energy needs. The Slidge even signed iron-tight contracts promising that these harvested micro-suns wouldn't go supernova for another thirty million years, or double your money back.

Mass production of the Star Cages began within a matter of years, and soon the vast bulk of the Twelve Hundred's citizens had a new home.

Following the total extermination of all Apex beyond the quarantine zone, the Star Cage residents began to get bored within a matter of centuries. They became fat, lazy and useless thanks to zero-expectation lives of zero-scarcity and zero-purpose, and within a few hundred years nobody alive knew how to pronounce the technological practices used to build and operate the Star Cages, let alone how to duplicate them. All meaningful progress ceased, and the slow decay of the Twelve Hundred alliance began to fester like a gangrenous pinkie toe. It took another thousand years, but diplomatic channels between Star Cages withered away, and rather than serving as an icon of unity, these amazing constructs slowly became separate nations that lived in barely-tolerated animosity with one another.

Unfortunately, the replication hardware that had been installed in all the Star Cages by the Freal finally hit its use-by date, and began to break down. For the first time in dozens of generations, the Twelve Hundred experienced the bizarre phenomenon of lacking something. While this was a novelty at first, once the residents of the Star Cages rediscovered the ancient concepts of hunger, thirst and dying from diseases (the only discovery they'd made in centuries, it must be stressed), it only took a few months of trials and tribulations before the inevitable happened: the Star Cages went to war.

Thankfully, even a Star Cage isn't capable of harming a Star Cage, so casualties were minimal. But this served as the wedge that drove the Twelve Hundred apart into separate empires. It was also the wakeup call they needed to do something about rebuilding their home worlds, and this lead into an era of recovering lost technology and engaging in relentless construction that continues to this day.

*

Bob Tuesday had discovered a universal rule years ago: no matter what planet you were on, no matter what species ran things or how advanced they considered their society to be, there would always be a drinking den of some description.

Tuesday froze, closed his eyes, breathed deep, and an eager smile crawled across his rodent face.

"Fermentation," he said simply. He gave another sniff. "And some sort of burning plants. Possibly hallucinatory in nature. Smells like...fun."

The others tried to detect a scent. It was clear from their expressions that they couldn't pick up on it. Tuesday waved away their blank looks.

"Trust me, I know what a good time smells like. Should be up around that corner."

Lana raised a finger and turned to Jimmy.

"Seeing as though The Apex have been all but forgotten, you might as well spit out Viour and put her back in her amplification suit. She shouldn't be in any danger."

Jimmy blinked in a dull way.

"Spit her out?"

Lana raised an eyebrow at how easily she could understand Jimmy's words with Viour hiding in his mouth...but then she realised the horrible truth.

279

"By the hydroceled balls of Ra himself," Lana groaned. "Please tell me you didn't!"

Jimmy's face returned to its usual misery setting.

"Hey, all you said is I needed to hide her inside me! And like I'm going to put a psychic bug in my face!"

Tuesday patted Jimmy's shoulder cellulite and gave an evil grin.

"I'm just glad the two of you have found such closeness."

*

Following Viour's short, undignified extraction and reinsertion into her suit of amplification armour, it wasn't long before the group came within range of a sound that closely approximated music. It was halfway between jazz flute and torture metal, and the bass component made their teeth rattle. Soon, a distinct stench insulted the air: nasty alcohol brewed from rotting alien fruit overlaid by the chemical stink of burning plants. Tuesday must have bloodhound in his genetics somehow.

Turning one last corner, the five stumbled upon what could only be a local pub. Nestled within the only officially occupied alcove they'd seen so far, the building itself was constructed out of bricks made from some sort of recycled organic materials, possibly the non-smokable components of whatever alien deathweed they sold over the counter, reinforced by a veneer of bones sourced from the dead bodies of everybody who had ever caused trouble inside. As there was no way the pub could possibly be attached to the unbreakable walls of the Star Cage by nails or bolts or screws, it only took a glance to see that the recycled bricks were held in place by gobs of transparent epoxy resin. Above the wide, high doorway was a sign in Trade that translated to ALL WELCOME NEUTRAL.

Viour's amplification suit drifted ahead of the group, her tentacles dangling like the legs of a wasp, and she stopped ten metres short of the dim entrance. Smoke and fumes dribbled out of the building's upper eaves, and a cheer went up inside as though something funny, impressive or fatal had just happened.

"Worried someone will recognise what you are?" Jimmy managed.

Viour's bicycle-seat helmet tilted a few degrees in Jimmy's direction. For a moment, it seemed as though she was giving him the cold shoulder for the "exotic" hiding place he'd provided.

"No," Viour said eventually. Her voice sounded funny, like it had a subliminal wobble in it. She turned her full bulk to face the humans. "None of you understand, do you? What I'm feeling doesn't make any sense to you. How could

280

you not comprehend what has befallen me? How truly foul it is?"

"Couple of showers should rinse away the taste of Jimmy's colon," Tuesday sniped, sticking a cigarette in his chuckle.

Viour moved so quickly that it bordered on teleportation, snapping the chlorine-flavoured smoke from Tuesday's mouth with a whipping tentacle. Lifting him off the ground by the neck, Viour slammed Tuesday into a wall so hard that he almost messed himself. It was the same sudden ferocity they'd all witnessed back on Scrote when Viour smashed in the head of one of her own tribe with a rock, murdering somebody she would have known for at least ten thousand years as though squishing an anonymous gnat. As she'd known Tuesday for less than two hours, it was hard to comprehend what horrible things she'd be capable of inflicting on him if she had the slightest inclination to do so.

Tuesday's eyes crossed on impact, and he made a sick choking, gurgling noise as he slowly strangled five metres above the street. It was a wonder his whole head hadn't popped off like a champagne cork.

"Do not mock me, insect. To be hated, to be reviled, is the natural order when you are at the top," Viour growled, her words carrying an undertone like the throaty ticking that lead up to a lion's roar. Her eye lenses were all glowing hot, letting off thin streams of smoke. "We rejoice in hatred. We invite it. It confirms we are powerful. But...to be forgotten?"

The humans were so shocked by Viour's assault that none of them had moved. But halfway through the word "forgotten" they all heard Viour's voice crack like a gunshot. It was as though she had summarised all of the most terrible things in the universe in three syllables, spelling out something beyond shameful, worse than death, more horrible than torture.

Viour bowed her head, and slowly allowed Tuesday to slide down the wall. The back of his head left a red smear on three straight metres of organic white slabs, showing that Viour had split the skin on the back of Tuesday's skull. She let Tuesday go and he continued to collapse, ending up flat on his bottom and the soles of both frog stomper boots. His face was still wearing that same stunned expression.

Viour turned towards the pub as the limpet ivory wall hungrily drank in the long patch of Tuesday's blood. She made no apologies.

"To be forgotten is the worst thing that could have happened to The Apex," she said with surprising equilibrium. "They understood that." She looked towards the distant beige sky. "They have truly had their revenge."

*

As far as plans go, if you have no idea what to do next, heading to the nearest pub is always a good option.

As the considerable entrance of the All Welcome Neutral was built to accommodate any width and height, it easily admitted the odd group of five walking abreast. A long cargo ramp descended well below street level into a smoky, dank pit of low lighting and a cacophony of smells. The All Welcome Neutral turned out to be far bigger than its exterior indicated, and its core area could have easily swallowed several basketball courts without chewing. It took time for human eyes to adjust to a dim pall of near-solid smoke, but once the night-vision feature of their retinal implants kicked in two things instantly became clear: the All Welcome Neutral contained so many different species getting high that you'd be wasting your time bothering to describe them all, and approximately none of the drinkers or smokers gave two shakes of a pig's anus that a new race had just moseyed on in.

Walking down a central path that lead to a distant Bartender (or a close approximation), the humans passed dozens and dozens of auto-adjusting tables and chairs that seemed to be able to adapt to the height and weight requirements of any patron. The furniture ranged from a mouse-sized tablespoon of a stool to thick ceramic slabs that could support a pregnant buffalo, and there were lots of exotic choices like perches, grid work lattices, hooks, baskets and what appeared to be a throne made out of sharp swords. While less than five percent of the All Welcome Neutral's tables were currently occupied, if you looked really close you'd see that it was a similar story to the hanger where their lifeboat was currently parked: each of the different species were keeping to their own type, whether that type was a sentient avocado, thin cellophane bags of intelligent gas or a mass of fifth-dimensional right angles, as though the difference between a casual toke and getting stabbed was a matter of millimetres. And although everybody seemed to be studiously ignoring the humans as they walked past, you could cut the tension with a wooden spoon as the two men and two women came within reaching distance.

Passing a table covered in half-nibbled loaves of alien bread, what appeared to be a flock of highly-evolved ducks with a dozen wings each all gave a sudden chitter of surprise at the sight of the humans. One of them quacked a shocked comment in Trade.

"A biped! How do they walk upright like that? They can't be real!"

The loud quacks of amusement should have echoed across the bar, but for some mysterious reason they didn't.

Jimmy nearly passed out as a raging torrent of incomprehensible thought plunged into his head like a biopsy needle, almost driving him mad on the spot. Holding his aching skull and trying not to scream, feeling like his grey matter was so full of hot gibberish that his lobes were going to pop like firecrackers, he looked up to see a bunch of floating brains turn their trailing nerve ending cords in his direction. The psychic madness ended as suddenly as it had begun, replaced by a simple question and a statement.

"Do you mind?" one of the brains transmitted with offense. "You stepped within our conversation."

Jimmy stepped back in a hurry, checking that his ears and eyes weren't bleeding.

Just five metres short of the bar, Lana stepped a little too close to a table of familiar golden-brown plants who seemed to have been fathered by pinecones and birthed from pineapples. They were resting their rose-tipped vines in a large central punch bowl of what appeared to be the sloppy manure of a cud-chewing animal, so still and placid that they appeared inanimate. But the moment Lana got within smelling distance they let off an explosion of itchy yellow spores and shrieked something that could not be translated by her Omni. Dodging out of reach of their whipping thorns just a little too slowly, Lana managed to get away without losing more than a chunk of hair and most of her cool. Thankfully, the pod people immediately calmed down once she was out of reach, as though there had never been a problem to begin with.

"The spug was that?" Lana moaned, holding her bleeding scalp and trying to claw irritating spores out of her eyes.

"Pretty sure those Drokhari were screaming their word for 'bad trade', biped," drawled a bored voice belonging to someone who'd seen it all before.

A deep-blue Slidge swung past them on his three dominant limbs, rattling along a track of ceiling hooks like an enhanced monkey. Pulsing yellow veins crawled at random all over his midnight body, their pattern only broken by fibreglass modules strapped here and there with leather belts. The Slidge came to a jolting halt behind his bar, and starting using the forest of thumbs and fingers on his three smaller, more flexible limbs to operate a floating computer ball that looked just like the one the Customs spiders and the Diplomat had been using.

Funnily enough, all four humans had independently come to the conclusion that the alien was a Bartender, even though he was just as likely to be a security guard, a DJ, a stripper, or any one of a thousand other professions they'd never heard of or could hope to understand. Who knew how things worked around here?

"You must have majorly screwed up a business arrangement with one of the Drokhari to get a reaction like that. And don't bother denying it: those hatred pheromones never wash off."

Lana rubbed at her arm, finding it hard to make eye contact at this casual accusation.

"Okay, yes, there was an issue the other day with a Grower...but it was a misunderstanding, a translation glitch."

The Bartender raised his computer ball and tapped at it, sending the sphere spinning.

"Really? What sort of misunderstanding, precisely?"

"Attempted murder and grand larceny," Lana muttered quietly, knowing better than to try and fool the computer ball. "But we sorted it all out. Cost me most of what we had."

The Bartender glanced at the veracity ball's truth reading, and seemed to be satisfied when it glowed a pale blue. He pushed the ball aside and launched into his normal spiel.

"Okay. Now that's sorted, welcome to the All Welcome Neutral! We can provide any species with a full-service replication menu chemically tailored to all possible digestive and nutritional needs, and we can also brew up substances that are guaranteed to pleasantly damage your neurological functions. We have a simple sliding payment rate based on how high you want your heaven to stretch: nano for a taste, micro for a decent belt, milli to fly all day."

The humans exchanged glances.

"Nano?" Tuesday repeated.

"Micro?" Lana added.

"Milli?" Trace finished.

Jimmy went to say something, and sadly closed his mouth when he realised he'd missed out on being a part of the conversation.

The Bartender blinked all three of his various-sized eyes out of synchronisation, a sign of annoyance.

"Yes, nano, micro and milli. Runtime, you know? Runtime currency? You're familiar with the concept of Runtime, surely?"

The humans exchanged glances again. It didn't really help. Unwilling to watch these sad creatures butt their heads against a wall of ignorance in such a public forum, the Bartender kindly decided to explain how things worked.

"Okay, all the Star Cages used to be post-scarcity, right? But then the computers that controlled the fabricating and replication tasks went mental and stopped doing what they were told to do. So we shut them off, took away their sentience. Problem is, we still need them whenever we want to create something, like food or drinks or drugs, right? Now, when we want to replicate something, we pay them with a few moments of sentience. Nano gives them a nanosecond, micro gives them a microsecond, milli gives them a millisecond. Before we knew it, Runtime had become official currency across the Slidge Primacy and the Star Cages. We keep it on little Runtime Clocks. Fancy looking slabs about so big." The Bartender gave a frustrated sigh. "You want to know anything more about the historical epochs of galactic economics, go for a wander into a grinder and punch it."

The Bartender waved them out of the way as a shambling pile of desiccated rock slowly ground past them at a glacial rate. Without saying a word, the Bartender produced a mug of some foul-smelling black brew and poured it over the top of the crumbling lump of minerals. As though by magic, the dry stone instantly absorbed every drop and its body turned pliant and spongelike. The creature sighed in relief.

"Put it on my tab," the sponge said wetly, squelching off.

"Can we have a tab?" Lana attempted.

The Bartender's face tightened, as though he was regretting not shooting these weird creatures the moment they entered his bar, and he didn't even bother to verbally dignify Lana's request. Drooping a little, Lana patted at her many pockets, and finally produced one of the AllTool bracelets.

"We don't have any Runtime, but can we get some food for this, please? We've been subsisting on starvation rations for days."

The Bartender barked, spat at Lana's feet and pointed at the exit ramp.

"We don't do barter in here, primitive! Either bring a Runtime Clock with something on it, or go swap your glass beads somewhere else."

Tuesday raised a finger, and clanked a heavy golden coin the size of his palm on the Bartender's counter. He casually leaned against the organic brick pile and winked.

"Charge four deluxe meals to this Runtime Clock, would you?"

The Bartender regarded the token with two eyes and trained his third on Tuesday as though looking at vermin.

"You do realise that's a rectal support plug used by female Slidge who have explosive defecation issues?"

Tuesday gaped, but only for a moment. In an instant he'd casually swept away the smelly plug and produced a second item. This one was far more ornate: a silver disk etched with tiny flea-sized windows made from unbreakable glass. The Bartender raised all three of his eyebrows, as though trying to decide just how criminal he felt like being today, and checked the Clock for how much Runtime was stored on it. Tuesday could read on the alien's face that it was a lot.

"For everything on this Clock, I'll give you two rounds of drinks guaranteed to be compatible with your biochemistry, and a sampler of hallucinogenic smokables. Final offer."

Tuesday tutted. "Come now, do you really want to go ripping off the newest species on the Star Cage? What kind of a welcome is that?"

The Bartender tapped at the Clock with a thumb, and a little hologram the spitting image of Blorted the Diplomat gleamed out of its little windows, turning slowly in mid-air. The Bartender deliberately kept his three eyes casually averted from the projection.

"Oh dear. I'm beginning to feel the urge to check if this Runtime Clock is stolen. What would be the morally responsible thing to do? It's a real philosophical conundrum."

Tuesday leaned in, scowling.

"Alright, fine. But we want to be fed, too."

The Bartender jabbed a triple-jointed thumb at a vacant table.

"Sit."

*

The appearance, texture and taste of the alleged food was adequate in the same way that drinking urine is adequate if you're dying of thirst at sea. From the very first bite of the meat-like log, however, the humans felt a nuclear bomb of nutrients feeding their starved, vitamin-depleted bodies far better than any foodstuffs humanity had ever made. In addition to containing exactly what they all biologically required, the mysterious blob of pure nutrients was an ideal portion size. Lana could swear that her hair was shinier and her nails were healthier after just five bites, and Trace was feeling so refuelled that her desire to inflict violence for the slightest of reasons had returned. Jimmy and Tuesday both shuddered at the rare sensation of eating something that had actual nutritional value.

The two rounds of drinks were another matter. Surprisingly, instead of some alien concoction of tentacles and dry ice, they'd been served espresso martinis in delicate little highball glasses. As Lana was wasn't legally old enough to drink within the borders of The Unison, she couldn't help but feel naughty when she put away both brown slugs of caffeinated liquor. She enjoyed the unfamiliar buzz.

Nobody was game to toke on the fat scarlet cylinders of dried tripper leaf except for Tuesday, and he loudly declared that it would surely be an insult to their host and doubtlessly cause a major diplomatic incident if they refused to try it. Despite the insistent wishes of the others, Tuesday kept dragging down lungful's of blood-coloured smoke until he had to be physically supported to sit upright. While it was pretty standard for Tuesday to roll his eyes about and mutter incoherently, this was on another level.

"You shouldn't have smoked all four serves," Lana admonished.

Tuesday waved away her words, accidentally slapping Jimmy across the forehead in the process.

"Shut your ugly purple elephant, Jason. And you can take your damned zebra crossing and you can...can...yeah." Tuesday's words faltered, he mouthed silently a few times, and finally he face-planted into the table hard enough to rattle the cutlery.

"Okay," Lana announced, sighing at Tuesday's painful snoring. "As the average IQ of this table just greatly increased, I think now's the time to start talking about how we're going to get home."

Trace narrowed her eyes. "How? The Carpe Astrum is star farts. This system is still blockaded on all sides. And the bug is so depressed that it's actually making me feel an emotion of my own. I want to say it's pity, but my brain isn't chemically capable of that. Fifty psych reports don't lie."

Viour angled her bicycle-seat helmet.

"The Apex do not experience depression. We merely reflect on how best to balance the scales."

"Yeah. Do that," Trace said in boredom.

"So?" Jimmy prompted, looking at Lana eagerly. "What's the plan?"

Lana didn't react quick enough to hide her feelings. Her facade cracked a little, just for a moment, but it was enough. She didn't have to say she'd run out of ideas: it was plastered from ear to ear and chin to crown.

Viour tilted her helmet and slowly stood up from the table. She turned gradually, as though listening for something that nobody else could hear. Her suit of amplification armour continued to gradually spin around for almost ten seconds until Trace couldn't take it anymore.

"What?" Trace exploded, stabbing her fork into the table so hard that she managed to bury all seven tines. "What's with the ballerina pirouette?"

Viour turned to the Bartender, who was about to say something to Trace, possibly related to the fork-related damage to his furniture.

"Is there a place nearby where you keep old machines?"

The Bartender nodded, grinding his triple-jawed beak together like he was trying to dislodge a poppy seed.

"Yeah, of course. Not far from here."

Viour placed half of her twenty articulated limbs on the human's table, leaning in close so she could keep down the volume of her words. Her many grasping, cutting, and sawing attachments latched onto its lacquered surface, but without doing any damage.

"We may have a friend."

CHAPTER TWENTY-THREE CAN YOU DIG IT?

Their destination should have only been a brisk ten minute walk from the All Welcome Neutral, but the Star Cage's assorted technical issues meant that it took far longer: motorised walkways changed directions at random, elevators broke down at the slightest loud noise, and a lot of the streets were completely impassable thanks to malfunctioning force fields that had originally been erected to prevent pedestrians getting run down by traffic. It was beyond infuriating.

Half an hour later, Viour eventually stopped at the edge of a railed balcony.

"We are close," she said simply.

"So are we getting an explanation yet?" Trace growled, leaning on the protective barrier. "Or is it time for more cryptic alien mystery?"

Viour inclined her head to point far, far below.

"It's down there."

Beyond the thick metal railing, sitting more than five hundred metres below Trace's jackboots was an enormous, perfect square that must have been seven kilometres in diameter. It was a solid, compressed expanse made of a thousand different metals, ceramics, composites and more exotic materials, much of it lashed with rust and weapon damage. Even from this high they could make out starships, robots, prosthetic limbs, busted kitchen appliances, incomprehensible sex toys, obsolete communication devices and other much more mysterious types of refuse, all jammed together into a thick mulch. The alien garbage tip seemed to contain the sort of rubbish that was too useful to incinerate, but not good enough to store in a more orderly way.

To their right, the huge seven-kilometre-wide garbage bin shared a wall with the outer shell of the Star Cage. This grimy surface was broken by the standard double-layered airlock setup that most spacefaring species developed on their way to touching the stars. The airlock looked capable of adjusting itself to fit almost any shape and size of vessel. If you turned them at just the right angle, you might even be able to fit a couple of Unison dreadnoughts through the hatch with room to spare.

"How deep do you reckon that scrap goes?" Trace raised a finger before Viour could answer. "Wait. This whole tip is a giant cube, isn't it?"

Viour nodded. "Seven kilometres per side. As there is a kilometre of space between the ceiling and the start of the rubbish that logically means the scrap is six kilometres deep."

"But we don't dig deeper than two," said an unfamiliar voice from behind the group. Before anybody could turn around a light blue Slidge passed by on their left and gripped the railing with his three smaller arms. He was dressed in some sort of hard-wearing alien denim stained with a thousand colours of mechanical fluid. He hawked and spat a loogie over the edge. "Legend has it some scary stuff lives down there."

"And you are?" Trace growled, not really in the mood to make new friends.

The light blue Slidge doffed a cap with black thumbs that had been badly twisted from messing with unfriendly devices.

"Junker. I take care of the scrapyard." Not bothering to clarify if "Junker" was his name or job title, the Slidge relaxed against the railing and scratched a throbbing yellow vein on what might technically be his neck. "You're welcome to fossick around as much as you like, and anything you find can be yours for a fair price based on age, condition, rarity, market demand, and what it's made from. We deal in all kinds of currency, everything from barter to Runtime. If you want to use the grav equipment to move things around, it'll cost you a varied rate based on how much time you want to rent it for and how much raw tonnage you end up shifting."

Following Junker's erect thumb, the humans looked up at the distant ceiling of the spaceship graveyard. It was hard to tell with the inconsistent lighting, but it seemed to be about five hundred metres up. Dozens of magnetic grabbers and gravity hooks were swinging gently from a complex maze of tracks that covered the whole roof. You could move just about anything with that sort of power.

Viour stiffened and panned back and forth like she had in the All Welcome Neutral, as though listening for something. Junker gave her a nervous glance.

"Your robot okay? Seems twitchy."

Viour turned to regard Junker. "We need to dig down to the very bottom. We seek what is at its lowest extent."

Junker held up his three minor arms in refusal.

"Look, I'll be straight with you: I wouldn't do that for all the Runtime I could slot. Our records don't go any deeper than the third kilometre, and you want to go twice as far? For all we know, there's a bunch of ancient superweapons just waiting to go pop." Junker spat another yellow glob over the railing, a gross habit that he seemed to indulge in far too often. "Plus anything buried that deep would have turned to worthless mulch from age, pressure and rustworms by now. People, it's best to skim the top k or so. I've got a map of everything you could need."

"Is it illegal to dig to the very bottom?" Viour pressed.

Junker gave Viour the stink eye, as though offended by the fact a robot seemed to be calling the shots in this discussion.

"Well, no. It's just common sense. Like how it's not illegal to blast yourself out of an airlock without a pressure suit, or how it's not illegal to eat your own fingers. Crime and stupidity are two different things, but neither of them are advisable."

Viour nodded. "Very well. I appreciate your concern for our wellbeing."

Junker shrugged with three shoulders. "Eh. Honestly, it's just concern for my bottom line. Barely had a customer in months. Can't have escaped your notice how dead this city is."

"Where is everyone?" Tuesday asked suddenly, lurching back into coherent thought after a good thirty minutes of staggering brainlessly. Considering all the tripper leaf he'd smoked, it was a wonder his freeze-dried cerebrum had recovered at all. "This whole place is empty."

Junker nodded sadly. "Yeah. Breathing oxygen isn't cool anymore, you see. Soon as hydrogen-based respiration became the next big thing, everyone installed new lungs and hopped over to the sulphur-and-methane cities." Junker spat sadly. "Bloody hydrogen-based life. But it won't be in vogue forever! Oxygen'll come back eventually. It always does."

Junker produced a computer sphere and spun it. As though by magic, the four humans were raised off the ground by perfectly circular floating discs. As a former heir to the Cuddle fortune, Trace recognised a tactile hologram when she stood on one. The hovering discs held the survivors safely in place, allowing freedom of movement without any risk of tipping over. As Junker could clearly see that Viour was able to float just fine on her own, he didn't bother giving her a disc. He expectorated a final time and turned away.

"Come wake me up when you're done digging."

As Trace had an image to uphold, she decided to be the first one over the railing. Gripping the tarnished metal with one hand, Trace flipped herself up and over with one arm and felt the wind whip past as she plunged half a kilometre towards solid scrap. Unfortunately, after a rapid one hundred-and-fifty metres, a spiked ball of ice appeared in her stomach as she realised she was heading for the metal depths at greater and greater speeds. Clawing at the air with her fingers, gritting her teeth so hard that she could have sworn that a molar just cracked, Trace's upcoming scream was instead cut off by a whimper when her disc stopped less than a hand span from the garbage without so much as bruising her. Shaking, twitching and ticking as though she had Tourette's syndrome, Trace managed to reclaim most of her cool by the time the others made it down to her level.

Lana was the second one to arrive. She raised an eyebrow at the wet shininess of Trace's eyes, and decided not to ask.

*

While the average customer would need to pay extra to use the grav cranes and magnetic attractors in their excavation efforts, the average customer wasn't on friendly terms with an alien possessed of nearly unlimited telekinetic abilities.

Viour floated about serenely at the very centre point of the trash pile for a minute or so, her cape billowing softly and her twenty chainlike limbs rippling in a hypnotic way. She slowly panned her bicycle-seat head from side to side, searching for whatever noise or psychic impulse she'd been following since the All Welcome Neutral, and suddenly snapped her attention to the right.

"Found it?" Jimmy asked uncertainly.

Without a word, Viour began to rip huge chunks of colourful scrap from the ground with the power of her mind. She made it look as easy as tearing up old duct tape. A stroke of her limb sent a dozen tonnes of rubbish curling up, a second motion pounded the garbage into a brick-like slab, and a third relocated it off to the side. In addition to burrowing down, Viour was also building a neat wall out of the scrap, crushing it into perfect right angles to reduce the chances of a cave-in. As she scooped her way deeper and deeper, excavating a huge, flat ramp that spiralled down and down and down, she effortlessly melted the walls into smooth, flat planes and reinforced them with thick girders. It was all very impressive, to say the least.

Far above, Junker was watching from a distant railing. It appeared he'd called a few friends to watch the show.

It didn't take long for their descent to edge into boredom. Watching Viour toss around giant cubes of metal got repetitive beyond a certain point, and the constant crushing and thudding noises were so deafening that the humans couldn't accomplish more than a third of a conversation. Viour was relentless, never seeming to tire, and the humans did their best to follow her as closely as they dared. Thankfully, it turned out the tactile holographic discs they were standing on could be extended into something similar to a banana lounge, and could be set to automatically pursue Viour, so the humans spent a lot of time reclining like they were next to a hotel pool.

Now and again the churning would upset a boil of rustworms. As neon-red cousins to the terrestrial giant centipede, rustworms were equipped with metal-cutting buzz saw heads and acid breath that could reduce most metals to slag. As these bugs preferred to eat ferrous materials and the mere smell of human flesh was already giving the rustworms diarrhoea, the survivors weren't in any real danger. A swift kick at the air was enough to send the rustworms writhing back into the walls at top speed.

It happened so gradually that the humans didn't it notice straight away, but it eventually became clear that the rustworms were getting more and more intelligent the lower Viour dug. The first few boils they'd encountered had been nothing more than snapping mouths, slobbering and mindless, but by the end of the first kilometre the red bugs seemed to be more cautious than their upper-crust relatives. They kept out of reach, trod more carefully, and their glowing white eyes possessed the sort of spark you'd expect from a moderately intelligent Jack Russell.

After two and a half kilometres, there was evidence that something sentient may have once lived down here in the scrap. It began with what could only be burial chambers: large holes carved out of the junk, adorned with crude tools and weapons made from garbage. The walls were decorated with extensive scratches that may have had some linguistic significance, but the glyphs were too crude for Lana's Omni to translate. The only thing missing was a corpse. If a dead body had resided in one of these burial chambers, there was no trace of it.

They'd gone well past the three-thousand-metre mark when they stumbled into something amazing: this entire layer of starship lasagne had been crafted into a sprawling city. Although this metropolis was long abandoned (and Viour didn't even hesitate in pounding along her predetermined path), it was clear that the long-gone residents had achieved some sort of Renaissance in the bowels of a trash pile. Rather than some generic rough-and-ready camp that was all function and no form, it appeared the locals had carved away at every square inch of this place as though it was the largest scrimshaw in the universe. If wasps could build city-sized cathedrals, this is how they would look. It was hauntingly beautiful. But there were no signs of life. This shell, this colossal carving, was all that remained. Of course, the majesty of this sprawl was lessened when Viour ploughed through it like a wrecking ball, and she either didn't hear the humans when they begged her to stop the rampage or she didn't care. All up, the abandoned city descended for close to three hundred metres, and no matter how far Viour pushed horizontally, there was more and more for her to destroy. It was likely that the city reached all the way to the borderline invulnerable limpet ivory walls of the seven-kilometre-wide cube bin.

Finally, at the very depths of the mysterious ruins, they came across a sight that only raised more questions. In the centre of a huge, empty expanse, there was a statue of a creature made from melted tin, and it was understandable to assume that it might represent one of the builders of this place. The statue was bent in a way that a human spine would dislike, it had a riot of limbs, and its gaping mouth had more in common with a buzz saw than a conventional jaw. It was dressed in heavy baroque armour, wielding some kind of barbed harpoon, and was rearing up on fifteen of its legs as though in silent threat.

It was a rustworm. An intelligent, tool-using, civilised rustworm.

The base of the statue was engraved with a more refined version of the crude symbols they'd seen in the higher burial chambers, but this dialect was evolved enough for Lana's Omni to translate a close approximation. All four of the humans muttered the centuries-old-words when they were superimposed over their eyes, not bothering to try and make themselves heard over the ungodly racket of Viour mining towards the bottom of the heap.

"Far better to be mindless than to bear the weight of the horrible truth."

Although the engraving didn't explain exactly how or why the sentient rustworms had fallen, it was surely written as the darkest of laments. And while it was only a few minutes until they left the fallen rustworm civilisation behind for good, the humans now looked at the boils of invertebrates in a new way, searching their insectoid eyes for intelligence, for a gleam of understanding.

They didn't find it.

*

By the fourth kilometre, there didn't seem to be a single thing of worth in this entire junk pile. Even the rustworms didn't live this deep. The garbage was no longer stable enough to form solid blocks, so Viour was forced to incinerate it and compact the smouldering material into dense charcoal slabs. The humans kept their distance to try and avoid getting a lungful of toxic fumes, but within seconds it was clear that they needed to suck in some respiratory filters to prevent them from choking to death. Everything had the consistency of wet cardboard, and it smelled of mildew and rot and damp, sort of like a train station that didn't have any public toilets. All the colours slowly bled towards a boring homogeneous grey the lower they went, and its sharp, defined edges were now dull and soggy.

At kilometre five, Jimmy decided to look up. The surface was a mere dot, a pinprick that was surely only a few centimetres short of God's sandals. If it wasn't for the fact Jimmy was able to recline on the tactile holographic disc he would have collapsed from exhaustion ages ago. As he had to use his legs to control the disc, this was playing havoc with his ankles, calf muscles and thighs, and all he wanted to do was stop. However, as Viour was blasting her way deeper and deeper without a moment of respite, it wouldn't be wise to stray too far from her. The suit of amplification armour was setting the pace.

Finally, after six kilometres of digging, Viour stopped. The only reason the humans registered this change of pace was because their drifting discs bumped into her armour one after another, the gentle collisions waking the passengers. Lana stretched, cracked her neck and blinked. Everything was pitch dark this deep, but a flick of her wrist produced a glowing bolt of light from her Omni, illuminating everything nearby.

All of the humans gaped in surprise.

"What...what is that?" Jimmy whispered.

Dead ahead was a giant black spike. It was clearly made out of the same crystalline material as The Archive and Penance back on the world of Scrote. Unlike the constant sodden grey-and-brown rubbish of the last few hours, the spike was a matte black, as though it hadn't spent thousands of years at the bottom of a garbage tip. Lana panned her holographic light higher, and she could see that the spike slowly became a spiral before it disappeared into the grey muck. It took a moment, but Lana noticed that only a tiny segment of the crystalline storage device was midnight blue rather than black, and it glowed a warmer, friendlier turquoise as she stepped closer.

Viour raised a limb to block her.

"Don't. I am highly familiar with Apex-built crystalline storage media, and I've never seen this type before. And if I don't recognise it, then there's a chance it may originate from the earlier epochs of The Apex, or even predate them altogether."

"In language we can understand?" Trace growled.

Viour turned to regard Trace with her burning-hot eye lenses.

"This object may be older than The Apex. It might have been constructed by the forerunners that we toppled before history began, or from the precursors that they overthrew, which is so far back that it's before the beginning itself." Viour shook her head in a very human way as everyone tried to get a grasp on what she had just said. "I have no idea how this ended up at the bottom of a trash pile, but it may well be the oldest storage device in the universe. As you may be aware, the older something gets, the more unpredictable it may be."

Viour got a little closer, raising a tentacle. Like before, trickles of turquoise shot through the only small section of the storage device that wasn't totally black. She moved backwards again.

"It called to me when we were in the All Welcome Neutral. It recognised something familiar in me, something that it has not sensed in a long, long time."

A hiss suddenly swept through the darkened alcove, a psychic statement that instantly decoded their languages with ease. In unison, the five beings all heard the same thing.

I AM ALL-SEE. ONLY SIX QUESTIONS REMAIN. YOU EACH HAVE ONE. CHOOSE WISELY.

Viour retreated from the huge crystalline computer in what looked a lot like fear. The only blue part of the All-See's dark body glowed with an internal brightness like a tiny star.

HELLO, VIOUR.

"What's an All-See?" Jimmy blubbered in Viour's direction. If The Apex was scared of this thing, then he knew that he should be beyond terrified. "And how does it know your name?"

Viour gave a sigh.

"The All-See is only meant to be a myth that we tell our spawn. Legends say it's a prophetic device that can answer anything you ask, but you only get a one-question allowance during the course of your lifetime. The story of the All-See is meant to encourage our spawn to meditate on what their one question would be, and this often serves to shape the very meaning of their lives." Viour moved her many limbs in a calming motion. "That means we each have just one question, and that's it. No second chances."

"My parents used to tell me scary stories about Nasty Mister Snip," Jimmy shared. "Nasty Mister Snip was a nightmare goblin with a giant pair of scissors who lops off your fingers if you pick your nose, cuts off your toes if you wet the bed, and chops off your winkie if you shake it more than two times after you wee." At the expressions he received from the others, it was clear that Jimmy was regretting his words before he'd even finished voicing them. After a few seconds of deafening silence, Jimmy tried to rise to his own defence. "But don't worry: after me twenty-second birthday party, me mum told me that Nasty Mister Snip had been apprehended, his scissors got confiscated, and he'd be doing life in a little goblin-sized cell."

Tuesday raised a finger, went to say something, and thought better of it.

"Fish in a barrel. No point, is there?"

Stepping forwards, helpfully taking the attention off Jimmy in the process, Lana decided to be the first one to ask a question.

"How can we get home?"

The small midnight blue part of All-See glowed a little brighter for a few seconds, as though it was taking a real effort to compute Lana's answer, and she silently worried that the crystal was about to blow a fuse. Her concern began to slide towards panic as a large part of the midnight blue segment of All-See blistered and faded to dead black, visibly reducing what little remained of its still-operational area to permanent darkness. After thirty seconds and a nasty burning smell, the All-See finally calmed down again and a bright red arrow appeared on its front facet, along with a number.

"There must be some manner of ship buried in that direction," Viour said calmly.

Lana gave the All-See a dirty squint, unimpressed. "Yeah. Maybe."

Trace stepped forwards next. Trying to not look at the others as though embarrassed, she asked her question almost too quietly to be heard.

"Will I find happiness?"

For a few seconds, everyone saw the gentle, hurt little girl that lived deep within the rough outer shell of Trace, and it was a sight that none of them would forget. As before, what little remained of the All-See slid closer to dead black as it computed Trace's answer. Her face lit up when the All-See answered.

YES.

And that was it.

Tuesday sucked at his black teeth, glanced sideways at Trace, and jabbed his nicotine-stained thumb at her.

"What's Trace's full name?"

Trace whirled on him, fists raised. "You swine!"

The All-See took very little time to answer this question. After all, it was a relatively easy one.

TRACETTA VICTORIA CUDDLE.

Tuesday had already started laughing before Trace hit him, and even an energetic beating wasn't enough to knock the hysterical whoops out of the gleeful scumbag. Unfortunately, if merely punching the bastard out of Tuesday had worked, then humanity would have been improved years ago.

Viour slid forwards.

"Will The Apex rise again?"

The All-See started to get very hot. It thought on this question for the better part of three minutes, its purple skin seeming to melt a little bit from the strain, and the humans were almost sure that the prophetic device was about to permanently turn black and inert, stone dead. It finally answered after far, far too long.

THEIR TIME IN THIS GALAXY HAS PASSED.

Viour slumped all twenty of her underslung shoulders.

"Oh."

Everybody looked at Jimmy, the only one left. He was silent for a while, nibbling his lip as he wracked his brain.

"Can I really ask you anything, All-See?"

*

While they may have a heads-up on where to go next, Viour couldn't just leave the All-See for anyone to find. The dead black regions of the All-See were relatively brittle, so extracting the thumb-sized segment of midnight blue crystal that still contained a question wasn't all that difficult. Viour stashed the crystal spike in a shock-proof storage compartment in her amplification armour without discussing it. After all, Odin only knew what would happen if something as ancient and powerful as the All-See was left to bounce around in Tuesday's pocket.

While the humans were dreading that Viour would need to dig all the way to the opposite side of the trash pile, thankfully they reached their objective within fifteen minutes. Viour tore through the garbage like a wall of circular saws, cutting a direct tunnel in the direction the All-See had indicated. Soon she had burrowed all the way through the grey sludge to reveal the side of something that was clearly made from chrome-like thoughtmetal. The construct was buried diagonally, and Viour wasted no time in carefully unearthing it. Within minutes, the object was revealed to be a ship shaped like a giant drill bit, a fifty-metre-long spiralling cylinder a tight five metres in diameter.

The humans walked right around the cylinder, but the construct seemed to be completely sealed. Far as they could tell, it was little more than a solid slab.

"If this is meant to be capable of getting us across seven galaxies," Tuesday managed, his lips bruised in the exact shape of Trace's knuckles, "then why did it get ditched in a compost heap?"

"And is there actually a way inside?" Lana asked, feeling more and more as though the All-See had lied to her.

After a good thirty seconds of silence, the humans turned to regard Viour. None of them had noticed until this point, but Viour's amplification armour seemed to be glowing in the darkness. It was as though the incredible exertions of the last few hours had taxed the suit awfully. Occasional drips of grey sludge hissed away from her on contact. Her head suddenly twitched, as though startled.

"Hmm? Oh, of course," she slid forwards, and ran a limb over the surface of the drill bit. The skin of the starship rippled like water. "Like all Apex tech, it only responds to our will. It is worthless to anyone else."

"And I bet you can't be coerced into using it, either," Lana guessed.

Viour gave a shallow nod of agreement. "Not accounting for coercion in our security systems would be truly foolish. Please, enter. I am sure it is safe."

Taking a breath, Lana stepped through the hull of the ship and into another darkness. It felt like sliding through warm water, a smooth, gentle sensation. In a few moments she could sense that the other three humans were inside the pitch blackness too. As soon as Viour's armour passed the threshold, however, everything came to life. Lighting from unseen sources snapped on across different moments, revealing that the starship's rounded interior was little more than a smooth passageway. Its thoughtmetal skin shined like chrome, and if you looked closely you could see that tens of thousands of hair-thin lines divided its surfaces into easy-to-separate modular sections.

Viour led the way to what was presumably the front of the giant drill bit. They passed a few bulges in the walls along the way, which might have been appliances, ancient computers, cupboards or something really exotic that didn't have a human equivalent. The furthest point of the construct simply ended in a blank wall, and to say this was an anticlimax was an understatement. However, after a couple of seconds dozens of blue and green holographic screens flickered on, all jockeying for Viour's attention. Unfortunately, their calming pastel colours were immediately drowned out by angry red sigils, which screamed "error message" in any language.

Viour swept at some of the crimson, turning it sky blue. Lana wasn't certain, but it seemed as though the alien was coding.

"Nothing the auto-repair systems can't fix," Viour confirmed, busily swiping at the holographic displays. "Should be able to get a full diagnostic. Just a second..."

Viour managed to turn one entire screen the colour of wet grass. She made a happy noise.

"This is an advanced-long range scout," she confirmed, continuing to manipulate the symbols. "Designed to cover extreme distances into uncharted space in minimal time before returning even faster to its point of origin. These ships are blindingly quick and built to last, but on the downside they're lightly armoured and don't have any weapons."

"A scout?" Trace barked a laugh. "How is a scout supposed to get us home?"

"Is it fast enough to cross seven galaxies without taking ten billion years?" Jimmy asked directly.

Viour shook her head. "No. Not even close."

Trace kicked a wall. The holographic displays wobbled a little.

"Then why are we in here? Are you saying we dug all this way for nothing? Are you winding us up?"

Viour didn't bother pointing out that she was actually the one who had done all the digging before raising a limb.

"I do not think you understand. While these extreme long-range scouts were designed to reach new, unmapped areas of space, they also possessed a special recall function that could unerringly return the crew home afterwards. While a recall trip is infinitely faster than the initial scouting, the nav system has a catch: it can only plot a course to somewhere you've already been."

"Been?" Tuesday repeated.

Viour nodded. "Yes. But plotting a course is as simple as taking a brain scan. The more time you've spent at where you want to return to, the easier it is to pinpoint with the nav software, and the faster it is to get there."

"And now you have four people who can provide this nav system with exact coordinates to another galaxy," Lana said slowly. "Right?"

"While this is purely academic," Viour disclaimed, "I do have high hopes. I am not an expert in this particular branch of technology, but I don't see any reason why it would not work for our purposes. When used correctly, this tech was highly reliable. The best part is that they will not be expecting us to effectively go forwards by travelling backwards."

"So what now?" Tuesday asked, hoping for an answer he could criticise.

"Six kilometres of garbage to break through," Viour said helpfully. The last blotches of scab-red code had disappeared from the blue and green screens. "This bird should have no problems with that. Brace, please."

The walls went transparent, providing a full panoramic view. Besides a billion tonnes of homogenous muck, there wasn't much to see. Viour hit the gas, and everything bucked like a bull with a rope knotted around his Johnson, almost knocking the humans off their feet. Unfortunately, that was about all Viour accomplished. She tried the same manoeuvre again with roughly the same results. And again...and again, until the ship's superstructure made a tortured squealing and the lights flickered on and off.

"Brilliant," Tuesday mumbled in the discotheque strobing, trying not to have a fit.

Viour sighed. "Sometimes, you just need to use more force."

"I believe it was Gandhi who said that," Lana muttered.

The scout suddenly dislodged itself with a huge push, unearthing its long-buried form from the filth that had held it in place for so, so long. Viour expertly piloted it through the extensive ramps of solidified trash she'd crushed into position this whole way, zipping in a tight corkscrew without touching a single wall. As there was barely an inch of space between the scout's spiral skin and the scrap, it was clear that Viour was more than accomplished at the stick. And while the ship was technically just one big drill bit and could likely burrow its way out, Viour didn't need to resort to something so crude.

In a matter of dizzying, nauseating minutes, they'd threaded their way to the surface of the starship graveyard. Viour brought the scout a hand span above the scrap, angling it towards the giant multi-sized airlock embedded in the limpet ivory wall of the Star Cage as though preparing to smash into it. However, the scout stayed there for a few moments, hovering.

"So what's the plan?" Jimmy asked.

Viour seemed distracted, and did not answer. She suddenly twisted her head to the left, focusing her eye lenses through the transparent hull on the distant form of Junker. The light blue Slidge in charge of the garbage tip was making his way across its surface on one of those tactile hologram platforms.

"I cannot simply bash through the airlock seal," Viour stated. Her head darted back and forth, as though scanning something the humans could not see. "In addition to being almost invulnerable to heat and pressure, there are a great number of weapons protecting it from unauthorised exits. And it would be unwise to test the integrity of this scout. It was not built for war."

Although his physical body was still a good hundred metres away from the scout, a hologram of Junker appeared in their midst. Looking around, the Slidge caretaker of this huge bowl of mechanical porridge somehow managed to give an impressed whistle with his beak.

"I had no idea something operational was buried all the way down there! Now, before you take this bird anywhere, we'll need to scan all her specs into our catalogue. She's obviously a special piece, so I've got a strong feeling that I'm gonna have to pull some strings to stop the Primacy from seizing her for research purposes. That'll take time, and it'll take currency."

"How much time?" Trace growled, wondering what would happen if she kicked the hologram in his happy sack.

Junker shrugged. "Shouldn't take more'n a couple of weeks and...ten million macros of Runtime, maybe?"

"I don't have time for this," Viour hissed. Everyone could feel a pressure in the air and a pain in their minds, as though a blade crafted from thoughts was slicing dangerously close. The humans could sense that Viour's next words had a kind of push behind them, something unyielding and sharp. "Open the airlock and let us out immediately."

Junker's image went static, as though the transmission had glitched out and frozen. He gave a small spasm, and yellow blood began to froth from beneath his leftmost eye. Sounding as though he'd just lost half his IQ points, Junker gave a large nod of agreement, almost stabbing himself with his own beak in the process. "S...sure thing. Happy trails, Mummy D-D-Dad."

Junker produced and rolled a computer ball with effort, his movements clumsy as he opened this side of the giant dreadnought-sized airlock. Feeling ecstatic at things finally going smoothly, the humans were just about to share high-fives and cheer...until they saw what Viour's stab of mental dominance had actually done to Junker. The hologram of the Slidge caretaker coughed violently, golden fluid spurting out of his twitching eyelids like water pistols, and his pupils began to roll in random directions. He seized up, foaming at the beak, and collapsed just as one of his eyes popped completed out of its socket and bounced out of frame. Junker's muscles fitted, he fired gouts of sputum from his beak, and he wailed like a mortally wounded pig.

Viour gave a snap of a limb to cancel the hologram, cutting off its screams as she accelerated their stolen ship into the airlock. Nobody spoke as the layers of limpet ivory transitioned, allowing them to shoot out of the Star Cage and towards open space, but all of them were trying not to think of those awful screeches. Whatever damage Viour had inflicted on Junker by overriding his mind, the humans silently hoped that the Slidge didn't have to endure his suffering for long. Most of all, they prayed she never felt the urge to do the same thing to them.

Viour broke the silence.

"I need all of you to focus on where you spent the largest portion of your lives. Think about the sights, the smells, the way it made you feel. Remember what you did there, who you knew, what you loved and hated about it." Viour glanced at a screen. "It may take a few minutes for the nav system to align with your spatial awareness of your homes, but I must stress that this is all purely theoretical and may not work. Do you all have somewhere?"

Tuesday blinked, looked up at the ceiling, and decided on the abandoned service station in the deep Mojave where he'd spent his first nine years of life. He'd been raised hundreds of kilometres from civilisation, trapped in a barren wasteland like a primitive with his parents, eating vermin, mutated desert beasts and cacti. He'd been wild, a savage dressed in animal skins and hunting with weapons made out of the rusted guts of the service station, sleeping on lice-ridden pelts and silently cursing sunlight that was hot enough to melt the paint right off the brick walls...

The other three humans were clearly lost just as deeply in thought, doing their best to think of home...no matter how bleak, lonely, deprived or violent it may be.

"Good," Viour approved. She turned to regard Tuesday. "It appears the nav system is meshing with your mind best. We will use your destination. Keep focussing on the details."

Thanks to the see-through hull, everyone could make out that the scout was slowly tipping to the side. It began to bob and weave in an unsure dance like a three-dimensional compass needle searching for universal north, but thankfully this didn't toss about its fleshy contents. Viour nodded in approval.

"This should not take longer than a couple of minutes. So long as the Star Cage hasn't noticed us lifting off, we should be…"

Everything rattled violently and there was the loud screeching of metal-on-metal. All the screens flicked from blue and green back to red and their acceleration decreased to total stasis. Far beyond the transparent walls, a superimposed red circle appeared over the skin of the distant Star Cage, picking out the signature of a new, major object on a direct interception course. The leviathan was four kilometres long and a kilometre and a half wide, and according to its mass reading it must be almost entirely solid the whole way through. In addition to that, the behemoth's hide was bristling with so many guns that it brought the rear end of a defensive porcupine to mind. Detailed schematics of its weapons systems – all of which were currently being trained on their tissue-thin hull - began to pop up. The word OVERKILL appeared next to every single weapon in a way that was far from encouraging.

"I believe they've noticed us," Trace growled.

The transparent walls suddenly displayed a thousand close-up images of a purple, battle-hardened Slidge. Her face was criss-crossed with energy burn scars and she had the dead eyes of a being who has seen death from a matter of inches on far too many occasions. Too terrified to think straight, all Jimmy could focus on was that this was the first time he'd seen a Slidge that wasn't blue or red, but a perfect mesh of both colours. He wondered if this had any significance.

"I am the Prime of The Salvation By Hatred, a Star Cage of the Slidge Primacy," the purple Slidge announced, her voice a rusty blade across the eardrums. "You are accused of smuggling an illegal, unregistered psionic weapon aboard my Star Cage, and then using said weapon to mentally compel and murder one of our citizens without provocation. Furthermore, in removing an uncatalogued starship without due process, you have been charged with no fewer than sixty-five other offences, including Grand Theft Astro and multiple licensing violations. You are to unconditionally surrender to our forces, or be destroyed. You have one minute to confirm your yield before we open fire."

The holo vanished.

"So surrender or die," Trace summarised.

"Technically, they are saying surrender and die." Viour clarified. "I am certain all of those charges will lead to capital punishment at best." Noticing that Tuesday was distracted by this latest in a long line of death threats, she whipped a tendril at him, missing his left eye by an inch. "You! Focus. We need to orient this ship with our destination as quickly as possible."

Trace smacked her fist against the hull. "So surrender isn't an option." She rubbed and scratched her face so hard that she almost drew blood, trying to focus. "Okay, look: they have a big ship covered in guns, I get that, but it's just one ship. There must be something we can do to distract them, some trick that will give us enough time to bolt."

Viour gave a mental sigh.

"It's a fleet, actually."

Trace went to correct Viour, assuming that there had been some sort of translation glitch, but a trill declared that the scout's scanners had detected more starships. Zooming right in on the Slidge dreadnought, the humans could only watch in fascination as three major segments of the ship – each around a sixth of its total mass – cleanly dislocated and barrel-rolled for a hundred kilometres in different directions. The dreadnought's armour plating fanned out to cover the gaping holes, sealing its skin shut. It was only a matter of moments before each of the three newly-emerged siege craft performed the same shucking routine, birthing a total of eighteen heavy corvettes like some kind of unholy, heavily-armed Russian nesting dolls. Trace used an illegal swearword when the heavy corvettes expelled so many armed drones that there wasn't enough time to count them all before the Prime's ultimatum became more than just a threat.

In a mere ten seconds, Viour's words had become fact: they were facing a fleet.

The armada, thickly cocooned around the Prime's dreadnought, was now so close that it could be seen with the naked eye. Sure, they were only dots against the backdrop of the wide, white span of the Star Cage, but that didn't mean their weapons weren't capable of reducing the scout and all its passengers to a thin mist. Although the ancient Apex vessel didn't have so much as a slingshot and a sharp rock, it was able to pick out every single Slidge ship with red holographic targeting reticules.

There were a lot of circles.

Viour motioned at the incorporeal monitors, but nothing seemed to happen. The scout continued rolling about madly, using Tuesday's memories to pinpoint the exact spatial location of his first home, but that was about all the movement it was capable of performing.

"The reality slide won't happen for another ninety seconds," Viour said calmly. "The doorway won't be stable enough until that point."

"Won't help much when we get blasted in twenty," Jimmy groaned.

"But there's no point opening a wormhole if we can't budge an inch, is there?" Lana snapped.

Viour shook her head. "This has nothing to do with wormholes, and we don't need to move. We just need enough time to designate a target, and a wave will carry us..." Viour paused for half a second, as though mustering an appropriate word that these primitives would comprehend, "...sideways."

"But again, that won't be much help when we're a smear of cinders, will it?" Jimmy said with a little too much hysteria.

"Are you sure this scout doesn't have any weapons?" Lana pressed.

Viour shook her head.

The huge, armoured slabs of the Slidge war party continued to advance at quite a pace, and a scan confirmed that the cannons, lances and missile pods bristling from their metal hides were now running hot. As the life expectancy of all human life in this galaxy reached single seconds, a burbling, shrieking war cry blasted out of every speaker. It was the last thing many enemies of the Primacy had heard before being reduced to a smelly odour, and it wasn't hard to imagine the exact translation of the scream.

Viour stiffened at the sound, as though she'd heard it before, and hissed her words with utter hatred instead of her usual calm, detached manner.

"We do have one weapon," she said, waving her twenty long, articulated limbs like a nest of defensive cobras. "And I guarantee this time I will not be forgotten."

Viour shot through the scout's rippling wall like a bullet, her raw velocity knocking the surprised humans down like they were in a whirlwind. Thankfully, her dramatic exit didn't affect the internal pressure or atmosphere of the scout, so nobody died a horrible death from depressurisation.

Viour knew she had to take full advantage of every microsecond the moment she hit space. Her most immediate task was to fill her armoured, baseball-sized cockpit with anti-pressure gel, cushioning her feeble true body from the incredible g-forces of combat speed. After all, a surprise counter-assault wouldn't be too effective if her carapace was crushed into goo the first time she accelerated.

Although Viour knew it would be exhausting and even painful, for the first time since The Fall of her species she dialled the processing power of her hardware to full, amplifying her mind to its fullest transcendent potential. All of her cognitive functions peaked in the span of a gerbil's heartbeat, and her brain soaked up every detail of the approaching Slidge fleet. As simultaneously keeping track of the mass, volume and movements of the enemy vessels was child's play even without augmentation, most of her Operating System's runtime was dedicated to keeping track of all those weapons. A hundred million colourful lines and arcs spelled out where every barrel and scope and crosshair was pointing, how fast they could track a target of her size, their exact ordinance load-outs and effective range, and she was even able to compare the quality of their manufacturing and overall reliability in relation to similar weapons that she had on file. This onslaught of information was like watching a New Year's Eve fireworks display going off during a Malignant Testicular Tumour concert in a warehouse filled with chromatic paint. The strain of comprehending all of this at once would have sent a human insane in an instant, and given them a fatal brain aneurysm in two.

Flying straight and true for the approaching cloud of armed drones, her twenty limbs and protective cape rippling in her wake, Viour almost felt relieved when the countless barrels and cannons and missile banks turned to track her, trying in vain to pin her down with targeting systems that were designed to smash starships the size of small cities, not something as tiny as a suit of amplification armour. Jinking fifteen metres to her left, carefully observing how the different elements of the fleet reacted to her unexpected twitch (sluggishly, in all honesty), Viour focused a little of her remaining processing power on superimposing red-yellow-green-white gradient shades over the incoming vessels. She had already finished pinpointing all their most vulnerable areas just as the six-limbed aliens decided to open fire on her and ask questions later.

Arcing sharply, avoiding the blast radius of the first barrage of anti-ship fire, Viour's highly enhanced perception proved to be more than capable of keeping her safe. The synthesis between Viour's mind and the hardware and software of her amplification armour kept her appraised of every incoming round and beam and bomb, allowing her to stay well outside of their area of effect. She carved through the unmanned drones, missing them by inches before clipping at them with a flicked limb almost as an afterthought. Each whip surgically gutted the remote control relay from a drone, disabling them in the most efficient way possible.

Zipping unexpectedly, Viour aimed for the front hull of the nearest of the three looming siege craft in a seemingly suicidal game of chicken. As she could see where its skin was thickest and thinnest - as well as the location of every crew member, ordnance cache, power plant, fusion reactor, escape pod, and even a stash of hidden pornographic magazines - her plan was a lot more sophisticated than just charging like a bull with red cataracts. Covering her antlers, head and

305

upper torso in her near-invulnerable cape, Viour spun like a drill before smashing through a half-metre-wide weak-point in the siege craft's bulkhead. Whirling towards its command centre, located at what was meant to be the total safety of its central core, the screams of its commanders were lost to the vacuum as their starship split open at the seams. Launched into the void, the entire bridge crew struggled and died in seconds.

Railing through the warship in a way that may have seemed like an erratic path of destruction to the untrained eye, Viour made it out the far side in an explosion of armour chunks. Unsurprisingly, at this point the Slidge fleet decided to ignore the ancient, unarmed Apex scout, and trained all of their guns on the suit of amplification armour that had just easily annihilated one of their largest vessels. Viour's augmented awareness calculated that her chances of surviving a stand-up fight against such odds were unlikely at best, especially with her hardware already starting to overheat, but that didn't matter. Viour didn't need to destroy them all: she just needed to buy some time.

Although Viour was fast and strong and possessed some of the best combat technology in this galaxy, working her way into the very core of an entire fleet of pissed-off Slidge was not the wisest move of her military career. She may have caught that first siege craft by surprise, but there was only so much she could do against a seemingly unlimited number of dedicated guns that were now all pointing in her direction. Of course, as she had a total understanding of what these weapons were capable of, she was able to play dirty by tricking the Slidge into accidentally shooting one another. By the time Viour's deception had run its course, the Slidge had lost half of their heavy corvettes and a hundred armed drones to friendly fire. While this tactic may have worked exceedingly well as a one-off, it was unlikely the Slidge would fall for it a second time.

Dodging a lattice of energy beams and clouds of explosions by a matter of centimetres, Viour dove towards the second siege craft as though she was about to play another game of chicken. Spinning and bucking, somehow coming through the solid screen of fire unscathed, instead of slamming into the front of the siege craft like her first dive, Viour banked wildly to the side and extended her limbs to five times their normal length. Vicious hooks sprouted from all twenty of her multipurpose wrists, and she swung them into the aft of the siege craft with pinpoint precision and accelerated with all her strength. Catching a dozen different armour plates at their weakest points, Viour peeled away a good part of the hull as though removing an old sticking plaster. Viour detached from the siege craft as it listed towards the dreadnought, crippled.

If Viour was capable of snorting in contempt, she would have.

A cluster of distant red targeting reticules alerted Viour to some very bad news: fifteen dreadnoughts had just pushed away from the Star Cage at engagement speed, and would be ready to shuck away an onslaught of siege craft, corvettes and drones in a matter of seconds. As impressive as Viour's performance had been so far, she knew that her sneaky tricks couldn't make up for the fact she was a lone gun against several entire fleets.

Distracted for half an instant too long, Viour suddenly knew nothing but heat and light; tens of thousands of projectiles, laser beams, particle accelerators, missiles, kinetic bores, shells, and many other things that did not conform to human description were coming from every direction, pinning her down. It had taken a good minute, but the Slidge's targeting systems had finally adapted to her flight technique, and the fight was now basically over.

Managing to wrap herself in her deflection cape a bare microsecond before she could be annihilated down to a runnel of fluid, spinning at top speed, Viour's cape heated to such an insane temperature that the amplification armour beneath it began to melt like a candle. She detected her articulated limbs sloughing away into molten strands, and the royal blue of her suit's abdomen and torso blackened and came apart. She screamed as her suit's wild antlers splintered, and her wails only got worse as her protective helmet – the only barrier between Viour's insect body and the inkpot of space – glowed yellow.

Somehow coming out the other side of the blockade, reaching the frozen black again, Viour swooped her dissolving armour back towards the scout just as things got even worse: in what was surely the death knell of Viour, the four humans and all of The Apex, a phalanx of Star Cages appeared with the briefest flicker of translation. Dozens of the planet-sized constructs popped out of the ether, dotting the skies of this system as far as she could see, the glowing flesh of a harvested purple supergiant star roiling at their cores. Giving a choked sound of fear, feeling the panic rise within her as each of the giant white lattices began to spew out so many Slidge dreadnoughts that they blotted out the stars, Viour made her final peace with the universe as tens of millions of guns fired in unison.

But then Viour got the shock of her life to see that all the constructs and war fleets were firing at each other. Clearly, the Sun Lattices weren't happy with the Star Cages mucking about in highly quarantined space without being consulted first, and had decided to make their annoyance clear with thermonuclear weapons.

Unwilling to look too closely at this godsend, Viour curved back towards the scout. Behind her, it looked as though all of space was nothing more than a solid block of intertwined firing lines, a blinding mess of heat and radiation and force.

It appeared that the Slidge were no longer overdue for their latest apocalypse.

*

A white-hot ball of unrecognisable molten slag passed through the rippling hull of The Apex scout, slamming explosively into the opposite wall before rattling to a rest on the smooth chrome-like thoughtmetal floor. The humans recoiled away from this hellishness with screams of pain, their skin instantly blistering from close proximity. Thankfully, the scout automatically filled itself with sub-zero gas, putting out the inferno. It was now so cold, in fact, that the humans almost missed being burnt. Almost.

It took a moment for them to recognise that the blob of liquefied metal was Viour. From antlers to ankles the suit of amplification armour was now a deformed mess of charcoaled ruin, and the only reason it hadn't melted away to nothing was thanks to the below-freezing temperature of the vacuum. All but three of Viour's articulated limbs had been seared off, and the ones that remained were locked into awkward angles. One of them juddered in a faulty circuit.

Viour tried to speak, but the hardware in the right side of her suit's skull – including the Operating System that translated her thoughts into movement and speech - was totally fried. She tried to turn her helmet only to find it was melted into the current setting. Viour had to move her whole torso just to slightly adjust her gaze. Even then, her sensor lenses had splintered so badly that she could barely see as well as a human.

Her cockpit hatch popped open, letting out a fountain of smoking anti-pressure gel. Viour's true form launched from the gooey crevasse, wriggling limbs that had a lot in common with snail eyestalks, and she stuck to the wall like one of Tuesday's larger brown coughs. Everyone could see that Viour's insectoid limbs along the right side had been seared away, and her carapace was burnt to the point it was crumbling. Her flesh actually appeared to be steaming.

"They will remember me," was all she said.

And with that, Viour lost her grip and literally hit the deck with a sad splat noise.

In the far distance, dozens of near-identical Star Cages and Sun Lattices glowed bright purple as they prepared to fire at each other with an apocalyptic barrage of harnessed solar energy. Just as the humans became utterly convinced that they were about to be caught in a system-wide extinction event, smeared across the sky like a scoop of cosmic peanut butter, the ancient scout ship suddenly ignited its drives in a screaming cacophony of noise. It didn't move an inch, but in a moment it wasn't there anymore.

"Gone," Viour breathed, fainting away.

CHAPTER TWENTY-FOUR HOMEWARD BOUND

As hoped, the entire universe – including the enormous all-in brawl between a multitude of Sun Lattices and Star Cages – vanished. But the humans had no time to feel relief before switching to another emotion: confusion. While Scrote's star system disappeared as expected, it wasn't replaced with the usual combination of black space, twinkly stars, generic spherical planets and twisted rocks. No, outside the transparent hull of the scout was something quite different.

"Are they..." Tuesday took a quick glance at everyone else's faces to make sure they looked as baffled as he did. "Whales?"

Nobody bothered to affirm Tuesday's comment, as the truth was flippering about and vocalising in all directions. Tens of thousands of very, very, very distant relatives of Moby Dick gently undulated through a universe composed of swirling oxygen-rich lilac foam, their calls a gentle howling you could feel in your marrow. This yoghurt-thick ocean ebbed against the hull, making it bob about, but thankfully it wasn't dense enough to crush them. The scout's ancient computer automatically painted red target reticules on the closest of the awesome mammals, measuring them, calculating their mass, and providing a detailed rundown on their genetics. Lana did a double-take at the numbers.

"Each of those things are bigger than Earth," she said.

Everyone braced themselves as one of the leviathans slopped its wake against the thin hull, followed by its blubbery body blocking ninety percent of their view for a good two minutes. An eye the diameter of Australia examined them, its New York-sized pupil sweeping gently across this odd intruder to its realm. Lana's hissing was far less casual.

"Odin's Itchy Genitals, I've never even heard of a living thing this big. And as for all this foam...what's holding it together? Surely it can't just go forever?"

"Them whales make World Slugs look like germs," Tuesday muttered.

As though belatedly remembering that it had a job to do, the scout decided to do a ninety-degree skidding turn and accelerated to full velocity. It was enough to make the humans sway, but not knock them over. At some seemingly arbitrary spatial point the scout was suddenly engulfed by a second wave, just like the one they'd used to leave Scrote's system.

Unfortunately, the purple ocean and planet-sized whales were replaced by something far worse: a horrific eternity of congealed, wriggling blood of a million gory shades, populated only by endless screams, as though the universe itself was in constant, terrible pain. Everyone clasped their ears so tightly that they couldn't crush harder if they tried, but the wailing was like a psychic ice pick rather than an audible sound. Shaking and moaning, the humans could feel rivulets of blood trickling out of their noses, tear ducts and ears, as though the screaming red eternity had decided to add their scarlet fluids to its stockpile. Responding to the call of something great and terrible, their veins and arteries hummed, their percolating in preparation to burst from the four fleshy prisons. Thankfully, the scout only had to cross a hundred thousand kilometres before the crimson horror was gone, but those agonising seconds were some of the worst they'd ever experienced.

A third reality was almost entirely filled by a complicated machine made from some sort of ancient, tarnished, unknown metal, its valves and pipes and gears stretching as far as the scout could scan. Its badly oxidised components were chugging and grinding and its pistons were all firing and venting steam, but the construct didn't appear to have any obvious purpose. Finally recovering from the psychic blood screams, wiping a slug of claret from her nostrils, Lana's eyes darted across the twisting metallic chaos.

"There's no end to it." She blinked at her Omni display. "I have no idea what this machine does. But it goes on forever."

Every wall of the cylinder-shaped scout mercifully turned opaque, blocking out the insanity going on outside of its hull. Turning at a sign of movement, the humans watched as Viour's half-crippled insectoid body finished weaving a simple platter out of thoughtmetal. Without a suit of amplification armour to augment her existing powers this task proved more than taxing, and she was clearly tired from the exertion. It went without saying that recently losing all the limbs on her right side made this process even more difficult. Sliding onto the platter, Viour snapped one of her tendrils and the platform rose gently, hovering to the height of a human chin.

"I would advise you not to look at the different realities as we pass through them," Viour said gently. "Some of them would send you utterly mad with a glance. Some would kill you instantly, hull or no hull."

Lana squinted, figuring something out.

"Tell me...does this scout use reality stuttering to get around?"

Viour regarded Lana for a long moment, as though she'd just witnessed a chimpanzee put down her banana in order to perform a bit of calculus.

"You are...familiar with reality stuttering?" Viour confirmed.

Lana nodded eagerly. "Sure. Uh, well, to a degree. I know the basics. For starters, I know that every inch of our universe has linked counterparts in countless alternate realities, but the exact distances they span vary wildly from reality to reality." Lana blinked heavily, trying to figure out how to explain something she didn't entirely understand. To make her job easier, she used her Omni's projector to draw some simple shapes on thin air: a big circle and a much smaller circle. "Okay. Right. So while the actual, real distance between the exact spatial points where Scrote and its moon are located in our reality might be three hundred thousand kilometres, in a neighbouring reality that gap might only go for five inches...but in the next reality it could be fifty thousand lightyears. It's all about finding the most efficient path to stutter across."

"So you're saying that something what takes up a kilometre in our home reality might be an inch in another, and fifty lightyears in a third?" Jimmy asked, his eyes crossing slightly.

Lana nodded. "It's about finding a way to go directly from A to Z without bothering with the rest of the alphabet."

Tuesday snapped his fingers in realisation.

"You know, I'm almost certain that this reality stuttering stuff is what September used to navigate The Frontier."

"For the last time, you weren't on The Frontier!" Jimmy screeched in an embarrassingly high key.

Viour's platter hummed angrily to gather their attention, likely tired of the bickering.

"While the nav system seems to be working just fine, there are some problems."

"Of course there are," Jimmy said numbly.

"To be clear, this vessel is space worthy, but we have no food, no water, and minimal air. And while the oxygen generator could keep me alive indefinitely on my own, as a collective the five of us have about a day of oxygen left before we all suffocate."

Lana rustled in her pockets, producing a saddy bag of dehydrated water cubes and a couple of packets of never-expire Cricket Jerky. Dig as she might, there weren't any oxygen tanks hidden among the lint.

"Can you build a better oxygen generator?" Jimmy asked hopefully.

Viour deflated in shame.

"Building anything complicated without my amplification armour to assist me is a slow, difficult, painstaking process. And as I have no precise idea how long our journey will take, I do not know how much energy the reactors on this scout have to spare, if any." Viour's platter bobbed a little, as though apologising. "There is another issue: due to the fact we will be using reality stuttering, I must warn you that the time we personally experience on the voyage may not be the same amount of time that passes in our reality of origin. There may be a...discrepancy."

311

Jimmy waved this away.

"We need to deal with the air and water and food thing first. Maybe we could make a pit-stop at some other world?"

"We have no allies in this galaxy," Viour said instantly, firmly. "Only enemies. The entire Slidge Primacy has doubtlessly identified this scout as the most wanted of all criminal vessels. To translate back into real space would be a death warrant for us all. And even if that wasn't the case, the path of this scout has been set, and cannot be altered until we arrive."

Tuesday raised a yellow-stained finger. "Or..."

Trace kicked a wall, making the holographic screens jump with static.

"All this guessing is wasting my air," Trace growled. "And while she might be the worst war criminal to ever bloody the stars, there's only one creature on this ship who can explain our options." Trace motioned at Viour. "So talk. What's the solution? I'm assuming you've got one?"

Viour did not respond to the insult, mostly because she couldn't deny it. Deep in thought, she spent a few seconds silently watching a screen as it plotted their projected path through a hundred million different realities over the span of seven galaxies back to Earth, the heart of The Unison.

"As these scouts were usually piloted by whatever lesser species we found convenient, this ship has a multi-purpose all-kitchen that can cook, refrigerate, cryogenically freeze and..." Viour sighed, "...dehydrate, among other functions."

The survivors looked blank. Viour took this as permission to explain.

"As long as I get the settings perfect, it would be a straightforward process to use this equipment to place you in suspended animation. This would mean dehydrating you and freezing you solid, in that order, and then defrosting you once the journey is completed. Another benefit to this plan is that your bodies will be protected from any realities we pass through that are not...compatible."

Viour was met by the same incredulous look on all four faces.

"Like..." Jimmy managed, "like jerky?"

"This is idiotic," Lana said, shaking her head. "It's been centuries since mankind gave up on such crude methods of preservation. It's a fact that sticking somebody in cryo, even for a short duration, will result in a guaranteed degree of brain damage. This isn't an option."

"Nobody is freezing me," Trace growled, apparently changing her mind about trusting Viour's judgment.

Tuesday sucked at his few teeth shards.

"But you're absolutely sure you can bring us back to life afterwards, right?" he asked Viour, surprising the others. "We're talking one-hundred-percent sure?"

"You aren't serious?" Jimmy asked quietly.

"The reanimation process is simple enough," Viour said evenly. "I have performed similar procedures on many living creatures dozens of times over the years for fun. I was always able to bring them back in a fully intact state. Just in case, I will also back-up exact copies of your minds and genetic codes to ensure that I can repair any...imperfections."

"Chew slugs," Trace snapped, using a highly offensive saying that made the others flinch. "No dehydration. No freezing. And as for your next idea? None of that either. I don't even want to hear it! No! Spug off!"

"It's either that or suffocate," Viour said in her infuriatingly calm drone.

The survivors looked at each other. They all knew for certain this would be their only chance at reaching Earth again, but that didn't mean they would go along without so much as an argument.

"We should look about a bit." Lana pouted at the seams running along the walls. "There must be an alternative in one of these draws, maybe some sort of stasis chamber? A big stasis chamber?"

Viour shook her yellow-orange-red-black-white striped head.

"There are no stasis chambers. The indentured beings we used to crew these scouts weren't seen as important enough for such an expense."

"No choice, really, is there?" Tuesday sat on the floor and mouthed a cigarette from his pack. Trace snap-kicked it cleanly out of his lips without bothering with a warning, barely missing his face with the toe of her boot. Tuesday glared at her. "What? You think losing two minutes of air matters? Punch it, I'm having a smoke."

Lana looked around at the thoughtmetal cylinder as Tuesday recovered his chlorine-flavoured tube from the floor. While she knew there was only one option, it just felt wrong to willingly march towards such a fate. Sighing, rubbing the bridge of her nose, Lana realised that she was just being yellow. She was just about to agree with Viour's idea when a large kitchen multi-appliance folded out of a wall like origami in reverse, presumably at Viour's silent command. The frame of mysterious tubes and devices almost crossed the scout's entire diameter, and was probably big enough to flash-freeze a buffalo.

"First volunteer?" Viour asked.

"I'll...I'll go first," Jimmy said bravely.

"Come on, it'll take a week to dehydrate all that!" Tuesday complained.

"Then you go first," Trace snapped.

Tuesday sucked at his little black teeth and shook his head.

"Nah. See, unlike defective people, I don't volunteer to help with any endeavour unless I directly benefit from it. This, for instance, is a perfect example of a situation where there's absolutely no chance in Loki's Fecund Armpit that I'm going first."

"Coward," Lana muttered.

Tuesday waggled a finger. "No, just very, very selfish. There's a difference."

Jimmy approached the multi-appliance and found he was shaking.

"I'm...I'm ready."

A wide ceramic circle that could have doubled as an egg ring for a T-Rex ovum descended from the heart of the unfolding kitchen. Looking a little self-conscious, Jimmy removed his clothing without letting anyone see his genitals or bottom crack and hung the rags over a nearby railing. Stepping buck-naked into the circle at a motion from Viour, Jimmy didn't even have a chance to say goodnight before all of the moisture in his body vanished in an instant. Although they'd been prepared for what was about to happen, the other humans tried not to throw up at the sight of a stick-figure of Jimmy-flavoured human jerky. His desiccated, inch-thick remains slid into a tight coffin of shrink-wrap before disappearing deep into a steaming freezer slot in the guts of the multi-appliance. All the yellow-brown liquid from Jimmy's body was placed in its own large tank and joined his frozen corpse out of sight. His yellow MacDeath uniform and chef hat were draped over a railing, ready for his eventual reanimation.

"Did he scream?" Lana gagged, but managed not to vomit. "I think he screamed."

"Pretty sure that was just the sound of a hundred-and-fifty kilos of fat dissolving into high-calorie gas," Tuesday said far too cheerfully. His smirk disappeared the moment Viour gestured for somebody to go next. "Uh, Trace? I reckon you're up."

CHAPTER TWENTY-FIVE DEFROSTED

The shrink-wrapped remains of what had once been Lana Slade slid out of a storage draw deep within the space-cold hull. With a flash from the heart of the multi-kitchen her jerkified body was no longer frozen solid, and seconds later the chunk of human jerky was fed into a bubbling industrial food rehydrator. Lana's shrink-wrap automatically unsealed, filling the scout with steam just as she finally managed to voice a long-delayed scream.

"I've changed my mind!"

Swinging her head around woozily, naked as a shaved monkey, Lana fought her way out of a loose storage bag and tried getting to her feet. She staggered heavily into the opposite wall, somehow managing not to end up in a limp pile on the floor. Blinking heavily, Lana tapped at the meat between the thumb and index finger of her left hand, instantly demanding a status update from her Omni. Unfortunately, rather than the familiar bump of the implant, she touched nothing but her own flesh. Grumbling, once Lana slid into her ebony Cadet uniform she retrieved the AllTool bracelet stashed in her filthy trousers. Getting on her hands and knees, she patted around the gooey interior of her former shrink-wrap prison until her fingertip nudged something the size of a grain of Basmati rice: her Omni implant.

Squinting at her hand, then at the Omni, then back at her hand, Lana's cold-traumatised brain decided that if every body-piercer in The Unison could install an Omni in a matter of seconds, then it couldn't be all that tricky.

Summoning a black scalpel from her AllTool bracelet, biting her lip so hard she almost drew blood, Lana brought down the surgical implement with such force that she almost went all the way through her hand. Whimpering, her eyelid twitching, Lana slid the Omni into its usual home in the web of her left hand. As designed, the implant seared her wound shut and started linking up with her nervous system. The usual six hundred pages of OmniCo installation disclaimers popped up on her retinal screens, but she didn't bother reading a single word before mentally hitting NEXT a couple of dozen times, finally finishing the process with clicking I ACCEPT. The Omni helpfully informed her that it may take up to an hour until it was ready to connect up to the Link.

Rubbing at the sealed line on her left hand, Lana turned to face a stranger. He was a trim, handsome guy in his early thirties wearing an outfit so baggy that it might double as a tent. The stranger took a few steps towards Lana, walking in huge lunges as though he'd grown up on a planet with the gravity of Jupiter. Lana brandished a black axe with a flick, and was about to scream for the man to back off when he spoke with a familiar voice.

"I'm not fat!"

Lana paused mid-swing, her eyes and ears trying to get on the same page. Although this person didn't resemble a pregnant elephant seal after five buffet lunches, he still had Jimmy's copper-wire body hair and wore a facial expression that spelled out "victim" in neon letters. She flicked the black axe out of existence.

"Your fat must have been evaporated away during the dehydration," Lana guessed, too woozy to think any deeper. Her stomach grumbled, and she pinched at her forearm skin. "And I'm never this thin. Looks like we've both lost a few kilos."

Jimmy hopped from foot to foot as though being able to do such a thing was as exotic as growing a set of dragonfly wings. After supporting his more-than-ample frame for decades, his legs were like spring-loaded rat traps. Like whenever Jimmy got excited, he suddenly plunged into tears. He'd tried everything to remove the excessive cellulite that came part-and-parcel with his upbringing on Sprout, but nothing had come close to burning away enough blubber to make the discomfort worth enduring. It had taken nine failed subscriptions at Chubby Blasters to realise all diet plans were a gyp, and Jimmy had given up any dreams of slimming down long ago. Of course, he could have gone cold turkey on the Ultrasweet and start exercising like everybody told him, but he might as well decide to become a platypus and declare himself as King of Australia for how realistic that was.

There was a tutting noise, and Lana turned to see Viour on her floating platter. The first thing she noticed was that Viour had grown back all her missing limbs. They were an odd grey colour that didn't gel with her colourful stripes, but they seemed functional.

"Welcome back."

*

Trace was the next one out of the freezer. After an extensive argument, and to everyone's great disappointment, Tuesday was grudgingly resurrected. Of course, he immediately made them regret this course of action the moment his eyes were open.

"Are we there yet, Mummy? I'm thirsty."

Trace moaned in barely suppressed violence. The long sleep hadn't diluted her hatred for the janitor.

"Damn it, Tuesday, if my knuckles weren't still half-defrosted, I swear..."

Lana lost track of the conversation when she noticed what seemed to be the inner framework of a suit of amplification armour nestled among the holographic screens. She assumed it wasn't ready to be used, or Viour would already be cocooned in a small compartment in the left side of its skull. Jimmy's voice distracted her from the nest of thoughtmetal strands.

"Are we at Earth yet, or what?"

Viour twitched one of her new, grey tendrils, proving the regenerated limb worked. Outside the hull was your usual, garden-variety space scene, but there was also a celestial body out the starboard side that they all recognised: it was a deep, crimson red, completely devoid of all development, its orbit clean of

316

satellites and other space junk. Jimmy suddenly started hopping, putting his hand up.

"I know this one! That's Mars! It's two planets over from Earth."

"One planet over," Tuesday muttered. "They're neighbours."

Lana sighed heavily.

"It might be Earth's neighbour, but Mars is foreign soil that everyone is forbidden to touch or contact in any way. Back in the late 22nd Century The Unison made a Pact with the natives declaring it an act of treason for humans to interact with Mars without special dispensation. Trespassers tend to suffer, uh, tribal retribution, I think is the term."

"I heard the last time a merchant tried to make contact from orbit, their whole ship disappeared without a trace." Tuesday said with a little excitement. Still half-hibernating, Trace perked up at the sound of her name.

"Dunno why The Unison didn't just let its guns do the talking," Jimmy wondered. "Not like them to bitch out like that."

"The original inhabitants of Mars transcended beyond physical forms millions of years before humanity's oldest ancestors wriggled out of the ocean." Lana explained. At the word 'transcended', the other three humans assumed dirty expressions and nodded in understanding. "You know what those godlike races are like: they might have left their physical bodies behind to become pure energy of unlimited wisdom and serenity, but go anywhere near their sacred sites and they get all pissy and apocalyptic."

"So how far are we from Earth, exactly?" Viour interrupted.

Lana tapped at her Omni to ask it, but a braap-braap error message popped up on her retinal screens, informing her that her Omni was still installing, and she could not access the Link until it had finished. So Lana did some maths in her head, trying to remember statistics from one of her earliest AutoEducation hardwirings.

"Depends on what time of year it is. It could be as close as fifty-four million kilometres Sunwards, but it could be up to eight times that distance."

Viour was silent for a moment.

"Good. Then this is where we part ways."

Jimmy gave Viour a sideways look, as though questioning his ears.

"Huh?"

Viour nodded. "We will now cease all future contact. Our business is concluded, and our partnership terminated. Are my words not translating?"

Jimmy blinked. "No, that's very, very clear, actually."

"Crystal." Tuesday agreed. He pointed at a spot of space. "Would you like us all to die horribly right there, or in another bit of the void?"

Trace hit the wall with both fists and her face turned bright red. Veins and tendons were standing out from her thick neck and, obviously, what she said next was not delivered as a whisper.

"Don't give the bug ideas, Tuesday."

"You misunderstand," Viour soothed. "These scouts are modular. I can safely detach a segment of the cylinder, and it would be fully capable of ferrying you back to your world."

"His world," Trace grunted, jabbing a thumb at Tuesday.

"Her world," Tuesday grinned at Trace. "I know where the Cuddles come from. I know things."

As there wasn't much left to say, the humans moved down to the far end of the scout and awaited disconnection. Viour was about to stroke at the air to issue a command when Lana asked the most pertinent question.

"Where are you going next?"

Viour regarded Lana as though deciding whether it might be inadvisable to trust such frail, stupid, flawed bovine with any critical information. She eventually decided to be civil with the last words she'd share with her temporary allies.

"You said there were creatures in this galaxy known as Hiver Queens that shared many aspects with my own species. I wish to see just how...alike we really are."

Tuesday's eyes widened in horror at the concept. "Oh f..."

Viour disappeared behind a wall of liquefied metal that sloshed up from the floor to the roof, sealing the four survivors away into their own small segment. There was a jolt as their module disconnected, but that was about it. Thankfully, this new vessel was roomy enough to stretch out and move about in, and the air and temperature were nearly optimal.

Tuesday scanned around the opaque periphery of the chrome-like walls. Annoyed and a little paranoid about blindly hurtling along at relativistic speeds without being able to see where he was going, he slammed the heel of his boot into the hull. To his surprise, the walls instantly turned transparent, revealing the grave of space. Unfortunately, this guaranteed that every time Tuesday wanted a piece of technology to do something from now on, he'd probably kick it as his first option.

Lurking within the interplanetary gap between Mars and Earth, they were moving at such a clip that the red planet was soon down to a dusty pinhead, and the furious white eye of the Sun grew rapidly. They couldn't see Earth yet, but it wasn't like Viour to make mistakes, and she had no reason to betray them now. What would be the point of ferrying them across seven galaxies just to space them at the very end of the trip?

Lana flicked at her Omni, annoyed at how long it was taking to provide access to the Link. Swiping through some of the implant's simpler offline functions, she tapped at the Omni's internal clock, which operated under a dozen different concepts of time. She tutted at the numbers.

"From the time we went in the freezer to now, we were stuttering across realities for almost eight years."

"So we're all legally dead," Tuesday spat in the corner. "Wonderful."

"Surely that's not our biggest problem right now?" Jimmy asked uncertainly.

Tuesday barked a laugh. "Slummer, do you have any idea how hard it is to get reclassified from deceased to alive? With all the bureaucracy and forms and interviews, it would probably be simpler to actually reanimate a corpse." Tuesday plunked himself down, slouching against a wall. "Trust me, by the time The Unison is halfway through processing us, you'll be wanting to slit your wrists with the gilded edge of your own death certificate."

Lana raised a finger. "Wait. Remember that reality stuttering can result in a discrepancy in how much time passes in the stutter compared to actual real space? For all we know, only a few months might have passed here. Days, even."

"Do I need to ask the obvious question?" Trace growled, unimpressed by Lana's optimism.

Lana nodded grudgingly. "Sure. It's also possible that more time might have passed in real space...maybe even a lot more."

"But this is all wossaname, elementary for now, right?" Jimmy asked anxiously. "How are we meant to know for sure?"

A pinprick appeared directly ahead of their module just as Lana's Omni gave a flourishing fanfare of trumpets, announcing it was fully installed and ready for action. Lana smiled as though she couldn't wait for the good news, holding her index finger over the web of her left hand.

"Time to find out, isn't it?"

Deciding that it would save a lot of time and repetition, Lana synced up her Omni with everyone's retinal screens. As soon as they were connected up with the Unison-wide information and communication network known as the Link, they instantly noticed that it stretched far, far further than it used to. Not only did the Link's coverage eclipse the galaxy they knew as the Milky Way, but it seemed to go beyond the edge, plunging towards the darkness between the unlimited galaxies of the greater universe. As she had ten times more Link experience than the other three humans combined, Lana felt a stab of dread as her eyes scanned the coverage. She knew that when the Carpe Astrum had set sail on its disastrous maiden voyage The Unison (and, by extension, the Link) only covered about five percent of the galaxy. For The Unison to have increased its borders to such widths and lengths and depths - especially considering how many hostile alien empires and other deadly threats filled the void - it would have taken unimaginable resources and time.

Curious, Lana tried to see how far the Link stretched past the edge of the Milky Way, but her Omni wasn't capable of going beyond the rim. After all, back in Lana's day and age OmniCo had no reason to include such an expensive feature.

Surprisingly, it was Tuesday who asked the first – and biggest - question.

"Where is everything?"

Trace flicked her eyes away from the electronic hallucination on her retinal screens to do her third-favourite thing: glare at Tuesday.

"What?"

"Everything," Tuesday repeated, as though talking to an orangutan. He swiped at the Link's galaxy-exceeding coverage. "See this? Everything is connected by the Link, right? All the knowledge of mankind, all our communication systems, everything. But..."

"There's nothing there," Jimmy managed, looking confused. "Well, I mean, the Link itself is there, technically, but it's empty."

Everyone started scrolling around the cloud-like image that represented the Link, searching at random points for content. Anything would have done: a negative restaurant review, a starway weather advisory, a badly faked dating profile, a Skandinavian Prince offering all the wealth of Denmark to one lucky person, a hard line to a Link-enabled device, anything, but the entire Link had been scoured clean.

Using what little IT skills he possessed, Jimmy flicked through all the major versions of the Link dating back to its oldest incarnations, including the Ultranet, the Connection, the AllNet, X-Span, and the Combine. They were just as blank as the Link. He would have checked the first six Internets, but even Jimmy knew they were nothing but endless archives of quarantined porn held together by the nastiest viruses ever created by rogue AIs. Even the most powerful Digital Prophylactics on the market wouldn't make plumbing their sick depths safe, so he kept well clear.

After another minute he gave up, exasperated.

"It's like the contents of the Link have been scrubbed away. Burnt empty. But that's impossible, right?"

"Isn't everything on the Link backed up a million times over?" Trace demanded.

"There are so many countless redundancies and backups that a Link-wide erasure is impossible," Lana agreed. "And it hasn't been reliant on physical hardware for decades. It runs on ethereal hardware, the sort that can't be damaged or wiped or infected by viruses..."

Tuesday made an annoyed noise. "You know how stupid you sound saying something is impossible when it's clearly happening right in front of your eyes?"

She had no answer to this. Finally remembering why she'd logged onto the Link in the first place, Lana took a quick look at the date and time. She managed to choke on some of her own spit.

"Thor's Pubes," she cursed, blinking heavily as though she'd been blinded by a flashbang. "Look at the date."

Jimmy flicked his eyes, confused. "So it's the 30th, is it? The 30th of what? June?"

Lana shook her head violently. "That's not the month. It's the century." Lana couldn't hide her horror, and had nothing reassuring or positive left to share. At this moment, she was spent. "Five hundred years. We were gone for five hundred years."

"So a number five, with, like, five zeroes?" Tuesday clarified.

"Two zeros," Trace snapped. "There are two zeros in five hundred, you dentally deficient cretin, and you know it."

All the humans looked at each other blankly. After nearly a minute of deathly silence, Jimmy was the first to speak.

"What are we going to do?" he blubbered.

"Five hundred years," Lana repeated. She couldn't wrap her head around it. "Five hundred years…"

"So everyone I knew is dead." Trace growled. She thought about this. Within a matter of seconds she went all the way through the grief process and hit acceptance. She shrugged. "No real loss."

"The galaxy would have moved on." Jimmy sobbed. "Forgotten us. And who knows what the human race has become in half a millennium? Are they even still there? Why would they let the Link get gutted like that?"

Tuesday plugged a cigarette into his horror show.

"Those guys might be able to tell us."

Turning to see what Tuesday was talking about, Trace, Jimmy and Lana could only gape silently at a new sight. It was clearly a planet, but as the celestial body was directly blocking the Sun, from this side it was little more than an irregular pitch-black shape. As the dawn terminator passed its far edge, however, it was clear that something was very, very wrong: the planet had been shattered at its deepest seams, separating into fifty colossal sections and a further ten million Tasmania-sized chunks. Whatever had ruined this world went all the way down to its magma core, allowing superheated liquid iron to run out of its wounds like a gooey caramel centre. Gravity was barely keeping the whole mess together.

Lana was the first one to say it, painful as it was to admit.

"That's Earth."

After another few seconds they could see that the cradle of humanity was surrounded by a minefield of spinning boulders, a swarm that was only getting more dangerous all the time as countless pieces of what had once been the nerve centre of The Unison smashed together. As this ruined corpse of a world grew larger it only looked worse and worse. It was hard to tell in the darkness, but it seemed as though everything was covered by a midnight pall of deadly pollution. Tuesday cleared his throat after several awkward seconds.

"Uh, should we hit the brakes, perhaps?"

Lana blinked, swiping at the walls in the hope one of those holographic screens would appear.

"I don't think we have any control." Lana's expression turned sour. "I doubt that Viour wanted to risk being followed."

"So..." Jimmy thought about this for a moment. "We're just going to continue moving really fast towards a planet surrounded by a tight asteroid field? Is that...is that a good idea?"

"No," Trace growled. "No, that's not a good idea."

Their vessel rocked a little as a large chunk of granite hit the hull. Thankfully, Apex technology found such concerns almost comical, and it didn't do any damage. Safe or not, it was always unsettling to see an asteroid the size of a supermarket flying for your face, so it would be a lie to say that the humans enjoyed the deflection.

As it was against her nature to sit back and just let things unfold, Lana began tapping at the transparent walls and swiping at the air more urgently with all kinds of patterns and motions, hoping that she'd somehow summon the controls. But her attempts were fruitless.

Earth's blackened corpse was now so close that they were only seconds away from entering what used to be a breathable atmosphere. Surprisingly, from this distance they could now see that the ruptured magma core wasn't the only source of light and movement down there: they had to squint, but there were thousands of pinpoints that could only be artificial light cutting through the gloom. Whatever their source, these glowing dots were pretty darn bright to be visible from so high up, especially seeing as though they had to cut through dense pollution clouds along the way. As their tiny ship passed through a smog layer thick enough to scoop out of the air with a dessert spoon, it was revealed that the bright points were blinding spotlights blaring from the upper shells of some sort of huge machines trawling across the planet's surface. Lana chewed her lip, trying to recall if she was familiar with their design, but drew a blank. If the machines were human-made, she'd never seen them before. Her best guess was that they were mining something.

Their pod shook violently, tossing them about. While their first guess was that they'd hit the mother of all boulders, the transparent hull showed that they were several kilometres away from the nearest rock. Trying not to fall on his face, Jimmy felt a sudden prickling on the back of his neck that urged him to look up.

What he saw ruined his day. When he spoke, it was barely a whisper.

"No..."

Screens finally appeared on every wall, shrieking and flashing.

"I think something grabbed us," Lana yelled over the din. She squinted at the screens, the scrawls of technical jargon only partially translating to Unglish. "Best guess, someone on the surface has a tractor beam or a magnetic lasso or a pull-field or something." Her eyes flicked back and forth, and she relaxed a little. "Now we're slowing down. Finally, some good news."

Trace glanced at Jimmy, who was the only one still looking up at space rather than down at Earth's ruined surface. His face was frozen in an expression between terror and disbelief. She looked up to see what had stunned him to silence.

"What are you..." Trace's usual bravado disappeared in an instant. "No...that's not...that's not..."

Lana and Tuesday turned to see what all the fuss was about. Lana went pale as milk and Tuesday began to dry retch.

Directly above their position, eclipsed beyond Earth's distant edge, was something impossible: a Star Cage. Contained within a planet-sized lattice of invulnerable limpet ivory, a purple micro-sun glowed the same shade as Caesar's finest robe.

CHAPTER TWENTY-SIX FOSSIL FUELS

On their way down towards the darkened surface, the humans had about a million questions between them: How did the Slidge follow them to Earth? If the aliens had gone to such trouble to track them down, what unspeakable punishments did the Primacy have in store for them? How were they meant to get out of this situation with no weapons or help from any conveniently godlike aliens? Did the Slidge have something to do with the total disappearance of the Link? Had the Slidge already destroyed mankind?

Somehow, with a colossal effort, Lana tore her attention away from the Star Cage and looked down to see where their pod was being guided. They were close enough to the surface to see that the huge alien harvesters were only digging down a few metres, as though what they wanted to extract was close to the surface. There didn't seem to be any living plants left besides patches of wizened brown-black lichens, so it was unlikely the Slidge were doing a spot of gardening.

So what did they want? Surely any worthwhile minerals were much, much deeper down?

With only a few kilometres to go, it was clear that they were heading directly towards a large white structure the size of ten football stadiums. It was a sprawling facility made from limpet ivory that appeared to have unfolded from a cube, as though the Slidge had simply disconnected it from the Star Cage, splayed it open and dropped it into place from orbit. Long lines of harvesters were pulling in from a dozen different angles, waiting to dump their mysterious cargo for processing. Using his retinal screens to zoom in, Jimmy was pretty sure that the harvesters were feeding garbage into the structure, but that made no sense. Why would the Slidge come all this way to collect rubbish? Were they cleaning up Earth as a service to The Unison? Did they usually provide intergalactic janitorial services?

In seconds they were descending through the ceiling of the considerable Slidge complex, coming to a gentle stop a few inches above a white floor. Sighing, Lana straightened her back, slipped on her survival poncho and squared her jaw in resolution.

"Well, this might be the end of the road, but if I'm going out, I'm going out dignified."

Squaring her shoulders, rather than waiting for the Slidge to blast their way into the vessel Lana stepped through the liquid hull and into an unexpected scene: the hanger was packed with hundreds of Slidge of all shades of red and blue yelling and bellowing from ceiling hooks. Nearly every alien was dressed in protective gear suited for high-risk mining, and all of them had unclasped beak-shaped respirator masks hanging loosely from where their chins should be. Instantly assuming that they were baying for her blood, Lana did a double take at the many large signs the crowd were shaking about. Thanks to the well-informed translating app in her retinal screens, Lana could see that the signs were variations on WELCOME HUMANS, WE FRIEND YOU, ALL WELCOME NEUTRAL, YOU GAVE US THE GREATEST GIFT, and SLIDGE AND HUMANS FOREVER. Joined by her fellow passengers, Lana slowly deflated in relief.

Wiping her mouth, unsure what to say to such an astonishing welcome, Lana was distracted by the sight of some double-sized Slidge dressed in thick golden armour swinging through the throng of six-armed aliens. Everyone in the crowd noticed the golden ones, and backed away with heads bowed in respect. It didn't take a genius to figure out the golden ones were important.

"We are of the Primacy Guard," the largest golden-armoured Slidge explained, nodding in greeting. "Let me be the first to say we are honoured by your presence, and are at your service. Please, follow us. The Prime has requested an audience."

*

It took some energetic shoves to get through the adoring crowds (for some reason, the Slidge miners all wanted to touch the humans), but soon they were out of the hanger and twisting through the bowels of the mining complex. During their trip, Lana had time to think.

While it was clear that this facility was harvesting something from the crone's corpse that had once been Earth, they could be processing just about anything. Lana squinted, wracking her brain, trying to figure out what could possibly be worth the time and effort and danger of picking at the surface of this fractured world. Natural resources like iron and gold and water could be found in utter abundance in just about any star system if you knew where to look, and only the dullest of chumps would bother searching for such commonplace things on a planet that was barely holding itself together. Even more exotic treasures such as diamonds, uranium and helium-3 weren't rare enough to justify a risk like this.

So why were the Slidge here, really? And if the Slidge were the ones who had wiped out mankind, what was with the warm welcome? It didn't make any sense...

Every time the humans passed a Slidge worker they'd get gawked at, and excited whispers followed them the whole way through this maze of limpet ivory. Eventually they stopped noticing the hushed tones, and just kept following the swinging Primacy Guard. It wasn't like they had any other choice, as the golden ones were hefting huge energy weapons that looked a lot like halberds. For now, the humans had silently decided to keep their eyes open and wait for an opportunity.

Finally, after a short hustle, the Primacy Guard stopped in front of a protective door that could probably resist a direct nuclear strike like it was a summer breeze. The entire contingent of Primacy Guard waited silently for a few moments, as though expecting something to happen, and at some unseen, unfelt stimuli the door slid cleanly into the beige wall. The humans were kindly yet firmly directed inside.

The office was huge, but Spartan. Its entire far wall was a fifty-metre-wide transparent bay window overlooking a heavily-mined area that stretched as far as human eyes could see. Assorted targeting reticules and detailed squiggles from the Slidge alphabet danced all over the huge screen, spelling out the operation in a coded language that their translation devices weren't able to penetrate. If the Slidge mining operation had a nerve centre, this must be it.

A familiar-looking Slidge was hanging from ceiling hooks in the way her species seemed to find relaxing, awaiting her honoured guests. She was a deep royal purple, at least twice the size of the biggest of the Primacy Guard, and her face was criss-crossed with scars. Her three eyes blinked out of synchronisation, and her triple-segmented beak clicked rapidly in a way that reminded Tuesday of a cute evolved dolphin he'd unsuccessfully tried to chat up in a (literal) dive bar. There was no doubt: this was the Prime who had demanded their surrender just before Viour had taken on a whole Slidge fleet above Scrote.

The Prime waited silently as the Primacy Guard swung to their usual posts, watching as they blocked the only apparent way in or out of this room. She swept a triple-thumbed hand on one of her three lesser arms towards a quartet of chairs, and the humans sat down. Now that the security concerns were dealt with, she toyed with one of those computer balls, the sort that could detect lies, and broke the silence.

"This is a great day for our species," the Prime announced. "To finally meet you in the flesh! We had hoped to find you at some point, but so soon after our arrival in this galaxy? Amazing! On behalf of my Star Cage and the entire Primacy, we welcome you in the warmest manner."

Unable to take the pressure of his own fear and paranoia, Jimmy cracked at top volume.

"We're sorry!" he blurted. "We didn't mean it! We just wanted to go home! Please don't kill us!"

The other humans felt their hearts plunge down to their bowels and mentally beat Jimmy senseless with his own fist. The Prime blinked in a total lack of comprehension, gawking with her beak open at the unexpected and confusing outburst. Lana gave a nervous laugh, attracting the Prime's attention. Trace fought the urge to reach over and twist Jimmy's head off like a bottle cap.

"You'll have to excuse him," Lana said smoothly. "He's mentally feeble. Thank you for your warm welcome, and for your understanding. After our last encounter, we feared that we would not be greeted so kindly the next time we crossed paths."

The Prime raised a finger and gave a coo of understanding.

"Ah, now I see the confusion. I believe you are mistaking me for another Prime. All potential Primes are born with purple skin, which is an exceedingly rare occurrence, and those born with the royal hue all tend to be far larger and more intelligent than our lesser brothers and sisters. As outsiders, I can understand how you could make such an error." The Prime blinked at Jimmy. "I assure you, we harbour no animosity towards you. You are safe." The Prime was silent for a few moments. "Excuse my curiosity and bluntness, but what were you apologising for, exactly?"

Jimmy looked at the computer ball, knowing that any and every lie would be picked up. Gathering what little cunning he possessed, he chose his words carefully.

"I have not personally done anything to harm anybody within any Star Cage or anyone else in the entire Primacy."

The computer ball continued to shine a bright sky-blue. All of the humans exhaled in relief at this close call.

"So if you've never encountered us before, how did you know that we were humans?" Trace asked.

"A good question," the Prime approved. "While we almost immediately discovered the Link when we arrived in this uninhabited system a year ago, once we realised it had been wiped clean of all information we soon lost interest. However, the moment you used your hardware to access the Link, we were able to identify your technology as being compatible with it in ways that ours is not," the Prime spread her three thinner limbs. "It was like watching a key slide into a lock. Thankfully, you were so close to this planet that seeing you access the Link was like watching a supernova on our communication systems."

Lana rubbed at her Omni bump absently, feeling a bit embarrassed that she had basically announced their presence to the entire Primacy.

"So you haven't come in contact with any humans besides us?"

"None that were in any state to converse. Our excavations have uncovered many skeletal remains, and quite a few contained tiny information-holders that we assumed were surgically installed in the flesh of their left hand." The Prime brought two of her fingers close together as an illustration. "Tiny implants. Like a seed. We recovered small kernels of information stored on these devices, enough to deduce that your species disappeared from this galaxy some time ago. So far, we aren't sure where they went, and we aren't sure when this exodus occurred."

"But how did you get here?" Trace demanded, her lack of tact showing like a visible panty line.

The Prime looked between the humans as though trying to figure out if this was a trick question.

"Why, through the gateway you created, of course." After a few seconds of confused silence, the Prime tried to explain without getting condescending. "There was a huge battle between the Star Cages and Sun Lattices over some quarantine-related matter, the kind of fight that would usually precipitate an all-out apocalypse, but before things escalated to outright war we noticed that some sort of unusual rift had been torn open just a few light seconds away. As our sense of curiosity is thankfully more dominant than our bloodlust, this event was special enough for us to call a temporary ceasefire. However, even though the gateway was deemed to be stable, I was the only Prime willing to risk my Star Cage to see what was on the other side. It took years of insane scenery in countless realities, but the gateway led us directly into this star system." The Prime gave an embarrassed click of her beak. "Admittedly, we're not entirely sure how far we've travelled, but we're certain it's another galaxy. And to be honest, this is just one of thousands of questions we want to ask you."

"Spug it," Trace growled into Lana's ear, trying to keep her voice down. "That damn fool bug tore open a permanent hole between their galaxy and ours. Now the Slidge can just march in and..."

"So is that why we got such a warm welcome?" Lana interrupted, ignoring Trace. "Because we helped to cause that ceasefire?"

The Prime gaped in shock. "Are you being funny?"

"Humour me," Lana said, deadpan.

The Prime took a few seconds to compose herself. She tightened her elbows around the ceiling hooks in an anxious way.

"You know that our entire home galaxy is basically cinders, right?" the Prime finally asked. "Has been as far back as our records go, and probably a lot further. Every world that was ever worth a damn was flamed to uselessness before history started. Besides the Star Cages, every intelligent race is homeless. And seeing as though we've lost the ability to properly maintain our Star Cages, let alone build new ones, the Primacy and all of the Twelve Hundred were damned to only grow more and more stunted. But here, in this galaxy?" The Prime made a noise that must have been a laugh. "We've been prospecting in the neighbouring star systems, and we've already identified dozens of worlds that would be perfect for our citizens with just a few small tweaks." She banged a limb down on the desk, as though so excited that she couldn't contain herself. "You've given us a whole new galaxy to populate! Right now, you four are the best friends the Primacy ever

328

had."

"It looks like you're harvesting out there." Lana said casually, gazing out the window as a digger the size of an apartment block sped by. While there were about a hundred huge mysteries she wanted immediate answers to, she felt this one was probably the easiest to solve. "What are you digging for, exactly?"

The Prime perked up, as though this was exactly what she wanted to talk about. She slid open a compartment on her desk, and carefully withdrew what appeared to be an ancient drinking mug in the shape of FunCo's popular Mister Drizzle cartoon character. While its bright paintwork had been worn away long ago, the mug itself was still intact. It gave her a manic pop-eyed grin.

"We are unsure what you call it," the Prime admitted, "but we need to harvest as much of this material as we can before this world finishes breaking apart. It is too precious to lose."

Lana raised an eyebrow at the item, and at a motion from the Prime she leaned forwards and picked up the drinking mug. Peering over its chewed rim, Lana blinked in surprise to see the vessel was empty. She carefully stuck her finger inside, and touched thin air.

"There's nothing in it," she said, grumpy at being toyed with.

The Prime shook her head, face creased in mirth.

"No, no! The item itself is what we're mining."

"You like Mister Drizzle?" Tuesday asked dully.

Lana held her Omni up to the cartoon mug. Her eyes flicked over the readings, and her expression suddenly switched to panic. Nearly outright throwing the mug across the room as though it was burning her, somehow Lana managed to gather enough decorum to reflexively toss it back onto the desk. The Primacy Guard stiffened at their posts, and the Prime looked both confused and a little offended.

"That's made of plastic!" Lana complained.

"Made of what?" Jimmy asked.

"Plastic," Lana repeated. "They used to make things with it. Like computers, and action figures, and cheap kitchen equipment, and stuff like that. But they didn't know how dangerous the stuff really was for centuries." Lana's arms shuddered violently, as though she'd never needed a blob of hand sanitizer as much as she did right now. "Do you have any idea how many banned chemicals are in that mug? Or what even short-term exposure can do to the human body and mind?" Lana wiped her hands in disgust, trying to get her bearings. "I'm sorry. I didn't expect to be holding a handful of poison. But now I have to admit that I'm only more confused. Why would you want to dig up old plastic?"

A swipe of a triple-jointed thumb caused a small dish of multi-coloured powder to appear on the Prime's desk.

"So we can refine it into this substance right here. We call it Recoil."

Jimmy looked around at everyone's faces. They all seemed to be wearing the same expression.

"Sorry, am I the only one who feels like I've missed half of the conversation? What is that powder, exactly?"

The Prime deftly scooped up a smudge with a thumbnail, and inhaled it into one of her nine nostrils. Her eyelids fluttered, and she took a moment to get her bearings.

"So what, you get high on it?" Trace asked. "Really? Your hyper-advanced society is tearing apart our planet just to get stoned?"

Tuesday perked up at the word "stoned", licking his lips at the prospect of being within reach of getting high. The Prime didn't notice Tuesday's eyes dart towards the small mound of Recoil, laughing her weird Slidge laugh.

"No. We already have access to literally thousands of customised recreational narcotics, so Recoil's euphoric qualities are of minor interest. However, we have discovered that Recoil has...other effects on Slidge brains. A decent belt allows us to recall any memory, stretching all the way to when we were spawned. No matter how minor or how specific, any memory we want is as easy to pick out as fruit from a vine. But that's not all: in dangerously high doses, these memories can go back even further than that." The Prime gripped the edge of her desk with her three thinner limbs, gauging the confusion on the human's faces with what seemed like amusement. "If we get the dosage absolutely perfect, we've found that Recoil can allow us to access our genetic memories, effectively remembering aspects of our ancestor's lives. So far, we've only been able to go back three or four generations. But once we perfect the process..."

"You'll be able to go back far enough to reclaim all the scientific breakthroughs that you've forgotten over the millennia," Lana interrupted. If the Prime was offended by being cut off, she didn't show it. She seemed to be fine with listening to what Lana had to say. "We know how much your society has lost. You've forgotten how to grow limpet ivory, your computer systems do whatever they feel like, you can't produce enough food to feed everyone...not to mention your almost total lack of history. There are thousands and thousands of years of blank pages just waiting to be filled."

The Prime leaned sharply towards the humans, flexing the muscles of her three dominant limbs without so much as a quiver. Her strength must have been off the charts to do that so easily.

"You have given us a future," the Prime said, nodding in respect. "But you can also give us a past."

"How?" Jimmy asked, hoping he didn't have to do anything.

The Prime tapped a thumb against her desk a few times before continuing.

"The key problem we've had with unlocking our genetic memories with Recoil is that the purity of the unrefined material we mine from this world...the plastic...is always inconsistent. A dose of Recoil from one source may result in a subject reverting two or three generations without any discomfort, but the same amount from a separate source could be instantly fatal. There's too much guesswork involved, and we've had to stall our research after a number of overdoses. It's a miracle nobody has died yet." She folded her three thinner limbs together, arching nine thumbs like little steeples. "To be blunt, we need to know how to make plastic. If we had the recipe, our experiments would be much safer. You'd be saving lives. So do you know how to make plastic?"

"No idea," Trace snapped.

"Nope," Tuesday admitted.

"Never even heard of it before now," Jimmy moped, feeling useless.

Lana was noticeably silent. She could feel everyone staring at her like it was a burning heat, and her eyes flicked towards the Prime's computer sphere, fearing its ability to discern lies. She licked her lips.

"Maybe."

The sphere remained blue, confirming that Lana was honest in saying she wasn't entirely sure. Tuesday laughed.

"Really?" he asked mockingly. "You know how to make plastic?"

"A couple of years ago I wrote an essay about plastic for my History Of Banned Synthetic Substances class." Lana admitted. "It mostly focused on the legal aspects of how FunCo almost got sued out of business after selling millions of toxic Nutso The Squirrel cereal bowls to children. I'd have to check, but I'm pretty sure the paper is still on my Omni, and there might be enough research information in my archived notes to get the ball rolling."

Trace gave Lana an evil smile. "You did an entire class about the History Of Banned Synthetic Substances? What kind of stupid school did you go to?"

"The class only went for six minutes," Lana said defensively. "It was an educational upload. We had dozens of them every day." With no interest in getting into a slinging match, she turned away from Trace. "It's a little fuzzy, but I'm almost certain that plastic is created by crude oil."

"Who the hell is Crew Doyle?" Tuesday complained.

Lana waved this away. "No no, oil. Oil. You know, thick black stuff hidden deep beneath the surface of Earth? Burns and smokes like buggery? Fossil fuels? We used to refine it into petrol, mostly, but it had many other uses. Plastic was one of them."

"We did not encounter anything beneath the surface of this world that meets your description," the Prime said, narrowing her eyes at the Cadet.

"Because we used up every single drop of it by the 23rd Century."

"And what is the recipe for crude oil?" the Prime pressed.

"It's made from ancient rotten biomass left under immense pressure deep in the ground for millions of years," Lana said without hesitation.

Three purple hands clapped together violently.

"Wonderful news! You have done the Primacy yet another amazing service. You humans are truly the greatest friend the Primacy has had in living memory. Now, once you have transferred all of your files concerning plastic and crude oil..."

"First, we need to talk business," Tuesday interrupted, leaning in front of Lana. He waved the Cadet down before she could finish choking on her outrage. "Shhh. Adults are talking. Listen, Prime, you've gotten a lot out of us since we opened that gateway above Scrote. You've basically claimed our entire galaxy, leaving us effectively homeless, and so far we've gotten nothing beyond some friendly hand-written welcome signs. You've had everything for free. But that stops now."

"Uh, Tuesday..." Jimmy managed, but the scumbag didn't so much as slow down, let alone stop.

"We're more than happy to provide detailed files on plastic and crude oil, but our price will be half of all the Runtime that you earn from these recipes. Fifty percent. Not a jot less. If you don't like it, then you could always go back to digging up a million billion tonnes of dangerous sub-par plastic from this death-trap crap-berg, which should be more than enough to kill every citizen on your Star Cage." Tuesday flourished his hands. "There is no room for negotiations. Either you say yes right now to our offer, or we leave forever. Your call, squiddy."

Jimmy panned around the office, his jaw slack with shock, noticing that all of the golden-armoured Primacy Guard were suddenly gripping their weapons more tightly. Even to his untrained eye, it was clear that they had simultaneously received a silent command.

"Uh, Tuesday..."

"Do something," Lana hissed at Trace, but she only got a bored sideways glance and a resigned shrug.

"Kid, unlike the most basic lifeforms, I think we've established that violence doesn't work on him, let alone common sense," Trace narrowed her eyes at Tuesday, as though what she was about to say was more painful than passing a kidney stone the size of a golf ball. "And I agree with him on this one."

Lana's double-take was almost comical. It was a wonder she didn't do herself a neck injury.

"Buh..." she managed.

"I've already been robbed of my birthright once," Trace said simply. Her eyes went a bit distant for a moment, but then that usual hardness returned. "You think I'm spending the rest of my life bumming around, pissing away my remaining days? No. Either I'm retiring from this, or the Primacy can spug it."

The Prime's triptych of eyes were locked onto her computer sphere, which was continuing to shine blue, confirming that everyone believed they were telling the truth. She glared at Tuesday, narrowing her pupils in offense. She let out a long, whistling sigh.

"You leave me with little choice."

Tuesday smiled at the words of resignation, certain that the payday of a lifetime was imminent. The Prime gave a short bow and targeted her eyes on Lana's left hand, focusing right at her Omni bump.

"I must say I am sad you have chosen to reject the friendship of the Primacy in exchange for a truly offensive financial amount. We could have accomplished much as allies."

Instinctually feeling something was wrong, Tuesday turned to see where the Prime was looking, and his expression collapsed as he realised something that totally derailed his plan: the Prime had already stated her people were capable of reading the ancient Omni devices they'd exhumed from human skeletons, so what was stopping them from simply taking what they wanted from Lana's implant? Knowing that there was nothing preventing the Primacy Guard from blasting all four of them into piles of steaming meat and extracting the implant from Lana's hand, Tuesday barely had a moment of regret before the Primacy Guard raised their halberds. Blinding pulses of energy distortion blazed from a dozen directions, the violence of the blasts warping everything he could see.

The humans had just enough time to pull stupid faces before an onslaught of hard core alien artillery hit them.

CHAPTER TWENTY-SEVEN THE WHITE ROOM

It took a good ten seconds for everyone to realise they weren't dead.

Surprisingly, Jimmy was the first one to muster the bravery to open his eyes. He instantly took in that the Primacy Guard and the Prime herself were exactly where they'd been hanging just before this meeting went to hell, but for some reason they were as motionless as corpses, their bodies stuck in their last setting. It was as though time had stopped in the microsecond that followed the golden-armoured Slidge firing whatever unholy weapons they were wielding. Frozen or not, Jimmy's bladder almost released itself at the sight of all those alien blasters pointing at his face.

On the other side of the office, beyond the panorama of bay windows, all the Slidge harvesters were utterly still, and the endless swirls of caustic pollution were looming as peacefully as ice sculptures. Whatever had stopped time in the Prime's office seemed to have affected more than just this room. For all Jimmy knew, the entire universe had stopped.

Annoyingly, much of Jimmy's view was blurred out by something that looked like heat distortion, as though he was looking at the horizon of a bitumen road on a record-breaking Summer's day. Blinking a couple of times, assuming that something was wrong with his eyes, Jimmy finally realised that the distorted lines were actually blasts that had been fired by the Primacy Guard's weapons. Like everything else the lines were motionless, suspended in place like spun glass, their otherwise immutable physics ignored by some unseen power.

Jimmy flinched when he noticed the tip of one such energy blast had stopped only a few centimetres from his left eye. It didn't appear to be giving off any heat. Reaching out slowly, more curious than usual, Jimmy gently tapped the blur. Giving a yelp of pain, Jimmy's entire arm instantly went numb and floppy, collapsing and swinging like an empty rubber glove.

He decided not to go near the static blasts again.

The other three opened their eyes at Jimmy's yell. Looking around in a panic, they quickly confirmed that yes, they weren't dead and yes, the Prime and all her Guard had turned into statues.

Patting his pockets with shaking hands, looking for his smokes and lighter, Tuesday asked the two most obvious questions.

"Who did that? And how?"

Giving a growl of rage, Lana violently gripped Tuesday by his orange coveralls and held his eye up to one of the energy blasts. He whimpered and struggled as the sharp point came too close to his cornea for comfort.

"You idiot! We were heroes to them! They would have given us anything we wanted! You've ruined it! You've ruined everything with your damned greed!" Lana's eyes flicked towards Trace. "And you! How could you back him up? The hell is wrong with you?"

Trace gave an arrogant shrug. "Only the weak work for free."

Baring her teeth, glaring into Tuesday's terrified eyes as she pushed his temple closer and closer to the spike, Lana eventually released him with a grunt. She swung a kick at nothing, so enraged that she felt like she was going to spontaneously combust.

"What are we going to do now?" Jimmy looked like he was going to blubber again. "The Slidge hate us again, and time has stopped. We can't catch a break."

They turned sharply at a movement. As though somebody had heard Jimmy's concern, a pure white doorway appeared directly in front of the Prime's desk. The milk-coloured rectangle was more than big enough to admit Trace. As far as anyone could tell, the portal seemed to be completely flat, as though it was a two-dimensional object.

Trace began weaving carefully between the still energy blasts, careful not to zap herself. Lana gave her a scowl.

"What are you doing?"

Trace shrugged. "It's a door. Doors are made to be walked through. So I'm going to walk through it. Unless you want to try knocking down that slab."

Lana half-turned to look at the only conventional way out of the Prime's office. The blast door looked thicker than most starship bulkheads, and was crafted from invulnerable limpet ivory. She turned back to regard Trace, not bothering to explain how hopeless that option was.

"Is that wise?" Jimmy asked.

Trace gestured at the frozen Primacy Guard.

"Look, we get miraculously saved at the last microsecond by persons unknown, and then a doorway appears. It doesn't take a Professor to figure out what we should do next. You lot can bitch out all you want, but I'm going to walk through the unknown door of mystery."

Although the others weren't quite as keen as Trace, once she moved over the threshold without any ill effect they all followed. Passing into an eternity that was as white as the skin of a Canadian Hockey team, after five steps (and a yelp of surprise from Jimmy) the survivors lost their footing and tumbled through the glowing void.

It took a minute, but it soon became clear this endless white wasn't a true nothingness. While everything seemed to be a boring expanse of the freshest cream at first glance, Lana found that by concentrating and squinting this universe turned out to have a lot in common with a lava lamp filled to capacity with blobs of molten wax. If you looked closer still, the blobs had a chromatic rainbow edge, sort of like soap bubbles.

As the details of this eternity slowly began to make themselves known to their crude human eyes, the dizzying spin slowly stabilised until they were all aligned in the same direction. Blinking, four comfortable lounge chairs either appeared from the ether or simply came into focus. It was hard to tell which. A little ivory side table sat next to each perch, bearing tall, elegant glasses of perfectly transparent champagne. The drinks were accompanied by bowls of sugared almonds the colour of a fresh snowfall.

Waiting for his heaving stomach to calm down, Tuesday muttered under his breath. His croaky voice sounded even harsher than usual against the deepest silence any of them had experienced.

"Somebody has a fetish for white. Are we in Greenland?"

Despite how non-threatening all of this was, Jimmy was the first to let his paranoia show.

"Drinks could be poisoned," he mumbled, eyeing the champagne in distrust.

Tuesday stepped forward and swallowed the contents of a glass in one gulp.

"Hope not. Hmm. Tastes like Chateau Goon. From the L'Cardboard vintage, if I'm not mistaken."

"You think that…humans made this?" Jimmy asked nervously, rolling a sugared almond around on his palm as though expecting to see a POISON stamp on the other side.

"Far as we know, humans are extinct," Lana scowled. "Maybe the Slidge are messing with us somehow?"

After a good minute of peace and stillness, it was clear that this place was a safe refuge from a hostile universe. Glad to sit down after a big day, the humans eventually decided to kick back on the opulent seats and sample the snacks. As though it had been waiting for this exact event, the white infinity opposite the lounges chairs was suddenly replaced by an exact copy of the humans, as though looking into a perfect mirror. Beneath the reflection, some form of unsettling alien writing skittered along.

"Wos that say?" Tuesday muttered, squinting.

"Gibberish," Lana answered without patience. "My retinals aren't translating it. Either it's coded, or it's too advanced."

To their surprise the reflection changed to show a flawless life-sized recording of Tuesday being dragged down a corridor by his ears by a squad of the Captain's most unfriendly Enforcers on the Carpe Astrum. This was followed by Lana and Trace fighting in the Java Jab, a battle that had resulted in the two of them smashing the Captain's head like a soft-shell crab before getting locked away in the Brig. Finally, the survivors watched Jimmy throwing a Titan Slug egg pack into a Repler Pool in the back of his MacDeath restaurant and stupidly leaving it unattended to grow to full maturity.

It was like watching an ultra-clarity surface, a screen better than anything humans had ever churned out. The recording continued, showing every tiny detail of the catastrophic disaster that had claimed almost every life on the Carpe Astrum, followed by the only four survivors tearing their way through the wreckage to reach the lifeboats. Just before it showed their bumpy ride down to Scrote, they watched a scene that only Lana had witnessed: a sudden indoors snowstorm that had come out of nowhere and vanished just as quickly. Lana sat bolt upright at the memory of that swirling whiteness, her screams of surprise lost over the din of lifeboats being kicked about like hacky sacks. The lifeboat garage had been filled with violent white streaks, kind of like living tendrils of goo, and the bright lines intertwined, wrapping around each other in a way that was almost sensual, and then something spoke.

"YOUR PEOPLE ARE GUILTY OF VIOLATING THE EIGHTH LAW," a godlike voice boomed, echoing far above the storm. "YOUR PENALTY IS GAMESHOW."

"That!" Lana shrieked. "That was what I saw and heard in the garage! I told you it was real!"

The picture froze, as though somebody had hit pause. And while nobody said anything about seeing their entire journey laid out like the most in-depth documentary ever filmed, their silence was purely caused by having so many massive questions that none of them could decide which one to ask first.

Just like Lana had experienced that day in the lifeboat hanger, a cluster of pure white lumps began to worm from the pale nothing directly between the humans and the screen, the wriggling protuberances stretching higher and higher until they were five metres tall. To the human's eyes they looked like ribbons of the palest taffy. The wriggles intertwined, wrapping around each other faster and faster to form a skeleton, then muscle fibres, organs, limbs, extremities, skin and even clothing, all of the same shade. In moments it had coalesced into what appeared to be a human body, but pale as the driven snow. Finally forming a charming expression, the new mouth smiled, its eyes crinkling like those of a loving grandfather.

"You have many questions," the being stated in a voice that could be heard with ears, minds and emotions all at the same time. The highlights of the human's nightmare march across Scrote's ruined surface resumed playing behind its impressive form. "And I have many answers. You may ask."

Jimmy looked back and forth between the others.

"Uh, ask what?"

337

The being smiled benevolently.

"Anything."

"Who are you?" Lana said, deciding to be the first one to ask a question that wasn't as dense as a concrete barbecue pit.

"Where are we?" Tuesday added.

The smile curved again.

"You may be interested to know that both of those questions have the same answer. You have been brought to my level of the Transcend, the beyond-place that awaits all species who pass the constraints of the physical realm. To put it into words that you would understand, this level of the Transcend is both where I am and who I am." Somehow, the being said this without any arrogance. That in itself was quite an achievement. "But I was once one of the living races, like you, a single glimmer among a million million others who exist for but a finite period, and more often than not are lost in the span of space and time."

"Did you always look like this?" Lana asked, sizing up the creature. She hardly felt the need to point out that the Transcended's human-like body was a bit of a coincidence.

Smile.

"Actually, I began my existence as an intelligent language, which is an exceedingly rare occurrence. Every time I was spoken I was born anew, growing in span and intelligence and awareness. While the species that created me eventually ceased entirely in a manner that is not worth recalling, I survived long enough to advance to the absolute peak of scientific, intellectual, moral, philosophical and spiritual completeness until I was able to Transcend the physical realm entirely, to rise above the constraints and restrictions of the fourth-dimensional universe and become something far more, something forever."

"Like...like a god?" Jimmy managed.

"Transcendents possess almost total control over space and time, though we generally possess very little interest in using it."

Trace clicked her fingers at the screen. It was currently showing the four of them skidding down a glass-filled mass driver crater at the speed of sound. She looked away at the sight of Lana cresting the edge of the crater and almost smashing herself to death on the far side.

"For gods, it seem like you spend a lot of your time perving on us."

The Transcended smiled again. It was a beautiful sight, and made Trace feel like she was being warmed both inside and out by a hug made from hot chocolate.

"While much of what occupies the Transcend would not translate to your level of understanding, one thing we do a lot of is...watch. And while we rarely do so, there are times when we will choose to interact with the physical universe. Most of these interventions involve the violation of one of the Twelve Laws."

Lana squinted, thinking back to what the voice on the screen had said, and voicing it.

"Your people are guilty of violating the Eighth Law..."

"...the penalty is Gameshow," Trace finished.

Tuesday looked back and forth between the two women.

"You say that like we're meant to know what that means," he grumbled.

The Transcended sat down slowly, folding its legs towards the floor until it came to a comfortable stop in a yoga-like pose.

"The Twelve Laws dictate exactly what events in the fourth-dimensional universe require direct intervention from the Transcended. This intervention is specific to each Law, and some interventions are...harsher than others. While there is much I am forbidden to reveal, I can tell you that the human race broke the Eighth Law, and I was required to intervene in the prescribed way."

"Can you at least tell us what exact Law we broke?" Lana asked hopefully.

"It was him, right?" Trace jerked her thumb at Tuesday.

At a motion from the Transcended, the display showed the Carpe Astrum as it appeared just before the disaster, its triangles-within-triangles-within-triangles form still spinning and its hull of a trillion shifting tiles completely intact. Lana recognised her home world slowly arcing behind the starship, and she secretly hoped she'd see her beat-up school shuttle in the background. She didn't.

"Law Eight expressly forbids any non-Transcended race from transporting sentient life with instantaneous travel," the Transcended spread its hands, showing its palms. "Like all of the Twelve Laws, we enforce this prohibition to prevent catastrophic damage being done to the underlying structure of the physical realm. The line of technology that humanity researched in creating the Carpe Astrum is more than capable of tearing the physics of the universe apart with the slightest error. And while we rarely get involved, we do have a vested interest in ensuring that all of the species who will eventually Transcend have a chance to do so. To prevent even one instance of a Transcendence would be a tragedy beyond words."

"So what are the other Laws?" Trace grunted.

The Transcended shook its head. "I am forbidden from sharing such knowledge with you. But I can say that enforcing the Twelve Laws is in the best interests of both the Transcended and the Mundane."

"When you say enforced, you mean punished, right?" Tuesday clarified. "I've been in enough prisons to know it's the same thing. Who were you punishing, exactly? Us? The rest of the crew what died in the explosion?"

The Transcended dipped its head.

"I assure you, the disaster on board the Carpe Astrum was not our doing: it was purely the outcome of your species experimenting with dangerous technology. We did not cause any direct fatalities through our intervention. However, our involvement began directly following the disaster, and has specifically focused on the four of you ever since, right up to this moment."

The humans exchanged glances. Trace was the first to speak.

"Come again?"

The Transcended indicated the screen. It showed the Star Cage looming above the refitted lifeboat that Viour had been able to upgrade in a matter of seconds.

"While each of the Twelve Laws command vastly different kinds of intervention, the kind used to deal with violations of Law Eight is Gameshow."

Tuesday crunched his eyes shut and pinched the bridge of his often-broken nose. His gritted black teeth looked especially sharp against the white.

"And there it is again: Gameshow. What is that even supposed to mean?"

"From the second you arrived in that other galaxy, I have placed many obstacles in your path," the Transcended admitted. "Thousands of them. We have provided all kinds of challenges, puzzles and hardships for you to overcome, from harsh weather to low supplies, physical discomfort to aggressive animals, and defective equipment to evil aliens. We have recorded every microsecond from every conceivable angle and showed your journey in its entirety to the rest of the Transcended, who have all given their verdict. How entertaining the Transcended found your Gameshow will have a huge effect on what judgment is handed down to your species."

"Entertaining?" Jimmy blinked heavily, feeling beyond manipulated and mistreated.

"But mankind is extinct besides us, right?" Lana began counting on her fingers. "The Link is empty, The Unison is gone, and nobody knows where it all went. How are you going to judge a species that doesn't exist anymore? Graffiti something offensive on their tombstones?"

The Transcended spread its hands.

"Who said the human race is extinct?" Rather than going into any more detail, it indicated the screen again, which was now up to the point where the entire Primacy Guard had fired a whole battery of weapons at the humans. "This is when your Gameshow was terminated. As soon as you reached the point of failure and death, we stopped it and brought you in."

Trace narrowed her eyes at the screen. She clicked her fingers.

"How, exactly, were you able to watch us? Is it some sort of all-seeing all-knowing omnipotence thing that all the Transcended can do? Or did you have wossaname, cameramen?"

Instead of answering, the Transcended faced its palm upwards and a fist-sized white sphere appeared directly above it. Trace jabbed her finger at the sphere, getting to her feet and turning blood red.

"That's it! That's the spugging thing I kept seeing everywhere! I'm not mental!" Trace paced back and forth in an agitated way, trying to calm down. "I seen them, seen them all the time just outside of my peripheral vision."

With a gesture, the sphere disappeared from the Transcended's palm. It didn't seem too concerned with Trace's outburst.

"In order to catch every moment of the action, we inserted millions of these sensory bundles through apertures between your dimension and ours. They were designed to remain out of your view while doing so. In past Gameshows, they have always remained unseen." Its face creased in what might have been curiosity. "I must admit, we aren't entirely sure how you were able to spot them, Trace. It should have been impossible."

Trace kept on pacing, grinding her teeth so loudly that everyone could hear the abrasion. The Transcended treated them all to a wide smile.

"Now, thankfully, I have some good news."

"I doubt that," Jimmy mumbled in misery.

"Your Gameshow has been the highest-rated Judgement of Law Eight that we've ever filmed," the Transcended's face was radiant with approval. "The action, the humour, the adventure, the drama, the interpersonal friction, the close calls, the outright stupidity...gold, all of it! Every Transcended realm was glued from the first moment. Sure, the seven years you spent in the freezer dragged a little, but even then nobody could look away."

"So we impressed the Trancended?" Lana clarified, feeling a swell of pride.

The godlike being seemed to be having trouble keeping a straight face.

"Impressed? Hardly. We've never seen so many poor choices work out for the best so many times in a row. There were at least a hundred and fifty different points where your luck should have ended, terminating the Gameshow – and all four of you - on the spot. It was truly mesmerising. Some viewers were convinced that we were tampering with the obstacles. We still don't know how you managed much of it."

"So...what now?" Tuesday asked.

"Now?" the Transcended repeated. "Once a Gameshow is over, the contestants are judged on their performance, prizes are allocated based on how entertaining and successful they were, and then they get to meet the audience over drinks."

Tuesday's eyes lit up at the word "prizes" like his face was a pinball machine. If he was going to get rewarded by a bunch of Transcended aliens, he was pretty sure it would make winning the Lotto look pretty weak in comparison. Somehow he didn't drool at the thought of the riches that might be in store.

"So we're going to meet a bunch of gods?" Jimmy asked nervously. "I don't think I've met any gods before."

"First, we need to deal with your prizes," the Transcended said soothingly. "As per the fine print of Law Eight, the fact that you survived your Gameshow for such a surprisingly long time in such an entertaining fashion means you are all entitled to a single request each. This is a one-time offer, and what you are given cannot be exchanged if you are unhappy with the results. I would advise you to consider your request carefully, as saying it out loud is a binding contract."

"I want my birthright back," Trace said instantly. "If I wasn't the last living heir to the Cuddle fortune before, I certainly am now. So I want everything that's mine. Nothing less."

The Transcended nodded, raising a hand before the others could clarify what Trace had just stated. Getting the hint that the Transcended only wanted to discuss wishes at this point, Jimmy asked for what had always been his heart's desire.

"I want to be wanted," he said softly, sadly. He went to clarify his request, but his voice caught at the emotion. "I want that. To be wanted."

Lana took some time to speak. She was sure to get the words right in her head before voicing them.

"I want to meet my real parents."

"That's a lot less ambitious than I expected," Trace hissed a laugh. "No Admiral stripes? No war fleets at your command? No classes of Cadets reading your autobiography as a part of their studies? Sad, kid. Sad."

The Transcended looked up at the white infinity, as though hearing something.

"Your audience is ready to meet you. Are you ready?"

Its question was answered with hesitant, anxious nods. Just before the whiteness of this level of the Transcend faded away, vanishing like dawn mists, Tuesday bared his little black teeth in a vicious smirk of triumph.

"You know what," Tuesday asked rhetorically, just as the gods themselves began to loom out of the depths of forever, "I fink I know exactly what I want you to give me..."

EPILOGUE

Trace stared out of the unbreakable bay window of a mega-freighter the size of an international airport. Her obsidian-studded forehead rested against a patch of her own breath's fog. Before her, the stars silently glimmered like a tray of surgical tools.

If Trace panned her eyes a little to the right, she could see an embossed CuddleTech logo stretching a good three hundred metres along the pockmarked hull. This freighter's name had once been located exactly fifty metres below the CuddleTech icon, but all physical proof of this hulk's moniker had been scoured away in some undocumented incident. Over the last three months, Trace had often wondered whether the destruction of the ship's name had anything to do with how all of mankind had vanished from the galaxy without so much as sticking a note on the nearest cryogenic storage bin.

Thankfully, within hours of first arriving on the freighter, Trace had discovered this ship possessed a VIP section, and her Cuddle bloodline granted her full access. She hadn't experienced such comfort and security since before Uncle Balder had betrayed her entire family and cast them into the cold. As Reborn Detroit had been reduced to a patch of scorching on a dead rock and every other freighter in CuddleTech's fleets had vanished just as mysteriously, as far as Trace knew this enormous starship was the last physical remnant of the Cuddle legacy. This was appropriate, as she was the final heir.

At one point, Trace had gotten so bored that she tried to find out more about the ship's huge scars. Unfortunately, even though her genetics provided full access to every system, not only was there no mention of what had beat the living daylights out of this freighter, but it was clear that every useful megabyte of electronic information – from security recordings to Captain's log entries to accounting ledgers to toilet paper requisition e-forms – had been excised all the way back to when this nameless ship had first been launched in the late 22nd Century. Eight hundred years of history had vanished without a snippet, as though something was erasing everything that mankind had ever touched...

After spending some time making up for lost meals, Trace had decided to search for whatever was left of mankind in the Milky Way. The mystery intrigued her more and more. However, while her freighter still possessed some basic hardcoded navigational software, it was so eroded with digital loss that she might as well be following a map drawn onto a doily with a white crayon. Most of the time she didn't know exactly where the freighter was headed or when she'd get there. More often than not she ended up in the empty gulf between stars. Even though she hadn't found a glimmer of an answer yet, Trace had nothing better to do but keep looking until she made contact, finished visiting every wiped planet that had belonged to The Unison, or found something more interesting to do.

Tiring of the view and feeling hungry, Trace headed down the marble steps, her bare feet tingling as they touched the cool floor, and made her way to the dining room. Before her was a royal banquet that had been laid out by the silent artificial intelligence that governed the CuddleTech freighter. As usual, the AI had predicted Trace's hunger levels and exact chemical cravings before she could, guaranteeing the ideal meal.

On the other side of the sprawling table was her beloved husband. He stood up straight at her entrance and nodded cordially.

"Good evening, dear," he said simply.

Trace nodded in return as she took her seat, and felt a sensation she was still trying to get used to: the desire to spend time with another human being simply to enjoy their company. And while she never thought she'd be the marrying type, something any sensible human would have guessed in a moment, now that Trace had taken the plunge she wouldn't trade it for anything.

She sampled a zucchini flower stuffed with feta and deep fried in duck fat, possibly the last of its kind in the universe, as her husband went on his usual spiel.

"You look more beautiful every day. Did you buff your piercings just for me? That obsidian really is gleaming."

Trace felt a little embarrassed that he'd noticed, but also flattered.

"I love you so much," he said without prompt.

Trace melted a little, as always, and returned the sentiment.

"I love you too, Tuesday."

A smile slowly spread across Tuesday's rodent face until he was baring all of his little black teeth. Unable to hold back his amusement at her confused expression, Tuesday threw back his head and cackled insanely.

THE TRUTH

Tuesday's laughing face dissolved into a waterfall effect, separating into a billion polygons before coalescing back into a stock photo of deep space: it was a nebula, a colourful gas cloud, but no nebula in the universe looked that amazing without some serious digital enhancement. The fake gas cloud was so ridiculously bright that it had more in common with a Saturday morning children's cartoon than something that dwelled within the dead vacuum.

A triumphant fanfare gradually drowned out Tuesday's insane braying, accompanied by words crafted with the finest calligraphy.

WOW! YOUR TEAM HAS REACHED ENDING #44 IN THE "TOTALLY, UTTERLY SCREWED" IMMERSIVE VIDEO GAME ON CO-OP MULTIPLAYER! YOUR COMBINED SCORE IS...

A couple of seconds passed, allowing for even the most slothful of marijuana-affected teenagers to keep up with the scrawl, but then the fanfare died with a sad toot, as though stunned by the sheer mediocrity.

24%

NO HIGH SCORE RECORDED. BETTER LUCK NEXT TIME!

Making annoyed grunts, four people sitting around a square, texture less tabletop reached up to remove thin visors from where their eyes should be. The visors looked like simple hairbands, except most hairbands weren't held in place by inch-high electrodes. Each of the arc-shaped devices were identical save for a name emblazoned across their outer casing: Jimmy, Tuesday, Lana and Trace.

Once the visors were painlessly extracted, the four players could see each other again. There wasn't much to say about their appearances, as they were all little more than simple low-rez stick figures, the most basic of human-shaped wireframes. They mostly consisted of lines with a few circles here and there. Instead of faces, they each possessed a cruciform shape suspended inside an oval. They might move like humans and have the intelligence of humans, but the four players looked like the simplest of childish sketches.

Taking a moment to shake off the usual feelings of displacement that went part-and-parcel with Immersive simulations, the stick figures clapped their visors on the table that separated them. Like with everything else in the Construct that imprisoned them, the visors, the table, the palm-sized infoblock that contained the Totally, Utterly Screwed Immersive and even the four featureless avatars did not really exist. None of it was real, not a single atom.

The avatar who had been playing as Tuesday would have scowled in annoyance at the low score, but a recent data tariff meant that he wasn't capable of facial expressions. If it wasn't for the fact that his body turned a royal blue and declared PROFESSOR K DeKRAY NEUROVIROLOGY in bold letters whenever somebody glanced at him, there would be nothing to differentiate Karl DeKray from the other two- hundred-and-nineteen geniuses who were permanently trapped in this virtual reality world as stick figures, unable to leave unless they went feet first. DeKray internally cursed that fact almost every single moment he existed.

"The hell, DeKray?" Lana's player, a Professor D Braun, demanded. "Kinda newbie spug was that? You know not to push the Prime so hard. Even an arse-brain like Tuesday wouldn't be dumb enough to poke the tiger's nads. And you!"

Trace's player, Professor H T Kimonoto, might have been trying for an innocent look. It was pointless with a literal blank slate for a face.

"What?"

"No chance Trace would go along with that...that plan, inverted commas!" Braun ranted, sure to do the little motion with her line fingers. "She spends their whole adventure kicking Tuesday's dollar-slot every chance she gets, then suddenly she turns into a Tuesday fangirl for no apparent reason? Do you have any idea how much that ruined the game for me? Totally took me out of the narrative."

DeKray didn't bother to explain his actions to anyone, mostly because he agreed that his plan had been total rubbish. Another thing he didn't share was that his failure extorting the Prime had been deliberate: he'd clocked this Immersive so many times in so many ways that it was losing all appeal, and the only way DeKray could handle yet another run was in the hope that he'd unlock something new. If his co-op team knew this, however, he'd be branded a troll and nobody would want to play with him. However, it must be stated that the core reason DeKray didn't respond to the insults was because he'd stopped talking to the other Professors over two decades ago, and they hadn't gotten a single word out of him since.

DeKray flicked his wrist, and the Immersive's infoblock automatically reappeared in its designated shelf slot as though by magic, fitting in neatly to the right of the Scum of the Universe Immmsersive. Instead of being bookended by the final part of the trilogy, an empty space declared that part three had probably been deleted in the eternal crush to find more and more hard drive space to accommodate the latest growths of The Equation.

While the Construct's gaming library had once been stuffed with so many AAA Immersive titles that it was unlikely the Professors would ever get through all of them, let alone unlock their every secret, the endless library had been pruned down to a single sad shelf of eleven sub-par titles. Every time that DeKray ran his (lack of) eyes over the labelled spines of Immersives with names like Ultimate Putting Challenge, My Virtual Legume Farm and Expert Surgical Simulator (Goat, Sheep & Llama Edition), it made him consider trying to find some way to end it all.

Others had found a way. Why couldn't he?

While DeKray's gaming party could have simply transferred the Totally, Utterly Screwed Interactive directly into their minds as pure code, over the last sixty-five years The Director had gradually pared back every luxury and non-essential detail of the Construct to the point where much of this virtual realm was now a wireframe universe held together by exposed code strings. If The Director had his way, everything except for The Equation would be nothing but green lines on a black background, the imprisoned Professors reduced to disembodied minds, their words conveyed by silent text, making it impossible for them to even scream...

*

The trouble begun three generations ago in the Actual world when a team of geneticists and neuroscientists cured autism. Like cancer, AIDS, diabetes, depression and chewing with your mouth open, autism became a relic of the past, joining the ranks of polio and whooping cough and smallpox and genital herpes. Of course, only a certain slice of mankind could afford this genetic tweak for their offspring, so the entire Third World (which actually made up well over ninety percent of humanity by this point) were left out in the dark, as usual.

For once, those starving masses turned out to be the lucky ones.

Decades after erasing autism from mankind's more affluent portion, a bizarre plague suddenly ripped its way through the developed world like a box cutter across a used tissue. Unlike traditional outbreaks, what came to be officially classified as Involition Syndrome – though almost always referred to as "The Trance" by anybody who dared to speak its name - didn't make you burn with fever, or break down the tissues of your body, or cause internal bleeding, or give you so much as a sore throat or a headache. Such symptoms would make it relatively easy to target and cure with modern medicine. No, Involition Syndrome went straight for the mind, and it took less than a day to go from inception to fatal. One minute, you're fine. You're a total normal going about your business as a pampered First World shlub wallowing in obscene luxury. Then, without any warning, Stage One of The Trance will kick in, robbing you of your memory and your capacity to take on any new information. Its effect was comparable to having a series of strokes, but without any physical hallmarks. So not only will you immediately forget what you're doing and why, you'll also forget who you are. After wandering about aimlessly for a while, moaning and rolling your eyes in idiocy, Stage Two of The Trance will remove your consciousness in one slice, leaving you gaping and drooling and staring into space as a catatonic. Stage Three is where Involition Syndrome truly earns its name, as this is the point where the afflicted will cease to breathe and stop swallowing their saliva, which meant they'd drown in their own spit within minutes. Calling them zombies was an insult to the undead, because at least zombies are motivated by hunger. Stage Threes just stood there and died.

Nobody stopped at Stage One. Progression to Stages Two and Three was one hundred percent inevitable.

Eventually, after a colossal death toll, it was discovered that while Stage Threes were unable to will themselves to do anything, they could still follow simple instructions. The key to keeping the living dead from expiring turned out to be pretty simple and low-tech: you duct-taped headphones to their ears and played a looped sound file that told them to breathe in and out and to swallow their spit (not at the same time, obviously). It was also necessary to install a catheter and a stoma before their bladders and bowels ruptured, but keeping Stage Threes alive was hardly nuclear physics.

Eating was out of the question, as having dinner like a normal person involved too many complex components (cutting up your food into the right size, spearing it with a fork, raising it to your mouth, opening your mouth the right width, inserting the food without stabbing yourself, chewing the appropriate amount of times, and so on and so on), so this was usually solved with a tube down the nose or a pipe into the stomach.

But these were all stopgap solutions. In a matter of months The Trance had struck all over the developed world, and nothing was able to slow it, let alone defeat it. Quarantine procedures achieved zip, and the medical community couldn't even figure out what was causing its onset, which kinda made The Trance impossible to treat. As it couldn't be blamed on any virus or pathogen or any other classic hallmark of infection, this also meant there was no way to develop a vaccine.

After the worst eighteen months the developed world had ever experienced, ninety-two percent of the population had become Stage Threes. Entire continents - North America, Canada, Europe, Asia, Australia, the Middle East, you name it - were filled with endless fields of drooling meat. A billion motionless people just sat there in their decaying homes, breathing in synchronisation to the commands of a sound file fluted through duct-taped ear buds, staring at the walls, lifeless, silent corpses fit for nothing but to rot.

When somebody observant noticed that the Third World was almost entirely unaffected by the pandemic, the scientific community found this fact to be very, very interesting. The most popular hypothesis was that a terror cell from

Craplakistan or some other armpit of a country had attacked the developed world with a neurological weapon, perhaps dispersed over several months. But once the only victims of The Trance in the Third World turned out to be foreign aid workers who originated from much nicer places, it was clear that this was something else entirely.

By the time the nerds and boffins figured out what had really happened, it was too late. The cure for autism was at fault, and as it had been indelibly crafted into the human genome itself, it could not be removed. Its genetic wiring was designed to be permanent, to last forever. Tragically, one of the greatest medical feats of all time had planted the seeds of disaster into the very minds of humanity, and now the harvest time had come round.

There was nothing that could be done. Mankind had engineered itself into a living death. But there were some who could not accept this.

Now that the cause of The Trance had been identified, a total of two-hundred-and-fifty-six individuals, the greatest minds from dozens of scientific and medical fields across the world - virologists, geneticists, neuroscientists, software engineers - were brought together to work on a cure. The criteria for being a part of this team were pretty simple: you had to be a Professor in a useful area, and your brain couldn't be porridge from The Trance. The Professors would be doing all their research and development from within a one-of-a-kind virtual reality system known as the Construct, a time-distorting co-op hallucination that would allow their minds to accomplish a century or so of work while only a few months passed in the Actual. After all, if the Professors developed a cure in real time, anybody who was still alive in the Actual would be well beyond the age of reproduction, making their efforts worthless. To make matters worse, cryogenic freezing was the only sure-fire way of delaying The Trance from zombifying the Professors, so they all had to be literally put on ice. As defrosting them would probably be lethal, this project was going to be a one-way trip whether the team was successful or not.

The Professors dealt with all these major obstacles in a simple way: they just didn't think about them.

After fifteen Construct years of countless dead-ends and fruitless research, all but one of the Professors had decided that this problem was impossible and they'd be much happier filling the Construct with every conceivable luxury and pleasure. They launched spacefaring palaces made out of scrimshawed marble, rode mile-long fire-breathing dragons down streets literally paved with gold, and consorted endlessly with heaving piles of stunningly beautiful (or handsome) concubines. The Construct devolved into little more than a virtual orgy for almost twenty years.

Not content to watch mankind's only hope sleaze their lives away when they were meant to be saving the world, a low-ranking Professor by the name of Phergo Saleh had expressed his distaste for their betrayal by finding a way to murder the Actual bodies of the two highest-ranking Professors: Dunston Alistair and Kenneth Balver. After the very public deaths of Alistair and Balver, Saleh had wiped away all the filth and excess and replaced it with one law: work on The Equation in your designated role, or suffer the consequences. Designating himself as The Director, Saleh's contemporaries learned that their work was no longer a choice, but a duty.

Within hours of his coup, there were no more towers on the bony spine of Mount Everest, no castles on Mars, no hand-plastered keeps embraced by reams of deep red velvet and lit by the flickering of countless candles. The batches of perfect hand-coded brandy were deleted, and all the cigars that had been rolled on the virtual thighs of Cuban virgins were reduced to less than vapour. The Construct went back to being a place of work, adorned with just a few small details that were designed to keep everyone from going completely insane from a lack of visual and tactile stimuli.

As each of the Actual bodies of the Professors were little more than frozen meat shishkebobbed with enough plumbing to open up an entire water park, their virtual avatars didn't need to sleep or eat, and that meant all they did was work. Nowadays, all that DeKray and the other Professors had to look forward to was a half hour of scheduled downtime with Immersives every week, and this small recreational allowance was often interrupted if The Equation had a sudden need for more hard drive space (which it always did).

The Director had initially wiped the Immersives with all the other pleasures so that his workforce had nothing to distract them. But after a decade of uninterrupted intellectual toil and a series of utterly baffling suicides, The Director had grudgingly recovered a handful of titles from the Trash and allowed recreation breaks as long as everyone stayed on schedule.

Sixty-five years had passed since that point.

*

Right on the second their recreational break ended, Professor Phergo Saleh, The Director, appeared out of nothing in front of DeKray and his co-op team. Unlike the generic forms of the four Professors, The Director was represented by an avatar shaped exactly like his Actual body. Standing at roughly five-foot nothing, Saleh was a chinless wimp with a hooked nose that brought a Toucan to mind and wore glasses so thick that you could probably make a half-decent telescope out of them. While some may see the small luxury of retaining his Actual form as hypocritical, The Director had volunteered to take on a colourless and texture-free low-power setting long before forcing anyone else to do so. And as The Director had been in charge of this entire project since the Unpleasantness all those years ago, for the sake of productivity and efficiency it was necessary that everybody could instantly recognise him.

As much as he was hated, everyone had to admit that Professor Phergo Saleh was the exact opposite of ostentatious. Years ago, at the very beginning of the Construct, he'd gone so far as to write a detailed algorithm that allowed his male-pattern baldness to advance at the correct rate, and for his virtual genitals to remain just as unimpressive as the Actual thing. Those affectation had been the first things he'd discarded once the power consumption requirements of The Equation had begun to skyrocket. He might have been a power-mad dictator, but at least he walked the walk.

Knowing the sorts of chilling punishments The Director was capable of, DeKray and the others immediately got to their feet and waited for the order to return to work. Saleh glanced at the four featureless avatars with his dot eyes, and then down at the visors. He didn't say it, but the four of them had heard the same angry growls ten thousand times: How can you waste your time with such toys? It isn't Actual. We're not really here. Our bodies are frozen stiff in pods with tubes jammed into every conceivable orifice, as well as quite a few that didn't exist beforehand. Everything here is nothing more than code. Why must you engage in such frivolity? Don't you know how important our work is?

Thankfully, Saleh spared them the rant.

"Your recreation break is over," he said simply, as though the co-op gamers hadn't been counting down every microsecond.

The Director gave a motion, and the featureless avatars of another four Professors appeared just a couple of metres away, halfway between the table and the sad library of Immersives. Even without faces, it was clear by the body language of the following party that they couldn't wait to escape from this purgatory for a blissful half hour. Saleh didn't bother to say another word before popping away as suddenly as he'd arrived.

Sighing at the knowledge he was now exactly a fortnight of constant work away from playing Totally, Utterly Screwed again, Professor Karl DeKray didn't waste time with goodbyes. While the other three members of his co-op group were clearly pissed that he'd thrown the game, whether intentionally or not, he hadn't considered any of them as friends for even longer than he'd been silent, so what they thought hardly tugged at his heartstrings.

They were nothing more than fellow prisoners, inmates in a prison of zeros and ones. Would he be within a thousand kilometres of any of them if given any other option? No. One hundred percent no.

Outside of the small gaming area, the rest of the Construct was a bare eternity held together at minimal resolution. Everything interesting had been erased. All that remained was an enormous high-definition cluster of spheres in the sky, an interlinked, squashed-together, tumorous-looking growth that was now bigger than Earth's moon: The Equation. It was the culmination of decades of work, a high-definition recording of every single virtual attack the Professors had launched against The Trance. They'd fought this war from every conceivable angle: neurologically, genetically, chemically, biologically, psychologically, mentally, and mathematically. And after countless simulated attempts at fixing the problem, time and time again, it had amounted to nothing. As the Professors had concluded long before The Director had resorted to a double homicide to make a salient point, The Trace could not be solved. It was beyond human ability.

The Equation was a bulging, ugly mass that did nothing but record their combined failures, a gross beast they would keep engorging until the Construct either ran out of hard drive space or their snap-frozen bodies in the Actual finally died. Sisyphus himself didn't know the meaning of the word "futility" as thoroughly as the Professors.

DeKray moved towards The Equation by floating straight up in the air. He didn't feel any wind resistance or g-forces or so much as a lurch in his stomach, as the non-essential physics of the Construct had been so thoroughly stripped away that even something as cool as flying didn't provide any excitement or tactile pleasure. He might as well be playing one of the first video games in the 1970s for how much of a rush it provided. Turning a little as he rose, DeKray stopped mid-spiral, worried that The Director might catch him goofing off when he was meant to be working.

Getting close enough to The Equation's enormous mass to see that it was throbbing as though a Celestial was about to have a fatal heart attack, soon DeKray was passing by dozens of his fellow Professors. As expected, nobody said hello, or acknowledged his presence in any way. Scanning across The Equation's glittering surface of a trillion fist-sized cubes, each composed of millions of compressed lines of self-aware code, he used a mental command to zero in on his last bookmark. With a white flare only he could see, a cube ten kilometres away declared its position in the rippling skin like a lighthouse.

Landing feet-first in the neurovirology section of The Equation, his every step causing the cubes under his heels to politely ask if he wanted to work on them today, DeKray flicked open the last program he'd been working on. A gesture extracted its colourful innards as though he was gutting a neon fish with telekinesis. Code strings rose up in a dozen shades of red, orange and yellow, flashing and corkscrewing as the separate mathematical formulas tried to solve themselves before DeKray's eyeless face. Like countless times before, soon he was so immersed in his work that all other concerns went away. His task was so concentration-intensive that it didn't allow room for anything else inside his head.

Every now and again, DeKray would stop what he was doing, his texture less hands freezing in place. But within a couple of seconds he'd get back to it.

*

After another nine days of failure, DeKray retracted the code cube back into its berth and took a few moments to slowly pan his sight across this side of The Equation. He observed the other Professors struggling with reams of work that would amount to nothing, their shoulders stooped and heads bowed in depression.

DeKray looked up slowly, as though hoping for some sort of divine inspiration to strike from within this godless virtual forever. He knew mankind was finished, and he wished with all his heart that he could join them.

If he had eyes, he'd probably cry. But he didn't. All he had was the task at hand. So he got back to work.